OBSESSED

Getting up, he walked to the locked door at the back of the room, which led to a stairway and his special room. He took a key from around his neck and unsnapped the hasp, pulling open the door. There was a cot inside and a shelf above it with a box. Ignoring the cot, he pulled down the box and reverently lifted the lid, which was only locked when he brought his prey back from the hunt and tied them to the cot.

Inside the box, the red-brown tress of hair was delicate within its tiny plastic bag. He touched it gently. The other items nestled in the box he would only touch with gloves, but his eye ran over them. Her things . . . drawings and chewed Crayolas and the *All About Me* book. Pictures of her childhood. A bounty that he'd discovered after much searching.

He'd waited *so long* . . . had fretted during long nights that it might never happen . . . had sometimes managed to forget for a while.

But now he knew they would be together. He knew where she worked and he knew where she lived.

Soon, very soon. She would be his last . . . and they would spend eternity together. But not yet. The hunt was on. The beast was in his prime.

There was much more to do before he allowed her to catch him.

Nine . . .

Books by Nancy Bush

CANDY APPLE RED

ELECTRIC BLUE

ULTRAVIOLET

WICKED GAME

UNSEEN

BLIND SPOT

WICKED LIES

HUSH

NOWHERE TO RUN

NOWHERE TO HIDE

Published by Kensington Publishing Corporation

Nowhere To Hide

NANCY BUSH

ZEBRA BOOKS
KENSINGTON PUBLISHING CORP.
http://www.kensingtonbooks.com

ZEBRA BOOKS are published by

Kensington Publishing Corp.
119 West 40th Street
New York, NY 10018

All Kensington titles, imprints, and distributed lines are available at special quantity discounts for bulk purchases for sales promotion, premiums, fund-raising, educational, or institutional use.

Special book excerpts or customized printings can also be created to fit specific needs. For details, write or phone the office of the Kensington Special Sales Manager: Attn. Special Sales Department. Kensington Publishing Corp., 119 West 40th Street, New York, NY 10018. Phone: 1-800-221-2647.

Zebra and the Z logo Reg. U.S. Pat. & TM Off.

ISBN-13: 978-1-4201-2502-3
ISBN-10: 1-4201-2502-8

First Printing: September 2012

10 9 8 7 6 5 4 3 2 1

Printed in the United States of America

Prologue

A hawk circled overhead. Something dead down below in the field. He watched its lazy circles and figured it was one of Avery Boonster's dead sheep. Shadows were creeping over the fields as he forged his way through the waving hay, trespassing without a qualm, at home in wide spaces.

Not a sheep, a large raccoon. No visible signs of struggle but he guessed the rodent was old enough to be at the end of its life. Probably just up and died. That's how things went, sometimes.

But sometimes you had to help them along.

. . . in fields where they lay . . .

He'd chosen fields as his staging arena. He'd read of others with his same affliction . . . same deviant sexual needs . . . same dangerous, aberrant behavior . . . same need to dispose of used-up bodies when they were finished with them. He'd molded himself accordingly and likewise had chosen fields where they would lie.

Closing his eyes, he tried to put himself into his other skin. His outer layer. The one the public saw. Beneath the skin lay a beast that answered to a hungry, sexual beat, a living thing within his skull and body. It was always there, lying in wait, especially when he thought about *her*. He tried very, very hard not to think about her, the one he'd believed in once, but she could not be denied. It had started long ago. He'd reached out to her, but she'd pulled back, repulsed. He'd been embarrassed and he could still hear them all laughing and laughing.

He'd managed to forget about her for a while . . . until he'd followed her . . . believed that she was laughing again . . . and the bad thing happened. He'd been scared, afterward. And when he'd been sent away he was certain they knew.

But *they didn't.*

He never stopped thinking of her. All those years in between . . . it had always been his unformed plan to have her. And then she started playing a game with him! He learned she'd joined the Laurelton Police Department as a homicide detective and he knew it was because of *him.* He could feel it inside, like a vibrating nerve. And suddenly he wanted to take her. Take her *right now.* But the time wasn't right. There was much to do before the final moment. And she was too clever, too sensitive by far. Like a skittish sea creature, an anemone, with little fibers always testing the surroundings. Upon the slightest whiff of danger they collapsed in on themselves, scurried away, disappeared. Gone.

His mind flooded with images and he awoke to the fact that he was on his knees, his blind-eyed face turned up to the circling hawk. He wanted to pleasure himself, but the time for that had passed. He was changing . . . morphing . . . becoming someone else over this long summer. His need could ultimately only be satisfied by her, but in the meantime he would take the surrogates.

He'd taken three of them already. Ones who knew too much. He'd taken them while he thought of *her*.

He hated her.

He loved her.

They called her Nine but he'd known her as September.

"September," he whispered to the dead raccoon and the soaring bird of prey. He would bring her to this field and let her feel his power. No more laughing at him. No more turning away . . . no more playing games.

They would be together. That was the way of it. Soon he would be tight within her sea anemone grip. Blood red, bright orange, and sunflower yellow. A kaleidoscope of heated sexual colors.

But not yet. Not yet . . . not till the right moment.

In the meantime he would find the surrogates.

"Do Unto Others As She Did To Me," he whispered into the shimmering heat of the day, staring up to the sky, into God's face.

Chapter 1

Her cell phone rang at four minutes after midnight. September Rafferty, asleep on her living room couch, half rose and thrashed around for the switch to the floor lamp, squinting across the room to her cable box, which showed the time in glowing white numerals: 12:03.

She smiled as she turned the switch and flooded the room with illumination. She knew who it was and why they'd called now. Blinking, she punched the cell's green ON button and said, "You couldn't wait till morning?"

"Twelve-oh-three," her twin brother said. "That's when you came into this world. That's when I'm gonna call. Happy Birthday."

"I should've called you six minutes ago instead of earlier in the day. Happy Birthday to you, too."

"But I called you at the exact time of your birth," he said with a touch of pride. "That was all me."

"You just like the idea of waking me out of a sound sleep."

"Well . . . yeah."

Her brother, August "Auggie" Rafferty, was her twin but they'd been born on either side of midnight on August 31, making it different days and even different months. His birthday was August 31 and hers was September 1, hence their parents had named them August and September respectively—a strange decision that went along with how they'd named their three older children: March, May, and July. Which said a lot about their parents, September thought, specifically their father, as their mother had died years earlier and had once alluded to the fact that she was sorry for manacling them with names after the months of the year.

"Did you field any other birthday wishes from the family?" September asked him, fighting a yawn.

"March called. And July."

"July's good about that stuff. I'm generally horrible about remembering birthdays."

"Yours and mine are the only two I'm really certain about," Auggie admitted.

"Yeah . . . well . . ." September thought briefly about her older sister, May, who'd died in a botched robbery at a fast-food restaurant when she was in high school, but that only brought on more melancholia than she was already feeling this birthday. "No word from Dad, huh," she said.

"Like there would be," he said.

Braden Rafferty had disowned his two youngest children when they both chose law enforcement as a career. He had firm ideas about family, though he'd been an unfaithful husband and an absent parent, and this naming of his children undoubtedly stemmed from his own desire for control and order. At least that's how September saw it. Had she and Auggie both been born in August, she wouldn't put it past him to have named them August and Augusta. That's just who he was, and was indicative of why she generally steered clear of him and most of the other Raffertys as well, except her twin. Luckily, the whims of fate had stepped in, delivering her and her brother on different days and different months, so he was August and she was September.

Or, maybe that was less about luck and more about Braden being able to bend the universe to his will. She wouldn't put it past him.

"So . . . have you done anything about your artwork?" he asked.

He meant her second grade artwork, if you could really call it that: the artwork with the phrase *Do Unto Others As She Did To Me* scrawled across its face in what looked like blood that had come to September at the station about a week earlier. She and her partner were the detectives on the Do Unto Others case where a killer was strangling victims, carving words and markings into their flesh, then discarding the bodies in fields around the city of Laurelton and in Winslow County. At least that was the prevailing theory at work, though they hadn't made that connection public yet.

"Still working on it," she told Auggie.

"Work faster."

"Hey," she protested.

"I'm just sayin'. I don't like you in harm's way."

When the "bloody" artwork had first arrived at the station, she'd told her brother about it, and Auggie had nearly come unglued. Not a big surprise, as he was known for his penchant of saving damsels in distress, and having a killer threaten his sister had sent him into overprotective mode, *toute suite*. He'd gone straight to their superior, Lieutenant Aubry D'Annibal, and insisted that he be put on the case. Hell no, September had told him flatly. It was her case, and she was bound and determined to hang on to it, especially now that it had become personal. She and her partner, Detective Gretchen Sandler, had been assigned the case and her interfering brother wasn't going to take it from her, no way, no how.

She'd pointed this all out to D'Annibal, adding that Auggie was still deeply involved in the Zuma Software case, where a masked intruder had stormed into the front offices of the software company and opened fire on the employees. That case was just wrapping up but there was still a helluva lot of work to do. Plus, she'd reminded him that he'd already yanked her off that case to put her on this one, and she really didn't want to be pulled again. Yes, her artwork had been sent to her. This killer knew her; there was something there. And that was exactly why she wanted to stay on the case.

So far the lieutenant had kept her on, with the caveat that September might be reassigned if things got too hot. She had then told her brother to leave it alone and get back on Zuma. He could damn well finish with that.

"But the two cases have overlapped," Auggie had argued at the time.

"And when we figure out how, maybe you can jump on this one, too," September stated firmly, holding her ground. As long as she and Sandler were the lead detectives, September didn't want her brother mucking things up.

But, all that said, she knew Auggie wasn't wrong. The third suspected victim of Do Unto Others, Glenda Tripp, had turned out to be related to one of the prime suspects in the Zuma case, so there had to be some connection between the two. It was too improbable, impossible really, that it was mere coincidence. Was Do Unto Others some kind of copycat of the Zuma killer? Maybe following that case and grabbing victims peripherally involved for the notoriety . . . or something? That had yet to be determined. It was early days still, and until they had more evidence connecting the three homicides to the Zuma killings and even to each other, they were treading lightly.

"Now," she said to her brother, "I've decided to go to Dad's house and dig through the attic or basement or both, looking for more of my grade school stuff. I want to see if I can find the rest of it. Wanna join?"

"You're kidding."

"You keep saying you want in on this case."

"I'm not going anywhere near dear old Dad." He and Braden didn't talk, didn't get along, didn't much like each other.

"Thought I'd ask," September said.

"But keep me in the loop," he ordered her.

"Yeah, yeah."

Auggie hadn't exactly acquiesced to having September and Gretchen handle Do Unto Others, but he was too busy to really protest much, and though, in reality, September wouldn't have minded working with him, regardless of what she said to him, Gretchen Sandler was her partner and they were in this together, for better or worse.

"I'm off till after Labor Day . . . kind of a forced vacation," she admitted now. "D'Annibal wanted me to think about things and decide whether I really wanted to stay on the case."

"You thinking of quitting?"

"Don't sound so eager. No. But when I get back to work I'll give you a call. Maybe we can talk over some stuff."

"What kind of stuff?"

"I don't know. About grade school . . . I'll let you know after I find the rest of my work," she said, then added, "If I find it."

"You know I'm always here for you."

"Oh, bullshit. You just want the case for yourself."

"I don't want my little sister involved with a psycho."

"Six minutes younger does not make me your little sister."

"Yes it does. Look it up."

"Bullshit again. Goodnight, Auggie," she said, switching off the light.

"Goodnight, Nine," he responded, calling her by her nickname. She was Nine, for the month she was born, a name that had stuck all through her school years and into her adult life.

The following Thursday she hurried past Guy Urlacher at the Laurelton Police Department's front desk, flashing him a look at her ID. He couldn't stop himself from asking everyone for identification no matter how many times they passed his desk. It was protocol, and Guy was all about it.

"Hey!" he called after her, wanting her to stop, but she was having none of it today.

In the squad room, she dropped her purse on her desk and walked over to stand in front of the bulletin board that held her piece of artwork. Beside it were pictures of Do Unto Others's suspected three victims: Sheila Dempsey, Emmy Decatur, and Glenda Tripp. They'd been reluctant to confirm they had a serial killer on their hands as they didn't want the FBI swarming on them until they were sure.

Detective George Thompkins, heavyset and squeaking his swivel chair, and her partner, Gretchen Sandler, who was seated at a desk, a phone at her ear, in the act of making a call, both stopped what they were doing as September plucked the artwork from the board and carried it to her desk. It was something she'd made in her second grade homeroom class. Now, she said to the room at large, "I don't care if it's ketchup or red paint or salsa or pomegranate juice, when I first saw it, I thought it was *blood*." She held it up for Thompkins and Sandler to see again. It had been tested for prints when it arrived but all they found were smudges, and she felt now, since it was hers, it didn't have to be tacked on the board. "This message came to me. The killer sent it to me."

"It's ketchup and something else," Thompkins responded.

Sandler skewered him with a scorching look. "We know, George. Jesus. Stay on point. It was meant to look like blood. It was meant to scare the shit out of her." To September, she said, "I still can't believe you can remember what grade you were in when you did that."

Sandler was slim and dark-skinned, half-Brazilian, with curly dark hair and slanted blue eyes. She was attractive in a cat-like, predatory way, and she was known by all and sundry as a bitch on wheels. No one wanted to partner with her, but September, being the newest detective at the Laurelton PD, didn't really have a choice. So far, it had been fine. Gretchen was a good detective, no matter what others thought of her. September had been watching and learning her style over the last four to five months.

Now September gazed down at the artwork, memorizing it yet again. It was made of light blue construction paper with glued-on, cut-out pictures of brown-, orange-, and mustard-colored leaves falling from the sky into a pile that was drawn in at the bottom of the page. An ink-stamped happy face and several gold stars ran across the top of the piece, with a teacher's handwritten note:

Your birthday cupcakes were terrific! Way to start the school year!

But underneath the teacher's words, new ones had been added in a bloody scrawl: **DO UNTO OTHERS AS SHE DID TO ME**.

"Mrs. Walsh was my teacher, and I really liked her," September said aloud. "The falling leaves were the first art project of the year, and my mom hung it up on the wall in our kitchen next to the refrigerator for a long time."

"So, the killer got it from your house," Gretchen said. Again. They'd been over this territory so many times since the envelope had arrived at the station it was like they were rehearsing for a play.

"Possibly . . ." September murmured.

"You're scared shitless someone in your family sent it to you."

This was a new wrinkle. To date, Gretchen had left the Raffertys out of it. "No," she denied.

"Oh, c'mon," Gretchen said, but September turned away from her. She wasn't about to trash her family to her partner even though she had entertained some of those very same thoughts.

It had now been two weeks since she'd received the message at the station. Two weeks since it had arrived addressed to her and wrapped inside a birthday card that read, "Way to go 3-year-old," where someone had handwritten in a zero beside the 3, making it 30. Two weeks since September had begun delving through the notes, files, and photos associated with the Do Unto Others killer and dealing with the fact that he'd sent this disturbing message specifically to her.

"They know my age," September had said when the

missive first appeared, brought to her at her desk by Candy from administration.

"Jesus, Nine," Gretchen, had responded on an intake of breath. "It really *does* have to do with you!"

She'd meant the Do Unto Others investigation because over the last several months, almost from the moment September had started as a detective with the Laurelton Police Department, this killer, or killers, had begun their rampage, leaving two of the victims' bodies in fields around the city of Laurelton and Winslow County and one inside her own apartment. The bodies were discovered in varying states of undress, but each of them had marks across their torso, maybe the beginnings of words, maybe something else, but Emmy Decatur's torso contained the full *DO UNTO OTHERS AS SHE DID TO ME* message that had later been sent to the station on September's artwork.

Two weeks ago . . .

At the time, September's thirtieth birthday had still been looming, so the card's timing was clear. But who knew the date of her birthday apart from her family? Not many people. And who knew it was her thirtieth? Even fewer. The thought that one of the Rafferty clan had sent it made for a very subdued birthday, and though her sister, July, had made noise about getting together when she called to offer best wishes, September had fobbed her off. She'd fielded calls from her father and her brother, too, though they'd merely said happy birthday and left it at that. Not exactly warm and welcoming were the Raffertys. Not since Kathryn, September's mother, had died, and then a few years later, her sister, May.

Now she looked up from the artwork and across the room to the board that still held Do Unto Others's suspected three victims' pictures. Tripp was the only one found inside her apartment. The prevailing theory was the killer had followed her home and attacked her, but had been scared away before he could fully carve his message into her skin. Since Dempsey and Decatur had been moved to fields, it was assumed he'd been thwarted in getting the body to its eventual "final resting place." Dempsey and Tripp's torsos had been carved with markings, but Decatur was the only one with the killer's Do Unto Others message.

So far . . .

After receiving her own warning, September had gone over every scrap of evidence and report on the case with renewed vigor, but still nothing stood out. They'd gotten back the lab evidence on Tripp, the last victim, but it hadn't given them anything new, either. There was no trace of DNA at the crime scenes; it was believed the killer had used condoms. He'd raped his victims and strangled them with a thin cord of some kind, but he was careful to take the cord away and it hadn't left any fibers. So far, they'd been unable to connect the victims apart from the fact that they all had darker hair and similar builds; he was probably going after a type—September's type, as her own hair was dark auburn and she had a lean, dancer's build. The killer had been quiet the last few weeks, which, though a good thing, didn't mean he'd stopped. Maybe he'd set his sights on September as the next victim? Maybe he just wanted to scare her, or play with her?

Whatever the case, she thought, *bring it on*. This waiting was making her edgy and snappish. And D'Annibal, though he was allowing her to stay on for now, was watching. She didn't want the feds involved until she knew more about how someone had gotten her artwork, but it wasn't her call, and the clock was ticking. She was lucky that Lieutenant D'Annibal loathed interference from outside agencies, so for the moment, the investigation rested with the Laurelton PD. She hoped to solve this thing before it became a joint task force investigation with the feds, but she was of the firm belief that the killer was one man and all three women were his victims.

How had he gotten her artwork from the *second grade*? Was it from her family home? She didn't want to think about what *that* meant. Just couldn't do it. Though she had more than a few issues with her family, she did not believe any of them capable of terrorizing her, let alone the terrible things he'd done to the three victims.

She glanced at the clock. Five P.M. She decided that tomorrow she would take it from the top again, start with reinterviewing the friends and families of the victims, see if there was anything else that connected them that they'd overlooked. She headed down the hall from the squad room to her locker to retrieve her purse and she realized Gretchen was hurrying after her. September stopped and half-turned, wondering what was up.

"I'm thinking about stopping by Xavier's for a drink. Wanna join?"

"Umm . . . I don't know," September said. She got along with Sandler okay at work, but the idea of socializing with her was a path she wasn't sure she wanted to take.

Still, returning to her empty apartment was even less appealing. And going to visit her father at the family home to dig into her own past and see if there was anything there—what she'd told Auggie she was going to do, what she *should* do, what she'd put off for two weeks—was the least appealing choice of the three.

"Well, it is Thursday, almost the weekend . . ." she finally said.

"Meet you there," Gretchen answered.

* * *

An hour later September was twisting a bottle of beer on the tan-and-black zebrawood bar at Xavier's, watching water condensation slide around beneath the bottom of it. The top of the bar was polished to such a high gloss it reflected like glass and the beaded water shone like diamonds under the lights. Lifting the bottle to her lips, September tried to shut her mind down, but if there was a way to stop the buzz in her head, she had yet to master the trick of it.

Sandler was making chitchat with one of the bartenders who was liking the idea that she was a cop. Idly, September wondered if Gretchen was thinking about going home with him. That would be fine with her. She really just wanted to crawl in bed and pull the covers over her head for a while.

She said as much to her, but Gretchen was zeroed in on the guy—Dominic, call him Dom—and didn't seem to hear her. Deciding it was time to vamoose, September headed outside into a sultry evening with a hot wind blowing the first leaves around, sending them skittering over her boots as she walked back to her silver Honda Pilot. She really shouldn't have come to the Laurelton steak house and bar wearing utilitarian black slacks and the button-up, short-sleeve shirt she'd worn to work. Even though it was popular with commuters Xavier's screamed for plunging necklines and chandelier earrings and CFM shoes with four-inch-heels.

Like that was ever going to happen.

She should go to her father's like she'd said she would and root through the attic and basement and garage and outbuildings in search of all the old flotsam and jetsam of her days at Sunset Elementary School. But like Auggie she didn't like going "home." *Ever.* She hadn't been comfortable there after her mother's car accident when September was in the fifth grade, and the thought of dealing with her autocratic father, who'd basically disowned her and Auggie when they went into law enforcement, wasn't a pleasant one, either. And then to have to explain about a killer who was targeting her . . . Braden Rafferty would have an apoplectic fit and the "I told you sos" would come raining down in a torrent.

And don't even get her started on Rosamund, the latest stepmother, whose age was closer to September's than her father's. The stepmom before Rosamund, Verna, lay somewhere in between; Braden's taste had apparently grown younger as he grew older.

Peachy.

Switching on the ignition and the Bluetooth, September dug out her cell and hit Auggie's number. That stuff she'd told him she wanted to talk about when he called on her birthday was bothering her and now she didn't want to wait until she'd found her grade school papers and such to discuss it. The phone rang three times before he answered, "Hey, there, Nine."

"Hey, yourself. I'm thinking of heading to Dad's now, finally, and looking around for my grade-school memorabilia," she said, negotiating into traffic.

"Took a while to work up the courage, huh. I feel your pain."

"I just wanted to talk about . . . growing up Rafferty, a bit."

He groaned. "Do we have to?"

"No one would have thrown our stuff out, would they? Dad? Verna, or Rosamund? I can't think they'd bother. I'm guessing my stuff—all of our stuff—just got shoved into the attic or basement and forgotten."

"Probably," he allowed.

"If Dad's there, I'll ask him."

"When was the last time you talked to him?" Auggie asked.

"He called me on my birthday, at a more civilized hour than you did."

"When before that?" he challenged.

"We talked on the phone on March's birthday," September told him. "And, of course, I saw him at July's birthday party at The Willows," she added, referring to her father's winery.

"Pretty good. Now tell me how long, every time, it took him before he suggested you seek other employment?"

"He's been better lately about keeping it to himself."

Auggie sniffed his disbelief. "Maybe going to the house will be okay, then," he said, but his voice said something else.

"The killer got my artwork from somewhere. Dad's house is the most likely place."

"If it even was the killer who sent it to you."

"Of course it was the killer," she stated.

"Not necessarily. Pauline Kirby let the world know. Could be somebody trying to shake you up."

Kirby was Channel Seven's best-known reporter and she was fast becoming the nemesis of everyone in the police department, September included. She'd blindsided September in a recent television interview.

"One of our family members?" she asked him. "That's what you're suggesting, right?"

"Maybe. I'm just saying the message could be from someone other than the killer."

"You just don't want to think he's targeted me. I get it. But yeah, it is a warning. And though I've got issues with some of our family members, I don't think any of them could be involved in any way with this killer. Maybe . . . the message was from someone who knows who the killer is and knows I'm on the case, but it's not our family. That I won't believe." Something in her own words tickled her brain, but when she tried to place what it was, it escaped her.

"You gotta keep your mind open, Nine."

"Well, *whoever* sent it to me got it from somewhere. That's all I'm saying. And the most likely place is the house."

"If you see dear old Dad when you're there, don't mention my name."

"Yeah, like he won't ask about you. 'How's your twin, September? Have you seen August lately?' That's pretty standard."

"He disowned us," Auggie said. "Not the other way around."

"You're preaching to the choir. But I gotta go see him."

She negotiated around a tight corner and back to her apartment complex with its matching sets of upper and lower units that gave it a faux townhouse look, each set separated from the others by different facades, colors, and design elements. September and her lower neighbor's unit sported tan shingles with black shutters. "I'm not crazy about going out there tonight, but I need to do something."

"Be careful, Nine."

"Oh, don't start that whole big brother crap with me."

"As soon as I can, I'm going to help you catch this bastard," he said for about the fiftieth time.

"D'Annibal took me off Zuma, and put me on Do Unto Others even before I got the message from the killer or *whoever*. Give Sandler and me a chance, for God's sake. We're capable. Okay? Capable."

"If it *was* the killer who sent you that artwork, then he's zeroed in on you."

"You're deaf, I swear. Let me do this! If you—" September stopped herself from saying something she would regret. She knew the main reason he was acting this way was because he was afraid for her.

"If I . . . ?" he prompted.

"Just don't do anything yet. I'll go to Dad's and see if I can find anything at the house. Gretchen and I are digging into the backgrounds of all the vics. Revisiting stuff we've already visited. Doing the work. Trust me, there's nothing for you to do, so just . . . wait."

After a long pause he finally said, "Okay."

"Go be with Liv and forget about me for a while. I can take care of myself. Even with Dad. I'm going to ask him about the kitchen wall where Mom hung up our elementary school stuff. He might remember something about it. Mom put the artwork that was sent to me at the station on the wall, the falling leaves. I remember that. She had it up for a long time."

"Your memory's faulty. She had mine up there, not yours," Auggie said.

"Uh-uh." September pulled into her designated spot in the carport, cut the engine, but stayed in the car.

"It was mine," Auggie insisted.

"She had your leaf artwork up there, too?"

"I don't know about yours, but mine was there. We both did a bunch of the same projects all through elementary school. I didn't remember it was from second grade, but if you say so I'll believe it. Mom was always tagging up some stupid thing we'd done and declaring it art."

"Mrs. Walsh was my second grade teacher. The artwork

that came to the station was from when I was in her homeroom."

"Well, there you go. But I know it was *my* artwork on the kitchen wall. Maybe yours was there, too."

"What teacher did you have?"

"Mrs. McBride."

"Ugh. She was no fun," September remembered. "And the third homeroom teacher was Ms. Osborne. She was younger."

"Uh huh." He sounded like he was losing interest in the conversation.

"You're sure it was your artwork?" September squinted, thinking hard as she got out of the car.

"I know it was."

"God, Auggie, maybe you're right. I left a lot of my stuff at school, I remember. You were always better about bringing everything home. It used to piss me off."

"Ah, yes. I was an approval-seeker in those days."

"So, what does that mean? That my project never made it home, and then . . . it fell into the hands of the killer . . . or whoever?"

"All I know is somebody sent you a message meant to scare you. If you find more elementary schoolwork at the house, it doesn't necessarily mean anybody at the house sent it to you. Maybe that project was found by someone else, someone with a twisted purpose."

"Someone who knew it was *my* second grade work and that I'm a cop, so they could send it to the station?"

"You were just on the news, weren't you?"

"Yes, but—"

"I gotta go, Nine. Take it easy with dear old Dad. Don't let him get to you. And call me later and let me know if you find some more artwork. We made so many beautiful pieces back then."

"I've always wondered if maybe we should have chosen a fine arts school instead of the police academy."

His snort of laughter was his sign-off, and she was smiling as she walked past the door to the unit below hers. She headed up the private flight of steps that led to each upper unit, then pulled out her keys, unlocked her door, and quickly let herself inside, closing the door behind her and throwing the deadbolt. She wasn't nearly as cavalier as she would like Auggie to believe.

She looked around the small space: U-shaped kitchen, living room with television and DVR. Along the back of the overstuffed couch was the quilt her maternal grandmother had given her. September had called her grandmother Meemaw when she was learning to talk and it stuck. Meemaw had died the same year her daughter Kathryn, September's mother, had been killed in an automobile accident. Meemaw had had health issues, or so her father had told her, but to this day September believed Meemaw's death was from a broken heart at the loss of her only child.

Before she could change her mind, September traded her work clothes for jeans, a black tank, and sandals, and headed to the Rafferty estate on the southern edge of Laurelton. The Raffertys, already wealthy, had been made wealthier by September's father, a businessman. After Kathryn's death, Braden had become even more single-sighted and hard driving, and he'd added to the Rafferty fortune, often on the backs of others, which had earned him more than a few enemies along the way . . . and lost him relationships with his youngest children, September and Auggie.

Braden Rafferty was known for his money, his influence, his business acumen, and his winery, The Willows, but he was not known for being a family man despite having five children. He was also not known for his fidelity and stick-to-itiveness. Though September still ached for the loss of her mother, and though she knew her father had loved Kathryn as much as he was capable of, she also knew Braden had made her mother's life a living hell. She liked to think Kathryn Rafferty had found peace in the hereafter. It made the "here" so much more bearable.

Now, driving through the pillared gates, September drew a fortifying breath. She pulled up to the sprawling Rafferty home and parked on the wide concrete apron, edged in travertine, that Braden had put in for his guests, which really, when you thought about it, was all September was to him anymore.

She climbed from her silver Pilot into a dense, black night, studded by stars, pushed the remote to lock the vehicle, then turned toward the house.

Showtime, she thought a bit grimly.

Chapter 2

The Rafferty house itself was a monstrosity. Built to resemble a Bavarian castle complete with front turret, gables, and pinnacles, its interior had been remodeled twice, once each by the two successive wives her father had married after her mother's death, both times to the serious detriment of the home. The last time September had visited she hadn't recognized one item of furniture, one dish, one picture from her growing up years. Everything had been changed. Everything had become something that either Verna, her father's second wife, or Rosamund, his current one, had added to the house, although Verna's contributions were slowly being eradicated: the crystal chandelier had been replaced with a modern one sporting polished nickel spikes that ended in bulbs; the heavy damask brown drapes had been replaced with even heavier damask black drapes; the kitchen cabinets, natural cherry once, had been painted burgundy during Verna's regime, and now were a malignant lime green.

September wondered briefly, as she had before, what had happened to Verna's sly, glance-at-you-out-of-the-sides-of-his-eyes son, Stefan Harmak, who was two years younger than September and Auggie. Verna had been married to Braden for about ten years before he met Rosamund, during September's tween and teen years. September's memory of that period was of just trying to keep her head down to stay out of the way of Verna's mercurial wrath. To this day Verna complained loudly and bitterly to anyone who would listen that Rosamund Bitch Reece was a money-grubbing slut (which actually had been said about Verna as well, though September wisely kept that to herself) and that the much younger Rosamund had seduced Braden with her sexual ways, otherwise she, Verna, would still be with Braden.

Which was, of course, utterly false.

September knocked on the front door, but, finding it unlocked, let herself in before anyone could answer. She headed down the thick Moroccan carpet that ran from the foyer to the living room and called, "Hello? Rosamund? It's September."

At the edge of the living room September halted, listening. Her eyes fell on the picture on the opposite wall. When Verna was queen of the castle, she'd put a photo of Stefan in pride of place on the mantel above the black, marble-faced fireplace, but now September saw that Stefan's picture had been replaced by a larger one of the beautiful Rosamund. She glanced away from the picture, then jerked back.

Was that a *baby bump* in the picture?

A moment later she heard footsteps padding toward her, and then Rosamund appeared in bare feet and a light tan linen sleeveless top and capri pants. To her disbelief the baby bump was now a full-fledged hill.

"My God, September! I thought some stranger had just walked in! Suma must have forgotten to lock the door after she left. Doesn't matter how many times I tell her, she always forgets."

"I didn't know you were pregnant," September said in a wooden voice.

Rosamund's eyes were a tawny brown, and her hair was a long, straight, lustrous, dark brown sheath. She lifted one brow and said obliquely, "If you and your brother would call Braden more often, you might learn things."

Sideways accusations. Her way. "If memory serves, he basically disowned Auggie and me over our career choices."

"He said he called you on your birthday."

"He gets points for that," she said without inflection.

"You carry such a grudge," she said with a tsk-tsk.

"A Rafferty trait. So, when is this blessed event due to occur?"

Rosamund placed a hand atop her belly. "January."

"I hope it's a girl," September said, "if you and Dad are sticking with the month-naming thing."

"It is a girl," she said. "I plan on naming her Gilda."

"Gilda. Good luck with that."

Her lips compressed and she said, "If you're looking for your father, he's at The Willows."

The Willows was about forty minutes away, in the Oregon wine country of Yamhill County. September took it as a good sign that her father wasn't in a closed-door conference with her older brother, March, heads bent together planning some sort of new business coup that would garner them a boatload of bucks while putting good people out of work, their usual modus operandi.

"I actually came to look in the attic for some of my grade school work," September told her, seeking to ease around Rosamund who was firmly planted between September and the back stairs to the attic.

"Grade school? What for?"

"I'm thinking of framing some of my artwork and selling it for some extra cash."

"Ha, ha. So funny. I don't really want you to go into the attic right now, if you don't mind. I'll tell Braden, and you guys can figure it out later."

"Are you serious?" September stared at her.

"As a heart attack," she answered coolly.

For the first time it occurred to September that the awful Verna might have been a better choice for a partner than Rosamund. And she might even have been right about that Rosamund-bitch thing.

She was debating on telling Rosamund the true reason she wanted to search the attic, when March strode through the front door as if he owned the place. He stopped short upon seeing September and Rosamund together. "Nine, what the hell are you doing here?"

"Visiting," she said. "Dad's at The Willows."

"I know. I'm heading there next. Since when did you start 'visiting'?"

"Oh, you know. Just missed my family."

He peered closely at her, trying to discern if she was putting him on. He looked like Auggie: dark hair, the Rafferty blue eyes, strong jaw, lean build. But where Auggie always had the light of amusement in his eyes, March was stern and cold, like their father. September's older sister, July, favored both her brothers' looks, whereas May, the sister closest in age to September—whose death when September was just fifteen shattered them all anew a few short years after Kathryn's death—also looked the closest to September: the same athletic build, high cheekbones, auburn hair, and, of course, the Rafferty blue eyes.

Now, it appeared they were about to have a new member of the family.

As if reading her mind, March glanced at Rosamund's rounded figure and frowned. He'd married a woman while in his twenties, but the union hadn't made it five years; Jenny, his ex, had liked the money and lifestyle, but had liked her Pilates instructor more.

March and Jenny had one child together: ten-year-old Evie, who lived with him half the time, Jenny the other half. Evie was downright beautiful with long, dark hair and eyes so blue they looked violet, but she was as unsmiling and uncompromising as her father. At least that's how September remembered her, and that's certainly how Evie had appeared two months earlier at July's birthday party at The Willows. But then Evie had been the only child at the outdoor picnic, so maybe that accounted for her attitude. September hated to think that, like March, who was as demanding, inflexible, and humorless as Braden, Evie had inherited those same Rafferty traits.

"Have you seen July?" he asked September and Rosamund both.

"She's not at The Willows?" September responded, as her sister ran the winery for her father.

"I just called there and they said she hadn't shown up today." He sounded irked.

Rosamund shrugged and said, "I'm not her keeper."

"I haven't seen her since her . . . birthday," September admitted, acutely aware that, though she'd gone to the picnic for July, she had merely called March on his birthday and had ignored her father's altogether.

If March noticed, he gave no sign of it, saying impatiently to Rosamund, "When you see her, tell her I need to talk to her."

"Text her. You'll probably talk to her first anyway,"

Rosamund replied, running a hand through her hair, looking bored.

"How's Evie?" September asked.

"Fine," he said brusquely. He mumbled something about papers in Braden's den, then strode on past them.

Rosamund watched him go and said to September, "He works with Braden. They're always bringing papers and folders and briefcases into the den."

"I didn't think March had much to do with July and the winery. Does he see her that often?"

"Oh, sure . . . we all do now."

"What do you mean?"

Rosamund gave an unladylike snort. "She's been living here the past month. Just moved in without even asking me! I told Braden she has to leave before the baby's born, but no one seems to want to listen to me."

September couldn't credit it. Though she hadn't kept up with most of her family, she was surprised her older sister had moved back in with their father. March had his own place, and he and her father practically lived in each other's skin. July had always, as long as September was aware, kept her own apartment or condo.

Rosamund was looking at her, waiting, and September thought about storming past her to the attic, then decided it just wasn't worth it. Even if she found her grade school treasures, she doubted there was anything earth-shattering amongst them that would give her a new lead in the investigation.

"Tell Dad I'll be by tomorrow," she said, then headed back outside into the still warm evening.

She felt depressed. Without Auggie, she had no one to relate to within the Rafferty clan. Her mother and May, the women she'd been closest to, had been taken from her before she was an adult. July had always been on her own path and September had been too young to ever really relate to her. Maybe it was time to bridge that gap; it was worth a try. She just wished she had someone else who was close enough to confide in; Auggie was there but he'd been undercover off and on, and therefore had been unavailable a lot of the time.

No wonder she'd fallen for Jake Westerly when she'd been a senior in high school. No wonder she'd made a fool of herself that year, dreaming about him like a lovesick fool, making love with him only to learn from his vile friend T.J. that Jake had merely been trying to score with a virgin. Was it true? To this day, she didn't know, and it didn't matter anyway in the larger scheme of things. September had wanted to be with him and she'd gotten that chance. He'd actually been nice to her during that time—or she'd thought he was being nice, hard to say with T.J.'s reveal—which had been wonderful after all the years of teasing she'd endured from Jake throughout elementary school. Jake's father had worked for September's and there was a bit of the rich kid/poor kid thing that he'd needled her about. It was like a backward way of flirting she recognized now, but it had hurt when she was young, especially because she secretly liked him. And then everything changed in high school when Jake came into his own and money was no longer any factor in his social status, and for a brief moment he split with his longtime girlfriend, Loni Cheever, and he and September spent a night together.

When he learned about it, T.J. had had a lot of unkind things to say about that. Embarrassing things. September had pretended to be immune as a means to get him to stop, but when Jake went back to Loni, she started wondering if some of what T.J. had said might actually be true. Did guys really want to score with virgins just to get that notch on their belts? Guys like Jake Westerly?

It just was so damn lame.

Shaking off the thought, September drove back the way she'd come, arriving at her apartment around seven-thirty. She'd barely parked when she thought of the empty contents of her refrigerator, so she started the ignition again and turned the Pilot toward the nearest fast-food restaurant, Subway Sandwiches.

Twenty minutes later, pastrami sandwich in hand, she returned to her apartment, stripped off her clothes, ran through the shower, then placed her sandwich on a plate and went to eat at the sofa, in front of the TV. Ever since she'd been interviewed about the Do Unto Others case a few weeks earlier, she'd set her DVR to record the Channel Seven nightly news at five-thirty and ten. Now she grabbed the remote and scrolled through the list of programs, punching up the recording of the five-thirty news as she took her first bite.

She was staring at the screen when the thought she hadn't been able to catch earlier came back to her: *he'd seen her on the news.* He had to have. The killer had seen her on the news and that's how he knew she was a detective.

And that very same night Glenda Tripp was murdered.

And shortly thereafter September had received the "bloody" message.

She set the sandwich down, and put the recording on PAUSE, catching Channel Seven's newswoman and resident muckraker Pauline Kirby's feral face in a really unbecoming moment where her eyes were half-shut and her mouth was opened in a snarl.

Was she making connections that weren't there?

No. It was too coincidental. He'd sent her that message and it was personal.

With a feeling of dread—she hated seeing herself on video—she switched from today's news to the interview she'd done with Pauline Kirby. She'd watched it once, horrified at how she looked. She didn't know how actors and people like Pauline Kirby did it. Whenever she saw herself on camera all she wanted to do was close her eyes and groan at the flaws.

Now, she exited the news program and scrolled through the lists on her DVR until she found the recorded interview again. It had been taken at the crime scene where Emmy Decatur's body had been discovered.

Setting her teeth, September pushed the button and the program started. She fast-forwarded to the clip with Pauline Kirby and the two hikers who had found the body, an interview that had occurred before September had arrived at the scene. Sitting on the edge of the couch, she braced for what was to come, determined this time to pay strict attention to the words and not get distracted by her own shortcomings, real or imagined.

It began with Pauline introducing the two hikers to the camera: "The body of Emmy Decatur was found by Brian Legusky and Dina Wendt, hikers familiar with this area near the foothills of the Coast Range. They called 911 and turned the case over to the Laurelton Police Department, but they agreed to come back to the site for us and give us a recap of just what happened." She pointed the mic toward Legusky and said, "Tell us what happened."

"Well . . . me and Dina had been on some trails and we were coming back and our truck was over there . . ." He motioned toward the gravel road that September had parked on when she'd joined the interview. "It was a nice day. We thought we'd maybe put our packs down in the field, have somethin' to eat . . . I dunno. And then, there she was . . ." He glanced over at Wendt, who was staring wide-eyed, looking sick with the memory.

Pauline then tried to engage Wendt, who could barely squeak out a word or two. Then back to Pauline, who said she was about to interview one of the investigators on the case, Detective September Rafferty of the Laurelton PD.

Enter September, wearing black pants, a black V-necked T-shirt, and her light gray, linen jacket. It had been hot that day, too, but she'd worried about sweat stains so she'd put on the jacket for her television appearance. Her auburn hair was normally clipped back, but she'd let it down for the interview and when the handheld camera brought her up, she looked too young to have any experience at all.

"Dammit." Lieutenant D'Annibal had asked her to be the face of the investigation and she'd been sent as a missionary of department goodwill. *Never fear, good citizens of Laurelton, the police are here to serve and protect and we've sent out our finest—youngest—detective to put you at ease.*

Pauline began by asking September about the circumstances that had brought Decatur's body to their attention, which was the 911 call, and then brought up Sheila Dempsey, the first victim discovered strangled and left in a field in the area, though Dempsey had been across the county line and not in the Laurelton PD's jurisdiction until D'Annibal wrested the case away after the discovery of Decatur's body. Then when the third victim, Glenda Tripp, was found within Laurelton city limits, it was understood the case had been given to Laurelton generally, and to September and Gretchen Sandler specifically.

But at the time of the interview with Pauline, Tripp's body hadn't been found yet, so the thrust concerned Sheila Dempsey and Emmy Decatur, a surprise to September as she'd hoped to keep the crimes separated, at least as far as the public knew. She'd had to go with the flow, however, and said, ". . . we're still checking the evidence to see if the two crimes are truly related," hoping to put an end to the speculation.

Pauline was nodding and regarding her with an intense, "I get you" look, but then she uttered her pièce d' résistance: "We understand there were markings on the bodies. Words."

September watched herself glance toward the hikers. They'd been asked not to reveal anything about the words carved into Emmy Decatur's body, but Pauline had apparently gotten to them. She then turned from them, faced Pauline squarely, and said, "Cause of death was strangulation in both cases."

"But there were markings . . ." Pauline also looked over to Legusky and Wendt. "There were words, cut into Emmy Decatur's torso. 'Do Unto Others As She Did To Me,' right?" The camera pulled back to include Legusky, who nodded several times. Pauline then focused on September again, asking, "Can you confirm, Detective Rafferty?"

"Not at this time."

"You're afraid of a panic? That people will freak out when they learn there's a serial killer whose signature is cutting a phrase into his victims' skin? Well, I think this is information we all need to know." Pauline looked directly into the camera. "Young women are being murdered and their bodies used as a crude message." She turned back to September. "What are you doing to protect us, besides keeping the truth to yourselves?"

September could see herself straighten with the affront and she fought a groan. Her onscreen self stated firmly, "There's an ongoing, full-scale investigation in progress."

"Really? Excuse me, Detective, but how can that be, given the other still-unsolved major case, the Zuma Software Massacre? Is that an ongoing, full-scale investigation, too?"

"Yes."

"Do you have the manpower for both? We all know there have been major slashes to government budgets and that includes law enforcement as well. Can you guarantee our safety? I mean, seriously?"

Watching, September almost wanted to cover her face and look between her fingers. She glanced away and heard herself say officiously, "Laurelton PD, in conjunction with Winslow County Sheriff's Department and the Portland PD, has qualified personnel working hard on both cases. We—"

"But has progress been made *anywhere?*"

"Yes, of course."

"On Zuma, or the Do Unto Others killer?"

"Both," she said. "I'm sure you understand we can't reveal details that would jeopardize—"

"What about Dr. Frank Navarone?" Pauline suddenly asked, and now September glanced back to the TV. Seeing herself blink in surprise at the unexpected question, she narrowed her eyes on Pauline's image, but her mind started traveling down avenues that had seemed like dead ends once, but now opened up to new possibilities. Pauline had brought up Frank Navarone who was Glenda Tripp's uncle and shortly thereafter Glenda Tripp was murdered by, it certainly looked like, the Do Unto Others killer.

The killer had seen September in this interview.

Pauline looked impatient, but finally September said, "Dr. Navarone is a person of interest."

"In which case?" Pauline pounced.

"The Zuma Software shootings," September was forced to admit.

And that was it for September. Pauline turned back to the camera for a close-up where she finished, "It may be just as Detective Rafferty suggests, that the police are doing everything they can"—her tone suggested otherwise—"but can we trust our lives to an undermanned, overworked local police force? There's a killer out there. Likely more than one. Take care and lock your doors. . . ."

September fast-forwarded to the end of the recording, but she didn't erase it just yet.

She'd been with the Laurelton PD for almost five months now. Sheila Dempsey had been killed around the time September was hired, but in Winslow County. Emmy Decatur's body was found in the Laurelton city limits, and then September had given the interview to Channel Seven. The next morning Glenda Tripp's body was discovered in her apartment.

And then the Do Unto Others message on her second grade artwork had arrived.

September stood up and stared across the room, out the window of her living room toward the backside of the building and the street. But she wasn't seeing anything, her mind was picking at possibilities.

What was it about *her* that interested the killer? Was he someone from her past, maybe seeking to even some old score she was unaware of? Or, was he someone who'd seen her on the news, and then found her artwork somehow? That didn't make any sense. Or, was it that he knew where her artwork was, and *then* when he saw her on the news, he was suddenly driven to send her the message? That maybe she happened to cross his path after he'd started his deadly mission? But then he still would have had to know the artwork was hers.

"He knows me," she decided. "He has to."

I need to find my stuff.

Tomorrow. Whether her father was home or not, she was going to attack the attic and basement.

The killer sat on the concrete floor, cross-legged and naked, his arms straight in front of him, his eyes closed. The blinds were drawn so if the bitch next door came snooping around she wouldn't be able to see in. New blinds, because the old ones had been bent and saggy and offered holes—windows—into his world.

New blinds because that was his outer self's current job: installer for Mel's Window Coverings and he ordered some for himself and haggled with Mel about the discount.

New blinds because the cords used to manipulate the slats had been lying there when he first needed them . . . with Sheila.

He inhaled and held his breath. For years . . . half his life . . . he'd kept the beast hidden inside himself and had managed to evade capture over his first human kills. He'd lived in pure fear, expecting the authorities to find him, but they never did. He'd fed the beast's need with an ample supply of pornography and sudden spurts of nighttime hunting for small, stray animals. And it had worked. He'd burned to prove them all wrong . . . the doctors . . . the medical staff . . . all the fuckers who'd passed judgment on him and labeled him a deviant. He'd been determined to fight the beast that was his inner self and he'd succeeded for *years*.

But the beast never slept, always wanted to prowl.

And then he'd read the article. . . .

Nine . . . the beast will have you. Soon . . . soon.

Outside he heard a noise. The bitch was coming toward his home!

But then he heard other sounds, the slamming of a car door, an engine roaring to life. He heard the crunch of gravel beneath the tires and wondered if she was backing all the way down the long drive. He hoped to hell there was nothing behind her because the bitch was half-blind.

All this land around him—all this isolation except for *her*.

He wished her dead, but not yet . . . he couldn't afford anyone sniffing around the area, asking too many questions. He needed nothing to give him away, now that the hunt was on.

Opening his eyes, he got to his feet and walked to the DVR, reversing to September's interview. He'd been recording the news since Sheila's death, combing the programs for anything about either of the women he'd left for Nine to find. And then suddenly there she was! Talking on camera with that woman reporter. Talking about *Navarone*!

It had sent him into a frenzy, seeing her so clearly. September . . . Nine . . . the beast had sprung loose and he'd driven frantically to the Laurelton station. He couldn't wait!

But then he'd gotten a leash on the beast and managed to pull the curtain down over his inner self. His brain cooled a bit and he knew he would be foolish to take September then. More planning was needed . . . more surrogates . . . but that mention of Navarone . . . .

He hadn't intended to take Glenda, but the beast needed to be fed and knew exactly where Glenda would be, her favorite bar, The Lariat; the slut just couldn't resist dancing. But when he got there, too many people were hanging around the parking lot. He couldn't chance anyone seeing him with her. So, he waited till she left the bar and then he followed her home. Easy for him to catch up to her by her car, easy for him to invite himself in, even though she'd been slightly skittish, but a little drunk, too. The beast knew her. Glenda Navarone Tripp. And she knew him. They'd screwed back in the day, screwed everywhere they could think of. She'd been particularly hot and nasty on her uncle's examining table, saying what a sick psycho he was and how she was only pretending to like him. He didn't care. He was just fuckin' horny and she had the right body, the dark hair. She'd been into it, too. Couldn't get enough. But in the end she'd dismissed him. Had even had the balls to tell him that she was worried about him. He was too obsessive, too intense. He wanted to show her the beast then, but he'd restrained himself. She drifted away, but he never forgot. Never forgot . . .

And she had a body like Nine's.

Now, rewatching September in the interview he grabbed his cock and brought himself to a climax before he could stop himself. As soon as he realized what he'd done he shoved his hands in his hair and pulled hard, threw back his head and howled in rage. No. No! Had to save it. For the surrogates . . . for the whores, if necessary . . . and for September . . .

The last time he'd allowed himself the pleasure was with Glenda. He'd taken his hunting knife, the cord, and a plastic baggie. As soon as he was inside her apartment, he'd backed her against the wall. With a pulse beating in his head and September's blue eyes imprinted on his retinas, he'd slammed into Glenda while she fought the hand covering her mouth. They wrestled a bit; she tried to bite and scratch, but he knew her game. He flung her down and she lay on her back, spent. Just like the others. Then he'd wrapped the cord around her neck and watched her try to beg for her life, but each time she spoke he cut off her words until finally there was utter silence.

He didn't like to kill them with the cord. He wanted the knife. The knife was the instrument that sang when he cut them.

It would be different with September, but for Glenda it had been what needed to be done to service the beast. He watched her eyes dim and grow glassy. He had to fight the urge to take her one more time but he'd purposely only brought one condom. He had to be careful. When he was finished he put the used condom in the baggie and yanked up her red blouse, exposed her black bra, and started to cut. But then the neighbors came back to their apartment, shouting and screaming. Through the thin walls he heard a huge, brawling fight break out, loud enough to be heard outside.

He couldn't stay. Couldn't finish. Couldn't risk it. In a cold fury he had to sneak away quickly.

Unsatisfactory.

Now, he watched September's interview in its entirety again. He reset the recording and watched it again. And again. Played it nine times, watching September Rafferty talk about the killer, acting like she knew *him*.

But she didn't know him . . . not like she thought she did.

His gaze lifted reverently from the television to the picture on the wall above it. An underwater seascape collage of sea anemones, some clinging to rocks. Some floating, one with its center opening to him . . . beautiful . . . vibrant . . .

In his mind's eye he saw her lying down in the field, opening to him.

She wouldn't be able to dismiss him again.

Nine . . .

Getting up, he walked to the locked door at the back of the room, which led to a stairway and his special room. He took a key from around his neck and unsnapped the hasp, pulling open the door. There was a cot inside and a shelf above it with a box. Ignoring the cot, he pulled down the box and reverently lifted the lid, which was only locked when he brought his prey back from the hunt and tied them to the cot. He hadn't been able to do that with Glenda, hadn't been able to later take her outside to the fields, and he could feel the pulse of the beast starting to thrum with need inside him.

Inside the box, the red-brown tress of hair was delicate within its tiny plastic bag. He touched it gently. The other items nestled in the box he would only touch with gloves, but his eye ran over them. Her things . . . drawings and chewed Crayolas and the *All About Me* book. Pictures of her childhood. A bounty that he'd discovered after much searching.

He'd waited *so long* . . . had fretted during long nights that it might never happen . . . had sometimes managed to forget for a while.

But now he knew they would be together. He knew where she worked and he knew where she lived.

Soon, very soon. She would be his last . . . and they would spend eternity together. But not yet. The hunt was on. The beast was in his prime.

There was much more to do before he allowed her to catch him.

Nine . . .

Chapter 3

September grabbed an iced coffee on her way to work the next day. The air was already hot and felt heavy with humidity at seven in the morning. Oregon rarely had serious humidity but since the beginning of the month the heat had been oppressive.

She seriously thought about going through the back door, the one the department used to bring in those under arrest. It was generally asked that all personnel come through the front along with the general public, but that meant passing Guy, who wouldn't know how to ease up on protocol if it clobbered him over the head, and he was such an overall pain in the ass "ruleser" that she felt like flouting authority and just going for it. Let someone call her out, if they saw her.

But she was also fairly new at the job and didn't have the power or clout to thumb her nose at the rules, like Auggie did. Whenever Auggie passed Guy he simply pointed at him, a silent, "Don't mess with me, asshole," that caused Guy much distress as he was a little afraid of Auggie who, since he spent much of his time working undercover, wasn't as regular as some of the other detectives and uniforms and Guy couldn't decide how to deal with him.

Gretchen Sandler also gave Guy the evil eye, and though he tended to sputter at her blatant disregard of protocol, she rarely deigned to so much as show her badge. Her theory was, Guy knew who she was, so why did she always have to prove it? Since the time she'd told him that they hadn't perfected cloning people, as far as she knew, and therefore he could assume she was the real Detective Sandler, Guy had tried harder to leave her alone, though it was against everything he believed in.

For September, it was a different story, so she now walked up to Guy and flipped out her badge, receiving his nod of approval before she passed through the door into the inner sanctum of the station, glad to find the squad room empty as she sat down at her desk. It was beastly hot. She suspected the air conditioning was on the fritz again.

They had compiled one massive murder book on the Do Unto Others case, and now she pulled it from her drawer where she'd stashed it yesterday. The locked file cabinets against the wall were where most documents in current use could be found, but the detectives all had a tendency to put the files of the cases they were working on in their own desks.

September had told Auggie she and Gretchen were re-working the information they'd gathered on Do Unto Others, and today she planned to go through the murder book and find names of people to reinterview. Maybe some of them could recall things now that had escaped them during the initial interviews.

She glanced at Glenda Tripp's information, looking down at the solemn-faced young woman. Her mother, Angela Navarone, had come down from Seattle to identify and collect the body post-autopsy, and now she'd returned home with her daughter's remains. Glenda's uncle was in jail awaiting trial; he'd been unable to post bail from what September had heard.

Glenda had worked as a teacher's aide at a nearby elementary school; not Sunset, but their rival Twin Oaks. Everyone at Twin Oaks whom September and Gretchen had interviewed had expressed shock and dismay, but no one knew Glenda very well and her employment seemed to be a dead end as far as learning more about her personal life went. None of her apartment neighbors knew her well, either, although one of them, the one who'd found her door open and had called 911, was pretty sure she was a regular at a local cowboy bar called The Lariat that featured country-western music and line-dancing. When September and Gretchen went to The Lariat and showed Glenda's picture around, the bartenders remembered her, but everyone said she was fairly serious and reserved and, once again, no one knew her very well there, either.

"A helluva dancer," the bartender named Nick said. "Always on the beat, but she stayed back, y'know, even though people urged her to get up front so they could follow. Didn't suit her, though."

"Ever see her with anyone? A man?" Sandler had asked him and the other employees, but their collective answers consisted of shrugs and head wagging.

Glenda Navarone Tripp liked to stay under the radar.

So, how was Glenda picked? September wondered now. Proximity? Had she fallen into the path of the killer and possessed the same body type and general hair color as the other two victims? Is that all it was? Or, was it something to do with her uncle, the once notable Dr. Frank Navarone who had lost his medical license owing to unorthodox methodology that had cost a patient's life, or so the yet-to-be-proven story went? Pauline Kirby had mentioned Navarone in the interview with September, and then Glenda Tripp was killed. Was she *that* connection? September herself?

She wished there was someone else to ask, but they'd bled dry every source they could think of when it came to Glenda Tripp. No one knew her. No one cared. Nothing.

September's gaze slid over Emmy Decatur's picture, and she grimaced as she recalled having to deal with the girl's parents. It had been a sad, uncomfortable scene when Sandler had asked them to identify the body. Emmy had been reported missing by her roommate, Nadine Wilkerson, who worked with Emmy at The Indoor Beach, a puce-colored tanning salon in a strip mall. Nadine had been the one who first raised the alarm that Emmy was missing, and when September and Sandler met Nadine at her apartment and went through Emmy's belongings, she said she and Emmy occasionally went to a local pub, Gulliver's, one that September had been to a couple of times. Gulliver's sported a suit of armor at the door and medieval weaponry displayed on the paneled walls, but its big attraction was Thursday Ladies Night—or more accurately, Wenches' Night, where the women were served dollar beers and, if they felt like dressing the part with a full skirt and peasant blouse, the lower cut the better—they might even get their beer for free. Emmy'd apparently had a thing for one of the servers, a guy named Mark who wouldn't give her the time of day. September and Gretchen had chased him down at Gulliver's and really put the questions to him, but he wasn't all that smart, and he was one of those "workout" guys who didn't have time for much of anything else. He just didn't seem to possess the imagination to commit the murders, so he'd disappeared into the background although they were keeping tabs on him.

The first victim, Sheila Dempsey, was the one they knew the least about. She'd been found outside the city limits and so, apart from hearing it on the news, the Laurelton police had little to do with the investigation, at least in the beginning. After the discovery of Emmy Decatur's body, September had interviewed the county deputy assigned to the case and he'd subsequently e-mailed her a list of people he'd talked to about Sheila, which September had run off her printer. She was scowling at it when Gretchen plopped down in the "perp" chair next to her desk and leaned an elbow onto the papers on its top.

"Anything new?" she asked.

"I keep thinking we need to learn more about Sheila Dempsey. Reinterview the people listed in Deputy Dalton's report."

"Start with the ex-husband," Gretchen said, her nasal tones more pronounced in the morning.

"Estranged husband." September wanted to talk to Sheila Dempsey's parents as well, but she didn't think Gretchen was wrong about Dempsey. The guy had given the deputy next to nothing, according to the report.

"Sounds like as good a plan as any. We need to kick-start this investigation before the feds learn about it and swoop in and take it away from us."

"I wish Wes were back," September said, thinking aloud. "He met Sheila once, or maybe twice, at The Barn Door. The bar with the mechanical bull."

"I know—the seventy-two-ounce steak place. Eat it all and you get it for free. Weasel tell you he tried that once?"

Wes "Weasel" Pelligree was another detective with the

Laurelton PD. He was African-American and had that lean, cowboy look that September found appealing. He'd gotten wounded helping Auggie on the Zuma case and had taken a bullet to the abdomen. Luckily, he was going to be fine, but he was still recuperating after surgery and in the care of his longtime girlfriend, Kayleen. No word on when he'd be back.

"He said he puked it up in the alley behind the place," September remembered with a smile. "But he said Sheila was cheering him on while he was eating it. A couple weeks later she was gone."

Gretchen nodded and looked at the bulletin board. Before Decatur's and Tripp's bodies had turned up, Wes had kept Sheila's picture on his desk, a reminder. Now all three victims' photos were on the board with pertinent data about each crime listed beneath them. Everything else was in the file.

"All three of them frequented bars," September pointed out.

"Who doesn't?" Gretchen stood up and stretched. "I mean, yeah, some people have problems with alcohol and all that, but these three women . . . that doesn't seem to be relevant with them. They were looking for a good time. Even Glenda, she just liked to dance."

"I was thinking that . . . maybe he picked Glenda after I talked about Frank Navarone in that interview with Pauline Kirby."

Gretchen frowned. "You think you influenced him?"

"She was killed that night. My interview ran at ten, and Auggie and I were called to her apartment the next morning. The neighbor saw the open door."

"Huh." Gretchen thought that over, then asked, "What's Sheila Dempsey's husband's name?"

September looked down at the notes. "Greg Dempsey. Sheila's parents live in Portland. Diane and Rick Schenk."

"Let's start with hubby. I like the idea of a face-to-face. Get something going. It's been like a morgue around here."

George showed up, yawning as he settled his bulk into his desk chair. "You guys are sure early."

"No, George. You're late. Again," Gretchen said.

"Shut up, Sandler," he said without heat.

"Get yourself some coffee and try to be nice."

He gazed at her blandly. "Like you are?"

Gretchen's mouth turned up at the corners briefly.

The Dempsey home was a modular house in a park of many such homes. Most of them were trimmed and tidy, but Greg Dempsey's was rampant with dandelions, the lawn brittle and bleached tan, the asphalt drive cracking at the edges and one big chunk of it had fallen and tipped into the yard. The front gutter had a big ding in it, as if struck by a rock, and when September rang the bell the plastic covering fell into her hand, exposing hanging wires. She knocked loudly twice instead.

"Think he's mourning his wife's death or just your average slob?" Gretchen asked.

"Guess we're gonna find out," September said as she heard heavy footsteps just before the door swung inward.

Greg Dempsey was somewhere in his mid-thirties with lanky, dirty-blond hair and that super-thin, fragile look of someone who'd been sick a long time or an inveterate junkie. He eyed them speculatively as both September and Gretchen introduced themselves and pulled out their identification.

"More cops? I thought I was done with you guys." He swung the door wide and walked back inside.

September started to step inside, but Gretchen held out an arm and called, "May we come inside, Mr. Dempsey."

"Sure. Whatever."

"You never know," Gretchen said in an aside to September. "You find something in the house, try to arrest the guy. His lawyer says in court that you weren't invited in. Unlawful search and all that. Besides, it's polite."

"Okay."

The living room smelled like sour beer, which wasn't a surprise given the cans that were tossed into every corner and spilled off a table onto the matted carpet. Dempsey was sprawled on a couch, staring at a television that had been muted. "What do you want to know now?" he asked.

"We're heading up the investigation of possibly three women, maybe more, who've been killed in essentially the same manner," Gretchen said. "Your wife is the first that we know of. We were hoping you could just fill in a few things for us."

"Me and Sheila were done," he volunteered. "Kaput. She'd moved on. Kicked me out of the place and started screwing every guy she could find. I moved back here after she . . . died."

September had a picture of Sheila living at the house and thought it had probably been a lot nicer then. "Do you know if she was seeing anyone in particular?" she asked diffidently.

"Jake Westerly, the miserable fuck."

Jake Westerly!

September hid her intake of breath behind a short cough. She'd just been thinking about him. But Jake . . .

linked to this investigation . . . it couldn't be. The idea
made her so uncomfortable that it took an effort to snap
herself back to the present.

"You know that she was seeing Westerly for certain?"
Gretchen was asking skeptically. "You didn't mention it
before."

"You mean to that deputy who told me my wife had
been murdered?" Dempsey sneered. "He was more interested in me and my whereabouts than listening to anything I had to say, so I just shut up. Fuck 'em."

"But you've thought it over now . . ." Gretchen prodded.

"Sheila knew Westerly from way back. She cut his hair
and they were . . . friends," he said with a twist of his lips.

September remembered, then, that Sheila had worked
as a part-time hairdresser. Deputy Dalton had reported
that Sheila had no particular client list and had only
worked at the salon a short time. He hadn't followed up,
apparently, so maybe he did put the blame for Sheila's
death at her husband's feet.

But *Jake Westerly!*

September suddenly recalled the slide of his hands
across her skin, the heat of his mouth, the shock and thrill
of intimacy. She felt slightly dizzy. Almost ill. She'd had
a few other relationships since Jake, but they'd never had
that same, throat-grabbing power. Now she clenched her
teeth together until her jaw ached and tried to stay in the
moment.

Gretchen asked Dempsey more questions about
Sheila: who else she was friends with, how she spent her
extra time, did she have any enemies that he knew of.
Dempsey didn't have much else in the way of real information. Kept circling around to the fact that "she couldn't

keep her legs together" after they'd split up, and that she had a real thing for the cowboy type.

September kept silent throughout. Jake Westerly had been a three-sport athlete in high school, tough and strong, but from her recollection, not a thing about him read "cowboy." At least not then. She wondered now if he hung around The Barn Door . . . his family had lived in the Laurelton area back in the day, and his father, Nigel Westerly, had worked as a foreman/overseer at The Willows when her father first invested in the winery, commuting the forty minutes each way every day. Nigel had been first on the scene of September's mother's accident as Kathryn had been driving away from the winery. He'd tried to save her, but she was gone before the ambulance arrived. Braden, in his grief, had half-blamed Nigel for not saving his wife, and even September, dealing with her own loss, had lashed out at Jake's father. But Nigel was as torn up as anyone. He'd liked Kathryn. She'd been nice to him, he'd said, over and over, like a litany. Treated him like an equal. It didn't stop Braden from firing him, though maybe it was a blessing in disguise because Nigel purchased a small vineyard nearby and began cultivating his own Pinot Noir grapes.

But September hadn't known any of that when she was a girl. She'd only known that her mother was gone, and then her sister, and that she'd wanted something special her senior year and she'd done her damnedest to make Jake Westerly notice her . . . and had succeeded.

She forcibly shut her mind down to those events, concentrating instead on the fact that, when they'd hooked up, Jake had mentioned the accident that had taken her mother's life, saying Kathryn's death had really hit his father hard. His words made September feel even smaller and meaner that she already had for the rash accusations she'd hurled when she was eleven. She'd been just a kid, sure, but the way she'd transferred her pain to Nigel— going so far as to tell him it was *his fault*, and she *hated him*!—was like a splinter under her skin to this day, one that still had the power to hurt at unexpected moments. Nigel's dismissal from The Willows by Braden was another attack on an innocent man.

"But she was still married to you," Gretchen questioned Dempsey, unable to keep from inflecting disbelief into her words.

"I didn't see her much," he muttered. "Stayed with her parents some . . . or at friends, whoever they were. That other policeman asked me all this, y'know."

Gretchen finished wringing Greg Dempsey dry of any useful information, and she and September headed back outside to the department issue Jeep. Gretchen swung into the driver's seat and September climbed into the passenger's.

"What a shithead," Gretchen observed as they drove away. "His wife gets strangled, carved up, and raped and all he can do is talk about what a bitch in heat she was."

September nodded.

"Weasel knew Sheila from The Barn Door. He ever meet this guy?"

"Called him a narcissist," September said. "We should talk to him about Dempsey. I know he checked on Dempsey's whereabouts during the time Emmy Decatur was killed and basically cleared him."

Gretchen snorted. "Yeah, what was that again?"

"Dempsey has the graveyard shift at a convenience store off Vick Road. The one in the strip mall. I think it's a 7-Eleven. He was there. Cameras on him all night."

She made a growling sound and said, "Maybe he switched the tapes."

"He's a bastard," September said, "but I don't think he's good for it. He didn't react when you introduced me just now. I was standing right there, but he barely noticed me. He didn't send my artwork to me."

"If it's all connected."

"You and Auggie . . . you think I'm reaching?"

Gretchen made a face. "Nope. I just wish assholes like Dempsey were wiped off the planet. All right, what's next? This Jake Westerly?"

September said carefully, "Let's go see the Schenks, Sheila's parents."

She made a grunt of acceptance. "I'm going to call this deputy—Dalton—and see what he thinks about Dempsey. I don't blame him for wanting to pin the thing on him, but he sure dropped the ball."

"D'Annibal basically squeezed it away from county."

"Only after Emmy Decatur's body was found," Gretchen reminded her. "Sounds like Dawson was just sitting around on his ass like George does instead of getting anything done."

"Is that the tack you're going to take?"

Gretchen turned to September, a little surprised. "You want to get warm and fuzzy on a homicide case?"

"No."

"I know you don't like my style. And you know what? I don't fucking care."

"Why don't you let me talk to him?" September suggested.

"Think you can do better?"

"Probably not," she hedged. She didn't want to get on Gretchen's bad side, but good God, Sandler could be a downright bully sometimes.

"Fine, you take Dalton. After you talk to him, let's go to The Barn Door, see if anybody knows this Westerly. Dempsey said Sheila liked cowboys and The Barn Door's got that going in spades."

Uncomfortable, September nevertheless kept her mouth shut. She would call Dalton and see if he had anything else to add to the investigation.

The Schenks lived in Portland on the east side of the Willamette River, and when Gretchen and September had explained what they wanted, Sheila's parents were more than happy to talk to them—maybe anyone—about their daughter. They waxed nostalgic on her days playing elementary and high school soccer. "She always wanted to be a cowgirl, though," her mother had said. "You just don't know how hard she tried to get us to buy her a horse. I always said, 'We live in the city, honey,' but she didn't care."

"We moved from Laurelton to Portland when she was a sixth grader," Mr. Schenk explained.

From the file, September knew that Sheila was about her same age. "What grade school?" she asked, her thoughts on Jake.

"Twin Oaks."

September exchanged a look with Gretchen. Glenda Tripp had worked at Twin Oaks and Sheila had attended elementary school there. Gretchen then asked the Schenks about Sheila's relationship with her estranged husband, and that was when the Schenks shut down as if someone had hit the GAME OVER button. It was clear they didn't much like Greg Dempsey, but when questioned about it, they kept trying to shift the conversation to happier days with Sheila. They finally admitted that Sheila and Greg just didn't get along, but that's all they would say.

An hour later, September and Sandler were heading back to the station when Gretchen took a detour into Taco Bell. "I can't face the vending machine today," she said, "and I don't have time for lunch."

"Tacos are fine with me," September said as they walked inside.

"That mighta been a huge waste of time with the parents," Gretchen said after they'd ordered, received their tray, and walked back to a table.

"Except for the part about Twin Oaks."

"Yeah . . ." Gretchen frowned. "I wonder how Glenda Tripp got her job there," she said as she bit into her taco.

"She didn't go to elementary school at Twin Oaks," September said, dragging from her memory information from Glenda's file. "She went somewhere in Portland."

"I remember that, too. . . ." She shook her head. "Could be coincidence."

"Could it?"

"We gotta be careful about making connections when there aren't any. Sheila Dempsey attended school at Twin Oaks until sixth grade, but she doesn't appear to have had anything to do with the school since. Glenda Tripp was looking for a job, and found one at Twin Oaks."

"Or . . . there's something the two women share that's centered around Twin Oaks," September said.

Sandler grimaced. "Okay. We should check the current staff. See if any of them were there when Sheila attended and knew Glenda."

"Okay." September's mind was already traveling back to the Jake Westerly angle, trying to figure out the best way to handle it. She didn't believe he had anything to do with Sheila Dempsey's death, but he did know Sheila, and he knew September, and well . . . she wanted to talk to him before Sandler or anyone else did.

They finished eating, tossed their trash into a bin, slipped the tray in its slot on the counter atop the garbage receptacle and headed back to the Jeep.

"I'll check on the staff at Twin Oaks," Gretchen said as they wheeled into the department lot. "And I'm gonna do some more background checking on that prick Dempsey."

"I'll call Deputy Dalton, and then see what I can find on Jake Westerly," September said casually.

"Have George look into it. All he ever does is sit like a stone in front of his computer. Give him something to do."

"Yeah . . ." September said, though she had no intention of doing so at all.

"If Dalton tries to do a little two-step, we might have to meet this deputy face-to-face and discover his level of incompetence firsthand."

"Dempsey didn't tell him about Westerly or much of anything else," September reminded her.

"Dalton didn't do shit," Gretchen retorted. Then, "Maybe it is better if you talk to him."

Ya think? September wisely kept that to herself as well.

As soon as she got back to the station she put in a call to the deputy, who wasn't in at the moment, so September was invited to leave a message. She told Dalton's voice mail who she was and that she was following up on Sheila Dempsey's homicide. After leaving her cell number, she hung up.

Next, she checked for Jake Westerly through her own computer and came up with an address not all that far from her apartment complex, and a number that, by the exchange, was clearly his cell.

Should she call him? Stop by? She didn't even know what the hell he was doing any longer, and wondered if she should revive her Facebook account and see if she could find him that way. She'd deactivated the account, which she only sporadically looked at anyway, after she'd received the artwork.

The artwork . . . Jake Westerly. He'd been a classmate of hers in second grade and pretty much every grade since. But there were a lot of kids who'd gone all the way through elementary school and high school with September. Jake was just the one who'd made the biggest impression on her. She, Auggie, and May had been enrolled in public school after their father had gotten in a furious wrangle with the administration of the exclusive private school that March and July had attended. According to family legend, Braden had bellowed that they were a bunch of arrogant hypocrites with too much power for their paltry little lives, or something like that. So, September had gone kindergarten through sixth grade to Sunset Elementary, then moved on to Sunset Junior High, and finally Valley Sunset High. Jake Westerly had done the same.

Sheila Schenk Dempsey had attended Twin Oaks, but the family had moved and September had never known her, though they were the exact same age. But Sheila had been Jake's hairdresser, so it was possible that Jake Westerly had known her before her parents moved from Laurelton to Portland. Could be random. Gretchen was right about making too many connections, too soon.

All September needed to do was ask him.

What did she know about him today?

Nigel had started his own winery shortly after Kathryn's death, his fight with Braden, and his subsequent dismissal from Rafferty Enterprises. September had asked her sister July about the Westerly winery at July's birthday party, which had taken place at The Willows. She'd learned that Nigel's sons, Jake and Colin, had taken over the business, which was known as Westerly Vale Vineyard. Though September had pressed for more details, July hadn't seemed to be interested in anything but her "date," Dashiell Vogt, who stood on the fringes of the outdoor party, a glass of wine in hand, surveying the crowd but not really a part of it. Though July's attention seemed riveted on him, September didn't get the same hit from him. He was too aloof, his attention more often on Braden and March than July or any of the other women invitees. But September hadn't seen July since and didn't know what the current status was between them.

Another trip to The Willows might be in order, she decided now. And maybe one to nearby Westerly Vale Vineyard. Maybe that was the way to contact Jake.

Jake Westerly. Good God. Her mind wanted to slip to their time together, but she wouldn't let it. With a sound of frustration, she dragged it back to the present. It was an effort to put thoughts of Jake aside, but she managed.

She put in a call to Detective Wes "Weasel" Pelligree and, after chatting with him about the state of his injury, which was healing fine and pissing him off more than anything because it was keeping him away from work, she asked, "You met Greg Dempsey face-to-face, right? Sheila's husband?"

"Eh . . . I only went to The Barn Door a few times, especially after eating that seventy-two-ounce steak," he said. "Dempsey was there once with Sheila, and they were in a corner, havin' a big fight. He was mad 'cause she was there and he had to go to work. He told her to go home and she told him where he could stick that. Got kinda ugly and I was startin' their way, when he stalked out."

"You called him a narcissist," September reminded him.

"Yep. From what Sheila said. You know the type: they're only thinkin' about what's next for them. They're bored with everythin' you say. Don't even hear ya. And everythin' that comes out of their mouth is about them."

"I know the type," September agreed, thinking about both her current and ex-stepmother.

"You lookin' at Dempsey for Do Unto Others?" he asked.

"Well, he sure can't say anything nice about Sheila."

"His kind can't say anythin' nice about anyone. Much as I'd like to take it to that guy, he didn't kill Emmy Decatur, and if you check, he was probably puttin' in the hours at work when the Tripp homicide went down, too."

"You sound just like I feel."

"How's that?"

"Depressed. I want it to be Dempsey, too."

They talked for a few more minutes, then September hung up, a smile lingering on her lips. Her cell phone rang a few minutes later and she recognized the ring tone as the one she'd assigned to her brother. She'd put a call into him and it had taken him a while to call back. She answered, "So you are still on the planet."

"I've been busy. Portland's got another task force and they want me to be a part of it."

"It's hell to be popular."

"Yeah, well . . . you know what I want to do."

"And you know what I said about that," she responded.

"Don't worry. It ain't gonna happen. D'Annibal's practically assigned me to the task force before I was asked. You guys are down to a skeleton crew with Weasel laid up."

"Wes is getting better. I just talked to him."

"Huh. Well, what's the big news you alluded to?"

September smiled faintly and said, "Just checking to see if you're ready for another sister."

"Another sister? What do you mean?"

"Our current stepmama is pregnant with a girl."

There was a suspended moment, and then he barked, "Rosamund? No way!"

"'Fraid so, Bro."

"What month?"

September grinned. All of them always went to the same place. "January. But never fear, she's naming it Gilda."

"Bullshit."

"That's pretty much what I said."

"This isn't some kind of joke, is it?"

"No joke."

September had left a message on Auggie's cell when she'd gotten back from seeing Rosamund and March and told him to call her. She was glad Auggie was so sought after and unavailable so he would quit bugging her about Do Unto Others. Especially now, when Jake Westerly's name had cropped up.

"I'm going to have to talk to our father," he said in a long-suffering tone.

"Ah, you can skate for a while more. Rosamund's already pregnant. A little late for changing anyone's mind."

"Man, I don't want to deal with him."

"Then don't," was September's advice. "You've got along this far without him, let it go. Maybe after the blessed event you might want to meet your new sibling, but I wouldn't sweat it till then. Me, I've got to go back. Rosamund barred me from the attic and basement, so until I talk to Dad, I can't get to my grade school artwork short of pushing her out of the way and making a run for it."

"Pregnant . . ."

"Ruminate on that some more. Meanwhile, I've got some interviews to take care of."

"What interviews?"

"I've got three homicides. You know the drill. There are always interviews."

"Who, specifically?"

"Good-bye, Auggie."

"Damn it, Nine!"

"I can't hear you. I think my cell's breaking up. . . ." She clicked off and took a deep breath.

Jake Westerly.

Chapter 4

Jake Westerly shaded his eyes against a blasting September sun and thought about grapes. Specifically Pinot Noir grapes. Fall was harvest time and this lingering heat was helping the sugar levels as long as the damn sun didn't blister the hell out of them.

Westerly Vale Vineyards grew and processed their own grapes, but the greater portion of the wine they produced was from grapes from other vineyards. That was the bulk of their business. His current personal favorite was a blend of three: Malbec, Pinot Noir, and Merlot.

But then don't ask him about wine. He could drink Three-Buck Chuck—Charles Shaw—and be happy as long as the company he was with was good. The true wine connoisseurs were his brother, Colin, and Colin's wife, Neela, and they were the ones who sweated over the weather (this year's cold and wet spring had put the growing season back a few weeks), the grape harvesting (handpicking was best so the grapes weren't smushed but gently split, releasing more of the juice), and the running of their B&B, a rambling early 1900s farmhouse that they'd rehabbed and added to and was Neela's pride and joy.

Not that he would tell anyone that. He was in partnership with Colin—the financial end of the operation—and people in the business expected him to know something about wine. Saying he was the numbers guy didn't cut any ice with those who worshiped the grape.

The grape.

Nigel had been a worshipper, too, though it had taken being summarily fired by that rat bastard, Braden Rafferty, for him to finally realize his own dream. His father sure knew the business, though, and he'd passed that knowledge on to Colin who'd sucked it up with the same fervency Jake had sucked up Three-Buck Chuck—which he'd heard was Two-Buck Chuck in California.

Pricing . . . that's what Jake knew. And loan mongering with skinflint bankers. And the cost of every aspect of wine-producing down to the cute little coasters and napkins and wine corks and glasses in the gift shop— another of Neela's specialties, along with running the Westerly Vale Bed & Breakfast with Colin.

What Jake didn't know was how his brother could stand it out here. Sure, the scenery was gorgeous. But Oregon wine country was too bucolic and the pace was extraordinarily sssllloowww and whenever Jake came to the vineyard, a clock started in his head, counting down the minutes until he could race back to Portland and his downtown office and think in terms of stocks, and bonds, and accruing interest and maybe even a commercial real estate deal or two. Colin professed to like living here, but then, Jake thought, maybe it was marriage that had made his brother slightly mental. Jake lived in Laurelton, in a dumpy, 1950s two-bedroom rambler with mahogany-stained board and bat siding, a driveway that really needed to be rid of the tree whose roots were popping it up near the two-car garage—the right side of which had been added on sometime during the rambler's life and now was about an inch below the edge of the drive—and a neighbor dog that liked to sleep on Jake's front porch and bark at any bird that flew overhead, apparently designated a "no fly zone" according to his canine brain. The dog was a lab and every other breed mix, and had a habit of pulling its lips back in a smile and panting, even when the temperature wasn't this high.

I should sell the place and buy a downtown, high-rise condo, he thought, the same thought that circled his brain every time he pulled into the rambler's driveway. He'd bought it because he knew the previous owners, and they were having serious financial problems and he liked them and they needed help and . . . well . . . he just . . . bought it. He could afford to fix the place up, but he just couldn't seem to find the energy or time or inclination. Neela teased him that all he needed was a woman to push him. Maybe it was true.

Sheila's image superseded the view of the vines that rose across the field and up the terraced hillside, heavy with fruit. Four months after her murder he was still having trouble processing that she was gone. It was weird. He'd known her some during elementary school—she went to Twin Oaks; he was at Sunset—then about six months earlier he'd walked into a unisex Laurelton hair salon, His and Hers, recognized Sheila, and had become one of her clients. She'd learned he was associated with Westerly Vale Vineyard and had made a "date" with him to meet there one Saturday afternoon with some of her friends. From that, he'd shared a couple of get-togethers with her and these same friends at The Barn Door, a shitkicker kind of bar off Highway 26. He'd thought she was divorced, the way she talked about Dempsey, but he'd learned later that they were separated and living apart but still married.

Not that anything had happened between them, but it almost had. He'd been certain that Dempsey had killed her; he'd encountered the man once and learned Greg Dempsey was a crazed, jealous maniac with control issues.

But just when Jake had decided the authorities were a bunch of idiots who couldn't tell their ass from a hole in the ground for not arresting Dempsey, another body was discovered in a field and it was rumored that maybe a serial killer was at work. As much as Jake thought Dempsey could have killed Sheila, he wasn't as convinced the guy was some kind of random killer.

And then September Rafferty did a segment on the news with Channel Seven's Pauline Kirby. *Detective* September Rafferty, who was involved with several high-profile homicides and happened to be the daughter of Braden Rafferty, his father's ex-employer, and the same girl Jake had spent one reckless night with amongst the grape vines of her father's vineyard.

Nine Rafferty. Everyone called her Nine.

She was investigating the death of another young woman who'd been left in a field. Something Decatur. Emily . . . no, Emmy. Emmy Decatur. He'd been fascinated at seeing Nine on the news for a couple of reasons. First, she looked great. So young and serious and her body was compact and muscular, like a gymnast's, or Sheila's, for that matter. Second, Nine was a Rafferty and from what he knew of the Raffertys, they sure wouldn't normally choose law enforcement as a profession, so that was an anomaly. He wondered what had happened there.

Nine . . . He and his friends had sure given her a lot of

crap about her wealth when they were growing up. Her brother, Auggie, had been around, too; Jake had played sports with him and had known him well enough, though it was Nine with whom he shared the most classes. The Rafferty twins, and their older sister, May, had been sent to public school instead of private for reasons still unclear to Jake. He also still remembered vividly when Nine's sister May, and her friend, Erin, were killed in a robbery attempt while working at a local burger place, Louie's. The tragedy had swept the school and community, and Nine had looked shell-shocked for months. Maybe May's death was a reason for Nine's choice.

Or, maybe Nine just felt the same anger and injustice that surged through him when he thought of a life taken by someone else's hand.

Who killed Sheila? Was it that asshole Dempsey? *Was it?*

Jake shook his head and turned toward the house. He'd already walked through the tasting room and gift shop, which were both full of enthusiasts, looking for Colin, but apart from the young man with the trimmed beard and discreet diamond stud in his nose who was pouring, no one else was working.

There were two middle-aged couples sitting in the roughly-hewn fir rockers, each pair holding hands and gazing across the vineyards, so he did a quick turn and angled around the back of the house, opening the side door to the kitchen, which was verboten for guests. Jake didn't count on that score, and wouldn't give a rat's ass if he did.

But he did startle Bronwyn, the kitchen and all-around B&B helper, who slapped a hand to her chest and gasped as Jake entered unannounced.

"Sorry," he said. "Colin or Neela here?"

"Umm . . . no."

"Do you know where they are?" he asked.

"Uh . . . no."

A conversationalist she was not.

"All right," he said, then walked through the kitchen and into the hallway that led past Colin and Neela's apartment on its way to the door to the general rooms at the front of the house. He took a cursory look around their apartment—nobody around—then opened the door to the greeting room, which was a great room of sorts for the guests. In the winter, a fire would be blazing in the stone fireplace and a tray of cookies would be set on the oak side table. Today, though, fans lazily moved the air overhead, more for decoration than effect as there was air conditioning throughout. No cookies, but Neela would put out wine, cheese, crackers, and grapes for snacking as the afternoon wore on. The dining room was a rectangular offshoot with a swinging door to the kitchen that was locked except during breakfast.

The B&B was entirely Colin and Neela's operation; Jake wasn't any part of it. Personally, he thought it was a lot of work and kind of a money-suck, but each to his or her own. He'd spent most of his twenties in the financial arena and had made enough money before everything went to hell to put down a hefty chunk toward buying the vineyard from his father and the house that came with it. Colin had then struck a deal with Jake to turn it into a B&B and everybody was happy.

Sort of.

Lately, Jake had felt restless, and he knew it was an existential thing that had no real answer: Why am I here? Where am I going? What *is* the meaning of life?

The restlessness had started almost immediately following his final breakup with Loni, his on again/off again girlfriend since high school. He wasn't sorry that the relationship was finally over. Hell, no. It had been on life support for a long time and for a lot of reasons. But he was sorry for letting it go on so long. Way, way too long.

He and Loni had dated for thirteen, almost fourteen years—Jesus, was it really that long?—and at times they'd been exclusive and happy; at other times they'd been apart for months, once for nearly two years when Loni was in one of her low periods. Loni was bipolar but at the time neither he, nor she, realized what was wrong. Or maybe she had an idea, but tried to hide it from him. All he really was sure about was that by the time her condition was named, they'd invested a lot of years together, which made leaving her especially difficult.

And it wasn't all bad. After college Loni had gone into real estate while Jake was in the hedge fund/real estate game. For a while they'd been a power couple, wheeling and dealing like they knew what the hell they were doing. In the end Jake's basic conservatism had saved him, but Loni was hit much harder when the economy tanked. That's when the depth of her problem was impossible to hide. The only time he saw the bright young woman he'd once known was when they were talking marriage, either about some friend's upcoming nuptials, or better yet, the possibility of their own. Jake tried to steer clear of wedding talk, and finally this past January, Loni got fed up with his wishy-washy ways and laid down the law: either they were getting married this year or it was over.

So . . . it was over.

The ultimatum should have been a gift to Jake; it forced their final breakup. But the fight that followed, and Loni's subsequent spiral downward, had nearly made him change his mind. Guilt gnawed at him though he

knew that it was his one chance to be true to himself. To
do the right thing, really, for both of them. He held firm
even though Loni called him, incessantly in the beginning, begging to put things back together. Finally, she'd
quit calling.

He shook his head. He still felt low about it, though he
wouldn't go back.

And then, just as he was beginning to look around at
other women, ready to take a stab at the dating scene
again, his hairdresser, Sheila, was murdered.

He couldn't believe it, even now. Sheila and her
friends had come to Westerly Vale on a wine-tasting
junket with some women she knew from work. It was
then that she revealed she and her friends liked to go to
The Barn Door, and she invited him to join them. It was
in The Barn Door parking lot that things heated up between them, and he, four months out of his relationship
with Loni, had been more than eager to indulge in a
heavy make-out session with Sheila in the backseat of
his Tahoe . . . until she'd revealed that she was married,
a fact she hadn't mentioned while cutting his hair.

That had cooled Jake's ardor like a bucket of ice water
over his head. And it didn't matter that she and her
husband were estranged. Married was married, as far as
he was concerned, and Sheila had married a real piece
of work.

He clenched his jaw. If Greg Dempsey wasn't responsible for Sheila's death it was only because someone else
had gotten to her first, in Jake's biased opinion. The guy
was a bastard of the first order. And when Dempsey himself showed up at The Barn Door, confronted Jake, and
ordered him to stop fucking his wife, *or else*, Jake had
been a) glad he'd kept his pants zipped up in the Tahoe,

and b) damn close to slamming his fist into the son of a bitch's face.

And then, shortly afterward, Sheila was killed.

"Jake?"

He turned to find Neela pushing into the greeting room through the door he'd just entered. The door automatically locked behind whoever passed through it, so unless you had a key, or used the swinging door from the kitchen to the dining room, the only exit was out the front.

"Hey, there. I was looking for Colin," he told her.

Neela was a petite woman with chin-length blond hair and rounded curves. She and Colin had met at Oregon State where Colin had studied horticulture, specifically viticulture, and Neela had majored in education. Neither of them had much of a head for business, however, so that was where he came in. Unfortunately, owning and financing a vineyard, winery, and B&B didn't offer the same kickass jolt of adrenaline he was used to, so Jake kept his Portland office and pretty much steered clear of Westerly Vale.

"Colin's with your father," Neela said. "They're working out some details on the harvest. It's about to go full tilt. This weather . . ."

"Too hot. I know." Colin and Nigel loved to talk about the business in a way that made Jake a little crazy.

"Can I help you with anything?"

"Ah . . . nah. Not really."

"You can call or text him."

"I'll do that," he said, but he'd really just wanted to check in with his brother because he was feeling unsettled. Nothing urgent.

Climbing back into his Tahoe, he curved along Westerly Vale's long, paved driveway to Highway 99. Hesitating a moment, he then turned south rather than north, heading away from Portland and further into the heart of Oregon's wine country. There were wineries scattered around the state, a good many of them up and down the Willamette Valley, and a lot of those were within a ten-mile radius of Westerly Vale.

He drove past the open gates to The Willows, Braden Rafferty's vineyard, then turned around at the next light, came back and headed down the long drive. He didn't like Braden Rafferty, but he'd gone to school with three of his children; had been classmates with August and September . . . Nine . . .

She was the reason he'd decided to head to The Willows and check on his neighbors. Just thinking about her made him want to see if her sister, July, who ran the winery and vineyard was around. He didn't know her all that well; just remembered her slightly from when they were kids, though July, like their oldest brother, March, had attended a private school.

He'd slept with Nine when they were seniors in high school, one surprisingly warm spring night after a baseball game where his team had lost miserably and he'd played badly. After the game, he'd gone home to be alone, and then had gone looking for his father, driving to Westerly Vale from Laurelton as his father was supposedly at the winery. But Nigel had already left by the time Jake got there; they'd passed on the road, he'd learned later. Unsettled, then, like now, he'd gone on to The Willows, which wasn't half as grand then as it was now, and, in a funk, Jake had picked up a rock from the side of the driveway and hurled it out into the vineyard.

"What the hell are you doing?" a female voice had demanded from the shadows.

He froze, aware that he was trespassing, not really

caring until that moment. All the buildings were closed for the night and apart from a bluish security light above the parking lot, the place was in shadows.

"I'm . . ." He trailed off. He wasn't doing anything smart.

She stepped from the shadows and he recognized Nine at once. She was wearing low-riding jeans and leather flip-flops and a white tank that showed off a deep tan. Her hair and eyes were dark in the limited light. She was carrying a six-pack of wine coolers in one hand, a blanket tossed over her other arm.

"What are *you* doing?" he asked her.

"I'm supposed to be drinking with a friend who may have gotten caught," she said, as if she and Jake talked every day when they'd hardly said more than a few words to each other the past year.

He'd gotten the impression that September Rafferty was interested in him earlier in the year, but he'd been with Loni and he wasn't sure he wanted to go that way anyway. She was a Rafferty, after all.

"Which friend?" he asked.

"Barb Caplan. You know her?"

"Sure. Bambi."

"I knew you were going to say that," she declared in disgust. "You and your friend, T.J."

"I'm not like T.J."

"Yeah?" she challenged him.

"Yeah," he said, eyeing her wine coolers.

"Why'd you throw the rock?"

"Why're you drinking wine coolers at a *winery?*"

"I'm not drinking anything yet, and I might not be. *Bambi*, apparently, isn't going to show."

Barb "Bambi" Caplan had a set of the biggest boobs

at Valley Sunset. T.J. had said her porno name should be Bambi, and that was that.

"There's a lot of really good wine around here," Jake said, "or so I've heard."

"Your father's are getting good reviews," she said stiffly.

"Yeah, I guess."

"I'm not crazy enough to drink the stuff around here," she told him. "Dad would kill me if I took anything from The Willows, so I brought my own."

"Wine coolers, though?"

"They're drinkable. And this isn't a bad place to be, after hours. Auggie's a master at sneaking into the arbor and having a private party."

"Where is your brother?" Jake asked.

"Not invited, although Barb wouldn't have said no. . . ."

"So, what are you going to do now?"

"Drink alone?"

It was the end of senior year. Jake had tried drinking a few times, but he was more interested in sports, academics, and graduation. Alcohol was fine, but he'd always figured he'd wait till college rather than risk getting thrown off a team. But baseball was nearly over and the night was warm for May and he suddenly wanted to sit down with Nine Rafferty and swill wine coolers.

"I could join you . . . if you want . . . ?" he said tentatively.

She stared at him, thinking hard. "C'mon, then," she said, and he followed her past the buildings and into the lines of grapevines. It felt like they walked forever, but it was probably only half a mile when she tossed down the blanket and plunked the wine coolers on top of it. It was full dark with a sliver of a moon and he heard, rather than saw, her open one of the bottles, pressing it into his hand a moment later.

He took a tentative taste and licked his lips. "Strawberry," he said.

"I've got peach, too, if you're a connoisseur."

"This is fine."

What followed was kind of an awkward beginning where they each drank in relative silence, and then, as the alcohol started running through their veins, it loosened their tongues.

Eventually Jake lay on his back upon the blanket, his wine cooler balanced on his chest, one hand wrapped around it. He looked up at the faint moon, which had risen in the sky to a teeny crescent. Nine was seated cross-legged beside him, also staring into the sky. The vines rose on either side of them, giving the illusion of a wall.

He reached out his free hand to her, touching her arm. She looked over at him and when his hand slid further up her arm, she didn't move away.

"It's almost summer," he said. He had a buzz going. Not totally drunk, but things definitely were just a little softer around the edges.

"Are you and Loni going to the same college?"

"Nuh-uh. I'm going to U-Dub. She's going to Oregon. We're not . . . together anymore."

"You will be again," she predicted.

"What school are you going to?" he asked her, ignoring that last remark. He'd sensed even then that she was probably right.

"Oregon State."

"That's where my brother is."

"Colin," she said.

"Colin," he agreed.

And then . . . it was a little fuzzy after all this time. He thought he maybe wrapped his hand around her arm and tugged her to him. Or, maybe she just leaned in. But whatever the case, she was suddenly half-lying atop him and they were kissing and then they had their clothes off and suddenly he was pushing inside her and she was holding on to him tightly, her breath coming in short gasps, and he was kissing her face, her throat, her lips, and climaxing in a haze of conflicting emotions.

He'd wakened, as if from a dream a few minutes later, still inside her, and didn't know whether to apologize or tell her how wonderful it was. He levered himself onto his elbows and looked down at her.

She inhaled on a shaky breath and said, "I didn't . . . hmmm . . ."

That's what he remembered to this day. The "hmmm . . ." She'd called him a couple of times afterward, but he'd been too conflicted to do more than act like a complete jerk, mumbling excuses of why he had to get off the phone, too uncomfortable when they met to look into her steady blue eyes.

T.J. tried to make something more out of it than it was when he overheard Jake on one of the calls from Nine. Jake had gotten totally pissed at him, but T.J. was unrepentant and had then turned his attention on Nine, teasing her and embarrassing her and after that, Nine had stopped calling, which had bothered Jake at the time, but he let it go.

It had almost been a relief to go back to Loni after that, although when college came around that fall he was glad to be away from her, as well. He should have stayed away . . . left himself open to be with other people . . . people like Nine Rafferty.

Now, he pulled into one of the lined parking spots outside The Willows' tasting room and told himself that he was a rat bastard, always had been, probably always would be.

He was debating on turning around and leaving again, wondering what had possessed him to come—uneasy memories that still burned, probably—when he saw Nine walking across the tarmac toward a silver Honda Pilot. He stared. Blinked. And stared some more. It wasn't a mirage. She was *right there!*

No way in hell, he told himself. She couldn't be there in the flesh when he'd just been thinking of her.

But it sure as hell was September Rafferty. Before he could think it through, he scrambled from his car and yelled across the parking lot, "Hey, Nine!"

She half-turned his way, her hand on the door to the Pilot. Her hair was pulled back and clipped at her nape and she wore a black tank with a gray linen jacket and dark pants. He realized, with a start, there was a gun in a holster clipped to her hip. He caught a glimpse of it when she moved away from the Pilot toward him.

She stopped ten feet in front of him. "Jake Westerly."

She looked a bit wide-eyed, but her tone was cool and careful.

"It is you . . . September," he responded. She looked fantastic. "I saw you on TV. You're a—cop."

She asked, "What are you doing here?"

"I was in the area. I don't know." *Remembering . . .* he thought. Although his memories of her were nothing like the way things stood today. She carried a gun, for God's sake.

"You're on my list of people to see," she said, her face giving nothing away.

"I am?" He was flattered. "Why?"

"You were friends with Sheila Dempsey."

"Well . . . yeah . . ." He recognized, then, the way

she was staring at him. Like he needed to be carefully observed. The thoughts floating around in his head coalesced into one startling conclusion. "You want to know if I had something to do with *her death?*" he realized, his jaw dropping.

"I'd like to ask you some questions. Do you mind going back inside, or we could meet at the Laurelton police station if you prefer . . . ?"

The way *everyone* at ... She needed to be careful, observed. *Ahh* thought ... seemed wound in his head now, when ... other ... the ... whole ... want to know if The ... something to ask ... Jake ... he replied, try something "I'm sure ... had he not ... he ... if she ... for to ... know to ... and the ... plain feeling ...

Chapter 5

Jake—all-around athlete—Westerly. God . . . damn. Still good-looking. Still athletic in that lean way September found so appealing. She got the cowboy thing now, too; he wore jeans and cowboy boots and there was something about his dark hair and afternoon beard shadow. A dusty Stetson would just top off the whole look, except he was bareheaded, his hair a bit longish, as if he'd been too long between cuts or had just given up.

Sheila had cut his hair, she remembered with a cold zing through her veins. Of course.

She was walking ahead of him toward The Willows' tasting room and gift shop, and she immediately took a sharp turn around the back to the offices behind them. July was probably still there. September had just spoken with her and her father.

Her father. God, she hoped Braden was gone. He'd said he was leaving and had taken off a few minutes before September, but the last thing September needed right now was to have him catch her *interviewing* Jake Westerly for any and all information he possessed concerning Sheila Dempsey's homicide.

Damn.

She opened the door to the main office, took a quick look around and was gratified that neither her father, nor July, was anywhere in sight.

"Have a seat," September said, gesturing to the two occasional chairs tucked in the corner away from the main desk and file cabinets.

"No, thanks."

She slid him a quick look. His gray eyes were regarding her steadily and his demeanor had changed since he'd first hailed her. Then, he'd been surprised and glad to see her, she was pretty sure, but now . . . not so much.

"I spoke to Greg Dempsey earlier today," she began, feeling a little out of her element. "We're doing some more follow-up on Sheila Dempsey."

"Okay."

She was glad she'd made a point of leaving Gretchen behind. She'd planned to meet with her father and get his okay to search the house for her belongings and she didn't need her partner involved in that. Gretchen was rechecking with Emmy Decatur's parents anyway, so she was busy, but she'd also wanted to meet with her family, and possibly Jake Westerly, on her own.

Well, she'd gotten that wish in spades.

"Why now?" he asked, before she'd formed a question.

She had to fight back telling him the excuse that county had first been in charge of Sheila's case until Emmy Decatur's body was found but thought he was probably aware of that fact. "Mr. Dempsey mentioned your name as someone who was friends with his wife."

"Yeah? She cut my hair," he stated flatly.

"Did you ever go to The Barn Door with her?"

"Am I a 'person of interest' here?"

"Mr. Dempsey intimated that you had a . . . sexual relationship with her."

Jake swore a string of epithets beneath his breath. "I can't believe this is happening. You . . ." He thrust out an arm toward her and shook his head, as if he couldn't find any further words. But then he did. "I know you," he said in a low, urgent voice. "I mean, we went to high school together. We had *friends* that we shared. I haven't changed that much, but you . . . you're a *cop?* And you think I had something to do with Sheila Dempsey's murder? Really. That's what we're doing here? Instead of greeting each other like old friends?"

"I'm not sure if that's a yes or a no," September answered stiffly. They hadn't shared any friends. They'd scarcely shared anything together except antipathy and one night she would rather forget.

"It's a no," he grated out. "Sheila cut my hair. And, yes, I did go to The Barn Door a couple of times when she was there. But no . . . we were barely friends and we did not have sex."

"How long had you known her?"

"A couple of years. Something like that."

"Did you know her in elementary school?"

He stared at her. "Uh . . . I knew of her. She went to Twin Oaks. I met her . . . but . . ." He found his heart was starting to pound. "Jesus," he muttered.

"Do you know any of her other friends?"

"She came with some coworkers to Westerly Vale on a wine tasting. I know them by name. And we went to The Barn Door a couple of nights, but I don't know much about them."

"What are their names?"

"Why didn't you guys do all this back when she was killed?"

"County had jurisdiction first. Laurelton PD has the case now," she said.

"Is that an aspersion on the sheriff's department?"

"I'm just trying to gather information," she said evenly.

"Didn't Dempsey tell you about her friends?"

She slowly wagged her head from side to side, and, as if finally realizing he needed to stop being such a wall, Jake gave a snort of disgust but he did take one of the occasional chairs, the one that swiveled. He put a toe out and rocked back and forth in agitation.

"She hung out with two girlfriends, Carolyn and Drea. Carolyn had a boyfriend who we met up with, Phil. Phil . . . last name was a cigarette name. Marl . . . no . . . Merit. Phil Merit. Sheila knew him because she knew Carolyn, I think. She was friends with the girls."

"And you don't recall their last names?"

He almost smiled. "If you're trying to jog my memory, forget it. If it doesn't have to do with numbers, I'm a lost cause."

September tried to steel herself not to react. He sounded just like her father. And it was overwhelming talking to him like this, but in a way she was glad for the interrogation. She didn't know what the hell she'd say to him if called upon to make small talk.

"You never went on a date with Mrs. Dempsey?" she asked.

"No." He paused, and then remarked, "The 'missus' part got in the way."

September tried to think up more questions to ask him, but she only circled and recircled the same ones. In the end, she merely thanked him. He got to his feet, and as she was trying not to look up and meet his gaze, he said, "I'm waiting for you to order me not to leave town, or something."

"Don't leave town . . . or something."

She said it before she could stop herself. Stupid. She was looking for his approval? Still wanted him to like her?

A smile spread across his lips. "You're still in there, aren't you? The September Rafferty from high school."

Instantly she thought of their night together, and the flare in his eyes said he remembered, too. She'd been too bold that spring night. Too eager. Wanted too much. She'd called him a couple of times but he'd been unavailable and she'd been embarrassed and let it go. She'd wanted Jake Westerly like she'd never wanted anything before, and, if she were completely honest with herself—something she *hated* being, but sometimes it was a necessity—she could admit one taste hadn't been enough to quench her thirst.

He could never know.

"I'm sure we've both changed a lot," she said repressively, and was startled when he chuckled and shook his head.

"I'd like to talk to you and share a drink, *or something*, and find out everything about you that I missed the night we were together."

The way he said *together* made her feel uncomfortable. "If you can think of anything else about Sheila Dempsey . . ." she began.

"I should have never gone back to Loni. That time, or any time since. It took till last January until it was completely over, but it is over now. And no, I didn't pick up with Sheila afterward, or anyone else for that matter. What about you?"

September made herself meet his searching eyes.

There was humor in their gray depths. Teasing. She felt herself prickle up and had to remember that this wasn't high school, or even grade school.

"Are you married?" he asked.

"No."

"Engaged or involved?"

"I'm . . . single."

"You keep up with Bambi?"

She snapped out of the trance-like feeling surrounding her and said shortly, "Barbara's the one who's married and she's got two kids, a boy and a girl."

"She live around here?" he asked.

"We keep in touch on Facebook," September said. *Before I deactivated it.*

"I'll take that as a no. I think I have a Facebook account," Jake said reflectively. "Might have to try using it more." He got to his feet and peered at her speculatively. "Anything else, Officer?"

"One thing . . ."

"Yeah?"

September gazed at him seriously and said, "Didn't you have Mrs. Walsh in the second grade?"

He gave her a long look, thinking that over. "Mrs. McBride."

"Ah. Do you remember an art project we did at the beginning of the school year? The whole class did it. It was of cut-out crayon-colored leaves pasted onto construction paper. The leaves were falling into a pile of more leaves on the ground."

"And the leaves on the ground were just crayoned in, not pasted. Sure. My mother saved everything, and that 'piece of art' was one of her favorites. I kinda peaked out in second grade, so she hung onto that one for years." He squinted at her. "Okay. You got me. Why . . . ?"

September's gaze searched his eyes, but he seemed completely lost. "Someone recently sent me my leaf picture with a message scrawled on it."

He frowned. "What do you mean, 'my leaf picture'?"

"It was my art project. From second grade. Someone sent it to me."

"*Your* art project."

He was as pedantic as Auggie, for God's sake. "Yes. It was a warning."

If he was faking his confusion, he was doing an excellent job. "But how? Who would . . . how could they get it?"

"I don't know."

"What did it say? The message."

They were walking toward the parking lot now and September drew a breath. She wasn't sure what she wanted from him. Proof that he wasn't involved in either Sheila's death or the warning to her, she supposed, though she couldn't believe there was any connection, really.

That why you hid this from your partner? a voice inside her head asked.

"You said you saw me on my interview with Pauline Kirby?"

"Yes, I did. I thought you looked young."

"Huh." That seemed to be the general consensus.

"You were holding your own though. . . ." He stopped suddenly and said, "Was that the message? That phrase that Pauline quoted? Do Unto Others as she did . . . or something?"

"'Do Unto Others As She Did To Me.'"

"Holy Christ, Nine." He stopped short, stunned. "You were sent that same message on your *second grade artwork?*"

"Yes."

"Wait . . . wait . . . it was carved in her skin. Not Sheila's. Decatur's."

"That's right."

"But Sheila's body wasn't carved into. That was never reported."

"We think there's a connection. There were mark-ings—" September admitted.

"*Sheila?*"

He seemed so shattered she had to fight the urge to offer comfort. *Don't get personal.* "Sheila and Glenda Tripp both had markings cut into their torsos with a knife, but they weren't formed letters. Wait, no." She held up her hand when he would have interrupted again. "We believe the killer was aiming toward his message. Maybe he hadn't worked it out exactly when he killed Sheila. Didn't know what he wanted to say, or just didn't have time. Then he killed Emmy Decatur and left the message. And this same message looks like it was started on Glenda Tripp, but he may have been scared off by some-thing and couldn't finish. Unlike the other two, Tripp was found in her apartment. He didn't take her to a field, so he may have been interrupted and wasn't able to complete his mission."

"You were trying to keep this under wraps," he real-ized, "but Pauline Kirby already outed you."

"If it's a serial killer—and though we're leaning that way—we're moving cautiously, gathering proof. Then we'll go public but yeah, the hikers who discovered De-catur's body told her and she put it on the news. We're not releasing that Dempsey and Tripp were carved on as well to the general public until we have more evidence."

He gazed down at her searchingly. September did her

best to appear unaffected. "This killer . . . he sent you the message because he knows you're on the case?"

"Auggie suggested maybe it's not the killer. Maybe it's someone closer to me who's got their own agenda."

"Somebody screwing with you?"

"Something like that."

"Well, it might explain how he has your artwork, but then . . . why? It makes more sense that it's a real threat. I would take it seriously."

She was gratified by the concerned look on his face, "I am. And Auggie is, too. I just think at some level he thinks it might be someone in the family, and he can't wrap his head around that, yet."

"Is that what you think?" Jake asked.

"I'm concentrating on connections between the three victims. See what the common denominator is."

"And you're looking at me because I knew Sheila . . . and because I went to second grade with you and just happened to do the same art project." His gray eyes turned a bit glacial. "Maybe I shouldn't have remembered it." When she opened her mouth to respond, he cut in, "No, I get it. You're making connections, and I'm weirdly connected. So, is this interview over? Have I answered enough of your questions?"

She nodded. "Let me give you my card, in case you think of anything else."

As she fished it out and handed it to him, he said tautly, "I didn't save your second grade artwork, Nine. And certainly not to terrorize you with it. Better stick with Auggie's theory and check with your own family."

With that parting remark, he climbed into the Tahoe, started up the engine, and tore away.

She watched the taillights of his car until he turned onto the main highway and they winked out.

* * *

Suma, the maid, was just leaving the Rafferty house when September pulled up and parked.

"They're not here," Suma said with a faint Asian accent. She had black hair threaded with gray and dark eyes and was from a mixture of Far Eastern nationalities. She'd come with Rosamund and wasn't the warmest person on the planet. Or, maybe she just didn't like September.

"I talked to my father and told him I was going to look for some of my things," September told her. She looked worried, so September pressed, "Call him. Or Rosamund. Whoever, if you need to confirm."

Suma reluctantly unlocked the front door again and said, "The door will lock automatically behind you. Please make sure it's pulled tight when you go." She headed across the parking area to her older-model Toyota.

"Sure," September said to no one in particular as she entered the house. The front door possessed a mortise lock and it shut behind her with a satisfying click. September didn't have a key and didn't want one, most of the time.

It was six o'clock and the shadows were growing long. Surprisingly, now that she was in the house, she felt beaten down and weary and really didn't much want to start her search. Entering the living room, she saw Rosamund's picture again, the pregnancy very evident. At July's birthday party, Rosamund hadn't really been showing, though she'd only popped in for a minute or two, claiming another engagement. At the time September had scarcely noticed her; she'd been too absorbed in navigating small talk with the rest of the Raffertys, none of whom she really wanted to see except July. Auggie, of course, had been a no show, but then he'd been working undercover at the time, and September had used that excuse to explain why he was absent when they all knew it was because he didn't want to see his father and he didn't really give a shit in the first place.

Exhaling heavily, she walked down the hall, opened the door to the stairs to the attic and trudged up the steep flight. At the top, she looked around. The attic was large, with a number of rooms created by dips in the roofline over several wings of the house.

There was a lot of junk in piles, everything from forgotten furniture to boxes and boxes of financial papers and old tax returns, to out-of-date electronics that should have been thrown away years before. September rooted around in the boxes of papers, unstacking them, restacking them, sneezing from the swirling dust she created, sweating from the heat that had built up. She went through twenty boxes before she gave up, swiping her inner elbow against the perspiration forming on her forehead and running down her temples.

Finally she sank down into an old toile-covered chair with worn arms and tufts of stuffing sticking through the seams. There were more boxes than she'd counted on, and it looked like it might be a fruitless task anyway. She thought about going down to the basement, but couldn't get up the energy. Besides, she hadn't even made a dent in any of the attic stuff.

What was she looking for? More artwork? What would that prove anyway? She knew the killer had the one piece. If she found more in the attic did that mean hers had been discovered by someone in her family? Maybe . . . but so far she hadn't found any of hers or her siblings' childhood memorabilia. Had it been moved somewhere?

There was a whole pile of stuff in the furthest room

from the stairs but it was barricaded by more forgotten
furniture: chairs, tables, mattresses. . . . She glanced over
it but it would take more effort than she was willing to put
in to figure it out.

The basement . . .

Leaning her head back against the chair, she gazed up
at the cobwebbed rafters and thought she could use a
drink of water, or lemonade, or an ice-cold vodka martini.
She would check out the basement in a minute, but she
just wanted to sit a moment and think. What a day. She
almost wished she'd gone with Sandler to interview
Emmy Decatur's parents again. She might have learned
something more rather than just come here and get dis-
heartened.

And that meeting with Jake Westerly. She searched
her feelings and shook her head. She didn't want him
involved in this.

Pulling out her cell, she put in a call to her partner.
Gretchen picked up quickly and said she was busy but to
meet her at The Barn Door later. "Okay," September
agreed, then hung up, feeling a little left out. The only
good thing was she didn't have to explain about her interview with Jake, something she wasn't ready to go into
with Gretchen just yet.

She thought back to the way he'd looked at her when
he'd realized she'd put him specifically under the micro-
scope. She'd seen disappointment and aversion in his
eyes, and it had about killed her. She almost preferred
thinking about the earlier meeting with her father, which
was saying quite a lot about how much she didn't want to
think about Jake.

When September had arrived at The Willows, Braden
was in a deep discussion with July about the upcoming
harvest and a possible "Crush" weekend, where guests

were invited to help crush the grapes, taste wine, basically eat, drink, and be merry in a kind of festival. Braden abhorred the idea while July was thinking it would be great publicity for the winery. September thought it sounded like fun as long as she didn't have to head it up, and said as much, which earned her a cool look from her father.

"How's your brother?" he asked her in return.

"Auggie's fine."

"You're just like him, aren't you?"

His tone reflected what he thought about that, so she'd quickly changed the subject and told him about her desire to search the house, figuring she was on a downward track of his goodwill and she'd better get out what she needed fast. He brusquely told her she was welcome to look around the house and that he would talk to Rosamund about it, then he was gone. September and July had been left looking after his tall form striding away.

"Is he as much of a pain in the ass as I think he is?" July had asked.

"Auggie and I can't do anything right, so yeah, he is."

"That's only because you went into law enforcement and thumbed your nose at all things Rafferty."

"You, at least, have a job," September pointed out to her older sister. "I wasn't going to hang around and hope there was something I wanted to do in the company, and that it would also be something he would allow me to do."

"I don't know why he's against Crushin' It. You ever been to the one in Washington? It's fun. And it would create great goodwill, and put our product out there. We don't have time to really put together a big thing this year, but we could get started, get some buzz going, and make it a regular event."

"Sounds like you've been giving it a lot of thought."

"Our wine's too expensive," she said. "That's a fact. If we priced it better and got it to more people, it would sell better, but Dad and March are such . . ." She shrugged. "They don't listen to me."

September just nodded.

"The weather's bound to break soon, too," she went on. "Then it could be really nice. Harvest is starting. This is when it's all happening and he *knows* that."

"The fact that you can work with him at all . . . you're a better woman than I."

"You don't believe that for a minute, Detective Rafferty," she said with a smile. "So, what brought you here. Dad, I know. But you could have connected with him in Laurelton if you'd really wanted to."

"I like it here," September admitted. "And I went to the house once already and was stonewalled by Rosamund."

"Can you believe she's pregnant?" July asked grimly. "Verna was at least smart enough to keep from getting pregnant. But then she already had Stefan, and that probably cured her for good."

"I think Rosamund really wants this baby," September said.

"Yeah, well, it ties her into the Rafferty money at another level, something Verna never managed to do. January . . ." she muttered, testing it out.

"She wants to name the baby Gilda."

July snorted. "It'll be January, bet you a case of Cat's Paw," she said, referring to one of their most expensive Pinot Noirs.

"No bet," September said.

"I'm the one who should be pregnant," July said a moment later.

"You want a baby?" This was news to September.

"I'm thirty-four and counting. Sometimes I think I should just get pregnant and figure the rest out later."

"Thirty-four's young. Lots of women get pregnant in their late thirties and into their forties."

"But it gets harder and harder, not the other way around. We all know that . . . and now Rosamund . . ." She exhaled heavily.

"Well, what about Dash? Maybe things'll happen between you two," September suggested lightly.

"Dash and I are just friends. He's . . . it's not like that." She shook her head.

July looked pensive and September wondered what the deal was between them. September had watched Dash as he'd wandered around The Willows at July's birthday party. The long-haired guitarist had a lean, hungry look about him that held September's attention. He'd seemed familiar, somehow, and she'd wondered, for a moment, if he'd been involved in a crime, but the penny hadn't dropped and it was July's party and September didn't want to ruin it, so she let it go.

"I heard you'd moved back with Dad," September said into the silence.

"Temporarily. Rosamund had a shit-fit over it, so I decided to stay longer than I'd originally planned."

"Good thinking." September smiled.

"I sold my house. It needed so many repairs it was a money-suck like you've never seen. Anyway, I'm trying to get a place closer to the vineyard." She gave September a considering look. "What about you? Still chasing after killers with Auggie? I hate Channel Seven news, but Dash watches it and he told me he saw you with that woman reporter who's such a bitch."

"Pauline Kirby . . ."

"So, some sicko really wrote something on that body you found?"

"Yes . . ."

"She warned us all to lock our doors. Is that for real?"

"We don't know enough yet." September thought about bringing up her artwork, but decided against it for the moment. "We're still investigating," she added, then July was called by the foreman in charge of the harvest and September headed toward her car. She'd been toying with the idea of stopping in at Westerly Vale; she knew that Jake's brother Colin and his wife had taken over the running of the vineyard and she thought maybe approaching them first might help warm her up for the interview with Jake.

But then . . . Jake himself had called out to her. Could that be mere coincidence? She'd recognized his voice immediately, and in mild shock she'd turned to meet him while strange sensations chased up and down her spine as she looked upon her long ago crush.

Jake Westerly. She'd sorta hoped he'd aged poorly. She'd sorta hoped that she would take one look at him and wonder what the big deal was. But no . . . one eyeful and she was thrown back to that May night among the vines with a skinny crescent moon riding overhead and the scent of loam and vines and strawberry and peach coolers hanging on the warm air. She'd lost her virginity right there and then, and though she'd never regretted it— hell, no, she'd *cherished* the memory—she did sometimes wish she'd just picked someone a little more emotionally available. Maybe even someone she could have had a relationship with of some kind. Sure, they'd been kids but sometimes those relationships had real weight and even lasted.

And then T.J. and his announcement that Jake had

been looking for a virgin. She knew T.J. was a bastard, and you couldn't believe half the things he said. Nicknaming Barbara "Bambi" sort of spoke for itself. But that said, it had still stung to hear his words.

So, yeah. She'd wanted Jake to be a dog, but he was still just as handsome, tall, lean, and athletic as ever, his hair still dark brown and maybe a little longer behind his ears, his cool, gray eyes lit with inner amusement as he gazed upon her.

He looked . . . good enough to eat, and it really pissed her off.

Now, she tried to review their conversation, but her mind kept circling around to the same two issues: 1) that he'd realized she'd been wondering about his involvement with Sheila, and 2) whether she'd seemed professional enough. She'd been so desperate for him to take her seriously, that she thought she might have come off a little too Joe Friday—just the facts, ma'am—when she really did want to just roll back the years and treat him as an old friend, even if he wasn't one exactly. She'd been concentrating on seeming capable and successful and well, interesting. Yes . . . she'd wanted Jake Westerly to find her *interesting*.

So, sue me, she thought, annoyed with herself. It irked her to no end that inside she still hadn't completely washed him out of her system. Even with him on the periphery of a murder investigation . . . or worse.

September got up from the chair, not liking her thoughts. She couldn't let herself be blinded by her own attraction to him. That was reckless and dangerous. Still, he just didn't seem the type to seduce and attack women. He was too easygoing. Too normal. Too involved with people, with humanity as a whole. She wasn't exactly sure what his job was; she would check that out along with a lot of other things when she was back at the station. She had been avoiding driving the investigation at him for a number of reasons, one being she was too susceptible to him. Still.

Grinding her teeth together she headed back downstairs and through the kitchen to the cement stairs that led down into the basement. Flipping on the fluorescents, she looked around, but as she ducked beneath the low-beamed ceiling she saw only outdoor tools and gardening supplies. There wasn't one cardboard box. Nothing paper except some bags of mulch. The place smelled faintly musty and the narrow windows were dirt-smeared. She doubted anyone but the gardener had been in the basement for years.

She would do another search of the attic, another day, though she was fast losing interest and energy for the task. And even if she succeeded in finding her old schoolwork, she wasn't sure she'd learn anything from it.

Back upstairs, she was heading toward the front door when she heard a noise, the creak of a floorboard. Pausing, feeling the hair on the back of her neck rise, she called, "Rosamund? Dad . . . ?"

There was no answer, but the air felt different, in that way that sometimes meant that someone was near.

"I know you're there," she said calmly, even while her heartbeat escalated.

She waited, then felt a jolt of fear when a man suddenly emerged from the shadows.

"I didn't think anyone was here," Stefan Harmak said, eyeing her carefully. He'd been silently waiting somewhere in the dining room, beyond her sight.

"Good God, Stefan. You still have a key?" she asked a bit harshly. Verna's son had always been a skulker, but it had been years since Verna was the reigning evil stepmother and Stefan had the run of the house.

"Yeah. Of course," he answered.

Of course? "But you haven't lived here for years."

His answer was a shrug, and, as if losing interest in her, he sauntered off in the direction of the kitchen.

September and Auggie had gone to school with Stefan; he'd been several years behind them. But the last time September had seen him was at July's birthday party at The Willows. Both he and his mother had shown up—uninvited—but there were enough other people around that July had simply waved off Rosamund and March's suggestions that she should kick Verna and Stefan out.

"Who cares?" July had said with a shrug. She hadn't wanted to spoil her good time and she'd been a little wine-drunk as well.

September hadn't spoken to Stefan at the party, nor had she paid him much attention. She'd spent most of the time staying a couple of steps ahead of her father, who'd been, as ever, bent on learning information on Auggie. The war between Braden and his youngest son would never be mitigated by September or any of the other Raffertys. The only way they would get past it was by one or the other of them making a big concession . . . which was about as likely as the moon being made of green cheese.

"What are you doing here?" she asked Stefan. He had dark hair, a little unkempt, dark, penetrating eyes, and a stony expression. She didn't think she'd ever seen him smile from joy.

"Just waiting."

"For . . . Braden?"

"Mom told me to meet her here. She wants to talk to

your dad about some stuff." His gaze flicked past her, to the picture of Rosamund.

"Verna's coming here tonight?"

Stefan nodded.

September wasn't sure what to make of that, but she'd had enough of the house, her family, and now Stefan and Verna. She moved to the door and heard Stefan ask, "Wait. What are you doing here?"

"Looking for things," she said as she slipped into the surprisingly warm evening air.

"Like what?" he demanded.

But the door was already shutting and automatically locking behind her. With a shiver sliding down her spine despite the heat, she hurried to her car.

Chapter 6

The Barn Door was aptly named with its red and white sliding door that led into a huge room with a loft overhead. The loft sported real hay bales, from the look of it, and a roughhewn bar that ran all along one side of the room, a smattering of wooden tables, and a small dance floor with a raised stage where wooden crates were upended for stools amid varying mics, amps, and assorted instruments. A row of overhead fans hanging on long stems from the rafters were whirling madly in an effort to keep the outside heat from suffocating the patrons. The fans were only marginally effective.

September walked in without paying a cover because it was still early for a Friday night. She chose a spot at the bar, and sat down, wearing only her sleeveless black T-shirt and black pants. No jacket, and therefore, no gun. She wanted to blend in as much as possible and had stopped by her apartment to change her shoes, eschewing the practical, clunky black flats for sleek black boots with wooden heels. She'd brought a black messenger bag along as well, and now she lifted the strap over her head and searched around underneath the bar for a hook to hang it on. Failing that, she set the bag on the bar, effectively saving Sandler a seat at the same time.

"What'll you have?" a blond, female bartender asked her, flipping a white cloth over her shoulder.

"Club soda with lime," September answered. She was still working, or more accurately, working again, as stopping by the family home had been more of an off-hours thing, though she could undoubtedly argue that it was all in pursuit of the Do Unto Others killer and claim overtime. Didn't matter. At this point she just wanted to find the psycho as soon as possible, whether she got paid for her efforts or not.

She was delivered her drink and then the bartender moved on. There was a male bartender as well, but he was much further down the bar, closer to the front door, and he wasn't as young or ripped as Dom at Xavier's, so September figured Sandler wouldn't be pouring on the charm.

Gretchen had called September as she was driving back toward the station and said that she was getting ready to leave and to meet her at The Barn Door. She would fill September in on her reinterview with Emmy Decatur's parents and they could ask questions of The Barn Door staff together.

September had received a call back from Deputy Danny Dalton, who'd caught her as she was leaving her apartment after the footwear exchange. Dalton hadn't been all that thrilled to talk to her.

"I already gave you guys the file," he said smartly. "Everything I learned was inside. I write a damn good report, Detective. You should see what you could've got."

"I'm not denying the report," September said. "I just wanted to get some impressions from you, if that's possible. Anything you might have thought. An observation, or anomaly . . . anything."

"It's all in the report," he said again, not giving an inch.

"Let me ask you a specific question," she said, giving up the pretense of trying to keep up relations between county and the Laurelton PD. Dalton didn't care, and neither did she. "Greg Dempsey suggested that his wife— his estranged wife, Sheila—was seeing other men. There was no mention of it in your report."

"He never said anything to me."

"From your impression of Dempsey, do you think he just made that up for us? Or, maybe he added it after he thought things over?"

"Dempsey's a dickhead. I'll go with made it up."

"Maybe," September answered, though she knew she was too personally involved to make that kind of judgment.

"Look, you want to get together and talk, I can do it. But everything I learned is in the report. I was pretty damn careful about getting it all down, especially when I heard you guys were taking over."

"Okay, good," September said, sensing an insult in there somewhere but not caring much. "If I need anything else, I've got your number."

"Sure. You won't though. It's all in the report."

That could be the epitaph on the man's grave, September decided now, sipping at her soda. It was damn hot in the bar despite the fans. She thought about switching to a chilled glass of white wine, but then wine reminded her of The Willows and that reminded her of Jake Westerly and she decided to stick with soda.

Damn the man. He'd invaded her thoughts as much as he had in high school, and she'd thought she was way over caring a whit about Jake Westerly. She should be way over it. She really should.

Gretchen came in wearing what she'd started the day in: gray pants, a white blouse, and a gray jacket. She was still carrying her Glock at her hip and the expression on her face said: Don't fuck with me.

Hmmm . . . September thought. Why was she looking so hard-nosed? A finger of guilt slid down her bag. Had Sandler learned about September's relationship to Jake?

"God, I'm tired of assholes," she said, grabbing the stool next to September and shoving her satchel out of the way.

"Who's the asshole?" September asked.

"Thompkins. I asked him to check on Glenda Tripp's employment and instead he checks with the lieutenant, like I've overstepped my bounds. He thought it had something to do with the Zuma case, I guess, and that's not ours any longer."

"What did D'Annibal say?"

"Told George to get the fuck on it . . . in nicer terms, of course."

Lieutenant Aubrey D'Annibal was known for being put together in creased slacks, fresh dress shirts, shined shoes, tailored jackets, and his silvery hair was combed, clipped, and styled. His conversation rarely fell into expletives. Reading between the lines, September guessed he'd said something like, "Go ahead and do the research, Thompkins. It's for the Do Unto Others case."

"So, did George learn anything about Glenda?"

"Not really. Looks like a dead end as far as connecting Tripp to Dempsey. Tripp applied all over the city for a teaching job, and was finally given summer classes at Twin Oaks. She took the job because she needed the experience, but she got paid next to nothing. She was hoping to get on staff this fall, but well, we know it never happened."

"Any staff members still there from when Sheila attended?"

"We can look into that when school opens Monday. For now, I need a drink." She tried to catch the female bartender's eyes, but she was busy with a group of cowboy types and it was the male bartender who caught Sandler's raised hand and came down the bar to help them.

"What can I do for you?" he asked.

"Cranberry juice, a little lime and vodka."

"Cosmo?"

"Whatever."

As he turned away to get her drink, September asked her, "Did the Decaturs offer anything more?"

Gretchen shook her head. "Mostly it was more of the same. What a wonderful girl she was. What a bright light. They just want to talk about her, like the Schenks did about Sheila, and they do not want to even brush on Emmy's murder and sexual assault. Remember Emmy's coworker, Nadine, who said Emmy's parents had kicked her out her junior year? That they didn't care about her?"

"And you said, 'Don't believe it.'"

"Well, I was right on that one. The parents are really having trouble with her death. I did ask them what schools she went to. Brandyne Elementary and Junior High, and Rutherford High. Not Twin Oaks. Same district, different lineup."

September made a "hmm" sound. She visualized the Decaturs from the time she and Gretchen had interviewed them at their home on Sycamore Street, which was on the opposite side of town from September's Sunset Elementary, Sunset Junior High and Valley Sunset High. Emmy Decatur had attended schools in the same district, but hers didn't funnel into Valley Sunset High like September's, and since Sheila hadn't stayed past sixth grade, she hadn't attended either Brandyne Junior High or Rutherford High where Emmy had been until she dropped out. Rutherford High and Valley Sunset had long been rivals within the same district, and though a lot of students knew each other from sports, or family friends, or because they'd crossed from one high school to the next, a lot of them only knew their own classmates. It didn't appear there was a connection between Emmy Decatur and Sheila Dempsey through their schools. They hadn't attended the same elementary school and Sheila never made it to junior high or high school in the district where she might have met Emmy. If there was a connection between them, she and Gretchen needed to keep looking for it.

"Glenda Tripp went to a Portland school. Lincoln, maybe," Gretchen said.

"Do you think the killer changed his m.o. with her?" September asked.

"Nah. It's just like we're thinking. He didn't have time to move her body to a field. He kills them somewhere else and drops them off. He was interrupted. Does it seem to you he's just targeting a type—athletic women with darker hair? It seems that way to me." She slid a look at September.

"I know," she said. "I fit the part. But he picks them up outside of bars and he sent my artwork to the station, which is different, too."

"All three vics lived in the Laurelton area, so maybe he's from here."

"If he did them all," September said.

"Do you think it's a question? I know we're dancing around, keeping it from the public, keeping the feds from taking over before we know, but really?"

September locked eyes with her partner. "He did them all."

Gretchen nodded once. "I agree. We'll go on that assumption from here on out."

"And I do think the killer's the same person who sent me my artwork and the card with my age."

"Okay." She pressed her lips together. "Then it's someone who knows you. Maybe he's even lived here all his life. One of your classmates?"

"At least you didn't say it was my family." September drew a breath. "So, that's how he has my artwork? Because he knows me and he's saved it all these years and decided to send it to me now . . . ?"

"How'd he get access to your grade school project?" she asked, nodding, circling back to the same basic issue.

"I don't know." September shook her head. She didn't believe for an instant that either her father or March could have sent that "bloody" artwork. Stefan was a possibility, she supposed, but he was an odd duck whose interests seemed more juvenile than alarming. He'd never had a girlfriend, or boyfriend, for that matter, that she knew of, and, since he'd never shown the least little bit of interest in moving out, she'd just kind of always thought of him as a Peter Pan type. If he had a job, she didn't know what it was. And the killer wasn't July, or either of the two stepmothers. Besides the fact that she just couldn't imagine any of them as the killer, the three victims had all been sexually abused and unless somebody found irrefutable evidence to the contrary, September was sticking with the theory that their doer was male.

But for September, that meant that Gretchen had been right the first time: the killer was one of her classmates. Jake Westerly was a better candidate. He'd gone to second grade with her. He remembered the project. He knew Sheila.

"So, if it's not one of your family," Gretchen was going on, "then how does he have your artwork? I really don't believe anyone held onto your second grade leaf project all these years. *All* these years. Gotta be some other explanation."

September knew she was going to have to tell Gretchen about her personal association with Jake Westerly soon, but she wasn't ready to barrel down that road just yet. She wanted to do some more digging into the case. Logically she could see that turning the department's attention on Jake could actually eliminate him as a suspect, but she just needed a little more time to process everything. Her gut told her it was a coincidence that he was anywhere near this investigation. She just didn't know whether she could trust her gut.

"So, where'd you go when I was with the Decaturs," Gretchen asked, unaware she was touching on the very issue September was struggling with.

"My father's house," September said. "To the attic. I thought I might find my old artwork, but there were enough boxes and junk that it just made me feel tired. I'm going to go back, but maybe I'm on a wild goose chase. I don't know."

"What about this Jake Westerly? Did you follow up on him?"

There it was. She wanted to lie, but she curbed the impulse. And it would just cause further suspicion if she were found out. "I did," she said. "I had a face-to-face with him, actually."

"Yeah?" Gretchen was surprised. "You track him down to his office?"

"I went out to Yamhill County. His family owns Westerly

Vale Vineyards, which is just up the road from my family's vineyard."

"Really. And you didn't think to tell me that?"

"I wanted to do some checking first."

Gretchen thought for a moment, then said, "Well, la-di-dah. The wine country . . . So, what'd he say? Did you ask him if he was sticking the old johnson to our vic?"

"More or less. I tried to use the D'Annibal approach and keep it a tad less lowbrow."

"I'm too crude for you? That could hurt my feelings."

"Could, but didn't."

She gave September a shark-like smile. "All right, then. Tell me the whole thing."

"He said, no. He and Dempsey were just friends, maybe more like acquaintances. She cut his hair, and she showed up at his vineyard and invited him to The Barn Door. He went, but she was with another couple. A guy named Phil Merit, his girlfriend, Carolyn, and a woman named Drea. He couldn't remember the women's last names."

"That's a helluva lot more than Dawson gave us."

"Dalton, who said very clearly that everything he'd gotten was in his report." She then related her conversation with the deputy.

"He doesn't deserve to be pissed at us," Gretchen said when she was finished. "He didn't try hard enough. Sounds like a guy just putting in the hours."

Her drink materialized and she made eye contact with the bartender, but almost immediately her gaze slid away. September had been right, at least; not Gretchen's type.

But then Sandler called him back. "Excuse me," she said, pulling out her identification. "You know a guy named Phil Merit? Might come here some?"

The guy squinted at her ID as if he didn't believe it. "I don't think so."

The female bartender glanced over from pouring a Widmer from the tap. "Phil Merit, yeah. I think I know him. Maybe. You looking for him?"

"We heard he came in here with some friends, one of them being Sheila Dempsey," Gretchen enlightened her.

"Oh . . . yeah . . . Sheila Dempsey. The one they found in a field?" the woman asked.

"Uh huh."

"You can drink on the job?" the male bartender asked.

"I'm off regular hours," she said with forced patience. "Doesn't mean I can't ask questions."

The female bartender glanced from Gretchen to September. "And you think the killer came in *here?*"

"We're really just trying to follow up on Sheila Dempsey's whereabouts her last week."

September added, "We're trying to determine whether Sheila's death was personal, or if the killer chose her at random."

"At random . . ." she repeated, throwing a look of apprehension around the bar.

"What can you tell us about Sheila, or Phil Merit, or any of them?" Gretchen pressed.

"Well, Phil used to come in here, but he really hasn't been around since Sheila . . . died. He was generally with his girlfriend, Carolyn. Sheila cut their hair. I heard Sheila say once that her customers were also her friends."

"And there was another friend? Drea?" September added.

"Yeah. They all came in together. And there was this good-looking guy, a few times, that Sheila was interested in. I don't know his name."

Gretchen slid a glance toward September. "How'd you know Sheila was interested in him?"

"Oh, she just couldn't stop touching him. A hand on his arm, or around his waist, or holding his hand . . . stuff like that."

"What'd he look like?" Gretchen asked, and September's heart started to pound, slow and hard.

"Tall, dark, and handsome," she stated promptly. "Athletic. That's how come I noticed him with Sheila. He was memorable. He didn't seem all that interested in her, though. At least not that I could tell."

"Think maybe he was more into her than he was letting on in front of people?" Gretchen suggested.

"Maybe." She didn't sound convinced. "But Sheila's ex came in hot one time and *he* thought they had something going. They got into it."

"Physically?" September asked.

"Just words, I think. Sheila was not happy with her ex. But the other guy . . . his name starts with a J. . . ."

"Jake?" Gretchen asked.

"That's it. You know him?"

"His name came up during an interview."

"Well, he's not the guy that killed her, if that's what you're thinking. He's too perfect."

"What the hell do you know, Diane?" the male bartender asked her, shaking his head. "Anything in pants, huh?"

She flushed and glared back at him. "Wishful thinking, Egan."

September broke in, "You see Sheila with any other man? Or, is there anything else you can remember?"

Diane shook her head. "That deputy came in and asked all kinds of questions right after it happened, but he wasn't . . . much of a listener. We were all kind of stunned. I didn't know Sheila well. She was just somebody who came in sometimes, but it's been weird."

"You talked to Deputy Dalton about Sheila?" Gretchen questioned her.

"Not me. I wasn't here. I just heard he was kind of a . . ." She shrugged.

"Prick," Egan said. "I was the one who talked to him."

Gretchen swung back to him. "Anything more you might remember?"

"I didn't know this Phil guy or his girlfriend. But I remember Sheila, and the"—he shot a look toward Diane—"'perfect' guy."

Diane rolled her eyes and went back to helping customers.

"Sheila was hot for him all right," Egan went on. "And I was there when her ex showed up and got in the guy's face. They headed out the back like they were going to get into it, but Mr. Perfect didn't go there. If I were him, I woulda pounded Dempsey, but he just was trying to keep everything copacetic, I guess. I didn't see him after that. Sheila came in by herself a few times afterward and then we heard the news that she'd been killed. It was sick, man. Sick."

"Do you have any idea how long it was after Sheila was seen with Jake, that you heard she'd been a victim of homicide?" Gretchen asked.

This was all wrong, this focus on Jake, September thought uncomfortably. It couldn't be him.

"Oh . . . not long . . . maybe a week . . . or two . . . ? When that deputy came in and started asking all those questions, I couldn't remember anything. It was later, that I started thinking about some stuff."

"Happens that way a lot of times," September encouraged him. "When the shock wears off."

"Yeah . . ." Egan frowned. "There was one thing . . ."

"What?" Gretchen asked quickly.

"One of our customers came in later, like after she was killed, and said he thought he'd seen her with some other guy who was pushing a little too hard. He kinda stepped in and asked if the guy was bothering her, but she intervened and said she'd gone to school with him. Something like that, but Ray got the feeling she didn't want the guy around her. Like maybe she thought he was a problem."

"Ray . . ." Gretchen prompted.

"One of our customers," he reiterated.

"What's Ray's last name?" Gretchen asked.

"I don't know. Been trying to think of it."

"Did you mention this to Dalton? The deputy?"

"Didn't think of it right off, and Dalton wasn't . . . I don't know. I didn't like talking to him."

"Think anyone else might remember Ray's last name?" September glanced at the other patrons in the bar.

"I can ask around," he said dubiously.

"It would really help," September encouraged him. She snatched up her bag and pulled out her wallet, extricating a business card. "Call this number, if you find out anything." She handed him one of her cards with the station number and her extension. It also had her cell number.

"Detective September Rafferty," he read, then lifted his brows and smiled at her.

"Yes." She smiled back as he returned to his customers. The bar was starting to fill up.

"I think he likes you," Gretchen said as she finished her drink. "Add him to your fan club."

September let that one go by. Since Glenda Tripp had been killed almost directly after September's interview with Pauline Kirby, Sandler had been giving her grief about her "fan club," which represented anyone who'd watched her on the news, apparently, the killer included. She'd cooled off after September received her own warning, but now it looked like she might have gotten over that.

As if recognizing she'd stepped over the line, Gretchen muttered grimly, "I want us to catch this bastard. You and me. But if you want to step back . . . get out of his crosshairs . . . I get it."

"You know that's not what I want," September retorted. "I want to see this thing to the end." They were walking back outside into a night where the air had begun to feel thick and still and hot. Odd weather for sure. By this time of night it was usually cooling off. "And I want to get him. More than ever."

"Okay. Just thought I'd check." They reached their respective vehicles; Sandler's was only three over from September's. Inclining her head back toward The Barn Door, Gretchen asked, "So, what're your thoughts on the case?"

"Deputy Dalton could improve his interviewing techniques."

Gretchen grinned. "What else?"

"I hope Egan, or someone else, remembers Ray's last name or sees him come into the bar and calls me."

"You don't think Jake Westerly's our man."

She said it casually, but September sensed her sharpened interest. "He sounds like the guy who pissed off Greg Dempsey, but I don't see him as the killer."

"Mr. Perfect. You might be right, but it very well could be Westerly. Gotta keep your personal feelings out of it."

"What do you mean?" September asked, slightly alarmed that she was evidently so transparent.

"You don't want it to be him, that's all. You're all twitchy whenever his name comes up. Something you're not telling me?"

She hesitated. "Well, I know Jake some. Like I said, his family's vineyard is right next to ours."

"That all?"

Not by a long shot, but September wasn't quite ready to reveal the full extent of her relationship with Jake. "Pretty much," she said. "I'm going home and take a bath and think about things. See you Monday, if not before." Sometimes they were called in on weekends, especially in the heat of an investigation.

Gretchen grunted and headed toward her car. "We'll check with the staff at Twin Oaks and see who remembers Sheila," she said.

"Okay."

The beast was in control again as he prowled around his home, stalking from the upstairs room with the cot downstairs to the main room and back again.

The need had been there when he was young, but he hadn't understood it until he'd killed the raccoon. The rodent had entered the garage and he'd struck it with a two-by-four and then stabbed it with the hunting knife while the old lady shrieked and screamed. He'd seriously thought he was going to have to bash her over the head, too, just to get her to shut up. She wasn't anything to him. Not a friend. Nothing. But he'd been too young to go after her then.

Afterward, he'd relived the killing of the raccoon, over and over again, especially the stabbing. It was the first time he felt powerful . . . the first time he felt *right*. He started sneaking out at night and hunting small animals, always with the knife. He learned he needed to immobilize them and so he grew handy with a noose, letting it hang loosely in his left hand, the knife in his right. He lured the beasts to him with food while slowly moving the noose closer. He grew excellent at flipping the rope around their necks and hanging them until the spitting, growling, and clawing slowed down. Then he brought out the knife.

The nights were the only time he felt right, though. Like a real being. The days were hell. Going to school was torture. Their faces . . . and their laughter . . . he *hated* all of them. September most of all—now—though he'd felt love for her once. She'd been nice to him in the beginning, but then she'd turned away. She'd been sickened by him. He'd felt it then, he felt it now.

All he wanted to do was fuck her and keep her as long as he could.

And then the killing. It would be done exquisitely.

Like she'd done to him.

His head pounded and he looked through the eyes of the beast where everything was tinged with red. Once in high school the beast had escaped and triumphed and that had been a bloody fiasco. No one knew what he'd done, but there had been a change in him that was apparent and shortly thereafter he'd been sent to the doctors. They never knew the extent of his rampage, but they knew about the small animals. Someone had told . . . one of them who knew the truth . . .

If the doctors had known, he'd still be locked up; he knew that. They'd sent him away for a time—too long— because he'd been deviant and anti-social. "A sociopath," one pinched-faced woman psychiatrist had proclaimed to his primary doctor. Luckily, she'd been mostly ignored.

He'd been good after he got out. He'd been afraid. But that fear had dissipated and then suddenly the newspaper article brought everything flooding through him in a sudden rush. The edge of his vision receded and he could barely see the words on the page. There had been no picture, but it was *her*. Detective September Rafferty! Newly joined up with the Laurelton Police Department.

September.

He'd thought of her dark hair shot through with red.

He'd thought of being inside her. Choking her into compliance, or maybe she would like it and scream for more.

He'd thought of his bone-handled hunting knife in its buckskin sheath, nearly forgotten in the closet he'd fashioned for himself, the one he'd used so long ago.

The beast had awakened, slavered, and *wanted*.

"Nine," he whispered now to the empty room, his gaze dragged to the hot center of the sea anemone on the wall. Not yet, he warned himself . . . not yet . . .

There were others who could slake his need. More than just those who'd tried to betray him: Sheila, Emmy, Glenda.

The expendable ones were still out there.

Grabbing his knife, the cord, and the keys to his van, he headed out.

Chapter 7

Nine spent the rest of Friday night lost in thought about the case and it created a sleepless night. Early Saturday morning she went out for a bagel and cream cheese and brought the to-go sack and a paper cup full of coffee back to her apartment, dropping them both on the kitchen counter. She then pulled out the white Ikea drop-leaf table she had shoved up against a wall, flipping out one side of it and pulling up a chair. Normally she ate every meal at home on the couch in front of the television. Today, she needed a desk.

She cut the bagel in two and spread the cream cheese over both sides, then bit into one half and carried it in her teeth to the table, balancing the coffee cup, a pad of paper, and a pen in her hands.

She hadn't brought home the murder book full of the case files. It wasn't to be taken out of the station and besides, she practically had the Do Unto Others file memorized. She munched on her bagel and stared into space for about a minute. Being off for the weekend didn't really work for her because she couldn't think about anything but the killer.

He'd sent her the artwork. He knew her. He had to. It had been a warning from the killer, not a prank from another party.

Maybe Gretchen was right about one thing, though . . . maybe he was someone she'd gone to school with. How else could he have gotten the artwork? No one had broken into her father's house; she would have heard about that.

Unless the killer was a Rafferty family member . . . or someone who had access to the family home.

She made herself think about that for a few tense moments, then she slowly shook her head and moved on.

Was she in the killer's sights? He'd sent her the artwork for a reason. He wanted her to recognize that it was hers and undoubtedly shake her up, and in that, he'd succeeded. But was she the next target? Or, was she part of his game, part of the hunt? Someone to crow to and taunt. Maybe it was a little of both. . . .

How long had he been planning to send her the message? Years, decades, maybe . . . ? Or, was it something new?

Earlier this summer she'd had the sensation she was being watched. Nothing big. Nothing concrete. She hadn't even mentioned it to anyone because she'd just gotten the job at the Laurelton PD and she didn't want to seem too skittish and paranoid to be effective. She didn't want to be *that* woman.

But it had been there, all right. The sensation that she was being followed, and it had been strong enough that she'd taken circuitous routes home from the station. She still had a tendency to look all around her whenever she got into her Pilot.

Accepting that the same man had killed all three victims, what then had first triggered Do Unto Others? Sheila was the first victim they knew about, but maybe there were others that just hadn't been found yet. It was generally believed, though not proven yet, that the man who'd blasted his way into Zuma Software had also strangled women and left them in fields some twenty years earlier. Then, right on the heels of his capture, Do Unto Others had jumped onto the scene with a similar m.o. September had the feeling that the one had influenced the other, maybe even kickstarted Do Unto Others into action.

Or, maybe there were no new ideas, even with serial killers, she thought sardonically.

So, why Sheila? And Emmy? And Glenda? They were all dark-haired women with athletic bodies who lived and/or worked around Laurelton. All three women frequented bars around the area. Is that how he selected them? Was there another common denominator, and if so, what? The schools . . . ?

She wrote down the list of schools each of the three victims attended and the fact that Glenda Tripp had been teaching summer school at Twin Oaks.

What about mutual friends?

She circled "mutual friends" several times. The three victims might not know each other, but maybe they had friends who made up a larger circle that could even include the killer.

Unlikely. From everything she'd seen to date, this guy's profile would be that of a loner. Someone who had trouble fitting in.

Someone who knew September Rafferty . . . ?

She grimaced and then glanced over toward her cell phone. She hadn't asked for Jake's number when she'd given him her card, but it was a simple matter of getting it. She had the resources.

With a snort of derision directed solely at herself, she dragged her attention back to the paper with her notes, and when that didn't work, she jumped up and headed down the hall for her workout gear. When all else failed, go for a run.

His pulse was deafening . . . a tribal drumbeat that fed the beast. He sat in the dark outside the bar, shivering in his van though he was consumed with heat. In his left hand was his killing cord. Thin and taut. It bit into flesh like a wire and constricted until they simply gave up.

He stared through the windshield at the back of the dirty building. This wasn't his area, nor was it his type of woman. Cheap whores hung out here, all tits and ass and hair. They'd been the bait for the Rock Springs Strangler and look what that got him. Bars . . . jail bars until death.

That wouldn't happen to him. If the police caught up with him he was going to shoot his way through them. Except for September . . . she would be his before that final reckoning.

But not yet . . . not yet . . .

He chewed at his fingernails, caught himself, curled his hands into fists. He couldn't afford even the slightest drop of blood. DNA. The word was like an ice pick to the heart.

They came stumbling out, hanging onto each other, a john and his whore. The guy was dead drunk, but she was probably faking. His lip curled as he imagined her slipping one hand inside his front pocket to ostensibly give him a little stroke while the other one was loosening his wallet from the rear pocket.

Yes, he knew her game.

He watched as they staggered toward his car, a Subaru Outback way past its prime. The guy was in the driver's seat, cajoling, wanting her to get in with him, but she was

resisting, playing coy and cute, and finally it looked like
he'd opted for a blow job because she got on her knees
and stuck her head into his lap. He musta been too pissed
for anything to happen, however, because she finally gave
up and when he threw the car into gear and drove off
without paying, spraying some loose gravel in the broken
asphalt, she simply let him. Why not? She had the cash.

He watched her walk in that mincing way all hookers
in four-inch heels seemed to do. She was trying to hide
the wallet down by her side. If he closed his eyes and
dreamed, she could be September. A little older, a little
more weathered, a lot less desirable. When she got close,
he could see the inches of makeup on her face but her
hair had a red glow . . . fake, probably . . . but his fantasy
took flight.

Nine . . .

"Hey," she said.

"Don't talk," he growled back.

"Don't talk," she repeated. "Well, now . . . how will I
know what you're lookin' for, huh? Ya gotta talk."

He hated the way she went into her routine. "Shut the
fuck up."

"C'mon," she wheedled. "We could have a little fun
together. . . ."

His outer self crumbled and he bared his teeth. His left
hand came up with the cord and it was around her neck
and he was pulling with both hands before she could utter
one more fucking syllable.

He yanked with all his strength, the cord biting flesh
and into her windpipe, and her hands scrabbled and her
feet clambered and she was falling off those platform
shoes.

Relax . . . he told himself. Stop the pressure. *Stop.*

He let go just in time and she went down gasping and

flopping on the ground like a dying fish. Quickly, he hauled her up and dragged her to the back of the van. Looked around furtively. No one. He threw her inside and slammed the doors before she could make another peep. She could be dead, he supposed. He hoped not.

He drove back out of Portland toward Laurelton and beyond, down a twisting road that led through long tracks of sparsely wooded land to a field. He knew the area well though he didn't know who owned the property and didn't care. This was his land. Always had been.

He parked on a gravel road that separated this property from the smaller tracts further west. Sometimes kids cut through there—climbing over the fence with its barbed wire top. He got his wire cutters and snipped open a hole that he would conceal on the way out, making the fence look whole.

Pulling her out of the van, he saw her tongue loll from her mouth but she was still breathing. He'd put her in a coma, he suspected. Cut the oxygen a bit too long.

Well, good. He liked warm flesh.

He half-dragged, half-carried her to the fence, rolled her forward, then followed through into the open field, far from the road and close to a small stream. Above there was a three-quarter moon chased by ragged clouds. He paused for an instant, counting his heartbeats, savoring the moment. He'd been unsuccessful in his hunt last night, but he hadn't been focused. He'd tried for some of those cleaner girls outside a Laurelton bar but it was too risky. He'd had to wait till tonight and go into a deep, dark corner on Portland's southeast side where he knew the prostitutes trolled.

Stripping her of her clothes, he was disgusted by the bruises on her flesh. Someone had beaten her but good.

Then he took off his own clothes, set them neatly in a

pile, pulling out his sheathed hunting knife and a condom
from his pocket. He removed the blade from the sheath
and then laid it on the ground beside him. He stared down
at his flaccid member, then he closed his eyes and there
she was—Nine—her hair in a long red-brown ponytail,
her blue eyes smiling at him in that lustful way she had.

"C'mere," she said, through her pink lips.

He felt himself harden and quickly put on the condom,
afraid the image might shimmer away.

"C'mere . . ." She moved her finger, urging him to her.

He was on her in a flash. He couldn't wait. Pushing
into her. She was HIS and she always HAD BEEN and
she always WOULD BE.

He was panting and thrusting when the whore woke
up. She floundered beneath him and gave one aborted
scream and he grabbed the knife, held it high, then
plunged it into her chest.

He was still bucking against her when she died and
he deemed it a good kill. He lay upon her for a moment,
wondering how long it would take till her body grew
cold. Could he be here that long? No. He pulled out, carefully, and naked, he began cutting her flesh. DO UNTO
OTHERS AS SHE DID TO ME.

When he was done he listened to the quietude around
him and heard his blood singing in his veins. He waded
into the stream, cleaned the knife, then lay back, staring
up at the moon, washing himself of her, lulling the beast
back to sleep.

It would be good for a while now, he thought, though
he could already feel the turn of the beast's head, nose to
the air.

He donned his clothes quickly and gave one glance

down at the woman. The dark lines of blood on her torso were visible in the moonlight.

. . . in fields where they lay . . .

September's eyes popped open to a room black as pitch. Her curtains were made to block the light and they sure as hell did the job. She was hot and had thrown off the covers. Now she fumbled for the light, then stopped herself before turning it on. What had awakened her?

Pulse speeding, she climbed from the bed and parted the curtains, looking out her bedroom window to the road below. There was hardly any traffic so it had to be the wee hours because the street behind her building was nearly always busy.

She turned back, listening hard. Had she heard a noise? Was that it? When you were asleep, it was hearing that came back first. Throwing a robe over her pajama bottoms and tank, she carefully picked up her Glock from its shelf in the open closet, then cracked her bedroom door and peered out, gun kept down at her side.

She waited several long moments, then stepped out. "Who's there?" she asked loudly, flipping on the hall light.

No one.

She stood for several moments with the Glock now held in both hands in front of her, then she backtracked to the bathroom. The shower curtain was open. She was alone in the apartment.

Relaxing a bit, she went into the kitchen and poured herself a glass of water. Fragments of her dreams came back to her: a skulking shadow working its way toward July who was a baby, Rosamund's baby . . . Jake's smile and a woman's voice saying he was damnably attractive . . .

her own voice maybe . . . on television saying she'd just started as a detective and it wasn't her fault . . .

September set the water glass down with a thunk. A noise hadn't woken her, she realized. It was a thought . . . a breakthrough, maybe. That's what had snapped her eyes open.

Sandler's words, just before September received the bloody artwork: *How long you been here, Nine?*

And her response: *About four months.*

And then Sandler: *About the time Sheila Dempsey was murdered. That's how I remember it.*

Gretchen had actually said something similar more than once. She'd only been half-kidding when she'd pointed out that this current rash of murders coincided with September joining the Laurelton Police Department.

But why . . . what . . . ?

The newspaper article. In the *Laurelton Reporter.* Right when September began with the Laurelton PD, there'd been an article in the local paper about her, detailing both her training and where she'd attended school.

Someone had seen that article, she realized now. Someone with mal intent. And shortly thereafter Sheila Dempsey's body had been discovered. She'd never put it together before because Sheila's investigation had started with county and didn't become part of the Laurelton PD investigation until Emmy Decatur's body was found and Lieutenant D'Annibal basically appropriated the case.

But what did that mean?

Was the fact that she was a Laurelton PD detective the kickoff to Do Unto Others's killing spree? How could it be? She'd been in uniform with the Gresham PD and had patrolled her beat and arrested drug dealers and muggers and been to the scene of many domestic disputes before she ever made detective. But there was nothing remarkable about it other than the fact she'd been instrumental in talking down a father who'd kidnapped his own kid and had threatened both their lives before he surrendered. As a direct result of her actions she'd received a commendation and a chance to work at Laurelton with her brother.

But that father she'd talked down was currently serving five years in prison and he'd completely broken down anyway, admitting guilt and feeling remorse. He didn't blame September for her involvement. He'd actually *thanked* her, after the fact.

No, if her theory was right, Do Unto Others had begun because he knew her, knew she lived in Laurelton, knew where she went to school. She was at a loss to imagine who it could be. Her family? Someone from her criminal courses at PSU? Someone from high school, or better yet, *grade school*?

Not Jake, she told herself immediately. It just didn't feel right.

She put the Glock back in the closet, slid back her curtains, and opened her window a crack, letting in some light and air from outside. She stood there a moment, then went back to bed and stared up at the ceiling.

Not Jake.

Jake stood on the back patio in the dark outside his living room and kitchen. The moon was disappearing into daylight. A glass of red wine sat on the glass-topped side table behind him. He'd poured it thinking he would drink it while sitting in one of the lounge chairs he possessed. He'd been meaning to buy more furniture but he'd been meaning to do a lot of things that hadn't gotten done because after his final breakup with Loni; it was like he'd hit the PAUSE button on life.

He wore a pair of boxer shorts and it was almost too much clothing. Oregon had the most pleasant of summers as a rule, but there was the occasional blast of blistering heat that might run a few days, maybe even a week or so, in July or August or September, and right now they were in the thick of it.

Since running into her at The Willows yesterday, he was bothered about September Rafferty. She really thought he could be involved in Sheila Dempsey's death? And that maybe he'd kept her artwork from second grade all these years? *Really?*

What kind of cop was she? he thought angrily. Suspicious and closed off and seeing criminals behind every tree, bush, and blade of grass?

It wounded him that she thought so little of him, whereas all these years he'd carried a small torch for her. The memory of their night among the grapevines was a really good one. He'd held it close a long, long time, whether he was with Loni or not. He'd *used* it as a feel-good, as a means to remember that yes, there were other women in the world besides his problematic girlfriend who would be great to date and hang with and just generally enjoy.

And Nine had ruined that. Taken it away. Shattered his one sacred memory/fantasy from high school.

Well, to hell with her.

But what about the message? Some sick bastard is out there, maybe stalking her?

He didn't like thinking about that. It bothered him deeply. Not that September Rafferty would appreciate him worrying and caring; she'd be more likely to slap some cuffs on him and throw him into a holding cell than listen to anything he had to say. But Jesus Christ . . . who was this sicko? Her brother, March? Her *father?* It wasn't Auggie. That just didn't compute on so many levels.

And didn't she have a stepbrother, or maybe two? He could ask Colin. His brother was more up on the Rafferty family dynamics than he was. What Jake remembered most was that Nine's mother, Kathryn, had died in an automobile accident and his own father had lost his job right afterward, basically because of it. And then Nine's older sister May was accidentally killed in that robbery attempt at Louie's. Talk about your string of bad luck. But then some families seemed to have more than their share of tragedy that even wealth couldn't save them from.

He went back to his glass of wine, thinking about Nine. He'd sensed at that arrogant teen level that she'd had a thing for him. She hadn't been overt about it, like some girls. He'd just known it by the way she seemed to laugh and talk with her friends, but when he showed up her animation fled. That wasn't always the way it was. When they were younger and he'd run into her at school or at home—his father did work for hers and there were a few times when they actually played together at the vineyard—they had fun together. He'd given her grief about her family money as a dumb way to relate and luckily she'd ignored his jibes. She wasn't inhibited, and she tried to keep up with him and Auggie and Colin in whatever game or competition they planned. But then junior high and high school arrived and everything changed. At first he'd thought she didn't like him any longer, and he'd tried hard to change her mind any chance he got. He made the rookie mistake of going back to the well and teasing her about her family's wealth again—one of those "I know you so well" kind of things that only earned him the cold shoulder. Then he tried to seem interested in what she was doing, when he was so self-absorbed in himself that he could scarcely listen to what anyone else was saying, so she saw right through that, too. Finally, he stopped trying so hard, settling instead for a quick smile of hello when he saw her in the halls or at some school event. Over the course of their senior year he sensed a bit of thawing on her part, and when he stopped actively trying to make her like him, he noticed that she was hanging around his usual haunts more, attending baseball games that spring, becoming a fixture around the periphery of his sphere of friends.

And then he and Loni had a BIG breakup—they were all big, but this one was colossal—chock full of all the high school drama that made him groan aloud now. Loni had accused him of having a make-out session with Patrice LaVelle, which had pissed him off but good because, though Patrice was only a friend of his, Loni just couldn't seem to grasp the concept of friendship between a man and a woman, possibly because she never felt it herself. They broke up before the end of the school year and Jake felt nothing but relief. Then he'd had his night with Nine Rafferty and he'd kinda thought maybe something more would come of that, but she'd shut down right afterward—his friend, T.J., hadn't helped—and Jake, in his infinite teen wisdom, had drifted back to Loni.

Why had he spent so much of his life with Loni? Why hadn't he chased after September Rafferty with everything he had? How could it be that she thought he could be a sick stalker of some kind at the very least, and a *killer* at the worst?

Okay. No need for hyperbole. She was following an investigative road and he happened to be one stop along the route. It wasn't any more sinister than that. It just bugged the hell out of him that the thought even whispered across her brain.

Now he gulped down half the glass of wine, then took it back inside and dumped the rest down the drain though it wasn't half bad. But if he was going to drink he wanted something stronger, and the last thing he needed was to drink himself into a stupor for no goddamn good reason.

Half an hour later, as he lay in bed, unable to sleep, he realized what he really wanted was a woman. And not just any woman. He wanted Nine Rafferty. She'd been a fire in his blood twelve years ago, and, seeing her again, that fire had been rekindled with a blowtorch.

But how to do it? How could he get past her very strong defenses?

He fell into an uneasy sleep thinking about her, his mind worrying, his dreams full of Nine's image, always just out of reach, as shadows chased her through the dark.

Chapter 8

Sunday morning dawned hot and mean and slightly overcast, the kind of day that happens after a buildup of heat. September took a shower and then put on shorts and a tank, sat down, and felt herself start to sweat. She changed into running gear, but the air was so humid when she stepped outside that she defaulted to a fast walk and even that took its toll. By the time she cruised into a favorite Laurelton coffee shop, Bean There, Done That, she was sweating freely and didn't give a damn what anyone else thought as she ordered another iced coffee, her favorite drink this summer and fall.

She sipped it as she stood by the glass door to the outside, looking through the pane and debating whether she was ready to brave the blasting heat or stick with air-conditioned splendor.

In the light of day she was wondering if she'd made too much of the fact that Do Unto Others had started his killing spree after the article about her in the *Laurelton Reporter*. It felt a little like she was making herself the center of the universe.

After a few minutes she pulled out her cell phone and

called Auggie. He answered sleepily on the fourth ring. "Did you forget I'm working that drug task force with Portland and Saturday nights I don't get home till you get up?"

"I need to pick your brain," she said, ignoring him.

"Coffee . . ." she heard him say to someone, undoubtedly Liv, who'd asked him if he would like anything. "Go ahead," he said, sounding less than thrilled.

September stepped outside, walked down the sidewalk away from other ears, and filled him in on her thoughts about the Do Unto Others killer and how the killings started almost immediately after she began with the Laurelton PD. She stopped beneath a maple tree for some relief from the heat and briefly she gave him a rundown of what she and Sandler had picked up in their interviews on Friday, finishing with, "And I ran into Jake Westerly and questioned him some."

"Westerly? Where?"

"At The Willows. He just—dropped in."

"Did he know you were there?"

"No." She heard herself, and then added, "Not that I know of. He didn't come to see me."

"Well, why did he come?"

September realized she had no idea. "He'd been at Westerly Vale and was in the area."

"So, what did you question him about?"

"When Gretchen and I talked to Greg Dempsey, he brought up that Sheila was friends with Jake."

"You didn't mention that before," Auggie said, sounding wide awake all of a sudden. "How friendly?"

"That's what I asked Jake," September said.

"And . . . ?"

"They were more like acquaintances."

"Did Dempsey bring up anybody else?"

"Not really."

"Just Jake Westerly?"

It felt like he was picking at a sore. "He said Sheila and Jake were having an affair."

"Ahhh . . ."

"But it was a lie. Sheila cut Jake's hair at a place called His and Hers Hair Salon. She went to Westerly Vale once with some friends for wine tasting and invited Jake to join them at The Barn Door. He met her once, or maybe twice, I don't know. She had a couple of girlfriends with her, one of them was dating a guy named Phil Merit. We're running them down now."

"Okay."

"And the bartenders at The Barn Door said there was another guy, Ray, no last name that we know of yet, who saw some guy harassing Sheila. Ray tried to step in, but she said she'd gone to school with the guy."

"And this guy harassing her wasn't Jake."

"Nope. The bartenders called Jake 'Mr. Perfect,' and this guy sounded like he was pretty far from that."

"What does Sandler think?"

September inhaled quietly, exhaled, then admitted, "I haven't told Gretchen that I went to school with Jake yet."

Silence. Then, carefully, "Why?"

"I just didn't want to get into it until I knew more." She'd never told her brother about her one night with Jake, and now she gritted her teeth for a moment, poised to tell him, surprisingly nervous to do it.

He broke in before she could say anything, "Was Westerly in your homeroom with Mrs. Walsh?"

"No, he was in McBride's with you. But it doesn't matter. He wouldn't send me the artwork like that."

"Who else would send it to you? You're clearly thinking Westerly's connected somehow. That's why you don't want to talk about it. You're trying to protect him because you like him."

"I don't know him enough to even have an opinion," she stated firmly. "High school's ancient history."

"You liked him once. A lot."

A frisson ran through her. "What do you mean?"

"Nine . . . I know."

She closed her eyes and her grip on the phone was slippery from sweat. "Yeah?"

"I knew right after it happened. Guys talk."

"T.J.," she said through her teeth.

"All guys talk. I pretty much wanted to kill him and Jake, but it was your business and you weren't talking. If it makes you feel any better, I don't believe Westerly's good for any of this. He's not that guy. Trust Sandler. Tell her that you and Westerly have history. She's a pain in the ass, but she's not an idiot."

"Okay," she said.

"And if I'm wrong, at least you haven't held back on her," Auggie went on blithely while September's anxieties, which had begun to disperse, came racing back. *It's not Jake*, she thought.

Struggling to put things back on track, she said, "So, am I trying too hard, making the world revolve around me or something, or do you think maybe I'm onto something. That the killer chose Sheila after seeing my newspaper article?"

"It's possible."

"But you don't think so."

Auggie exhaled heavily. "You know I don't like thinking you're his target," he said. "But if you are, then he went after Dempsey and maybe got a taste for it, and then went after Decatur because maybe he knew her . . . ?"

"That sounds right," September answered, glad to

finally have Auggie thinking along the same lines. "And then he chose Glenda because I mentioned her uncle on television. You remember: you were with me when we found Glenda."

"Yeah . . . there was less planning involved in that homicide, and I've grown convinced he had to leave before he was finished. Otherwise he would have left her in a field. He knew all three of them," Auggie said. "And then he sent you the message."

She heard the thread of worry in his voice though he tried to quell it. "You know, I just assumed the message was only sent to me because I'm following the case. But maybe he sent something similar to his other victims."

"Their places were searched pretty thoroughly, weren't they?" Auggie asked.

"Yeah. No notes . . . But I just don't want to overlook something."

"If the killer wrote the message, which I'm beginning to think you're right, he did, then he's toying with you." A moment, then he said seriously, "You could be next on his list."

"I'm forewarned, Auggie," she said, hearing how grim she sounded.

"Be careful, Nine. Like I said, I don't believe it's Westerly. He sure doesn't seem like a sociopath." He hesitated, then added, "But again, I'd hate to find out I'm wrong."

Monday morning Jake drove with repressed fury through the commuters, squeezing the Tahoe between drivers in order to change lanes, earning himself blasting horns and stiff middle fingers.

"Stick it where the sun don't shine," he muttered, turning into the parking garage and shooting down the ramp to his designated spot, a parking space barely wide enough for his rig, much to the dismay of the BMW- and Lexus-driving lawyers on seventeen.

Jake's office was on the eleventh floor in with a group of other investment advisors who operated independently from each other. Across the hall was Capital Group, Inc., a conglomerate that dealt mainly in stocks and bonds, but continually tried to poach on Jake and his other business associates. They were called CGI, which fit in a way, as it also stood for Computer Generated Image, Hollywood magic made through companies like Pixel and Disney. That's how Jake liked to think of them, as substantial as fairy dust, as real as a series of computer bytes. They were tenacious, though. They'd moved in right on the same floor with their competitors without a qualm. If Jake et al. didn't like it, they could damn well move.

If it weren't for the signed lease, he'd be gone already. As it was he had to wait another year and a half and it deeply pissed him off.

But maybe it was another sign. A reason to get out of this business and find his "bliss," as the self-help gurus seemed to be always preaching.

Bliss, schmiss. He was simply looking for a clear path.

Nine Rafferty . . .

Her name was in his head like a neon sign, and he tried to shove it aside as he slipped into the central coffee room for their group of offices. He'd had a bad feeling hanging over him since seeing her again. She thought he was involved with Sheila's death. She did. She hadn't come right out and said it, but it was there all right. And the second grade artwork . . . he didn't get that at all. It was downright chilling, when you thought about it. Who would have it? Someone in her own family, was his best guess, but she'd talked like she thought *he had it*.

At least that's what it felt like after the fact. When he'd had a chance to digest everything she'd said, alluded to, and hinted at. Bullshit technique. Probably learned it in cop school.

"What are you scowling at, Westerly?" Carl Weisz asked him. He had the corner office and though his business was probably less lucrative than Jake's, he liked all the accouterments, the special bells and whistles, that represented SUCCESS in the business world. He would poach on Jake's clients as well, if he could. He was just *that* guy.

Jake couldn't give a rat's ass . . . which, he realized as the words crossed his mind, was what he thought about a lot of things these days. Not good.

"I'm thinking of going decaf," Jake said as a means to deflect.

"No fucking way."

"Sure, why not? Could be good for me."

"Wuss," Carl said with a doleful shake of his head.

Jake half-smiled and filled his cup with the high-powered coffee made by anyone who was willing to brew a pot, which usually fell to Andrea, one of the too-eager interns who fluttered through the offices. Her fluttering had slowed down after two months of service with no clear track to the big time and the coffee had become strong enough to chew.

Carl commented, "That ain't no decaf, brother."

Jake lifted a hand in good-bye and headed back toward his office, but as soon as he'd closed the door, even before he took his seat, his thoughts revolved like a gun barrel back to the first slot: Nine.

She hadn't changed a bit.

She'd changed completely.

He couldn't get the memory of that long ago love-making out of his head. Was this a case of being too long away from a woman? He and Loni had broken up in January but he honestly couldn't remember the last time they'd had sex. Musta been the year before . . . December? God, he hoped so, but he wasn't entirely sure. . . .

And there'd been no one since. *Almost*, with Sheila, but that was as close as he'd gotten.

He leaned his head back in his office chair and rotated to look out the window. He had a view of the Fremont Bridge in the distance, a suspension bridge like the Golden Gate only white. Today it stood bright and distinct in the sun above the dark green Willamette River.

Call her, a voice inside his head said. *Talk to her. Ask her to lunch.*

"She thinks I'm a serial killer," he said aloud.

She thinks you know more than you're telling.

His cell phone rang and he recognized the ringtone he'd chosen for his brother, Colin. Sweeping the phone off his desk, he answered, "'Bout time you got back to me."

"Phone works both ways, brother," Colin said. "What's up?"

"Nothing, really." Jake wasn't sure how to tell his brother, who seemed completely satisfied with his life, that he didn't feel the same. He wasn't even really sure Colin was the one to talk to about it. Instead, he moved into a general discussion about the winery and B&B, and finally Colin said, "I thought there was some big message. If that's it, I got stuff to do."

"Go to it," Jake said. "I'll talk to you later."

Hanging up, he was fully aware that he was going to have to figure out what he wanted to do with his life or drive himself, and everyone who knew him, crazy. He picked up a squeeze ball from his desk, designed to exercise the hand, and thought back to Nine Rafferty again. Did he know more than he was telling? More about Sheila? Was there something that had been said, something he'd heard or seen or sensed that might have stopped her from being killed?

No. He'd been down this road. There was nothing there.

But Nine had riled up all his nebulous fears. The ones that had been rolling around inside his head ever since he'd learned Sheila had been murdered. He knew a few of Sheila's friends, not well, but he'd met some of them. He could tell Nine more about Phil, Carolyn, and Drea. Conversations they'd had, as much as he could remember.

Or . . . he could make some calls himself, he thought, his mind moving in another direction.

Face it, Westerly. You're just searching for a way to be with her.

With a growl of impatience directly solely at himself, he pulled out her card, debated, then forewent the cell phone to call the Laurelton Police Department directly. She wanted it by the book, he'd give it to her by the book.

Sort of.

September and Gretchen were in the principal's office at Twin Oaks when the bell rang for first period class. The principal herself, Amy Lazenby, was short, busty, and about sixty with steel gray hair, clipped short, and a pair of readers perched on her nose. She looked over the readers at both of them, her eyes narrowed, as if she thought they were truants rather than police investigators.

"I wasn't here when Ms. Dempsey was a student," she said after Gretchen informed her why they'd come and said she'd check her files. "She left at the end of her sixth grade year. Mr. Abernathy has been teaching sixth grade for over twenty years. He's still here and may remember her." She pursed her lips and shook her head. "Such a shame about Ms. Tripp. She'd applied for a full-time position, but we didn't have the funding to hire someone extra, so she was only going to be here for the summer."

September nodded. Outside the office, students were shuffling down the halls to their homerooms. She could hear their movement, a dull wave of noise punctuated by a few yells. After they entered their classrooms, the quiet was surprising. Ms. Lazenby looked satisfied, her eyes on the overhead clock.

"Abernathy is in room . . . ?" Gretchen asked.

"I've asked him to come to the office. It will take about twenty minutes for him to get his students settled."

"Twenty minutes," Gretchen agreed.

It took more like thirty before Abernathy made an appearance. Some problem with a question of thievery between two students in Abernathy's room, which held him up, he said, when he appeared in Ms. Lazenby's office. He was somewhere in his early fifties with a receding hairline and was thin and precise in his dress. His mouth was pinched and his ginger mustache bristled, as he said, "No respect for others. None at all. You wonder how the world will survive in the next generation."

Ms. Lazenby excused herself and they were left with Abernathy, who looked from Gretchen to September and back again. From the expression on his face, it didn't appear that he appreciated being interviewed by the police. "How can I help you?" he asked stiffly.

September said, "We're investigating the homicides of Sheila Schenk Dempsey, who was a student here when she was in the sixth grade, and—"

"Yes, yes, I remember Sheila," he interrupted.

"—Glenda Tripp, who was teaching summer school here this past summer until she was killed."

He blinked, clearly surprised by the last part. "I didn't even know Ms. Tripp! I wasn't on staff this summer."

"We're not accusing you of anything," Gretchen soothed though the edge in her voice could have cut glass. "What do you remember about Sheila?"

But Abernathy was on his own path. "I wasn't here this past summer. Ask Amy if you need to know anything about Ms. Tripp." He paused, then added, "I thought the police would have already checked all this."

"We're following up," Gretchen told him tightly. "About Sheila Dempsey . . . ?"

"She was very popular," he said after a moment's thought. "She could have been a much better student if she'd applied herself."

"Do you remember any of her friends? Who she hung out with?" September asked.

"Well, she was always with the Schmidt boy . . . Ben . . . Benny. I remember because their last names were similar: she was Schenk and he was Schmidt."

September wrote that down. "Anything else?"

"He played soccer and went on to be a star in high school."

"At Rutherford High?" September asked, though she knew that's where he meant. "Ben Schmidt . . . I think I remember the name."

Gretchen gave September a look. "You went to Valley Sunset."

She nodded. "Rutherford was our crosstown rival. I never met Ben, but I knew the name."

"Sheila's family moved at the end of that school year," Abernathy said.

Gretchen eyed the man cautiously. "Do you remember all your students as well as Sheila?"

He bristled. "Not necessarily."

"Who should we talk to who might know Glenda Tripp?" Gretchen asked.

"Ask Amy," he said again, and his tone suggested the interview was over.

He left a few minutes later and when Amy Lazenby returned she gave them a list of teachers who were part of the summer school staff. "Maybe one of them can help you more with Ms. Tripp," she said, and they thanked her and headed out.

As Gretchen drove them back to the station, she said, "We'll put George on this list."

September, who'd been squinting out the window against the bright sun reflecting light off oncoming traffic, said, "I told you Jake Westerly's father worked for mine for a while. What I didn't go into was that he was a classmate of mine at Valley Sunset."

Gretchen shot her a look. "Okay . . ."

"He also went to Sunset Elementary and junior high with me. We were friends, sort of."

Gretchen digested that, and said, "Anything else you're keeping from me?"

"We were in second grade together. I've been thinking it through. I didn't want to jump to conclusions just because I've known him so long."

"You mean you don't want it to be Jake," she corrected her.

"I don't want it to be Jake, and I don't think it is," she agreed. "I talked this all over with Auggie yesterday and he knows Jake, too, and he said he didn't believe Jake was a sociopath, either."

"Sociopath . . ." she repeated as if trying out the word.

"They're the guys who almost make sense when you're talking to them, but then it goes awry. You know something's off, but you just can't put your finger on it."

"That's not Jake."

"You're a little quick to defend him," she pointed out.

"It's just that Jake's the guy every girl wanted. When I saw him the other day, I still got that hit," September admitted. "Sheila invited him to The Barn Door because he's . . ."

"Mr. Perfect," Gretchen filled in.

"Yeah. If we're going to concentrate on Sheila, it's more likely it's the guy this Ray saw hassling her."

"I'll go with that," she allowed after a moment and September relaxed a bit as she went on, "He picks them up at bars. He carves Do Unto Others As She Did To Me into Emmy Decatur, and probably would've done the same for Glenda Tripp if he'd had time. He sends you the same message on your second grade artwork."

"So, you do believe the killer sent that to me?"

Her gaze narrowed through the windshield. "I'm leaning that way. But the words 'As She Did To Me' . . . he's mad at a woman."

"He feels he's been abused by her and he's getting revenge."

"Something like that."

"Auggie suggested that maybe he knew them. That it wasn't just a physical type that drew him to Sheila, and Emmy and Glenda." A bit hesitantly, she told Gretchen her theory about the killer beginning his spree after reading the newspaper article about her, finishing with, ". . . you've been saying it all along. It started when I joined the Laurelton PD."

"So, he *knows* you, as well as the three victims."

"Well . . . yeah, maybe." September's thoughts flew right

back to Jake and she suspected Gretchen was thinking the same thing.

They'd reached the station and now they climbed out of the car and walked through the front doors. Guy Urlacher looked up as they entered and Gretchen growled, "Ask me for my ID, I swear to God I'll turn you over to medical, have them check you for OCD and get you put on permanent leave."

"It's protocol," Guy squeaked, alarmed.

"Don't ask me again. Don't do it," she warned.

They made it past him though his Adam's apple was jumping up and down as if pulled by a string and his eyes were wide. In the back hallway, September said, "Everyone says you're a bitch, no offense."

"I am. None taken."

There was a note with a phone number on September's desk from the front desk: *Jake Westerly called.*

Gretchen saw September freeze and glanced over her shoulder to view the message. "Just how good a friend is he?"

"Was he," September corrected her.

"Okay, how good a friend *was he?*"

"Good," September answered, after a telling moment.

"Don't meet him alone," she advised and then headed to her own desk.

Don't meet him at all, her conscience told her, even while she dug out her cell phone.

Chapter 9

September glanced across the squad room to where George was following up on the list of names and numbers of the instructors from the summer school program. Her gaze moved to the board that held the three victims' photos and bullet points on where they'd been located and whatever else was found at the scene. The women had similar appearances and they all lived in the Laurelton area. Emmy and Sheila were about the same age and had both attended school in the Laurelton School District, and though Glenda Tripp, who was also in the same age range, hadn't gone to school in Laurelton, she'd worked, briefly, for the school district.

Were they on the right track? she wondered as she slipped her cell into her pocket and headed down the hall to the break room with its his-and-hers locker rooms on either side. Gretchen had decided to check on Emmy Decatur's school record as long as they were on that track with Sheila and Glenda. Maybe she would find another connection.

September pulled out her cell and punched in the number Jake had given her on her cell but after a few rings it went to his voice mail. She left her name and hung up, kind of deflated. She didn't care what Gretchen or her conscience decreed, she was going to see him again to satisfy her own need for answers. Maybe he could provide those answers, maybe he couldn't. But she was going to meet with him, and she did not for one second believe he was the sociopath or psychopath or whatever type of deviant the killer was.

He returned her call as she was walking back to the squad room, so she slowed her steps and answered briskly: "Rafferty."

"It's Jake. Sorry, I was down the hall and didn't hear the phone ring."

"No problem. What can I do for you?"

"I didn't really like the way things went the other day," he said. "I got the feeling you were testing me with those questions."

"Mr. Dempsey had made some accusations and I was following up."

"Man, Nine. You're so damn neutral. Is that you, or is it a 'cop thing'? It's annoying as hell."

That brought her up short. "Sorry."

"Meet me for lunch," he said. "Let's have a real conversation."

"I . . . don't . . ." she said reluctantly. Yes, she wanted to see him, but no, she wasn't sure she wanted to share lunch with him.

"It's just lunch. I want to talk to you."

"I don't have a lot of time," she demurred.

"I'll come your way. I've got an appointment in Laurelton later anyway, and well, I live there."

"Your office is in Portland?"

"Downtown, yeah. But name a place in Laurelton. I can be there in half an hour."

She glanced at the clock. It was eleven-thirty. "Okay, how about Xavier's? They've got a rockin' bar scene at night, but in the day it's calmer and the food's good."

"Xavier's. See you at noon . . ."

He clicked off and she did the same, returning to the squad room but avoiding Gretchen's eyes. Luckily Sandler was in an involved conversation over Emmy Decatur's school records and didn't notice until September took her gun from her drawer and fitted it to her hip holster, slipping her light gray jacket over it. Then Gretchen started signaling her as she wound up the phone conversation, so September waited.

"You'd think I was asking to break into Fort Knox, the way they lock down those permanent records," Gretchen grumbled. "Christ, I hate schools. Are you going to lunch?"

"Xavier's," she said.

"Oh." She was surprised. "Meeting someone?"

"Yep."

She picked up on September's monosyllabic responses and said, "Jesus, Nine . . . Jake Westerly?"

"It's a public place. I think I'll be okay."

"Didn't I warn you?" Gretchen shook her head, and added, "Bad idea."

"Maybe I'll learn something."

She snorted. "Say hi to Dom for me, if he's bartending. And bring me back a sandwich?"

"What kind?"

"Anything." Her attention was grabbed by the phone again, so September strolled outside into the blasting sun.

By day Xavier's seemed less slick and glossy; the light streaming through the windows making it appear more like a restaurant, less of a pickup bar. September was early on purpose; she wanted to be seated to scope things out before Jake got there. She looked across the length of the zebrawood bar and noticed a dark-haired, buff male bartender but it wasn't Gretchen's Dom.

A young, female maître d' dressed in a black skirt and a body-hugging black, long-sleeved top stood by with a pile of menus in her slim arms. "Would you like a table?"

"For two," September said, and followed her to a spot by the windows that looked into a bioswale wetlands—which looked more like dusty weeds than anything—that lay between Xavier's and the row of commercial buildings beyond. She waited while the busgirl poured her a glass of water from a pitcher, a lemon slice slipping into her glass. She could feel the race of her heart and gave herself a mental tongue-lashing. This wasn't a date in any real sense. It was a meeting, an interview, an exchange of ideas.

Still . . .

Her thoughts turned to Wes Pelligree again. He was re-cuperating, which was great, but she missed having him around. In truth, she liked him a lot, though she'd never gotten the hang of calling him by his nickname, Weasel, which he teased her about. She'd quietly fantasized about him despite his longtime girlfriend, Kayleen Jefferson, who'd basically moved in with Wes since the shooting, from all accounts.

Oh, well . . .

Thinking about Wes, however, brought to mind thoughts of Jake Westerly. Maybe because she couldn't be with Wes and therefore was frustrated in love . . . maybe that was why she was still attracted to Jake. He was the epitome of the kind of guy she was interested in and couldn't seem to have. Either that, or she simply chose unavailable men.

Peachy.

She was trying to think of how to handle this upcoming interview when Jake himself appeared, wearing cowboy boots, denim jeans, and a collared white shirt with a suede jacket. Again, she got that sense that he could be the poster boy for "today's cowboy."

Wes Pelligree, she realized, had a tendency to dress the same way.

"What are you scowling at?" Jake asked with a grin as he seated himself across from her.

"Life in general, I guess."

"Maybe this job's getting to you, Nine. I don't remember you ever being so . . ." She waited while he searched for the word, but he finally just gave up. "You look great though," he said instead.

"Thanks." She felt tongue-tied and that fueled her self-directed anger; she could feel her scowl deepen. Time to take control. "You called me to talk about something?"

"I wanted to give you a chance to pick my brain about Phil and Carolyn and Drea. I know I shut you down on that before." He was gazing at her speculatively and she fought hard not to look away. "And, I was thinking about our second grade teachers."

"What about them?"

He shrugged lightly. "Mrs. McBride came just short of rapping knuckles a time or two. Everybody was afraid of her."

"She was a little short on warmth," September agreed. "I was lucky to have Mrs. Walsh."

"Maybe you should check with them, our old teachers. Ms. Osborne was younger, so I thought she'd be a good start, but I called and she's no longer at the school."

"You called the school district and asked if Ms. Osborne was there?" she questioned carefully.

"I called Sunset Elementary this morning," he said with a nod.

"You want to direct my investigation?"

He held up a hand. "All I did was ask a simple question. I gave them my name and told them I had Mrs. Walsh. Mrs. Peterkin, in the office? She remembered me, and she knew my dad had started the winery. She told me Mrs. Walsh died a few years back, but Mrs. McBride lives at Grandview Senior Care. She doesn't know what happened to Ms. Osborne after she left."

September wasn't sure what to make of him. "You've decided I should interview McBride and Osborne?"

"You know I always think of them with a Ms. or Mrs. in front of their names. They were so *big* when we were kids and had all the power." Amusement flickered in his eyes. "And you sound so hardass and professional calling them by their last names."

"Jake . . ."

"Hmmm?"

September could tell she was on slippery footing and she didn't like the feeling at all. "I suppose you have a list of questions I should ask them, too?"

"Somebody had your artwork. Let's just see if we can figure out who it is."

"You're thinking it's an old classmate."

He shrugged. "That's what you were thinking about me. I'd like to explore the possibility it's someone else."

The same idea had been floating around in her brain, and it irked her that he'd suddenly stepped in with the same idea. She realized she was feeling competitive about the ownership of whose idea it was to talk to Sunset Elementary and immediately decided she didn't care.

"Okay," she said.

"You'll go talk to them?" he asked, surprised at her sudden capitulation.

"If I can find them. Sure. Why not? I'll go see Mrs. Peterkin in the office and see what we can come up with."

Their waitress walked up and asked, "Have you decided yet?"

Jake's gaze was on September. "I think we just did," he said, faintly smiling. "But I haven't had a chance to look at the menu yet, though. Give us a few minutes."

The waitress looked confused, but smiled and said, "I'll be back in a few minutes."

September leaned across the table. "What did we decide on?" she asked tensely.

Jake leaned right back at her. "We're going to Sunset Elementary. Together."

"If you think this high-handedness is working for you, you're wrong."

He sent her a thousand-watt grin. "Oh, I think it is."

Sensing she was losing a battle she wasn't certain she wanted to fight, September pulled back and picked up the menu. She stared at the words but his mocking eyes seemed burned onto her retinas.

Muttering beneath her breath, she heard him ask, "Did I hear the word insufferable?"

Lowering the menu, September said, "I'll have the Santa Fe salad and a turkey club to go. I promised my partner lunch."

"We can drop it off on our way," he suggested.

"I'll buy it and I'll take it to her."

"I can buy."

"This is a police investigation. I don't want you mucking around in it."

"No mucking. You and I are just going back to our

grade school, trying to connect with our old teachers and maybe some old classmates. And Mrs. Peterkin remembers me, so maybe I can learn something before you get all official and cop-like."

"You're not an asset in this, Westerly."

"Westerly. Jesus." He shook his head. "I want to find the sick bastard who killed Sheila and sent your artwork to you. I want to help."

If I were smart, I'd shut this down now, September thought to herself, but the words out of her mouth were, "Okay . . . Jake. But if we do this, I'll do the talking."

He opened his mouth to protest, thought better of it, closed it, and said, "The turkey club sounds like a winner."

Forty minutes later September and Jake left the restaurant and got into their respective vehicles as September insisted on taking her own car to Sunset Elementary. He told her he'd wait for her, and she drove back to the station with Gretchen's sandwich, a little boggled by the whole thing.

Handing Gretchen the brown bag from Xavier's, she tried to head back out, but Gretchen asked, "No Dom?"

"No Dom. Maybe he only works nights." She edged toward the hallway.

"Where're you going?" Gretchen demanded.

"My grade school. Sunset Elementary."

"Good luck with those permanent records."

"I'd like to see some photographs. Maybe a class picture. I can't find my own."

"Whose idea was this?" she asked.

"Jake's," she admitted after a long moment. "He and I are going together. He's meeting me there." Gretchen looked startled and September added quickly, "Jake called ahead to the school and they're expecting him."

"He's all over this case. Jesus, Nine. What the hell are you thinking?"

"I'm playing this out. He knows I'm bringing you this sandwich, which he bought by the way. He's not going to kill me in broad daylight when my partner knows I'm meeting him."

"Do you know what you're doing? Are you clear on your motivations?" she demanded.

"I'm clear."

She shot September a sideways look and dragged the sandwich from the bag. "Tell him thanks. And text me the minute you leave the school. I don't like this."

"I gotta go."

"Text me."

September drove to Sunset Elementary, wondering if Gretchen was right. Maybe she was blinded by what she'd thought of him in high school. He *was* all over this case.

She pulled into the lot and had to squeeze the Pilot in a small spot; a lot of parents' cars were still around as people got used to the new school year's routine. It was probably a bad time to descend on Sunset Elementary as the school year had just started, but then she hadn't been the one who'd set this up.

She saw Jake climb out of his Tahoe and they walked toward the front door of Sunset Elementary School side by side. September automatically stepped back as her partner, Sandler, generally walked in first, but Jake swept out an arm to indicate she should precede him. Inside the school was fairly quiet, in that afternoon lull before bells started ringing and kids started hitting the playground. September thought she'd get that hit of déjà vu, heading back to her old school, but the inside of the building had been completely overhauled in the intervening years and was painted with bright colors instead of the beige she remembered. The administration offices had been moved to a new wing and hallway, and only a look through the hallway windows to the playground equipment reminded her of climbing up the metal and wood structure and sliding down the tall slide.

"Mrs. McBride used to say we were children, not kids," Jake remarked as they reached the administration offices. "Kids were baby goats."

"She was a stickler," September said.

"I always thought being a kid sounded better than being a child. More grown up. Someone calls you a child, it's an insult. They call you a kid, it's like an homage."

"If we go to Grandview Senior Care to talk to her, I'll let you tell her that," September said.

"I could get my knuckles rapped, but it might be worth it."

She felt herself smile and he shot her a look and smiled back. There was no way he was the killer. No way. He was just too damned personable and she knew him.

Mrs. Peterkin was the only person available when they walked in. September had left her gun in her vehicle, but she pulled out her badge for the woman to examine as she introduced herself as an officer and a former student. Peterkin's eyes were wide and she looked askance at Jake, who reminded her warmly that he'd called earlier asking about Osborne, McBride, and Walsh. She practically melted beneath the power of his smile and September watched their introduction with a mixture of amusement and impatience.

"Well, like I said, Mr. Westerly, Mrs. McBride is at Grandview Senior Care and Mrs. Walsh has passed on. I must admit, I took a peek at the file for Ms. Osborne after we spoke, and it doesn't say where she went, but there was a phone number. Looks like her home number. I could call her and ask if it's all right to give you information on her?"

September thought about pointing out, once again, that this was a police investigation, but when Jake said, "That'd be great," and Mrs. Peterkin smiled and gazed up at him, she figured it wasn't necessary.

"Is there something else I could help you with?" she asked, looking from Jake to September, then back to Jake.

Jake's brows lifted and he glanced at September. "Well . . . yes . . ."

"Go ahead," September invited him. She wasn't sure what he was planning to ask and kind of wanted to see what it would be.

Jake proceeded to tell the enthralled Mrs. Peterkin that he and September—the law—were looking for anything pertaining to his and September's second grade year. Were there files available?

"We can't have you look at personnel files without a court order," she said slowly, shooting September a glance filled with trepidation as if she expected her to demand to see them.

"How about class pictures? The composites of each of the three home rooms?" September suggested.

"Okay . . . I think they're on computer from back then," she said, turning back to her desk. She waved Jake and September around the counter, saying, "Mr. LeMonde's out for the afternoon, so it's just me and Linda B. She'll be back soon. She's just down the hall."

September and Jake followed her over to her desk where she touched the screen and woke the computer up. She searched through several menus before she found the archived photos and when Jake told her the year she zeroed in on pictures from their second grade year. When she clicked on the class picture, September asked her to wait a moment.

Looking at their bright faces, some missing front teeth, September had a playground memory of one of the boys wetting his pants and the other children clapping their hands to their mouths and running away, giggling. She looked closely through the photos of Mrs. Walsh's class but that boy wasn't there. Maybe he was in another class, or a different grade. Then she saw her own face with its messy hair and goofy look, the collar of her blouse kind of tugged to one side. She'd been a tomboy and it showed.

Jake commented, "That's exactly how I remember you," which didn't help.

They switched to Mrs. McBride's room and there was Jake, smiling at the camera, one front tooth in, one halfway down. Even so, his good looks were already evident, and Mrs. Peterkin even told him what a cutie he was. Her brother Auggie was there, too, his close-mouthed smile impish and maybe holding a secret. Both of them looked a helluva lot better than September.

Then they moved to Ms. Osborne's homeroom composite, but nothing stood out. September remembered most of the students, at least vaguely, but they all just looked like typical second graders and probably were.

Mrs. Peterkin clicked to another page, saying, "We try to add pictures from the rooms during each school year, but this was before we really started the program." She clicked some more and then a photo popped up. "Oh, wait. I think this is your year."

There were a series of pictures of the teachers in the classrooms, kind of fuzzy as they'd been taken with film and scanned. But one of them showed several pieces of the leaf artwork like September's.

"Can you zoom in on that?" Jake asked, focused on the same picture.

"This one?" Mrs. Peterkin asked, pointing to a photo of the classroom with snowflakes bordering the bulletin board behind Mrs. Walsh's desk.

"This one," Jake said, and touched his finger to the screen above the falling leaves.

"I should be able to," she said and did so.

September inhaled sharply, unable to stop herself. The picture pinned to the bulletin board was *her* falling leaves artwork! Auggie had been right. His artwork was the one at home on the kitchen wall. Her memory of hers being displayed was from her homeroom.

"That's mine," she said, staring at it.

Jake's gaze followed hers. "So, maybe you never made it home with it," he said slowly.

"Pardon?" Mrs. Peterkin said.

"Thank you, Mrs. Peterkin," September said, straightening. "If you wouldn't mind calling Ms. Osborne, that would be a great help. Here's my cell number." She handed the woman her card, which she took reluctantly, clearly preferring to deal with Jake.

Back at their cars, Jake asked, "What do you think about that?"

"I don't know. That was my artwork. Right there." She shook her head.

"Somebody got it from somewhere," he said. "Let's go to your father's house and find the rest of your school stuff."

"Oh, sure. That's what we're going to do."

"We can go after work. C'mon, you want to," he said, full of that surety and arrogance she remembered from high school. "What time do you get off?"

"Never. I'm always working."

"I was going to suggest dinner. You probably still eat, right?"

"You bought me, and my partner, lunch. She said thank you, by the way. I think we're good."

"You're really putting up the fences, aren't you?" Jake remarked, unperturbed.

"Hell, yes, and you're just trying to run them down."

"Well?" he asked, when September subsided into silence.

"You're pouring on the charm and it's pissing me off because . . . it seems like I'm responding."

"Just kills you, doesn't it?"

"Yes."

When she had to fight herself to keep from rolling her eyes he saw it. "I think you're afraid of me," he said.

"Not afraid . . . concerned, maybe."

"You don't seriously think I'm anything more than a bystander in these murders, do you?" he asked, watching her closely.

"I believe if you were the doer, you would have given yourself away by now."

"So, I'm a bystander?"

She nodded. "But you seem to want to be involved in solving the case, which is . . . unacceptable."

"I don't like thinking you're on someone's radar. And that's what this feels like."

September stared him down. "I'm just doing my job."

"You didn't ask for a copy of the class picture," he remarked.

"There wasn't anything there," she said, "and I'd like to find my own, eventually."

"Need any help looking?"

"You're overeager, Westerly. I don't know what you're angling for."

"It's Jake," he said firmly. "I knew you pre-cop. Let's not do that."

"Are you still friends with T.J.?"

It just popped out. She could still remember how T.J., after learning of her night with Jake, had made the "ok" sign with one hand and poked his other index finger through the hole, suggestively moved it back and forth while a wide grin spread across his face. It had hurt and September had made a habit of shoving Jake from her thoughts ever since.

"T.J.'s an ass. I really haven't seen T.J. since high school," he said.

September kept her face from showing her feelings with an effort. "I don't think spending time with you is going to work for me."

"Yeah?"

"What are you getting out of this?"

"It bothers me that my name's come up in this investigation, and that the killer sent you a message, and that you have some suspicions about me, whether you're admitting to them or not. I don't like feeling this way. And I don't want anything to happen to you."

September moved a few steps away and pulled out her cell phone, buying some time. "I need to text my partner."

"Have dinner with me tonight."

"You're . . . pushing."

"What do I have to do to get you to say yes?" His gray eyes gazed at her in a way that put a knot in her stomach. "I'll buy. Anyplace you want."

September could feel herself weakening. If she was smart, she would put up a barrier to his persuasiveness, but she wanted to be with him. Was that simple loneliness talking, or worse, some leftover unfulfilled need harkening back to high school? "I am kind of hankering for a seventy-two-ounce steak," she said, almost surprised by the words as they left her mouth.

"The Barn Door." He grinned like a schoolboy. "If we share it, that's thirty-six ounces apiece."

"Good God. That's over two pounds apiece," she said. No wonder Wes Pelligree was ralphing it up in the alley behind the bar.

"I'll pick you up at six-thirty," he said. "What's your address?"

With much trepidation and mental self-flagellation, September told him.

Chapter 10

It was late afternoon and Stuart Salisbury and his friend Matt were trudging away from Twin Oaks Elementary under a blistering September sun, hot and wilted.

"Fuckin' school just started and it feels like forever," Matt muttered.

"Fuckin' school just started and it feels like fuckin' forever," Stuart responded.

That drew a chuckle from Matt and a burst of energy from both boys and despite the heat they ran to the front of the school, waiting at the pickup circle for Matt's mom to pick them up. Stuart's mom worked full-time, but Matt's didn't. She just worked out at the gym like all the time, and drank wine with friends and didn't pay much attention to the boys, so Stuart and Matt were kinda left to themselves. She didn't really start the wine drinking till later in the day, so she was okay to pick them up, but she was kinda anxious, too, so everybody was happy when they were back at Matt's—Stuart had assured her that his mom was okay with him walking home from Matt's house and Matt said he'd go with him so she agreed that it would be okay. All they had to do was cross a couple of fields to get to his house and generally Matt came along 'cause his mom didn't really much care anyway.

They were both eleven, in Mrs. Bardelay's class, which was lame. They didn't like school and they really didn't like Mrs. Bardelay. She was old. Forty or so, for sure. And she smelled like cherry cough drops 'cause she sucked on them, like all the time. Said she was fighting a cold or allergies even though it was so blasted hot. Stuart thought maybe she was an addict, or something, and said as much to Matt who shrugged 'cause he didn't care.

Now they walked along the edge of a roadside ditch, on the field side rather than the asphalt side. Matt wanted to play video games at Stuart's which was what Stuart wanted to, but his older sister was probably around somewhere and she would tell his mom for sure.

They were halfway to the house when they saw the circling birds.

"Hawks," Matt said.

"Buzzards," Stuart responded knowingly. He knew about birds of prey. The kind that went after dead things.

"Something's dead out there?" Matt asked.

"Mebbe."

Stuart plucked a piece of grass and stuck it between his teeth, chewing on it. He'd seen a guy in a western on TV do something like that and even though the taste was bitter, he kinda thought he probably looked cool. He squinted his eyes, too, then shaded them with his hand as he looked up at the bird.

"It's over by the creek," he said.

"Uh-huh. If your sister's got soccer practice, she won't be there. We can play."

"Nah, she goes later. C'mon, let's go see what it is."

But Matt only wanted to play video games and wasn't

interested in a delay. "I don't wanna go all that way. It's too hot."

"I'm goin'."

Stuart climbed agilely over the fence. There was a strand of barbed wire across the top, but he avoided it carefully. He thought there might be some cattle around, but maybe not. As long as the bull was penned up he was okay.

Swearing, Matt followed after him. "Shit! I ripped my pants!" he yelled, but he kept on coming.

Stuart wondered if it was a coyote kill. Damn, but those bastards were getting bold. That's what his dad said. Could they take down a cow? Maybe a calf . . . His heart gallumphed as he thought about that. A pack of 'em could kill about anything.

Matt caught up to him, breathing hard. "What is it?" he asked.

They were nearing the creek, which smelled like rotting weeds and something worse.

"Gawd," Stuart said, holding a hand over his nose and mouth.

"Do ya think it's—" Matt cut off on an intake of breath that turned into a harsh, choking sound.

Ahead of them, lying on her back, naked from the chest down, was a dead woman's body. Blood was smeared on her skin and it stank to high heaven. Matt stopped short and Stuart could feel the hair standing on end all over his body. He took a step nearer but his legs felt encased in cement.

"Uh . . . uh . . . uh . . ." Matt stared ahead in shock.

Stuart said in a strangled voice, "Those are words . . . what's it say? What's it say?"

"We gotta get outta here, Stu," Matt whimpered.

But Stuart forced himself one step closer.

"Do Unto Others As She Did To Me," he read in a cracking voice. He turned slowly and looked at Matt. "Carved in. That's . . . blood."

The boys stared at each other unseeingly, and Matt felt faint, like everything was shrinking in and he could scarcely see. With all the strength he had left, he pivoted until he could see the fence and the road, far, far away. He took one step. Then two. Then he was running with everything he had, racing back across the field with Stuart hot on his heels.

September spent the afternoon placing calls and checking backgrounds and giving Gretchen, who wanted to know all the details of September's lunch with Jake, the bare minimum. She related that she was following up with the teachers at Sunset Elementary, and that she'd seen the whole grade's composite pictures, and her own leaf artwork displayed on a bulletin board in a picture from Mrs. Walsh's homeroom. "Auggie told me that it was his artwork our mom displayed, not mine, and I think he was right. I don't think I ever got home with mine," she admitted.

Gretchen absorbed all that, but when September wouldn't say much about her actual "date," she returned to her own work. September then looked up information on all Phillip Merits in the area—two—and hit the correct one on the first try when he said from his voice mail to leave either him or Carolyn a message. She did, and he called her back from the offices of James and Sessions, where he worked as an estate lawyer. It turned out Drea Bartelli, who'd lost her job, had moved back home to Colorado shortly after their excursions to Westerly Vale Vineyards and The Barn Door. Carolyn and Phil hadn't

returned to the bar since hearing of Sheila's death. "It just
felt . . . bad, y'know?" he admitted, sounding uneasy. "I
don't like thinking about it." He gave September Drea's
number and he said he would tell Carolyn she'd called.
He didn't appear to know much more about Sheila, however, as she was really the women's friend.

Putting that aside for the moment, she had a little
better luck with Sheila Dempsey's onetime boyfriend,
Benny Schmidt, who still lived around the area and was
a physical education teacher at a Portland high school.
When she couldn't find a phone number for him, she
called the school and asked him to phone Detective September Rafferty with the Laurelton Police Department,
which he did when he was finished with classes, his voice
rife with worry and trepidation.

"I'm just doing some follow-up on Sheila Dempsey's
homicide," September said to put him at ease. "Background work."

"I've barely seen Sheila. She got married," Benny said.
"I'm engaged. I don't know anything about her."

"What about when you were in school?"

"We were friends. We were kind of together in sixth
grade. I mean, does that even count? I'm really sorry
about Sheila. I was just shocked, y'know? But this can't
have anything to do with me . . . or school . . . can it?" he
asked, sounding like he was preparing himself for a firing
squad.

Yeah, it could, she thought, thinking about the message she'd received from her elementary school days, but
she kept that to herself. "Do you remember any of her
friends?"

"Sure. There was Caitlyn Carroway. She was really
popular and Sheila hung out with her some. And Andrew,
but he moved away."

"Andrew?"

"Andrew Welke. But y'know. We all just grew up."

"I know." September was writing the names down. "Anything about any of your classmates and Sheila that stands out? Some person . . . some incident?"

"Ah, nah . . . just the usual stuff." He was relaxing now that he knew September wasn't targeting him. "Well, she didn't like this guy who'd come from another school that she called Wart. A real psycho, she said, but then she called me a psycho sometimes, too. Just how she talked."

"So, psycho could be a meaningless term?"

"We were in sixth grade."

"You know him, though. He went to your school."

"I never talked to the guy. He kinda just stood around."

"With friends? By himself?"

"By himself. I never paid attention to him. He was like in his own world. I don't even remember what he looked like, much. He had brown hair, I think. He wasn't there long."

"But Sheila called him Wart?" September pressed.

"She mighta just meant it as a mean thing, y'know. I heard he died though . . . so maybe not . . . or maybe that was that other kid?"

"What other kid?"

"Just another one like him. No friends. Hanging around. There's always some like that, y'know?"

September nodded on her end of the phone. There were always some like that. "You said he came from another school. Do you remember which one?"

"Umm . . . I always thought it was Sunset Elementary." Her school.

September asked him a few more questions, but got nothing further. After she hung up she looked down at her notes. Maybe there was something there. Maybe not. Sheila had known a number of kids from Sunset Elementary . . . maybe this Wart was one of them. Maybe he'd even attended school with September?

She looked up the background on Andrew Welke and found one who lived in the Seattle area. She called the number and he answered right away. Turned out it was his cell phone and he thought her number was from someone he was trying to contact from the Portland area. When she told him who she was and she was looking for background on Sheila Dempsey, he was blown away.

"Wow. Sick what happened to her. Sick, man."

She could hear a television in the background and some other voices. As if reading her mind, he said, "Got a few of my posse here. Monday night football, y'know?"

"Do you remember anyone called Wart, that might have known Sheila?"

"Wart? Yeah . . . huh . . . maybe. That weird dude who wore the brown pants? I think he dropped out, or something. Probably got put away."

"Put away?"

"Locked up, man. In-car-cer-ated. He was . . . kinda into knives and stuff. Wait. Let me ask Caitlyn."

"Caitlyn Carroway?"

"No, man. Caitlyn Welke. She's my better half." Then he yelled, "Hey, babe? You remember that Wart-dude? Whatever happened to him?"

"Could I talk to Caitlyn?" September asked.

"Yeah, sure . . . here . . ." There was a shuffling sound and she could hear a woman hiss, "I don't wanna talk. You talk!", and then Andrew whispered something about the police, and a careful female voice said, "Hello?"

"Ms. Welke?" September asked. "Caitlyn Carroway Welke?"

"Yee . . . ess."

"Do you remember someone named Wart that Andrew said transferred in to Twin Oaks? Sheila Schenk Dempsey may have known him? He could possibly have attended Sunset Elementary first."

"Yee . . . ess. I kinda do. He came fourth or fifth grade, or sixth, maybe? Sheila talked about him a couple of times. Sheila said he was a freak."

"A psycho?"

"Well, yeah. I guess he kinda stood and stared and was weird, but there were guys like that, y'know? Sheila moved away in sixth grade, and I don't know what happened to him after that."

"He didn't go to high school with you."

"No, I don't think so. I don't really remember."

"Anything else you can recall?"

"Maybe I should put Andrew back on the phone?"

"Yes, thank you," September agreed, pretty sure she'd tapped Caitlyn out.

"Yeah?" Andrew said when he'd taken the phone from her. He sounded distracted and someone was yelling and then Andrew yelled back, "You lose, dirtbag! Go get the beer. Your turn to pay, cheap-ass." As if coming to himself, he said to September, "Uh . . . what was it you wanted?"

"Anything more on Wart," she said patiently.

"Man, I wish I could help you. Hey, try Benny Schmidt. He used to go with Sheila. Like they were the sixth grade power couple before she left." He laughed. "Geez, where's the time gone, huh?"

"Thank you," September said, hanging up.

How old was this "Wart"? she wondered. Did it matter? Could he really be someone who'd followed after Sheila since grade school?

"Anything's possible," she said aloud.

Lieutenant D'Annibal came out of his office and caught September's eye. She got up from her desk and followed him inside his glassed-in office, watching as he leaned against his desk, plucking at the crease in his pant leg as he half-sat on the corner.

"Pauline Kirby has been calling for you."

"I've purposely been trying to duck the press," September said, watching him. D'Annibal had told her he wanted to make her the face of the department, but since the debacle of the last interview, there was an order to keep your head down and say as little as possible.

"That still goes," he said. "But she's aggressive and if we don't give her something, chances are she'll make something up."

"You want me to call her?" September asked with a sinking heart.

"No, I'll do it. Just wanted you to be alerted, as she seems hell-bent on getting you back in front of her cameras."

Peachy.

At six o'clock, September told the squad room as a whole, "I'm heading out. See you all mañana." She walked down the hall to the locker room, picked up her messenger bag purse and her jacket, then walked past Urlacher into a baking September evening.

By the time Jake knocked on her apartment door, September had taken a shower, curled her hair, as much as it would allow itself to be curled, and changed twice. She was in gray capris, a light blue sleeveless top, and low black heels. The Barn Door wasn't the dressiest place to go. All afternoon, she'd tried to tell herself none of it mattered anyway, that she didn't care, but she did, and that was just the way of it.

She looped the strap of her messenger bag over her neck, aware that she'd brought her unloaded Glock and ammo, and threw open the door. Jake was standing beneath her small awning in a pair of pressed jeans and a black shirt, coupled with the ubiquitous cowboy boots. She didn't know why the way he looked appealed to her so much, it just did.

"Ready?" he asked.

"For The Barn Door and a trip to my family home's attic? Yes."

He smiled as they headed down the stairs to his waiting black Tahoe. "I asked my mother about my own grade school artwork," he said. "She says she's got a big box with all that stuff. And the class picture. And my brother Colin's work is there, too. He did a lot of the same projects a few years ahead of us."

September climbed into the passenger seat and absently put on her seatbelt. "I don't even know if finding my grade school work is important."

"I'm kinda intrigued to go through the Rafferty castle," Jake admitted. "I always wanted to as a kid."

"It's not a castle, though God knows my father sure wanted it to look that way," September muttered.

"It's got that turret."

"Yeah. Well." September had always been a little embarrassed by the place. It was just so ostentatious and odd amongst the regular suburban homes of around three thousand square feet.

At The Barn Door, September climbed from the Tahoe, and fell in step beside Jake as they walked inside. She almost said, "This is getting to be a habit," but thought better of it.

Egan, the bartender she and Gretchen had interviewed earlier, was wiping down the bar as they squeezed inside together, looking for an empty table. Glancing up, Egan noticed September. "Hey," he said excitedly. "He's here. Ray. I was gonna call you!"

"Ray?" Jake asked.

September said, "Where? Which one?"

Egan pointed down the bar to the end where a lone middle-aged man was eyeing a group of women in tight tank tops and sundresses, showing a lot of boob and skin. This was Sheila's would-be knight in shining armor?

She turned back to Egan and saw he was staring at Jake. Mr. Perfect. Figuring an explanation would take too long, she put her hand to the side of her face to shoulder past a heavyset guy wearing a cowboy hat that could take her eye out.

"Who's Ray?" Jake asked in her ear, moving with her.

"Another name." She stopped for a moment, turning slightly so she could see him. "By the way I got hold of Phil Merit."

"Was he helpful?"

"You go through a lot of people before you get any kind of information you can use," she said, thinking hard. She didn't want him with her while she interviewed Ray.

"I'll take that as a no."

She inclined her head toward Ray. "I need to talk to this guy."

"I'm right behind you," Jake said.

"Not a good idea. I'll be with you in a minute."

"If you think I'm letting you talk with Leisure Suit Larry, your detecting skills need work. I won't get in your way."

"Too late for that," September muttered, but she turned back and wove her way through the bar crowd in

Ray's direction. She wasn't sure what to do about Jake, but if she truly analyzed her feelings, she was kind of glad to have a partner with her, even if he wasn't strictly official.

As they approached Ray he ran a look over September's body, but his gaze slid to the well-rounded and buxom redhead with the Hello Kitty tattoo. Probably a copyright infringement there, she thought as she zeroed in on Ray, who, upon realizing September was approaching him, stood up straighter from the bar, as if he knew she was "the law."

"Hello, Ray?" September said with a smile. "It's Ray, isn't it?"

"Yeah . . ." he responded suspiciously, shooting a look past September to Jake. "Ray Dexheimer."

"I'm Detective Rafferty with the Laurelton Police Department. Is it all right if I ask you a couple of questions?"

"I guess."

Egan eased his way down the bar, eager to overhear. September told Ray that she was investigating Sheila Dempsey's homicide, and she'd heard that Ray had stepped in when it appeared some guy was hassling her. Did he know who that guy was?

"Oh, him," Ray said, relieved to learn what September's agenda was. "Nah. I don't know him. He was watching her and she caught him at it, and she told him to get a life, or something like that, and he just stepped up and glared at her real mean-like. Kinda scared her, I thought, so I asked if there was anything wrong, and he turned away and told me to fuck off."

"You didn't catch his name?"

"Nah. I asked Sheila but she just sorta shrugged and said not to worry about it, he was someone she knew."

"From school."

"Mebbe." Ray frowned, as if giving that real thought.

"What did he look like?" September asked.

"I don't know. Medium. Brown hair. Dark eyes, I think, he kinda turned away as I got close. Slim build, but sorta hard. I just got this hit of mean-tough, y'know?"

"How tall?"

"Five-ten or eleven, I'd say."

"You said you thought he scared her?" September probed.

"Looked that way to me."

"How about an age range . . . ?"

He thought a moment. "Yeah, I don't know. Pretty young. Late twenties? Early thirties?"

"Did Sheila ever say 'wart,' like that could be his name?"

"I don't think so."

Jake put in, before September could ask another question, "Had you seen him around before?"

"Yeah, I think so. Like hanging around the bar, mebbe."

September tried to come at Ray from a different angle, asking how well he knew Sheila, how many times he'd seen her, that sort of thing. He shook his head and shrugged through the questions, finishing with, "Look, I just saw this guy by her and she just looked . . . like she was trying to be nice, but he was coming on too strong. So, I said, 'Hey.' That was it. 'Hey,' like a warning. He ducks his head and leaves like he doesn't want me looking at him. So I ask Sheila, 'You okay?' and she says yeah. And I make some comment about him not getting the message or something and she says, 'Oh, I know him' and leaves it at that."

"Thanks," September said, then started back toward the door, Jake behind her once again.

Egan yelled, "Hey," over the noise of the other patrons and a couple of pissed off customers who were waiting to be served. He followed their progress on his side of the bar and September stopped and moved toward him. "Y'know, I've seen that guy Ray was talking about a few times. Kinda snuck in, watched a while, snuck out. I don't think he ever bought a drink."

"Have you seen him since?" she asked.

"Nuh-uh. After Ray stepped in, the guy never came back. And Sheila was dead pretty quick afterward."

A roar of excitement was coming from around the bar toward the dining area, and then a chant began. September glanced at Jake who leaned in and said in her ear, "Someone's close to the end of the seventy-two ouncer."

The maître d' was nowhere to be seen; or maybe there wasn't one and it was fend for yourself. "Maybe we should order at the bar," September yelled back to Jake in order to be heard when a big man with a stomach hanging over his belt came flying from the dining room, his hands covering his mouth, hawking and coughing, pushing through the bar patrons who were scurrying out of his way as he headed toward the back door.

He threw himself into the alley, gagging like he was going to upchuck his entire insides. Luckily, the door banged shut before he started to hurl.

Jake looked at September and she looked back at him. "Kind of takes the edge off dinner," he said.

"I know this great little Mexican place. Cheap and fast."

"Yeah?"

"Taco Bell. I'm making a habit of eating there."

"Not exactly what I had in mind when I asked you to dinner."

She shrugged. She was sort of over the whole meal thing with him. He made her feel a little unsteady.

"Taco Bell and then Castle Rafferty," Jake said.

A curious patron opened the back door and over the noise September heard full-on heaving.

"Let's go," she said with a shudder.

Chapter 11

The Rafferty castle, as Jake called it, was aglow with lights when they pulled into the parking area. September recognized July's car, and March's. If her father and Rosamund were home their vehicles were parked in the garage.

She thought about bringing Jake to the house and wondered if she'd lost her mind. She hadn't told her father when she'd called him earlier to ask if she could stop by and check the attic again that she was bringing him. He and Jake's father, Nigel, had broken off relations completely after September's mother's death, and Braden felt Nigel had poured salt in the wound by buying the failing vineyard nearby and turning it into one of The Willows' fiercest competitors. September didn't really know what her father thought of Westerly Vale now that Nigel's sons owned it. Was he envious that Westerly Vale's Pinot had been christened "Best in the Westerly" last year? July sure was, but her attitude was more positive, a kind of "we'll get them next year" thing, offered with a smile, where her father and March weren't made the same way.

And then, of course, Braden still blamed Nigel for Kathryn's death on some level.

Was that why she'd simply rolled over and allowed Jake to join her? To twist the knife a little?

"Are you growling?" Jake asked as they walked up to the front door.

"Did I make a noise?"

"Sounded like growling."

September smiled. "My relations with my family bring out the best in me."

"That's the first smile I've seen," he remarked. "You should do more of it."

She sobered immediately. She had to remember to keep him at arm's length. She sensed that being around him, though it made her uneasy in the short run, could become a dangerous habit, maybe even something she craved.

Taking a breath, she rang the bell and listened to its slow, funereal dirge of *bong, bong, bong* toll through the house. Shortly thereafter they heard heavy steps coming to the door, and then it was opened by Braden Rafferty himself.

"Hello, September," he said, his gaze shooting to Jake, brows bunching together.

"Hello," she responded as she entered, turning back to Jake. "I brought a friend with me."

"Braden Rafferty," her father said, trying on a smile as he extended his hand.

"Jake Westerly," Jake responded, clasping his hand in return.

Braden actually jerked as if waking up. His hard gaze turned to September, who countered it with a careful, waiting look in her own eyes. "Nigel's son?" he rasped.

"It's been a long time," Jake said congenially. "I don't know when I was here last. Maybe I was . . . ten? A while ago, anyway."

"September . . . a moment," her father grated out.

She threw Jake a look, and said, "Why don't you head on into the living room. I'll be right with you," then followed after her father into his den.

He stalked behind the massive mahogany desk and braced his hands on its surface, glaring at her. "What are you trying to do?"

September was counting the books on the shelves behind his head. Books that looked good in a library. Books not meant to be read. She'd counted them many times as a girl, whenever she was called in for a talking-to by, as Auggie said, dear old Dad.

"I'm looking for my grade school artwork and Jake—"

"What are you doing with *him?* In my house!" he interrupted.

September said coolly, "I was getting to that. Jake was in my class, as was Auggie. Do you want to know the reason I'm here looking for my old schoolwork?"

"His father . . ." Braden paused, gathering himself. "Nigel Westerly is the reason your mother died."

September regarded him silently for a few seconds. "You had me believing that for a lot of years, but it's not true. It was an accident, and Nigel would have done anything to save Mom. He liked her. From what I remember, and from what he saw, she was a good person, nice to everyone. I miss her. You miss her. But it's not Nigel Westerly's fault."

"That's why you brought him here? To make a point?"

There was some truth in there somewhere, but September only said, "I came to search through the attic."

"Well, he can't go with you." Braden straightened, his face flushed.

"Really."

"What's your relationship with him?"

"My business," September stated flatly.

"What does your brother think about this?"

"You're going to have to ask Auggie yourself."

His nostrils flared. He really struggled with insubordination, and from his point of view, that's all September and Auggie ever gave him. "I think I'm going to ask you to leave."

"Someone sent me a 'bloody' warning on a piece of my actual second grade artwork," she told him. "Came to the station. The words 'Do Unto Others As She Did To Me' were scrawled across the face of it in red ketchup, mostly. The same message that was carved into Emmy Decatur, whose homicide I discussed on air with Channel Seven's Pauline Kirby. Just hours after that interview was aired, another body with markings was discovered, and we believe it could be the work of the same killer. That's why I want to find the rest of my schoolwork. That's why I'm starting here."

Braden stood in stony silence for the space of five seconds, then he said softly, "This is exactly why I didn't want you and your brother in law enforcement. It's dangerous. You have constant contact with the scum of society. We lost May to a sick criminal. I don't want to lose you and August, too."

"May's death was random," September said.

"He targeted her," Braden enlightened her. "He went to that burger place when May and Erin were the only ones there. He took them into a back room and tortured

them and killed them. I lost one daughter that night. I
don't want to lose two."

September's heart was pounding. She knew some
things about her sister's death, but it was one of those
taboo topics that the Raffertys never discussed. Was it
one of the reasons she'd gone into law enforcement? Definitely. Was it the main reason she had? Probably.

"I can't live my life to your blueprint, Dad."

"Do you have to go out of your way to thwart it?" he
shot right back.

"Maybe," she said, after a moment.

A long period of silence fell between them and then
Braden sank into the office chair and waved a hand at her.
"Do what you have to."

This was about as much capitulation as Braden Rafferty would ever muster, so September nodded and left
the den, retracing her steps to the living room where Jake
was standing beneath Rosamund's picture and Rosamund
herself, the skin of her face blushing prettily, was talking animatedly to him.

"Can't believe we've never met?" she was enthusing.
"I've been past Westerly Vale so many times!"

"I'm not there on a daily basis," Jake answered casually. Seeing September, he moved her way, but Rosamund
wasn't letting him off the hook so easily.

"Are you staying for dinner?" she asked, sliding a
quick look September's way before her focus returned
to Jake.

"No, thanks. We just . . . dined together," September
told her.

"That's a shame. Suma put together a beef stew with
Asian flavors that's to die for. You have to try some,"
Rosamund pressed.

The corner of Jake's mouth lifted. "I'm afraid there's just no room. We're just off a four-course meal."

"Really? Where did you go?" Her face was turned up to his, bright and avid.

Oh, if Braden could see her now, she thought, then figured her father probably knew his wife better than anyone.

"Sorry, Rosamund. Thanks," September answered for Jake. "We're kind of on a tight schedule."

"Oh, you're not both going up to the attic?"

"'Fraid so. I still haven't found my old schoolwork," September said.

"Well, there's nothing up there."

"Guess we'll find out." She met Jake's gaze and said, "Ready?"

For an answer he squeezed past Rosamund and followed September down the hallway and up the narrow steps to the attic. Pulling the chain for the light, she was gratified to see the switch lit another light nearer to the pile of furniture and other flotsam and jetsam that had discouraged September last time she was here. That was the area she planned to tackle first.

"You want to move this stuff?" Jake asked, catching on to her plan.

"Can you help me?"

"Sure."

It was hot in the attic, the day's residual heat thick enough to eat. For the first fifteen minutes they shoved junk aside, concentrating on the unopened boxes behind the junk. Jake grabbed a couple of cartons and slid them out from behind the furniture. When they had all of the boxes, a pile of about twenty, they brought them to the old chair September had sat in before, and Jake found a folding chair that he set up beside the threadbare one with the tufts of stuffing trying to escape.

They systematically went through the boxes without having to speak to each other about it. There were only three that held papers and booklets and files. Of those three, none pertained to September's schoolwork, or any of her siblings', but one held some papers and books that had belonged to September's mother, and September pulled out a book of poems by Yeats.

"I remember she liked Yeats, especially one poem where Yeats wrote about not wanting his daughter to be too beautiful because he felt too much beauty in a woman would be her ruination, I believe. Something like that."

"Your mother was beautiful. I remember."

She was touched by his words but strived not to let him see it. "Yes, she was," she said, flipping through the book. A slip of paper fell out, a scratched out note, really.

September read: "'K at Willows til 7? Can meet you at 3.' It's signed with a heart."

Jake reached a hand out to it. "A clandestine meeting?" When September didn't make a sound, he gave her a quick look. "What?"

"That's Verna's handwriting."

He glanced at the note again. "You sure?"

"Oh, yeah. And she always sticks hearts on everything." Her voice was cold, then she inhaled sharply. "My God. It was the day Mom died."

"What do you mean?" Jake asked, regarding her with concern.

"I remember! I remember *that day*. Mom was at The Willows. She was supposed to be there till seven because of the charity auction. I know because there was this whole thing about her leaving way earlier, and we all kind

of wished she'd stayed so maybe then she wouldn't have
charged down the drive and into that truck. They always
said she was driving too fast. Your dad said so, too, and I
hated him for that. I wanted to scream at him, and blame
him, like my father did. It couldn't be her fault. It had to
be somebody else's. Had to be."

"September, slow down," Jake said, for once not
using her nickname. "There's no date on the note. You
don't know."

"I know." She gazed at him, her eyes hard. "I've
thought about this so much. It makes sense. Verna wrote
that note to my father. She was seeing him before my
mother died. Mom found the note and stuck it in this
book, her favorite. She kept it on the shelf in her bedroom
and I bet Verna boxed it up with this other stuff. Her stuff."

Jake shook his head, concerned, but September wasn't
having it. "Mom was supposed to be there all day. She
had to stay till seven to make certain everything was set
up. But then she tore out really early. She must have
found the note in the morning, then went to The Willows,
but then she thought about it, and it ate at her until she
just couldn't stand it."

"I don't want to say you're wrong, but you're not
thinking like a cop. You're thinking like a daughter," Jake
tried.

"She was going to catch them together. That's why she
left early."

"That's a lot of reading between the lines. You know
that, right?"

"Your dad tried to save her, but he couldn't. But he told
the truth. She was speeding and she lost control." September closed her eyes. "I guess I should be grateful no
one else was hurt."

A long silence ensued and then Jake got up from his folding chair and pulled September out of the armchair. He held her at arm's length for a moment, just looking at her, then to her ultimate surprise he leaned in and kissed her, a searching kiss that offered comfort and understanding.

When he pulled back to look at her again and see how she'd taken the kiss, she said flatly, "You don't believe me."

He exhaled slowly. "There's something there. I don't know exactly what. I just don't want you to start making accusations so fast. We came here looking for your schoolwork, which doesn't seem to be here, and now you've found this note and I think you want to confront your father."

"I do. I want to blast him. My father was never faithful to my mother. That's a fact, and we all understood it over time. But I really thought Verna came after my mother's death. I—I needed to think that to have any kind of relationship with my father.

"But now . . . their affair *contributed* to her death!" She sucked air between her teeth.

"Okay. Just . . ." She looked at him in anger, daring him to go on. "Okay," was all he said.

They were standing very close to each other and September could still feel the impression of his lips on hers. She flicked a glance at his mouth, thinking about him, thinking about her father, emotions colliding inside her.

She wanted him to kiss her again. To wipe it all away. Everything that had happened in her family, and at work, and everywhere. She wanted to disappear into the warmth of loving someone, or lusting after them, or maybe a combination of both. It didn't matter.

She looked into his eyes to find he was staring back at her. Wordlessly, he lifted a hand to her chin, raising it up and then he leaned over and kissed her again, his arms sliding around her back, pulling her tightly to him.

The kiss deepened and her lips parted, inviting his tongue. For someone whose experience with sex had been fairly limited, she could feel her body going liquid with need and she welcomed it. Finally, she thought, though other thoughts pinged around in her brain like tiny alarms, warning her to be careful, questioning her motivation. She tried to shut her mind down, but she wasn't good at that.

She pulled back and said on a gasp, "Fair warning. I could be using you to get back at my dad."

"Already thought it. Don't care," he bit out.

"Okay."

"Okay."

They grabbed at each other like starving people, ripping at each other's clothes. September laughed and then cut herself off, aware that there were other ears that could maybe hear from below. She knew this was crazy, but there was no way she was going to stop.

The sudden ring of her cell phone made her jump, however, and then she froze, listening to the tone. Not one of the ring tones she'd chosen for her personal use.

"Can you ignore it?" Jake asked. His shirt was unbuttoned and yanked from his jeans.

Her blue shirt had been pulled from her head and she stood in front of him in her bra and capris. "It could be the station. I don't know." Reluctantly, she pulled away from his arms and searched her messenger bag for the phone. By the time she found it the ringing had stopped. Checking her missed calls, she said, "It is the station," then the phone rang in her hand and this time she recognized the tone she had for her partner's cell. "Sandler," she said to Jake, then, clicking on, answered, "Hey."

"Two kids found another vic's body in a field. Do Unto Others's whole phrase was carved into her skin. Drop point was over the county line, so we just got the word. Deputy Dalton caught the 911 call and guess what? Now, we gotta deal with the fucking feds whether we like it or not."

Chapter 12

By eleven o'clock Tuesday morning the squad room had become a makeshift task force meeting room with federal agents Donley and Bethwick, two humorless, fortysomething white males, holding court. To September's mind, they seemed more interested in seizing control and making sure everyone at the Laurelton PD "got it" than getting down to brass tacks. But maybe that was just her inexperience showing.

However, D'Annibal was standing at the back of the room, his arms crossed, paying attention, but physically letting them know they were on his home turf, so maybe she was picking up the correct vibe. Her gaze moved from the lieutenant to George, who was silently sitting at his desk, watching, and then on to Gretchen, whose "don't fuck with me" couldn't have been clearer if it had been written in scarlet neon.

Deputy Dalton from Winslow County sat several desks over from September, looking uncomfortable. The agents had come to county first and Dalton had been quick to point out that Lieutenant D'Annibal had usurped his case, and that neither he, nor county, was in charge of Do Unto

Others. The agents had asked him to the initial task force meeting to report on the body, which he'd done, and though he seemed eager to stay—it would certainly look good on his resume—he was being kicked back to county and the dark look on his face revealed how he felt about that.

Auggie had insisted on coming, too, and the jury was out on what the agents thought about that. He was somewhere at the back of the room, behind September. He was still working his other case jointly with the Portland PD, so he wasn't going to be available full time, but today he'd been able to show up to hear what the agents had to say. September wished she could turn around and make eye contact, but didn't want to appear as if she weren't paying attention.

Agent Bethwick, who sported a short crew cut and wore a black silk shirt under a gray suit that looked expensive, was saying, ". . . fingerprints on the vic were in the system as she's a prostitute, working name of Lulu Luxe, out of southeast Portland. She was picked up outside of Richie's, a tavern off Powell. The bartender found a wallet on the ground Saturday night when he got off work. Belongs to the john who was with her. David Smith. Smith swears he left Lulu in the parking lot and that she lifted his wallet. Could be true. Melanie Cooke from Portland vice confirms that she knows Lulu and that's a definite part of her m.o. Are you with me so far?" He glanced around the room. Nobody said anything, and apparently he didn't expect it, because he went on, "Smith says she serviced him in his car and then he left. It appears our killer was waiting for her. Maybe he saw their interplay, then after Smith left, stepped in. He strangled her with a wire or thin cord, which fits with your Do Unto Others killer—we've asked for more in-depth lab reports on fibers from the cord—and then he raped her and stabbed her and carved his message into her flesh, sometime late Saturday night."

As soon as the county had found the body, they'd called the feds, and September had to admit they'd certainly jumped in feet first. When September had phoned into the station, she'd been told to call D'Annibal's cell. He'd wanted to talk to each of his detectives directly.

"The FBI's been circling this case ever since your television interview with Kirby," he admitted. "They're fast. They'll do a good job. Just wanted you to be aware."

She'd also heard the words behind his words: *And they'll try to take the case away from us.*

Now September thought about Lulu. A prostitute? This appeared to be a departure from what they knew about Do Unto Others. They'd been working on the assumption that he knew his victims personally.

As if reading her thoughts, Gretchen said, "Could this doer be a copycat? This is the first time he's actually killed in the field where he left her."

"We believe he's escalating," Bethwick said.

"Ye . . . ess . . . but this vic is different because, from what we've gathered, Do Unto Others seems to have personal connections to whom he chooses," she pointed out.

Bethwick stated flatly, "We believe it's the same doer. You have a picture of Emmy Decatur on your board. Lulu's message is the same as hers. Though the message was released to the press, the public never saw the lettering on the body."

Donley broke in, "It would be highly unlikely it's not the same doer."

Gretchen nodded curtly. September knew that she was only playing devil's advocate. That she probably agreed with them, but she didn't like their highhanded manner. Come to that, neither did she.

D'Annibal said, "So, he's moving from women he knows, or he picks up in bars, to women who may be more available to him because of their line of work."

Bethwick stated quickly, "Assumptions this early are almost always counterproductive."

D'Annibal straightened and September wanted to jump up and defend him, but it wasn't necessary. The lieutenant could hold his own.

Auggie drawled, from the back of the room, "We're all on the same side, compadres."

Donley and Bethwick just stared at him.

"You said he's escalating," September reminded them. "And his kills are getting closer and closer together." Bethwick looked like he wanted to argue, but since September had stated a fact, he let it go. September added, "My partner and I will continue looking for connections between the first three vics."

"All right." Donley nodded once. A concession.

Fifteen minutes later they were finished and September went to talk to Auggie who said in a low voice only meant for her, "You took Westerly to the house?"

"Thought you didn't talk to dear old Dad."

"July gave me a call. Said you ran out of there with your hair on fire."

"I'd just found out about Lulu."

"Also said you seemed a little . . . mussed up."

September narrowed her eyes on her brother. "We get called into a meeting with the feds and you want to talk about me being 'mussed up'?"

"Down, girl. Just saying you were with Westerly. Caution is called for. I—"

"Detective Rafferty?"

Both Auggie and September turned at the sound of Agent Donley's voice. He blinked a moment, apparently realized they were both Raffertys, and amended, "Detective September Rafferty?"

"I'll see ya," Auggie said, sliding away. September wanted to grab him by the sleeve and hang on, but there was nothing she could do. She gave him a "This isn't over" look and turned to the agent.

"Could I have a moment with you?" the agent asked her.

"Sure."

Donley led the way down the hallway to another room, one whose main purpose was interrogation. He was shorter than Bethwick, with longer hair and though he was in a suit there was something sloppier about him that made September feel less like she was enduring a military inquisition. Probably the point, she decided. Good agent/bad agent. Whatever, she preferred Donley, but that didn't mean she didn't have to be on her best behavior.

He took a seat at the table and invited her to do the same. She did, reluctantly, though she was beginning to understand D'Annibal's desire to stay standing. It just felt less . . . subservient.

"I'm not going to waste your time, Detective," Donley started right in. "You received a personal message from the doer, and we don't believe you should be on this case any longer."

September had been half-expecting this but it was a jolt nevertheless. "I wasn't aware it had been determined that it was from the doer," she said, borrowing from Auggie and Sandler's notebooks. It was a complete bluff, but she didn't want to be pulled off and would use whatever ammunition she had. "The message came on one of my own grade school projects, and I'm still trying to determine how whoever sent it to me got that information."

"What are you saying? That you think it could be a prank?"

"Whatever it is, I think it's to the benefit of the investigation that I remain on the case. I'm asking to stay." She wasn't quite certain of protocol here; she wasn't sure he had the authority to yank her off if D'Annibal said she could stay. But whatever, she figured she would just be straightforward and see what that got her.

He lifted his chin and leaned back in his chair. "Tell me about the investigation so far. What have you found?"

Drawing a breath, September explained about the Twin Oaks school connection between Dempsey and Tripp and that Decatur had attended school in the same district, if not the same schools. She brought up the similar ages and descriptions of the three victims, and the fact that they'd been regulars at different bars around the Laurelton area, a possible avenue for the killer to find them. "You say this prostitute—Lulu—was found outside a bar as well," she wound up. "Do we know anything about her background? Where she went to school?"

"She's a lot older than your first three." He gave her a look and she recalled with a faint flush that they'd been less than forthright about thinking they had a serial killer on their hands till now. On the other hand, until Lulu, they hadn't had the evidence to make that call, whether they were convinced or not.

"Cooke from Portland vice is pulling her background," he went on, "but at first glance, it appears he picked her because she was a prostitute. Nothing fancier than that."

"Of course, assumptions this early are almost always counterproductive."

Donley had hazel eyes with flecks of green. Those flecks seemed to light with amusement for a moment, but he didn't comment. "Your lieutenant has seen fit to keep you on the case, so . . ."

"I can stay," she finished for him.

"You can stay. For now," he added repressively as she turned toward the door.

Sandler was waiting for her apparently, as she hooked up with her as soon as September returned to the squad room. "What'd he say?"

"I'm still on the case. He told me I wasn't on the case, but he had a change of heart."

"How'd you manage that?"

"Niceness." She slid Gretchen a sideways smile. "Radical concept, I know."

She snorted. "Dalton caught the call after the two kids who found the body reported to 911. He's a putz. And Bethwick can kiss my ass if he thinks I'm helping the feds."

"See, it's that bad attitude that gets you in trouble," September told her.

"You've come a long way from the wide-eyed newbie," Gretchen observed. "Where's this newfound confidence coming from?"

"I had an epiphany last night of sorts."

"Yeah? About what?"

September shrugged. She didn't know how to say that the recognition of how her father's infidelity had contributed to her mother's death, coupled with her own undeniable attraction to Jake Westerly, had sprung something loose inside her, something that had just been waiting to be set free. "I think this guy Sheila called Wart is our man," she said. "I don't know what the deal is with him going after a prostitute. That's . . . something else. But this guy knew Sheila, and I think he might've known

Emmy and Glenda, too. If not personally, through some connection."

"The prostitute is just a quick fix to bring him under control," she said. "Let the feds chase that one around, but I'm with you. The other three—he knows 'em, or knows of 'em. They're specific targets. He goes for the Lulus out there because he's either losing control, or he's finished with his targets and has moved on. But the way we'll get him is figuring out how he knows those first three vics."

"So, what have we got?" September asked, glad that she and Sandler were on the same page. If nothing else, the FBI agents had brought solidarity between them.

"I don't know. This school thing . . ."

"I didn't find the rest of my stuff. Maybe it was thrown out after my mother died."

September thought about how she'd racewalked from the attic stairs to the front door, ignoring both July's "Hey!" and her father's dark frown as Jake followed after her.

Outside, she'd gulped air, realized she was sweating and quivering, and had looked at Jake and said, "I was crazy. That was crazy. I've got work to do and I need you to take me home."

"What's happened?" he asked.

"Another body. That's all I can say. I don't know any more than that, and if I did, I'm not able to talk about it yet. Take me back to my apartment."

He must've understood she wasn't fooling around because he did as she requested. She was grateful he didn't go over their moments in the attic. She needed time to process them herself. Not that she was sorry. Far from it. But she was completely aware that Jake was dangerous to her, not because of the investigation, but because she had a weakness for him. Always had.

As if sensing she was thinking of him, her cell phone rang and when she checked the number she saw it was him. She clicked it off without answering and Gretchen asked, "What?"

"My father," she lied. "Did I ever tell you that he cheated on my mother, like all the time?"

"No." Sandler was eyeing her carefully, as if she were a new species of animal, which in a way, she kinda was.

"You know how you know something. You didn't think you knew it, but you did. You just kinda let it go, and then one day it becomes so obvious you can't believe you didn't get it earlier."

"What happened?" she asked.

"My mother intercepted a note meant for my father from his lover, at the time. There's no date on it. I don't have proof. But I know. . . ." She inhaled and exhaled, shaking her head. "My mother was so upset that she was driving too fast and didn't look out and ran into a truck and that was it. I figured it out last night."

"And you had a powwow with your father about this?"

"Nope. Don't need to. Auggie's right. Best thing to do is stay away from dear old Dad."

Agent Donley had rejoined Bethwick and they were gathering their reports together and heading out. Auggie was long gone, and D'Annibal was back in his office, glaring at a computer screen as if it held terrible information, but he'd been in that position for long moments and it was clear he was pissed and thinking in his head. September sat back down at her desk. Her head was full of the events of the past few days and she sensed she needed some time to just collect her thoughts and put them in some kind of order. It wasn't like her to just run on adrenaline, but that's sure as hell what she'd been doing.

Just before six, George called, "Hey."

September and Gretchen both looked up. Thompkins was just hanging up the phone and swiveling in his chair, his bulk making the seat protest as if in agony. "I gotta callback from one of the summer school teachers at Twin Oaks, a Ms. Chapel. Looks like she had a sort-of friendship with Glenda Tripp," George said. "They got to talking one night and swapped stories. Tripp let it be known about her doctor uncle who's up on charges for practicing without a license et cetera, et cetera, and it comes up that Tripp was a little wild during those formative teen years and had sex with some guy on her uncle's examining table."

"Okay," Sandler said, interested. "But haven't we all got a few skeletons in the closet?"

"Tripp called the experience 'sex with a psychopath.' Said afterward she was weirded out and steered clear of the guy and where her uncle was practicing," George added with a lift of his eyebrows.

"Got a name?" September asked, knowing already that he didn't or he would have said so.

"Nope."

"Did she say where this examining table was?" September asked.

"Conversation didn't go that far. Ms. Chapel showed a little too much shock and Tripp clammed up. But it didn't appear to be Tripp's husband. Sounds like they were married less than a New York minute, but this was before him, apparently."

"The ex-husband lives on the East Coast," Sandler said reflectively. "He wasn't anywhere around when she was killed."

"We called him. He's remarried. Said he and the wife were home, but we talked on a cell phone," September remembered, her heart clutching a little. "Maybe we didn't follow up enough."

"Maybe," Sandler said, frowning. "But it'll be easy enough to check if he was around during any of the killings."

"Right," September said.

"Our doer's a local boy," Sandler said with a slow shake of her head. "It's not the husband, but I'll check him out some more just to eliminate him."

"Sounds good," George said, turning back to his computer.

September asked him, "This incident on the examining table? It would have been thirteen, fourteen years ago?"

"Sounds about right," George allowed.

"Wonder where Dr. Navarone was practicing then," September asked. "He moved around a lot, as I recall."

"Wonder if Tripp's fuck-buddy was a patient," Gretchen guessed. "She called him a psycho."

"Maybe it doesn't mean anything. That's what Sheila Dempsey called everybody when she was a kid," September said.

"But maybe it does," Sandler said.

"I'll ask Auggie," September decided, getting up and sliding her chair into her desk. "He was at that shoot-out with Navarone and he's still finalizing things on the Zuma case." She headed toward the back hallway and the locker room.

"What the hell are you doing?"

The killer felt the hairs on the back of his neck rise. He was cleaning out the van, at work. He'd cleaned it and cleaned it and cleaned it, but somehow the smell of the whore couldn't be removed.

He slowly straightened and turned to regard Mel, his drunken boss. Mel's eyes were red and he was a little unsteady on his feet, but he was still functioning at some level. "Cleaning the van," he told him.

"Fuck it, man. Get outta here." Mel waved one loose arm. "Go home. Get some rest."

He nodded and closed the back doors, glad Mel hadn't seemed to notice all the extra tools he had in the back along with the bottles of solvents and bleach. He'd already taken off the magnetic signs that said MEL'S WINDOW COVERINGS from both sides of the white van. It was his own van. Mel reluctantly paid some of his gas, but there was no company vehicle, which was fine because he changed the plates for his excursions. He was good at stealing ones with tags that would be good for a while.

Mel wanted him to leave so he had some time alone with the bottle in his office drawer before he went home to the wife, a nagging bitch with a voice that could cut glass.

He drove home with a feeling of anxiety rising. The beat of the beast's heart was starting to thunder again. How come? he asked himself, slightly alarmed. He'd been able to hold back the beast, contain it, but now it had escaped and was running rampant. The whore had been a good kill, but it wasn't enough. He needed more. Much, much more.

But he had to wait. Had to. He'd waited so long and he needed to draw it out, make it last, stop the laughing.

But the beast wasn't listening. The beast wanted.

The beast had wanted for a long, long, long time. He'd been afraid of it at first, afraid people could see.

He'd shivered in his bed. Had not been able to control his bladder and mistakes had happened. He'd been beaten for those. And then at school he'd wet his pants when the girls had played that trick on him, tried to pants him. They'd covered their mouths with their hands and run away screaming and he'd looked at Nine for help. She'd been nice to him, but she turned away. He could still see the way her ponytail swung in front of him, taunting him. Dark hair with red. And she'd given that report on the ocean. She talked of tidal waves and sea creatures and the anemone with its dark hole and waving fingers.

His erection had been impossible to hide, but luckily he was in the back of the class and neither of the boys on either side of him had given him away to the laughing girls. Laughing and laughing.

His hands squeezed on the steering wheel, his knuckles showing white.

He wanted to cut them all!

Twenty minutes later he pulled into the driveway of his place and looked quickly to the main house. It was quiet. The bitch was maybe sleeping. Pulling to a stop in front of his apartment, a converted garage, he locked the van and hurried inside before he could be seen.

He needed her to die, but could not afford to kill her. Couldn't have it traced back to him and it would be. It would be.

Quietly, he changed his clothes from the gray jumpsuit he preferred to work in, to a pair of brown pants and a sweatshirt. Then he moved back outside, listening for her, then he crept around the back of the main house and found his way into Avery Boonster's field, turning his face skyward.

The field where he'd killed the whore was several miles away. Too close. He'd killed her too close. He needed to be in the Laurelton city limits and away from here. Take the heat away from himself instead of bringing it near. He hadn't been thinking straight. He'd only been able to see through the beast's eyes and the beast was consumed with need, didn't think things through.

Dangerous.

He stalked across the fields toward the Boonster spread. The sheep looked at him as he approached and then moved away. They didn't trust him. He'd taken some of them when he was younger and Avery had found the carcasses. Told on him and his father had taken the strap to him with that glint of triumph in his eyes.

He escaped to a place where September Rafferty was his. They were together, but in his dreams she turned on him, opened her black maw and laughed.

He was moved to a different school; a secretive ploy because his father and mother sensed something wrong and they were through with him. The old lady took him in, but her eyes were dark and flat, like his father's, and she knew he was wrong. Winning her trust became an obsession to him, and he forcefully pushed the dangerous, black thoughts aside, would not listen to the beast's growls. He pushed thoughts of September aside as well, but he saw the other girls in school who reminded him of her. They didn't know the beast inside his breast, and they let him draw near to them.

His camouflage worked, at least in the beginning. He could be someone entirely different. He saw Sheila at school and she was so much like September that his thoughts turned to her. He saw her walking through the halls, smiling and joking, always with that moronic Schmidt. He stayed in the background and kept his eyes on them. Once he saw Schmidt slide his hand down to her rump and he had to hurry to the bathroom and beat off.

Later, he went hunting for raccoon and squirrel, failing in his quest, and he fought back the screams that tore him inside like razor blades.

The old lady suspected, but she didn't know. He did not approach Sheila. Like Nine, she was skittish. As he grew older he learned to put on the outer shell, and for a time he could walk among them, the laughers, and they didn't notice him.

But then he saw September again. One elementary school event between his old school and his new, and there she was. And Sheila was there. September and Sheila. He couldn't tell them apart. In a sexual haze he sensed there was meaning there, but it escaped him.

Then he saw the documentary on the ocean and he waited, heart pounding, for the sea anemones. He nearly passed out when they came on. He understood. September . . . she was the sea anemone. He wanted to stab her deep into her hot center. It was all he could think about.

And then it happened. The bad thing that no one knew about. He'd stolen the old lady's car . . . pushed it out while she was sleeping . . . and drove aimlessly into Laurelton. It was meant to be, because all of a sudden there she was: September, with a girlfriend, someone he knew, one of his neighbors. He followed them and learned their routine and then one night he put on the outer shell and met them.

But he was gawking. He could sense it, but couldn't stop it. And they saw him and understood and they laughed and laughed and laughed at him, tittering behind their hands.

Until he stopped them. The beast stopped them.

He'd killed September. He'd killed her, and maybe now he would be rid of the beast.

But she wasn't dead.

He understood then that she could not be killed without the ritual. There were steps to take, rules to follow. And when she died, he would die. But not before, and there was much work to be done.

Now he walked back to his apartment, carefully skirting the yellow-eyed windows that looked into the night from the old lady's house. He unlocked his door, locked it behind him, then pulled out the key to the upstairs.

That's where the treasures were. The mementos from the girls who laughed. He carefully searched through the drawers for his favorites and pulled out the sample of hair. Her hair.

He put that back, and pulled out the next box, the treasure trove. Before he reached inside, he pulled a pair of disposable latex gloves from the box he kept by the cot, then carefully, he drew out the book: *All About Me*. September's life carefully constructed by her loving parents. That's where he'd found the lock of soft, baby hair. He flipped through the pages and smiled. After a few moments, he put the book down and reached into the box for something else.

A report. The sea anemone report. His hands clenched, and he put it back in the box. He couldn't part with it. It was his. Forever. Instead, his hands roamed to the cardboard with the pictures she'd added about her family. He stared and stared at it. The brothers and sisters, mother and father. Perfection when he'd been given shit.

Turning it over, he saw her name printed in her unformed hand. With a smile, he took it downstairs, found a red felt-tip pen and scratched another message onto the back of the paper, next to her signature.

He almost kissed it, but froze, his lips a centimeter from the paper. Fucking DNA. Instead, he gently folded it and slipped it into a large envelope. He knew her address.

He knew all about her. But should he show his hand, or mail it to the station?

The station.

His chest began to pound.

The beast was on him again. How long could he wait? He needed to take Nine soon. He needed her.

His heart began to thunder in his ears. A silvery shiver of fear slid through him. What if, when he finally had her, it wasn't enough? *What then?*

But no. It would be the end. They would be together for all eternity and the beast would be put to death.

Soon. But first . . . another taste. There were other laughers out there. He could see their faces, but did not know where they lived, so it would have to be someone else. Another woman outside a bar. They were easy to pluck.

Chapter 13

Jake turned into the drive of his parents' modest three-bedroom ranch and noticed his mother's handiwork in the riot of zinnias and chrysanthemums surrounding the front porch. He parked behind his father's truck on the gravel drive, climbed out, and stretched.

He hadn't wanted to leave Nine last night. He'd wanted to stay with her, be a part of what she was involved with. Help, somehow. But after their brief make-out session in her parents' attic—she was right; that was crazy—and the call from work about another victim, she'd locked him out as if he didn't exist. He'd been unconvinced about her mental leap to the belief that her mother had received the note they'd found the exact day Mrs. Rafferty had died, but he'd let it go. It wasn't his call, though he'd certainly had experience dealing with that kind of blasting energy and surety. His years with Loni had taught him that.

Now, he knocked on the door and it was opened immediately by his mother, Roberta Westerly, who leaned up to give him a hard hug and kiss on the cheek. "I won't say it. I promise I won't say it," she said.

"Go ahead. Say it."

"We don't see you enough. But that's okay, you're here now. I won't even ask why. Your father said you called his cell, and I put a chicken in the oven and it'll be done roasting in twenty minutes. Got some fingerling potatoes . . . anyway, you're staying."

Jake hardly knew how to respond. He looked at his mother. Her steel gray hair was swept back in soft waves, and her face had faint wrinkles around the eyes and mouth, but she still had a youthful way about her that made him smile. That was why it was so hard to say, "I can't stay for dinner."

"Oh . . ." She tried to hide her disappointment. "What is it this time? Work, I'm sure. Something to do with that."

"Something to do with that," he repeated, though it was a lie. It was because of September he was here. Her sudden leap to conclusions about her father, that though he kinda understood . . . kinda . . . had thrown her into his arms, which was great, but he sensed it would be like dealing with a bipolar person at the peak of the cycle. All crazy, wild ideas and energy.

He understood about bipolar. Loni was classic. He was lucky she'd given him the ultimatum, and he was resolved not to go back, no matter what happened, though it still chilled him to be so firm in the face of her illness. But he'd been warned by everyone from his mother to Loni's own psychiatrist: he needed to save himself first.

"Where's Dad?" he asked.

"On the back porch, having a beer. Want one?"

"Sure. I'll get it."

He headed for the refrigerator, found himself a Henry's, twisted off the cap and opened the screen door to the porch. It was hot, but bearable in the shade. Hearing the screech of the door, Nigel looked over from where he was staring across the backyard to a vegetable garden, baking in the late sun. Some large pumpkins were visible, and Jake said, "Those look massive."

"Might be decent size by Halloween," his father allowed, getting up from his chair to shake hands with his son. His eyes were blue—a shade or two greener than Rafferty blue—and his smile was warm. "Have a chair."

It was a late summer/early fall tradition for his father. A beer on the back porch while dinner was being prepared, as long as the weather was good. It didn't matter that Nigel had all but retired. Some habits didn't need to change.

Jake sat in the other rocker. It was bucolic. Like Westerly Vale. He didn't know why he had such a hard time being part of this. It just felt like he was somehow marking time whenever he was away from the city. He couldn't explain it, didn't even want to try.

"I need to ask you a few things," he told his father, holding the beer loosely between his palms.

"Sounds serious." Nigel slid him a questioning look.

"It's about Kathryn Rafferty."

His father straightened in the chair. "Kathryn Rafferty."

"The day she died."

Now Nigel turned to give him a long, hard look. "What are you talking about?" he asked, half-bewildered, half-put-off.

"I don't know really. I was with Nine—September—Rafferty last night, and we found some—"

"What do you mean 'with her'?" he interrupted.

Jake opened his mouth to answer, but didn't know what to say.

"She's Braden Rafferty's daughter," Nigel stated flatly.

"I know who she is. She's also Kathryn's daughter," Jake responded, just as flatly. Then, realizing he was going about this badly, told his father how he'd run into September at The Willows, how she'd questioned him about the ongoing investigation into a suspected serial killer, how he'd taken her to dinner and then ended up at the Rafferty "castle." He finished with, "—and that's when she found the note that she just jumped on, sure it was an assignation between her father and his second wife for the day Kathryn died."

"Verna," Nigel said, sinking back into the chair and taking a pull on his own Henry's.

"Yeah, Verna. Nine just was sure all of a sudden that it was the note that contributed to her mother's death."

There was silence from his father's chair. Nigel, too, sported gray hair but he hadn't lost one strand. He, like Jake's mother, could have passed for ten years younger than their age except for the color of their hair.

"What are you looking for?" Nigel asked.

"Corroboration, I guess. You were first on the scene at the time of Kathryn's accident. Did you see her at The Willows that day? Talk to her? You were friends, right?"

"As much as Braden would allow. He really didn't like his wife consorting with the help." There was irony in there somewhere.

"Was it true about Braden and Verna? Did you know?"

Nigel inhaled and then exhaled, his chin dropping to rest on his chest a moment. "Braden Rafferty was not true to his wife. That was a fact. He wasn't true to Kathryn throughout their marriage."

Jake nodded. "I'm not sure how much Nine knows of that. Some. But she believes this note is responsible for her mother's death."

"Did she tell Rafferty that?"

"Braden. Not yet. Kinda think she might."

"What's your stake in this?" He gave his son a penetrating look.

Jake shook his head. "I don't know yet. I just thought if you had some information . . ."

"You would take it to her as an offering."

"Not exactly," Jake said, a bit annoyed.

A good long time passed without either of them saying anything. Jake could hear his mother moving around in the kitchen and he turned to watch her through the screen door.

"I don't like you getting mixed up with the Raffertys," Nigel said quietly, staring out across the backyard to the weather vane atop the outbuilding that stood perfectly still in the dense evening air. "But September might be right. I saw Kathryn as she was getting in her car. She was upset and I tried to get her to go back inside for a bit. She said she couldn't. She was going to face Braden with the evidence. I didn't really know what she meant, and she told me she'd seen the note. 'I've seen it,' she said. 'And I know they're screwing their brains out!' I didn't have to ask who. Verna was hanging around like a bad smell already. Kathryn was going to confront them in the act." He stopped, thinking a moment. "She tore into the road and was instantly hit. I ran down the drive like a madman. She was alive for a few minutes, but that was it. She was losing blood and I ran back to the house, to call 911, but it was too late."

"You never told this to anyone."

"I told it to Rafferty. You bet. He didn't like hearing it and he blamed me for her death. Guilt," he sneered. "I didn't have the money to buy Westerly Vale, but Edmonds knew I was good for it, and he hated Rafferty almost as much as I did. We struck a deal and I vowed I would put that bastard out of business." He made a sound almost of amusement. "Well, in that I didn't succeed, but the vineyard did okay."

"More than okay. It's Neela and Colin's total life."

"But not yours."

"No, not mine."

Jake stood up, thinking about what he'd learned, wondering if it would matter to September.

"What are you doing with her?" Nigel asked.

"Nine? Nothing. We're friends."

"You didn't come out here to talk to me about this if she's just a friend."

"I don't know, Dad. I just wanted to have the truth before she went off half-cocked, but . . . hell, she seems to know more than I do."

"About what?"

"Damn near everything."

To his surprise, his father chuckled. "Oh, boy. You got it bad. And a Rafferty. You be damn careful, son. They're rattlers."

"You don't know Nine."

"I know Braden. And I know March. I'll try to keep an open mind, but they're supercilious bastards with too much money and too little integrity. That's what I know. Be careful you don't learn that the hard way."

"C'mon, c'mon, c'mon . . ." September tapped her fingers impatiently on the dash, wishing her brother would just pick up, for God's sake. *Pick. Up.* But his cell went to voice mail again, and she was left frustrated.

Fine. She tossed her cell down on the passenger seat, twisted the ignition, and then it started ringing. Snatching it up, she realized it wasn't Auggie's ring tone. It was Sandler. "Hey," she answered.

"Where are you?"

"Oh, sitting in the parking lot of my apartment building, trying to reach my brother. He's probably turned his phone off so he can have dinner with Liv with no interruptions. Must be nice."

"He'll turn it back on soon," she said, uncaring. "Are you seriously done for the day?"

"Why? You working on getting some OT?"

"Yeah, just try to get some overtime in this economy. I was just thinking, though. I'd like to talk to those kids who found Lulu. See what they say."

"Tonight?"

"Yeah, if you're not too busy." A pause. "I could use you."

September half-smiled. "Because your particular style might not work with children?"

"Ya wanna come, or not?" she demanded.

September twisted the ignition and her engine rushed to life. "I'd like to see that field where they found her. Let's do it."

"Meet me at the station. We'll go in my car."

September was there in twenty minutes and Sandler was already waiting for her. They left her Pilot and climbed into Sandler's Jeep. Her vehicle was nearly identical to those used by the force. When September had asked her about it, she'd shrugged and said she was used to it, and that she tended to drive a vehicle hard and needed something that would go over rougher terrain. "And can you really see me in a luxury car?" she'd finished.

Enough said.

Sandler adjusted her GPS with one of the kids' addresses and they drove west into the setting sun. September put down her blind against the bright pink-orange glare, and Gretchen did the same, her eyes narrowed on Sunset Highway and the exodus of traffic from Portland, through Laurelton, and beyond. They left the city limits behind and turned south, cutting through several housing tracts, and then the rural landscape came up fast. Two-lane roads cut through farmland dotted with rambling homes separated by fields of grass and corn stalks and the occasional grape arbor.

September watched it flash by outside her window. "A friend of my sister's lived out here somewhere. May used to spend the night with her."

"This the sister that was killed?"

"Yeah. Her friend, Erin, worked at Louie's, a burger place off Hillside that's now a dry cleaners. I guess business never recovered afterward. . . ." She trailed off.

"I know where you mean. I wasn't here, then, but I know the place."

"It's kind of a blur for me. He locked 'em in the backroom, and tied 'em up, stole the money, and then came back and killed them. There were dollars found in the backroom, so they think he went back to kill them. Probably thought it over, the fact that they'd seen his face. Decided he didn't want to take a chance."

"What about cameras?"

"One wasn't working, so you can only see him from the back, and he kept his head kind of ducked down, anyway. He knew." She sighed. "Or, so I've heard anyway. Like I say, I was a kid and it was a blur."

Sandler slid her a look. "That the reason you're working homicide? For your sister?"

"Auggie's the main reason, but if we were psychologically examined . . . I'm sure that's in there for both of us."

Sandler glanced at the GPS. "Up on the right. About three-quarters of a mile."

They passed several fields and homes and then came to one with a white rail fence around about an acre with a split-level home in the front. Pulling into the drive, they saw a young boy look out the picture window.

"Must be who we're here to see," Sandler said dryly.

The porch light came on as they stepped out of the vehicle. By the time they reached the front door it was already open and a woman in her mid-thirties was standing there. "Are you with the police?" she asked at the same moment Gretchen and September lifted their badges.

The boy was behind her, looking at them with interest. Whatever state he'd been in after seeing the body, he clearly had brushed that aside in the face of his newfound celebrity. As if to confirm September's thought, he said, "TV people were here!"

"Shh, Stuart," his mother admonished, opening the door to allow them entry.

"TV people, huh," September said.

"Are you really a policeman?" he asked suspiciously.

"I really am. I'm Detective Rafferty, and my partner is Detective Sandler."

He took a gander at Gretchen and said, "Partner. I have a partner, too. Matt. Are you gonna see him, too?"

"We're just doing a follow-up," Gretchen said to the mother who glanced at the glass of white wine she'd set on a nearby table and introduced herself as Tori Salisbury, Stuart's mother.

"I didn't know where they were going," she said. "Those agents came by with that deputy and Stuart showed them where he was . . . wasn't supposed to be," she added, turning a stern look on her son, who barely noticed her.

"Is your badge made out of gold?" he asked.

"No." September smiled at him. "You weren't supposed to be in the field because it's someone else's property?"

"I don't know them." He turned to his mom for help.

"That's the Layton place," she said. "They have cattle, cows. The bulls are in a separate pen, thank God. There's barbed wire on the top of the fence, but it doesn't seem to stop them."

"That's how the killer musta got in," Stuart said with a nod. "Like we did."

"No, there was a break in the fence," his mom contradicted him. "That's what the agents said."

September knew, from Donley and Bethwick's notes, that a portion of the fence had been cut apart and the victim rolled through. They were checking for fibers caught on the fence, but September believed if they found anything, it would be from the victim's clothes. The killer was too careful.

"Could you point us to this field?" Gretchen asked Tori.

"I can!" Stuart cried.

"Hush, Stuart," his mother said to him, then she stepped back on the porch, inviting September and Gretchen to follow. "Straight ahead over that way. There's a gravel drive that splits between two of the fields. Drive down it and you'll see where the fence was cut. Mr. Layton put some temporary boards in front of the hole."

"How old is Mr. Layton?" Gretchen asked.

"Seventy-five. All of this is hard for him," she said with a sniff. "Do you mind? My husband's going to be home soon and I need to finish dinner."

"We'll be on our way. Thank you," September said, but Stuart was right on her heels as she stepped off the porch.

"I'll show you. I know where the spot is."

"Stuart . . ." His mother looked pained. She'd picked up the wine glass and was holding onto it as if her life depended on it.

"Thanks," September told him, "but you should stay here with your mom. We'll go look at it."

"You better check with Mr. Layton, then," he said seriously. "I don't think you'll make it over the fence."

As they climbed back into the Jeep, Gretchen eyed September with a kind of reluctant admiration. "I kinda wanted to tell the kid to shut up," she admitted.

"Niceness, Sandler. Niceness."

"That's what I've got you for."

Mr. Layton might be seventy-five, but he was wire tough and really pored over their identification before he would take them through the gate and across the field. They'd come in from the north side and a stream prevented them from passing to the spot where Lulu's body had been found.

Layton said, "Those agents and crime people went in the other side, but I blocked it up. Don't know what could get out, or in, I guess. Some psychotic, huh? Gave me a real bad feeling, seeing her like that. Why're you two here now?"

"We're on the case, as well," Gretchen told him stiffly. She looked around and then said to September, "So, you wanta ford the stream?"

"You think they missed any evidence?" September asked skeptically.

She shook her head. "Uh-uh."

They stood quietly for a moment. It had grown dark as they walked across the field and there was little to see.

"He's comfortable in open spaces," September said. "Fields."

"Farm boy," Layton said, and they both looked at him. "City folk wouldn't come out here."

"Maybe to hide a body," Gretchen argued.

"He spent some time with her," the older man disagreed. "He knew the area. Sick bastard."

They all worked their way back across the field. September and Gretchen thanked Layton, then climbed in the Jeep and headed back to the station.

"So, what did we learn, class?" Sandler asked her.

September didn't answer. She was thinking about the kids she went to elementary school with and where they lived growing up. She didn't know that many of them, but it was certainly possible to find out. That might narrow the list down a bit—the list of male classmates who knew about her second grade artwork, maybe had access to it, and who were also comfortable in open fields in a wide circle around Laurelton.

Chapter 14

September woke early and went for a run. Her head was full of so many things: Do Unto Others, Jake, her father. . . . She knew she was harboring a deep anger toward him, and kept debating with herself whether she should act on it or not. One moment she wanted to just bury all of it. Water under the bridge. The next she could feel the back of her neck get hot as she thought about screaming at him what a bastard he was.

Neither seemed like a good option.

She was back at her apartment by seven, through the shower by seven-fifteen, and out the door by eight. Her cell rang as she was getting in her car. Her heart fluttered momentarily. She'd half-expected Jake to call her yesterday, though she'd told herself it would be better if he didn't. Then when he didn't, she was disappointed.

And she was disappointed again, even though she'd been waiting for this call. "About time," she told Auggie. "And I don't want to hear any of this task force bullshit. You just turned off your phone."

"Guilty," he said. "What did you want?"

"I hardly remember, it's been so long."

"I'm sorry, okay? I wanted some down time."

"Yeah . . . well . . ." She gathered her thoughts, then told him what George had learned about Glenda Navarone Tripp's sexual encounter on Dr. Navarone's examining table from Tripp's coworker at Twin Oaks. "It may be nothing, but the guy creeped her out enough to bring it up years later to a new friend. I found it interesting that it crossed with your case."

"How old was she at the time?" Auggie asked.

"In her teens. Where was Navarone practicing then? He didn't have a private practice, did he?"

"Not then. Not from what I know. He might've been at Grandview Mental Hospital at that time."

"Grandview . . . the one that's now Grandview Senior Care."

"That's right."

"Huh."

"Huh, what?" he asked.

"One of our second grade teachers. Actually, *your* homeroom teacher, Mrs. McBride, lives at Grandview Senior Care now."

"I don't see how that fits in—"

"It doesn't. Just an observation."

"There was a woman I interviewed at Grandview Senior Care on the Zuma case. A nurse, Sofia, who said her sister worked at Grandview Hospital for a while. Hmmm . . . I'm trying to remember the sister's name. I'm not sure Sofia ever told me, but neither she nor the sister thought much of Dr. Navarone." He paused. "One other thing. Liv's brother Hague was at Grandview for a while during his teens."

"That's right," September said, absorbing that fact again. She'd never met Hague Dugan but she knew he had serious psychological issues that kept him from living a so-called normal life. He was somewhat agoraphobic, rarely leaving his apartment unless he went to Rosa's Cantina on the ground floor of his building and was in the mood to orate/rant to a small crowd of followers who hung around him. He also had a tendency to go into a self-induced coma, or fugue state, when he became overly stressed. "He's kind of a difficult interview."

"You could say that," Auggie said with a short laugh.

"Well, it's something," September said. "All right. I'll keep Hague in mind. And if I go interview Mrs. McBride, I'll see if Sofia's around and ask for the name of her sister."

"Mrs. McBride," Auggie repeated, making a shuddering sound.

"I was lucky I had Mrs. Walsh," September agreed with a smile before hanging up.

When she got to the station it was to find Agents Bethwick and Donley had taken over the squad room as their main command station. George had been moved away from his side of the room and was now closer to September and Gretchen's desk. He was not in a good mood about it. His creaking chair was protesting loudly with every move he made. Ah, well.

Inside his office, D'Annibal had a serious expression on his face. He could have been carved in stone.

Bethwick let it be known that they were all over the Lulu Luxe investigation, and they wanted everything on Emmy Decatur, too, as she was the other victim with actual words carved into her skin.

As she was getting settled in her cell phone rang again, and this time it was Jake.

Feeling like all eyes were on her, September got up from her desk and started down the hall in the direction of the employee break room and her locker. "Hello," she answered a bit stiffly.

"So, I waited a day to call you. Didn't want to act too eager."

She grinned, but then pulled the grin off her face. "What do you want?" she asked. "I'm working."

"I want to talk to you. I've got a couple of things . . . I want to clear up."

She sucked air through her teeth. "I'm sorry I was so—out of control the other night. I'm not like that usually. Really."

"I didn't mind the out of control part. Especially parts of it."

"Look, Jake, I can't talk now. I really can't."

"After work. Tonight. We'll go someplace nice . . . a step up from The Barn Door and Taco Bell. I really do want to talk to you."

He sounded . . . urgent. "Okay," she capitulated. What was she holding out for anyway?

"I'll pick you up at seven," he told her and then he was gone.

She wondered vaguely if he'd hung up so quickly because he expected her to change her mind. It wouldn't be that far off from the truth.

Her cell phone rang again and she didn't recognize the number. "Rafferty," she answered.

"Detective Rafferty? This is Marilyn Osborne. Marcie Peterkin called me from Sunset Elementary? She said you wanted to talk to me and gave me this number?"

"Yes. Yes. Ms. Osborne. I—uh—was a student at Sunset Elementary when you taught second grade. Mrs. Walsh was my homeroom teacher, and my twin brother was in Mrs. McBride's class."

"Oh, yes. I remember the Rafferty twins. How can I help you?"

September found herself at a loss for words. How could she help her? She wasn't sure there was any way. Taking a leap of faith, she explained about the artwork that had been sent to her at the station, the message across its face, how she'd made it in second grade, how it seemed as if someone from the school may have sent it to her . . . ? "Was there . . . do you remember . . . if anyone was called Wart?" she asked, fumbling in the dark.

"No, I'm afraid not." She sounded reflective. "I'm trying to think back. What year would you have been in second grade?"

September told her, and then added, "It's kind of a long shot. I just haven't figured out how someone could get my artwork and send it to me. I actually saw a picture of it on the bulletin board of Mrs. Walsh's room and thought maybe he took it from the class."

"It's possible, I suppose. . . ."

She sounded so dubious, that September said, "I know. It's been a lot of years."

"You think this is from the same man who killed those other two victims?"

Three, September almost said. And now four, with Lulu Luxe. "The words are the same, so yes, that's the theory."

"I wish I could help you more," she said.

"Thank you." September accepted defeat gracefully.

"If I think of anything else, I'll call you," she said before she hung up.

She walked back into the squad room and saw Gretchen give her a quick, low wave outside of the agents' view. She was on the phone, and she was listening hard, offering up surprisingly sympathetic noises. "I completely understand," she said, her voice sounding even more nasal with the effort. "We'll look into it. From everything you've said, she sounds like a lovely girl."

September's brows shot together. *Who is that?* she mouthed.

Sandler just shook her head a teensy bit and moved her eyes in the direction of the agents. She made a few more conciliatory remarks, then finally was able to disconnect from whoever was at the other end of the line and desperate to keep talking. "Thank you. Thank you. Yes, we'll get on it. You're welcome . . . I . . . I'll call you." She set down the phone.

"Wow," September said, surprised.

"Man, I'm hungry," Gretchen said. "Let's go grab some lunch."

September glanced at the clock on the wall. It was ten-thirty. "Sure," she said.

George said, "Bring me back something?"

"Fuggedaboudit," Gretchen muttered, then, as if realizing she was on some new tack, said, "Tuna, chicken salad, or turkey."

"How about a hamburger?"

"We're going to the Safeway deli," she told him.

"Turkey," he said, disappointed.

"The Safeway deli?" September asked, as soon as they'd made their way past Guy Urlacher.

"It's close. I'm not really hungry. You?"

"I take it we're making a break from the feds."

"You know who was on the phone? Mrs. Decatur. Emmy's mother."

"Ahhh . . . and you didn't want Bethwick and Donley to know, even though they're concentrating on Emmy and Lulu?"

"I put a call into Mrs. Decatur. Before when I interviewed her and her husband, they just went on and on about how wonderful Emmy was, and I just sorta tuned out. But when Frick and Frack took her case, it pissed me off. There was something else there, when I talked to them. Something they weren't saying. I kinda got the feeling Mrs. Decatur wanted to tell, but just couldn't do it when her husband was going on and on about what a lovely girl Emmy was."

"Emmy's roommate said her parents kicked Emmy out when she was in high school," September remembered.

Gretchen nodded several times. "So, I was thinking about your niceness thing. Decided to try it. At first Mrs. Decatur was reluctant to talk to me, but I figured this was my last shot before the feds got to her."

"But she did talk to you."

"Oh, yeah. You ready for it? Emmy's parents didn't kick her out of the house. They sent her away. To Grandview Mental Hospital."

September felt like she'd been punched in the gut. She inhaled sharply and felt the hair on her arms lift. Staring through the windshield as Gretchen wheeled into the Safeway lot, she said, "We've got to go there."

"It doesn't exist anymore. It's an elder care facility."

"I know that. But there are a lot of connections to Grandview, and we need to talk to somebody who was there. I've got a line on that. I'll tell you on the way."

"What about our FBI friends? They're gonna be . . . pissed," Gretchen pointed out, but her tone said she couldn't care less.

"I'd rather ask forgiveness than permission."

"Oho, you're learning."

"What about George's sandwich?" September asked, as Sandler put the Jeep into reverse.

She snorted. "It's way too early for lunch."

And she tore out of the lot.

Grandview Senior Care was a one-story brick building with wings that ran off it like spokes from a wheel hub. The wings connected to other wings, some added long after the original ones, creating a maze of passageways that were confusing to the newcomer. September and Sandler walked up to the woman at the front desk, whose ropy arms stuck out from her T-shirt. She was tanned and her nose was faintly burned. She might work at an institution, but it looked as if she spent a lot of time outdoors. September asked for a nurse named Sofia.

"We have a Sofia Markam," the woman said, eyeing her and Gretchen's badges with some alarm. "She's on West A. I can call her to the front, but it may take a while. Unless you want to go back and see her there . . . ? Most of the residents in that area require increased care."

"Can you direct us?" September asked, and the receptionist pointed to her left and told them to take the second turn to the right. Before they left, September asked, "And I understand you have a Mrs. McBride as one of your residents?"

She made a funny sound. "Mrs. McBride would never break the law!"

"It's more about gathering information," September told her.

The woman pointed in the opposite direction for Amelia McBride, and gave her room number as East C #222 in the assisted living section.

"McBride sounds like she has all her marbles, at least," Gretchen observed.

"I'd like to talk to the nurse first. Find out about her sister." September had filled Gretchen in on what Auggie had told her about his trip to Grandview Senior Care several weeks earlier.

"Hey, I could miss talking to your old teacher entirely, and it would be fine by me."

"She was Auggie's teacher." *And Jake's.*

Gretchen lifted her shoulders.

They took a wrong turn and had to retrace their steps before they found the correct hallway. There was a small area designated behind a half-wall where two employees were making notes and looking at a central desktop computer. Neither looked up when September and Gretchen arrived and they had to wait a few minutes before the one closest to them, a slim woman in her fifties wearing blue hospital scrubs and a serious expression, looked at them over the top of her glasses. "Yes?" she asked.

"We're looking for Sofia Markam," September explained. "The woman at the front desk said we could find her here."

"Sofia's with a resident." She turned back to the computer screen.

"Is there a place where we could wait?" September asked with forced graciousness.

"We're with the Laurelton Police Department," Gretchen said, holding out her badge.

The woman zeroed in on the badge, so September showed hers as well. She blinked several times and said, "I'll be sure and let her know. There's an alcove with a back door to the central patio. You can either wait inside or out."

"Inside," Gretchen said.

"It is hot," the woman said, trying on a smile that looked like it was a bit rusty.

September and Gretchen moved to the area she mentioned and sat down on a padded bench beside each other. They could look through the windows to the enclosed patio. Several elderly women were seated under the covered section, half in wheelchairs.

"You ever think about being old?" Sandler asked.

September turned to her in surprise. "Not really. Do you?"

"I just can't see it happening to me," she said. "I'm gonna burn out early." Before September could think of a response, she added, "Dom's off tonight, so we're going out, thank you, God. He's probably no better than any of the rest, but there's got to be something more than the job."

A large woman with heavy breasts and short gray hair appeared from around the corner. She wore pink scrubs and when she came toward them her brows were drawn into a line and her eyes were full of suspicion. "I'm Sofia Markam," she stated, stopping directly in front of them.

"I'm Detective September Rafferty," September said, standing to meet her. "You spoke to my brother, Detective August Rafferty, a few weeks ago about Dr. Frank Navarone. In that interview, you mentioned that your sister worked at Grandview when it was still a mental hospital, possibly when Dr. Navarone worked there. I was wondering if I could get in touch with your sister."

"I never met any Detective August Rafferty."

"He goes by Auggie," September said.

"I spoke to a man who said his brother was Hague Dugan. He didn't give me his first name."

September held a beat. "Um . . . yes . . . he was working undercover." This was a half-truth because, yes, though Auggie worked undercover on various task forces, it

hadn't been quite that way on the Zuma case. Damn him
for forgetting to tell her what he'd told Sofia.

"Could I see your ID?" she asked.

September dutifully pulled out her badge again, as did
Gretchen who was starting to look annoyed.

She examined the badge carefully, then handed it back,
and crossed her arms under her ample breasts. "You want
to reach my sister?"

"Yes. When did your sister work at Grandview Mental
Hospital?"

"About ten to fifteen years ago, give or take. The hospital closed over five years ago."

September quickly calculated that Glenda would have
been about fifteen or sixteen at the time. That fit.

"You want to know more about Navarone? I thought
he finally got put in jail."

"We're investigating the death of his niece, Glenda Navarone Tripp," September admitted. "And we're just looking for background on the hospital as well."

"I thought he killed her to cover up something."

"It doesn't appear that way," September said.

"My sister's name is Dawn Markam-Manning," she finally said reluctantly. "She didn't work there long. A couple
of years is all. Let me give you her number." September
pulled out her notebook and Sofia gave her the digits. "She
works nights at Laurelton General," she finished.

"Thank you."

As they walked back down the hall, Gretchen said,
"Laurelton General. Everything keeps circling back to
our area."

"Yeah."

"Auggie didn't tell her he was a detective. Any idea why?"

"I'm sure he had his reasons, but I wish he would've
told me. Sofia's a lot like . . . well . . . Mrs. McBride."

"Oh, that's just wonderful."

September smiled. "You don't have to go. I don't even want to go, but in the name of being thorough, I might as well interview her while I'm here."

"I'll meet you in the Jeep," she said and they parted ways at the reception area.

September walked down the hall, aware of an underlying smell of disinfectant and a surprisingly enticing scent of baking bread as they neared the lunch hour. She hadn't liked hearing Gretchen's assessment of how she expected to burn out early and realized she wanted the whole enchilada: career, love, marriage, and a family. She understood her sister July's desire to have a child, not that she was ready for that yet herself, but she certainly hoped that was part of her own life plan.

Jake's visage floated across her mind and she shook her head. A high school one-night stand did not a relationship make. Still . . .

It took a while for Amelia McBride to answer September's knock. The white-haired, stooped ex-teacher came to the door leaning on a cane and peered at September sternly through sharp, brown eyes. "Do I know you?"

"I'm September Rafferty. My brother, August, was in your homeroom when we were in the second grade."

She thought about that a moment, then said, "You're twins."

"Yes," September answered. Apparently she and Auggie's relationship was memorable enough that both Osborne and McBride remembered.

Her gaze dropped to where September's jacket had pulled away and she saw the badge clipped at September's right hip. "You're a police officer?"

"I . . . yes. Both my brother and I are with the Laurelton Police Department."

"Well, you'd better come in." She shuffled back from the door and September entered her apartment.

The place was stuffy hot, but McBride didn't seem to notice. Her age, probably, September concluded and decided not to ask to open a window or ask for the air conditioning to be turned on. "I retired shortly after your year," the older woman observed as she sank with a sigh into a La-Z-Boy chair and pulled an afghan over her lap. "That was a difficult year."

"How so?" September asked, as she perched on one of the two wooden chairs around a narrow table near the kitchenette. She couldn't believe she needed a blanket in this room.

"It's always a different mix of kids. Ratio of boys to girls. Social development rates. Temperaments of the families . . ." She said it grimly and September recalled the same "mean face" she'd exhibited to the kids—er—children when she was a younger woman. "We had a lot of boys that year," McBride finished.

"The boys were what made it difficult?"

"I don't remember their names. Wouldn't have remembered yours if you hadn't told me. I just see the faces." She sucked on her teeth and shook her head. "That one child . . ."

"Yes?"

"What is it you're looking for?" she asked.

September thought a moment, then launched into the tale of the artwork that was sent to her, how she'd seen it on the bulletin board in the picture from her homeroom class that Mrs. Peterkin had pulled up, how she was thinking someone from her class might have ended up with it.

"He would have had to have stolen it," Mrs. McBride stated flatly.

"Maybe he took it off the bulletin board."

She shook her head and sucked on her teeth some more.

"You were mentioning one child from the class. A boy, maybe?" September prompted.

She made a face. "We had several that were problems that year. Home life wasn't what it should be. One of them was an object of ridicule for wetting his pants at recess. Another one brought a knife to school. Another one kept pantsing his friends." She frowned. "Was that Tim . . . no . . . maybe he was from a different year. Had to keep sending them all to the office. It was a revolving door. Just get one back, send another one down."

"Was there anyone called 'Wart,' do you remember?"

"These were second graders, my dear. They bandy around bad names all the time."

"This might be a nickname."

She shook her head.

September felt like she might pass out if she stayed much longer, so she stood up, thanked Mrs. McBride, and then said she'd let herself out, when the older woman struggled to get up. McBride waved at her in acquiescence and ordered, "Make sure it's locked."

Once she was in the outer hallway, September tested the knob and found it secure. The staff had keys to all the rooms, but McBride was safe within her oven from unwanted strangers.

Gretchen was driving them back to the station as September placed a call to the number Sofia had given her for Dawn Markam-Manning. It rang four times before it was picked up. "Hello?" an impatient woman's voice answered.

"Hello, is this Dawn Markam-Manning?"

"Who are you?" she demanded.

September quickly launched into who she was, how

she'd gotten her number, and what she wanted to know in terms of information. "Anything about Grandview Mental Hospital that may have included Dr. Navarone's niece, Glenda Navarone Tripp. I also want to—"

"Glenda Tripp was murdered. I saw it on the news. If anyone did it, it was probably her uncle. Look, I was not a fan of Navarone. Didn't my sister tell you? He used dangerous, *dangerous* methods. He got his license revoked for damn near killing someone he was supposed to be helping!"

"Her uncle was cleared of any involvement in her death," September said, realizing she'd hit a hot button.

"Keep looking at him," she advised. "He's a bad'un."

Dr. Navarone was a zealot who believed in himself and his healing practices beyond all reason, but he hadn't killed his niece. September tried another tack. "Did Glenda visit her uncle at the hospital?"

"While I was there? Maybe a time or two . . . I don't know for certain."

September said, "We have information that she may have had a sexual encounter during that time on—er— her uncle's examining table."

Dawn made a strangled sound. "How did you hear that?"

"Do you know something about it?" September asked when Dawn didn't deny it straight out.

"Well, Glenda was kind of a wild thing, in those days. Something happened on the examining table. We all sort of suspected, so we hid it from her uncle." There was a bit of satisfaction in her tone.

"Could it have been with another patient?" September asked.

"I don't know."

"All right. Was there someone with the nickname of Wart there at that time?"

"Wart . . ." She turned that over in her mind for a few moments. "No . . . we tried to discourage that kind of thing. It was like name-calling, and it would send some of the patients into a rage." She paused, then said, "There was one, though, that stuck even with the staff. The boy's name was Hague, but everyone referred to him as The Hague, which I didn't get at first, until I found it was the center of government in Holland. This Hague was always ranting about something political, so he got tagged with that."

"Hague?" September repeated, with a sinking heart. Hague Dugan couldn't have been the one, *could he?* But then Dawn answered that question for her, by adding, "But he was there a few years after I left."

"Okay," September said with a kind of relief. It didn't sound like Hague and Glenda could have been at Grandview at the same time. "Let me ask you about another murder victim. There was a Grandview patient around the same time, Emmy Decatur. Were you there—"

"Oh, yes. I remember Emmy."

September gave Gretchen the thumbs up. "Was there something particularly remarkable about her?" September asked, because of the way she'd cut in.

"Only in the fact that her parents acted like she was off to college, or something. They never faced that she was in a mental institution. Bet they wish they could change things now, but it's too late."

"What was she being treated for? She is another victim," September repeated, even though she had said as much, in case Dawn decided to question whether she ought to spill private information without a warrant.

But Dawn had no such compunction. "Anorexia . . .

bipolar . . . recreational drugs. She was a hot mess, but she pulled it together, the last I heard. It's a shame, what happened to her." And then, hearing herself, she added, "I wouldn't put this past Navarone, either."

"Do you mind if I call you again? It might come up in the investigation."

"Sure. But you're wasting your time. Dr. Frank Navarone is your man."

"I'll keep that in mind," September said and clicked off.

"So?" Gretchen asked as she turned the Jeep into the station.

September brought her quickly up to date. "A lot of pieces, but no jigsaw puzzle," she finished.

"That's the way of it. It'll come together."

"I hope you're right."

"I am," she said confidently.

Chapter 15

By the time September was home, through the shower, dressed, and applying some new makeup, it was almost seven o'clock. Jake was undoubtedly on his way, but she felt rushed and a bit overwhelmed. She'd tried on three different outfits, frustrated with herself for caring so much, and in the end she'd chosen a mid-calf black skirt and a salmon-colored sleeveless top with silver hoop earrings, the kind she eschewed while on the job.

She'd put a call in to Auggie, wanting to basically chew him out for not being square with her about what he'd told Sofia, the nurse at Grandview Senior Care, and leaving her to fumble her way through the interview. He didn't answer, so she hung up and texted him her complaint, figuring he'd get that before a phone message.

Now, she slid her phone in a side pocket of her messenger bag, slipping her Glock into the bag's large interior along with her wallet. The whole thing felt too bulky for her outfit, but she didn't care. Slipping on a pair of black leather sandals, she took a hard look at the image in the mirror, seeing storm clouds in her blue eyes directed solely at herself as the doorbell rang.

"Okay," she told herself, not quite sure what she meant by that, as she went to answer the door.

Jake stood on the other side in a pair of black pants and a gray shirt, darkly handsome and surprisingly serious. She felt her smile of greeting fade on her own face. "What?" she asked him.

But he was gazing at her in a way that made her self-conscious. "You don't look like a cop," he finally said.

"That's good. I thought maybe there was something else wrong."

She gave him a long look, but he just said, "You ready?"

"Just let me get my bag." She grabbed up the messenger bag and then walked ahead of him down the stairs to his Tahoe. "Where are we going?" she asked, as they headed out of the lot.

"Have you ever been to La Mer?"

"No."

"Good."

He drove south, but though they held a conversation, it was all small talk. His mind was elsewhere, probably on whatever he wanted to talk to her about. Thirty minutes later, he pulled into the parking lot of the restaurant that looked high over Lake Chinook. September climbed from the Tahoe and glanced at the black and silver awning overhead as they walked to the front door. They entered an anterior room with rich, dark paneling and piped in string music. The maître d' smiled at them and led them past intimate booths with flickering votives to the back patio, also beneath a black and silver canopy, and to a table for two that overlooked the green lake far below.

As soon as they were seated, September leaned forward. "Okay, out with it. You're starting to make me crazy."

"I thought you weren't going to be a cop. Where's the small talk?"

"I'm not good with it," she said seriously.

"Point taken. Neither am I, really." He picked up the wine list, looked at it, then set it aside. "I saw my dad last night. Both of my parents, actually. I wanted to talk to them about your mother. After searching through the attic with you, and finding that note, and everything . . . I wanted to ask my dad about the day Kathryn died. I wanted his take on it."

September made a face. "Oh, Jake. No . . . I'm sorry I blamed him. I thought—"

"This wasn't about how you acted about him when you were eleven. After you found the note, I just wanted to know if he thought it could be true. About your father and Verna."

"I know you thought I jumped to conclusions."

"I did. I did think that. But my father . . ." Jake looked at her, his eyes searching hers. "He remembered that day. And he remembered the note your mother got. She was upset and driving fast and the accident happened. You were right, Nine. The note set her off."

Her throat felt hot. She hardly knew what to say. "It's not fair, you know," she said. "My father tried to shift blame to Nigel. He said . . ." She drew a breath.

"I know what he said."

"I knew it wasn't true. I always did. I just wanted to blame someone else besides my father."

He reached across and clasped her left hand with his right.

She felt a quiver overtake her from head to toe, and she had to pull back though she didn't want to. Emotion thrummed through her like a live wire. This was crazy wild, a seesawing ride that ran from low to high and back again. It was dangerous. Especially because it was Jake.

"Can we . . . talk about something else?" she asked on an intake of breath.

"Sure."

"I wish I were hungrier." She half-laughed. "Sorry."

"We can leave," he said.

"No, we can't leave. We just got here. Don't be so understanding, Westerly," she said.

"It's back to Westerly, huh?"

"Makes it a little easier for me. But, no, I don't want to leave. I'm just, absorbing." She nodded several times.

The waiter came and took their drink order. She asked for a glass of Pinot Gris and Jake had a scotch on the rocks. Then they both ordered salmon with a basil pesto sauce and September did her best to do it justice. By the time their waiter brought the check September had recovered a little bit of equilibrium, and when Jake reached for her hand again as they walked beneath the front canopy and across the lot to his Tahoe, she was able to clasp it without feeling like she was going to fall into a schoolgirl faint.

"Where do you want to go?" he asked.

"Home?"

When he didn't argue, she was almost disappointed, but then when he drove right past the turn that would take them to her apartment, she said, "Uh . . ." and pointed at the road they should have taken.

"Oh, I thought you meant my home," he said, fighting a smile.

She laughed. "You're too slick for your own good."

"Want to go back to yours?"

"No," she said after a moment.

They drove to another part of Laurelton and down a lane to a small rambler home that made her give him a long look as he pulled into the garage. He pushed the remote as they climbed from the vehicle and the garage door rattled down behind them. Then Jake opened a side door that led into the house.

"Not what you expected, huh?" he said, as he flipped on the lights.

They were standing in a family room off the kitchen, which Jake walked across on his way to a back patio. He slid open the sliding glass door and beckoned her to follow him outside.

September moved into the warm outside air and admitted, "I pictured you in a downtown high-rise condominium."

"My office is a little like that," he admitted. "But I'm moving when the lease is up."

"To where?"

"I don't know. Guess I need to figure out what I'm going to do for the rest of my life."

"Sounds . . . uncertain."

"Yeah, well."

The patio was lit by outdoor lights and Jake moved to the table, picked up a lighter, and touched the flame to the wick of a fat yellow candle that sat inside a large, clear votive in the center of a small table. There were two cushioned lounge chairs and he brushed one off with his hand, inviting her to sit down, which she did, lying back and looking toward the stars. She heard him brushing off his own chair, then he perched on the edge of it. "I have beer and not much else."

"Let me think . . . okay, I'll take a beer."

He flashed her a smile and headed into the house. She heard the refrigerator door open, then the snap of the tops being popped, and a few minutes later he returned, handing her a longneck Bud and keeping one for himself. "I should have asked if you wanted a glass."

"This is fine," she assured him, and it was.

They sat drinking in relative silence, feeling the heat of the day dissipating, watching the flickering candle. "How's the investigation going?" he asked after a while.

"I've got a lot of pieces that could mean something, or not, or I don't know."

"Can you tell me?"

"Some of it." She looked at the shadowed planes of his face. "There's definitely an elementary school connection somehow. I don't know if he went to our school, or knew someone who did, but it keeps circling back there. The FBI's on the case now, but I haven't really confided in them about this yet."

"Yeah?"

"They want to kick me off the case because of the artwork. I don't want to be kicked off the case."

"You want to get this guy yourself."

"I want to be a part of the posse, yeah."

"What's the grade school connection?" he asked.

"Well . . ." She shrugged, then she told him how Ms. Osborne had phoned her back and she'd told her about the artwork and asked her if she knew the name Wart, which she hadn't. From that, September ran through her meeting with Mrs. McBride where the teacher had mentioned theirs was a problem class, especially with three of the boys, for various reasons. She finished with, "Neither of them knew anyone nicknamed Wart. I tried that name out with a nurse who'd worked at Grandview Mental Hospital when Tripp's uncle was on staff there, but she didn't know it, either."

"Who told you about Wart, in the first place?"

"I heard it from Ben Schmidt, Sheila's sixth grade boyfriend. And then, I talked to a couple of her other school friends that Ben told me about, Andrew Welke and his wife, Caitlyn, and they said Sheila thought this Wart was weird. That he maybe had a real interest in knives, and that he possibly went to Sunset Elementary before transferring to their school, Twin Oaks. They also said they heard that he might be dead, or in jail, or something. No one seems to really remember, though. I'm not convinced that Wart isn't a catchall term that Sheila might have used. She used 'psycho' in her everyday language, so maybe 'wart' as well."

"Maybe when she was younger. I never heard her say that."

"But how well did you know her?" September questioned. "You said yourself, she was more of an acquaintance."

"She was." He peeled part of the label of the beer with his thumb, staring down at it thoughtfully.

The conversation lulled. She wondered how much she should tell him. It wasn't like she was giving away state secrets, but there was an unspoken understanding that the less civilians knew, the better. Still . . . "We learned today that Emmy Decatur was a patient at Grandview for a while. Her parents held that back because they were embarrassed. Emmy let her roommate think they'd kicked her out of the house in high school rather than admit the truth. She might've been there about the same time Dr. Navarone was on staff."

"You think Glenda Tripp and Emmy Decatur crossed paths?"

"With each other, or maybe with someone else," she agreed. "Glenda told a coworker she'd had sex with someone on her uncle's examining table. She didn't say exactly when, but it appears to be when she was a teenager."

"Huh." He shot her a look. "Sounds less romantic than in a grape arbor."

Her thoughts flew to the memory of that night and she pulled them back, aware that her pulse had increased at the fact that he was remembering that.

"So, you think it's someone who went to our grade school?" he asked, when she went quiet.

"Or, knew someone who did and was connected that way. Then, he met Sheila at Twin Oaks, but from there . . . I don't know about Grandview."

"Because Sheila never went to Grandview. Only Decatur and Tripp."

"I just wish there was some common denominator for all of them. So, if the killer knows Sheila, it's maybe through elementary school, but I can't make a connection to Grandview with her." She exhaled heavily. "But then maybe she just met him at The Barn Door and the rest is coincidental."

"Except there was that guy who hassled her at the bar. Someone she knew from the past."

"Yeah . . . maybe this Wart/psycho character. Maybe someone else." She made a face and took another pull on her beer.

"Don't get discouraged," he said.

"I'm not, I'm just . . ."

"What?"

He moved from his chair to perch on hers. They stared at each other through the uncertain light thrown by the candle. He put his hand on her knee and through the skirt she felt her skin turn to fire.

"Confused, mostly," she said.

He leaned over and kissed her, pressing his lips to hers, testing her response.

September closed her eyes, kissing him back, fully aware that she was recalling those moments amongst the vines, comparing. His weight pushed her further into the chair and she was conscious of every place their bodies touched: legs, hips, arms, mouth.

Am I going to really do this? she thought, with a quick calculation of her time of the month. She was close to her period, so she was sure she was okay; she was as regular as clockwork. And she wasn't sexually active enough to carry condoms with her. If you looked in her purse, you'd be more likely to find a gun.

"Why are you smiling?" he asked, his breath hot on her lips.

"Remembering . . ."

He propped himself up on one elbow, staring down at her face. "I didn't get the impression at our first meeting that they were good memories, but now . . . ?"

"I've had a change of heart."

He reached out and touched her chin, cupping it with strong fingers. "How much of a change?" he asked in a low voice.

For an answer she ran her hand over the edge of his beard-roughened jaw, then brought his mouth back to within a hair's-breadth of hers. "I think . . ."

"Yes?"

For an answer she reached her lips up to his, pressing her mouth to his, straining upward. He slid his body atop hers, never breaking the kiss, and his right hand moved downward to cup her breast. September's pulse was running light and fast, and when his tongue entered her mouth she felt herself go limp.

His hips moved against hers and she answered with the same age-old motion. She could feel the escalation of her rasping breath, and she slid her arms around him, sliding her fingers beneath his waistband, tugging up his shirt. With a muscular twist he was leaning away from her, balanced on one hip while he ripped at the buttons of his shirt. She swept his hands away and undid them herself, sliding his shirt from warm, hard shoulders.

As soon as he was shirtless he worked on her top, pulling her arms above her head and tugging the salmon-colored shirt up over them. Then his head bent to her flesh-colored bra and he placed his mouth over one breast, suckling through the sheer fabric and causing a shot of desire to streak through her inner core.

"Oh . . . God . . . I . . ." She held her breath, surprised, torn between a groan of desire and shaking laughter.

"What?" he asked, balancing himself on both hands, staring down at her, his hips pressed hard against hers. It was impossible not to feel his hardness and her legs moved apart of their own accord; September was sure she hadn't willed it, but then, later, she thought maybe she had.

"I'm . . ."

He waited.

"I think I've wanted this for a long time."

He flashed a white grin at her, and then very slowly moved down her body, his hands tugging on her pants, pulling them over her hips, and then following with her panties, pulling off shoes, socks, and everything in the process until she was completely nude. Swiftly, he pulled off his own pants, boxers and all, and then he lay half atop her, half beside her, his mouth nuzzling her ear and throat.

"I get the feeling you're more expert at this than I am," she said on a gasp as his mouth moved lower to capture her nipple. Heat shot through her and her head lolled back. She caught a glimpse of the sky and a billion stars before she squeezed her eyes closed.

"The only woman I've been with in forever was Loni," he admitted.

"But Sheila . . ."

"No. I told you." And then he shook his head. "She was married."

She believed him. Not that it could matter in the larger scheme of things, could it? If there was a bigger issue it was that he was involved in the case, at least peripherally, and she should know better.

And then she gasped, "Wait . . . don't . . . !" Her eyes flew open, because he was moving south to the center of her and her fingers were suddenly gripping his hair, hanging on for dear life.

He had the nerve to chuckle and then keep right on and a moment later, September bit down on her lower lip to fight back a scream of surprise and dark desire. And then he was kissing her and licking her and her hips were rising to meet him and she said, "Oh, God!" and pulled him to her, grabbing him and holding her arms around him and he entered her so smoothly that she was shocked it hadn't been more effort except that she felt like pure liquid.

She slid her mouth over his cheek and tasted the saltiness of his flesh, dragging his mouth to hers as he pushed against her. And then they were in rhythm, moving together, and he pulled back and looked down at her and she stared up at him and then his mouth crashed down on hers once more and within moments her whole body was shuddering and she was flying, flying, and there was so much desire, and love and emotion that she was afraid she would cry, or scream, or something, but all she did was hold everything inside in a deep crushing grip until the waves crested and she could let out that pent-up air on a huge exhalation at the moment of his own climax.

And then he lay atop her, their hearts beating wildly,

and for a few moments September just lay mesmerized, still staring at the clouds.

"I . . ." he said doubtfully, not lifting his head from her breast.

She froze a moment, her heart jerking. He wasn't going to already regret this, was he? She wouldn't be able to stand it.

"No condom," he said then, sounding stunned.

Her relief was so enormous she started to laugh, sounding half-hysterical. "I don't have any, but it won't be a problem, timing-wise, I'm pretty sure."

He lifted his head and looked at her. She could see the smile now on his lips. "This time," he said.

"This time."

"It's at the top of my shopping list for the future," he said, and then bent down to begin lazily kissing her and starting all over again.

Thursday morning September went to work in a daze. Agents Bethwick and Donley wanted a meeting but she barely heard one word of it. They had nothing much further to report on Lulu Luxe's killer, although the john thought there might have been a white van parked in the lot not far from his car. It had already been determined the guy was half-wasted, though he wouldn't admit to it and add to his transgressions by admitting to driving drunk.

Sandler looked her way to see if she wanted to report on their own investigation, but she signaled that Gretchen could take over. What followed was an abbreviated version of looking into Glenda Navarone Tripp's history that involved a possible sexual relationship with someone on the premises of what had once been Grandview Mental Hospital. She left out everything that had to do with

Emmy Decatur, and September's ongoing probing into the killer's possible association with Sunset Elementary School. The agents both stared at them silently. Maybe they thought Sandler and September were holding back, or maybe they just thought they were incompetent. From September's point of view, it didn't really matter which. They were following leads and that was that.

And all she could think about were Jake Westerly's hands and lips upon her skin, and twice she felt her face flush when a particular memory struck home.

Holy God.

"You okay?" Gretchen asked, looking over at her when the meeting broke up.

"Yeah, why?"

"You look, I don't know . . . shell-shocked, maybe."

"You said that the pieces would come together," September said, desperately trying to change the subject. "How can you be so sure?"

Gretchen shot a look to the agents, then at George, who was absorbed in a phone conversation that held all his attention. "Well, what do we know for certain, and what are we guessing at? Let's go someplace where we can talk alone."

"You want to leave the station?"

"Yeah, I'm due for a latte, aren't you?"

"An iced coffee. Sure."

They left a few moments later and this time September drove, taking her Pilot. The nearest coffee place was a Starbucks, and after they'd purchased their drinks, they sat at a tiny table for two in the corner rather than head into the growing heat of the day.

They spent about an hour hashing out what they had so far and it boiled down to a few facts and a lot of theories.

"You know we rechecked out The Barn Door, but we

haven't visited Emmy's Gulliver's, and Glenda's Lariat again," Gretchen said.

"We should do that," September agreed. "And I want to interview Hague Dugan, too."

"I thought you said the sister—Dawn Markam-Manning—said he wasn't at Grandview when Glenda and Emmy were."

"He wasn't. But his name keeps cropping up in both the Zuma investigation and this one, and we've always known there was something between them."

She shrugged and nodded. "How you gonna interview him?"

"I'll ask Auggie. He wants to help on our investigation. I've been trying to keep him out, but now with the feds here it hardly matters. Now, it's just whether he has the time."

"Hague is Liv's brother. If he can't help you, maybe she can."

"Maybe," September agreed.

Liv Dugan was her brother's newest love interest, and she'd been a person of interest on the Zuma case. September didn't know her all that well, but she sensed her brother was deeply involved with her. This was no quick fling spawned in the heat of the investigation.

"All right, let's go back," Sandler said. "Let's go to Gulliver's first, around four, and if we have time we'll hit The Lariat right afterward."

"I'll call Auggie and maybe Liv."

Back at the station, George was annoyed and frazzled. "Where the hell did you run off to? We've got a murder-suicide on East Blankenshire. Somebody's gotta go there."

"What's taking you so long?" Gretchen asked.

George flushed. He never liked leaving his computer and desk chair. "I don't have a partner right now."

"What's the story?" she asked in a long-suffering tone, rolling her eyes.

"Hey, fuck it," George muttered. "I'll go alone."

"You shoulda gone twenty minutes ago," Gretchen pointed out. "Fine, I'll go with you. Frick and Frack don't care what we do on the Do Unto Others case anyway." She gave September a long look full of meaning. She wanted her to continue forging ahead.

As they headed out, she heard George say, "They were losing their house and all their money. Foreclosure and bankruptcy. Looks like the husband couldn't take it, so he shot his wife, and then shot himself."

"So, the wife didn't sign on for this."

"Doesn't look like it. . . ."

"Son of a bitch," September hissed through her teeth to no one in particular. She couldn't stand these guys who became judge, jury, and *owner* of their wives or girl-friends, treating them like they had no mind of their own, as if their lives had no worth whatsoever.

She texted Auggie with a request to visit Hague, maybe with Liv.

While she was waiting for him to respond, Agent Donley cruised over her way, causing her to sit up straight. He leaned a hip casually against the edge of the desk and said, "What's with the guy out front?", hooking a thumb over his shoulder.

"Guy? I mean, his name is Guy," she said, falling into a familiar trap that all the newbies fell into when they first joined the force. Kind of like Abbott and Costello's "Who's on First" routine. "Guy Urlacher."

"I've passed his desk at least six times and yet every time I enter, he wants me to show my ID."

"Oh, yeah. Protocol. That's our Guy." She half-smiled. She didn't trust the feds' motives when it came to taking her case, but if he was going to make an attempt to be friendly, so would she. "I still get 'carded' and I've been here for months. He tries it on Sandler, too."

"How does that go over?"

"Just about like you'd expect."

He chuckled, then glanced back to his partner, then turned back to September. "We get the feeling there's some resentment around here with us taking over. That's all right. We're used to it. I just thought we might be able to get past some of it and work together."

His voice said he was just laying it out there. She could take him up on his offer, or not. No big deal. She had to admit, it was tempting to join forces, as they were expected to do, but something made her hold back. "I'm all for that," she lied easily. "Was there something in particular?"

"You and your partner are thick as thieves. Wanna share?"

"Oh, we've got a number of irons in the fire. She's out with Thompkins right now at the scene of a possible murder-suicide."

"And you're not with her."

"One of our investigators is recovering from a bullet wound, so we're short. Sandler decided to help Thompkins out."

"Thompkins didn't want to go," he observed, alerting her to the fact that he'd been paying attention. "If you'd jumped in, he would have been happy to stay. I think *you* wanted to stay, and that's why your partner's gone but you're still here. What's your next move, Detective?"

September just managed to keep herself from sliding a glance toward D'Annibal's glass office. He wasn't there anyway, but this political game-playing was making her sweat. Donley was fishing, trying to get a handle on what she and Gretchen were up to. "I'm following a lead," she said vaguely.

As if on cue her phone chirped at her. A text. Undoubtedly from Auggie. Feeling Donley's eyes on her, she picked up her cell and glanced quickly at the message.

could go see H in 2 hrs you in?

She clicked off immediately, processing, hoping the agent wouldn't be able to read what was on her face. "Did you have something I could help you on?" she asked him.

Hearing her dismissal, he straightened slowly from the desk, smoothing his tie. "No, I guess not."

"Then we're good?"

"We're good." He slid her a lingering look before he walked back across the room and September had the feeling she wasn't fooling anybody.

September drove her car to her apartment and waited for Auggie and Liv. They would have picked her up at the station, but September didn't want the agents to get too curious about what she was doing. It was strange; they were all on the same side, but the undercurrent of competition was strong and she felt like if she didn't keep swimming she might drown.

She called D'Annibal's cell and left a voice mail saying none of the detectives were at the department for the next hour or so and if need be, call on any of their cell phones. She was waiting in her Pilot when Auggie's newly repaired Jeep wheeled into the lot. A few weeks earlier it had sustained some major damage, but the bodywork and all other repairs had been made and it looked good as new.

She climbed in the back behind Liv, who rode in the

passenger seat, and said, "Thanks. I feel so clandestine about all this."

"Eh, the feds are okay. Just have to draw a chasm in the sand and make sure they stay on one side, you on the other," Auggie said.

September looked at the back of Liv Dugan's head. Her light brown hair was all she could see, but Liv's serious, hazel eyes, high cheekbones, and wide mouth were an attractive combination, and September couldn't help but feel a little like chopped liver with no makeup and her hair hastily clipped back at her nape. She'd left Jake's place in a rush after a lengthy morning shower together that had her now staring unseeingly out the window, her mind filled with the sight and feel of slick, hard muscles and a hot mouth exploring her in ways that made her feel limp and weak.

Good. God.

"What do you want to ask Hague?" Liv asked, breaking into September's heated thoughts. "You have to be kind of careful."

September didn't know Liv very well and wondered if she were trying to protect her brother. "What do you mean?"

She half-turned so September could see her profile. "I thought Auggie told you about my brother."

"He did. He said that Hague has difficulty staying on point in an interview."

"My brother sometimes rants and yells, and then other times he'll talk to you just fine. Until he slips into his own world. You can hit a hot button without knowing it, and then he's just gone."

"You want to talk to him about his stay at Grandview," Auggie said, meeting her eyes in the rearview.

"That's right."

Liv cocked her head and said, "Good luck with that."

"It's a hot button?" September suggested.

"You could say that. But then a lot of things are," she added almost as an afterthought.

They took Sunset Highway into Portland, driving through the Vista Ridge Tunnel and popping into the city on the other side. Keeping on the freeway, they crossed the Willamette over the Marquam Bridge and then took the Water Street exit to wind through the industrial buildings on the east side of the Willamette. Auggie pulled into a spot about a half block up from Rosa's Cantina, the bar on the first floor of Hague Dugan's building and the place where he sometimes came to hold court and orate to his followers about the evils of an oppressive government and people in power. His dissertations were rants just short of all out crazy, according to Auggie, though he would probably not say the same in front of Liv, though September guessed she knew anyway.

They took an open freight elevator to the third floor and when it bumped lightly to a stop, Auggie slid back the metal, accordion-type door and the three of them exited and walked to a door within sight of the elevator. Liv knocked loudly, muttering under her breath, "Get ready for Della. I called, but she never wants Hague to have visitors. She—"

The door opened before she could finish what she was saying. A woman with white blond hair pulled into a bun glared at them through icy blue eyes. Her intense gaze softened a bit when she saw Auggie, who said, "Hey there, Della. How're you doing?"

"I'm okay. It's okay," she said, allowing them entry.

September threw her brother a look. Auggie could really lay on the charm when it suited him, which kind of pissed her off.

They walked through the main living area to what was clearly Hague's personal living space. He was seated in a La-Z-Boy recliner and there were several trays and tables scattered around him. He was thin and his brown hair was unkempt and a beard darkened his jaw, though it looked like he was just growing it in. His eyes were closed when they entered, but when Della said, "Hague, your sister's here," they opened and regarded them with a faraway look.

"I brought Auggie with me," Liv told him. "And his sister, September. She's a police officer and she wants to talk to you about Grandview Hospital."

Hague's eyes shifted to September. "A police officer."

September pulled out one of her cards and handed it to him. "I'm trying to solve several homicides around the Laurelton area, and I thought maybe you could help me."

"What do you want to know?" he asked in a perfectly reasonable voice.

The buildup had been so dramatic that she was slightly taken aback at how normal he sounded. "I . . . like your sister said, I wanted to ask you about Grandview Hospital, what you can remember from your time at that place. There may be a connection there to the homicides."

Hague's gaze shifted from September to Liv. He said to his sister, "We know this. We know this already."

There was a thread of urgency to his voice, and Liv said, "Don't worry, Hague. We're safe now. September just needs you to recall anything about that time, what was going on, whether you knew some people."

"What people?" he demanded. "Navarone wasn't my doctor. My doctor was Dr. Tambor."

"Did you know Dr. Navarone's niece, Glenda Navarone?

She would have been a few years older than you?" September asked.

"Would have been?" He seized on the phrase. "Is she *dead?*"

"Yes," September said, after a moment. She hadn't thought she'd imbued her words with that information, but she couldn't very well lie to him.

A heavy sigh escaped him. "He told me he killed both of them, but I thought he was lying." His eyes stretched wide but it was clear he wasn't seeing what was in front of him. His view was from some inner torment.

"Both of them?" September repeated.

"Hague!" Liv said sternly, stepping forward. "You remember Glenda Navarone?"

He muttered, "He told me about them. They were behind the counter, laughing."

September's brow furrowed. "One of them was Glenda?"

"It wasn't me. I wasn't there. He told me about them. He would never listen to what I had to say, but he talked . . . he talked . . ."

September's pulse leapt. "Who is he, Hague?"

"He told me he would fuck me up if I told. I thought it was a lie." Now he gazed directly at September. "He said he took Glenda on the table. I didn't know he killed her. I thought I saw her again . . ." He faded out, confused.

"He didn't kill her at that time," September clarified. "We heard about Glenda having sex on Dr. Navarone's examining table. Is that what you're remembering?"

"Is it?" he asked, frowning.

Patiently, September asked, "Do you remember him? The one you're talking about?"

"He said he'd kill us if we talk to the doctors. . . . He talks to us because he wants to tell, but if we tell, he'll put the noose around our necks." His hands came up beside his head like blinders.

"When you say 'both' of them? Do you mean Glenda and Emmy Decatur?"

"Who?"

"Emmy Decatur," September repeated. "She also went to Grandview Hospital for a while."

"Was she one of them?" he asked, confusion filling his face. His hands turned inward and he pressed his palms to his eyes. A moment later he dropped his hands and looked around furtively. "Out of the sides of my eyes . . . I can see them . . ."

"What's his name?" September asked.

"Hague!" Liv practically shouted at him and Della snapped, "Stop it! You know what this does to him!"

"He's okay," Auggie said to Della and she glared at him for a moment but held her tongue.

But Hague's eyes had lost focus. They started circling around as if he'd lost control of them.

"Who is he?" September asked again, a bit desperately.

A faint smile crawled across his lips. "Wart," he whispered, then his eyes rolled back and he was gone.

Chapter 16

Liv and Auggie dropped September back at her car, and she lifted a hand in good-bye as they drove off, debating whether to run up to her apartment first, or head back to work.

Wart. Hague had said Wart!

She'd eagerly demanded, "Who's Wart? Who's Wart?"

But Hague was gone. To some alternate reality. Liv had turned to September and explained that this is what happened with her brother, this was the problem. It was all September could do to keep herself from grabbing Hague Dugan and shaking him. Sensing her frustration, Auggie had grabbed her arm and dragged her away. "I'll have Liv keep working on him. See if we can get something more."

"It's important, Auggie. I think this guy could be our doer!" September had urged.

"I know. I've been to this barbeque before, okay? Hague can't help it."

"Both of them must mean Glenda and Emmy. I wish I could talk to him more."

"It just doesn't work that way. You gave him your card.

Maybe when he comes back . . ." He let his voice trail off and she could tell he thought it was a long shot. "My advice: Don't get your hopes up."

She knew he was right but it didn't mitigate her frustration. At all. And the heat of the morning was turning into a blistering afternoon. She could feel the effects of her lovemaking, too; her body was sore inside and out, but it was the kind of minor pain that simply jolted her into recalling moments from the night before, and that left her breathless.

Now, shaking her head at her own susceptibility, she shot a glance to the second story of her building as she opened the door to her Pilot. Her brow furrowed. Was her front door ajar a little bit?

Shutting the vehicle's driver's door, she hit the remote and heard the chirp that said her car was locked. She headed up the stairs, her heart pounding triple time, her hand searching for the Glock that had been inside her messenger bag since her trip to see Hague.

She hesitated, thinking she should retrieve it, but as she looked again at the door she thought that it was a trick of light. Her door was shut firmly.

Still . . .

Reaching into her pocket for her keys, she moved quietly to the door, gently testing the knob. It was locked tight, but it was not a deadbolt. Easy enough to break into, she thought, if you had a little patience and skill. She'd thought before that she should install a better lock system; she was constantly alert and thinking someone was after her. Whether that was true or just her sensitive nerves, she didn't know.

Sliding the key into the lock, she opened the door and stepped inside, ears and eyes open.

Nothing. All was still and it had that dull feeling of

quietude that said the place was empty. She strolled through the kitchen and saw the crumbs from her hasty toast this morning as she'd raced through what passed as breakfast and changed into the clothes for work, clothes that had been tossed on her bed and discarded but were right there. She hadn't had time to come up with something new.

Recognizing her ultra-vigilance was not needed, she exhaled a couple of times, waiting for her pulse to decelerate. She used the time to change into new clothes, exchanging yesterday's navy slacks and blue shirt for a pair of jeans, a black shirt, and her gray jacket. It was hot, but she needed the jacket to cover her holster and gun, as much as it did.

She stopped by the bistro near her apartment and ordered half a pastrami sandwich, which came with a choice of fries, potato salad, or a green salad. She chose the green salad and a Diet Coke, and a few minutes later she walked out with the bag and drink, feeling heat prickle her scalp.

Jake had insisted on walking her to her door this morning, kissing her, refusing to let her turn away in case any of the neighbors were watching, branding her, she knew, in a way that she responded to even while she protested.

"It's too hot," she told him, swatting his hands away.

"Hot September," he said, grinning, and she groaned and pushed at him.

"Stop. We're not teenagers anymore."

"I'm going to think about this all day," he told her.

"Go away." She put her key in the lock.

"Not yet . . ."

And he followed her inside and kissed her some more and she found that she really liked it and she had to actually play a part of stony insistence to get him to leave.

Now her eyes looked around the room, remembering where they were standing and the feel of his hands on her.

God.

She actually covered her face with her hands and groaned. This was how she'd felt in high school. This was it. This all-consuming craziness. And her mind was definitely stuck on a lusty, sexual track.

If she could, she would call him up and demand he meet her and make love to her all afternoon and evening and into tomorrow morning.

"Get the hell out of here," she told herself, and that got her moving, and she twisted the button on the knob to lock the door and ran down the stairs to her car. At work, at least, she seemed to be able to push thoughts of Jake Westerly aside.

If there was one thing Jake never did it was daydream.

Sure, he took time in the day to think about things; his mind generally liked to work through knotty problems in those down moments. Business problems. But since reconnecting with September Rafferty all he seemed to do was daydream. How had that happened?

"Swear to God," he murmured to the walls of his office.

And after last night . . .

He was infused with happiness. The ennui of the past few months was simply not there. He felt energized and alive and ready for something. Like he'd told Nine the night before, he was trying to figure out what the next phase of his life was going to be and now he knew that, whatever it was, he wanted—needed—her to be a part of it.

Jake decided to go home and think it through. Maybe

he should just pull the plug on the operation now. To hell with his lease. Maybe he could buy himself out without having to pay the full amount. That's what he wanted. To be free.

Glancing at the clock, he grabbed up his keys and shoved papers into his briefcase, papers that had to do with more deals, possible deals, deals he didn't care anything about.

His cell phone started singing and the sound of the ringtone stopped him cold. He hadn't heard it in months. He should have changed it, but he hadn't.

Loni.

For a moment he thought about not taking the call, but then he did. But it wasn't Loni on the other end. It was Loni's frantic mother.

"She swallowed a whole bottle of pills," came Marilyn Cheever's choked voice. "A whole bottle. They've pumped her stomach, but it's . . . she's not awake . . . we don't know . . . Jake, can you come? Please? If you were there when she came to . . . ?"

"Which hospital?" he asked, aware how coldly serious he sounded, unable to prevent his tone. It wasn't the first time. It wasn't the second . . . it wasn't the third.

And he didn't want to go.

"Providence," Marilyn said on a hiccup. "Hurry . . ."

Wanting to say no, unable to be so cold to someone he'd cared about for so long, he said, "I'll be right there," then clicked off and headed for the elevators.

September ate her sandwich and drank her Diet Coke in the break room. She'd planned to sit at her desk, but she saw the federal agents look up when she entered and she decided she wanted some privacy. Sandler and

Thompkins hadn't returned and D'Annibal's office was dark. She needed a little alone time with her thoughts to think things through.

Hague had mentioned Wart. She'd heard that loud and clear, and yet no one, with the exception of Sheila's school friends, could recall the name. So, what did that mean? Was it a nickname that he'd used once with his peers, but had lost over the intervening years?

Ben Schmidt had said he'd thought Wart might be dead, and Andrew Welke had suggested he was in-car-cer-ated. Were those just guesses? And were they even talking about the same loner kid? Was any of it true, or was she just chasing shadows?

She finished her half-sandwich, wadded the plastic wrapping into a ball, tossed it toward a trashcan. The plastic opened up and lost momentum and dropped to the ground a foot short of the receptacle. Sorta felt like where she was in her investigation, just short of an answer.

What about Lulu Luxe? Why her? It was probably because she was available, but could there be a more specific reason? Was the reason he'd killed her in the field, rather than somewhere else first, because he was escalating, as Bethwick had suggested? Probably. The shortened times between his killings suggested the same. He was losing whatever control he'd had and his killings had become less well planned as the need increased. He'd also shifted focus, she believed, from women he actu-ally knew to convenient victims.

Except for herself.

She shook her head. She needed to stick with her own avenue of investigation and not get sidetracked until she either found some corroboration to her theory that this Wart was the killer, or reached a dead end.

As she was getting up from her chair, her cell phone

rang. She glanced at it and realized it was D'Annibal. "Lieutenant?" she answered.

"Detective, where are you?"

"I'm just down the hall in the break room."

"Could you come into my office?"

"Sure." So he'd returned.

She retraced her steps to the squad room, meeting Candy from administration coming from the opposite direction. Candy darted September a look, then glanced away, which did not bode well. September's heartbeat thudded once again. Last time Candy had made a delivery to the squad room it had been her bloodied second grade artwork.

Glancing back at Candy's disappearing form, September almost called her back. But then she decided not to borrow trouble. She entered the room and saw that neither agent was anywhere to be seen and Sandler and Thompkins were still absent as well. She shot a look toward D'Annibal's office, which was now brightly lit, though the curtains were pulled partway across, as if he'd decided he needed some privacy but then thought better of it.

"Lieutenant?" she greeted him as she entered.

His gray hair shined silver beneath the overhead lights, which also made his tanned face seem surprisingly colorless. He gestured her to come in and said, "Please close the door."

"Is there something wrong?" she asked as she complied.

For an answer he opened a drawer and pulled out a manila envelope, the same shape and size of the last one she'd received. Her ears buzzing, she took it from D'Annibal's hand. It was still sealed.

"Candy said it's like the other one. As soon as she saw

it, she brought it to you, and since you weren't at your desk, to me."

"It could be . . ." September trailed off, not sure what she thought it could be besides what she guessed it was.

"Do you want me to open it?"

She flushed, feeling foolish in front of her superior. "No." Wordlessly, he handed her a letter opener and a pair of latex gloves. She slipped on the gloves, slid the letter opener beneath the flap, sliced open the end of the envelope and, using her thumb and forefinger, slid the several stapled papers out.

She stared at the front page, recognizing another project from her grade school years. There was a colorful picture of ocean life glued onto the front page and she knew there would be more on each additional page. Immature handwritten text accompanied the pictures.

"It's my sea anemone report," she said woodenly. "This wasn't from second grade. It was third or fourth."

"It's definitely yours?"

"Yes . . ." She'd written her name at the top in cursive. Carefully turning the face of the report around so that he could see it, she stared at the back of it.

A big red IX stared back at her.

"Nine?" Lieutenant D'Annibal asked, and for a moment she thought he'd seen it, too. But no, he was just gazing at her with concern. Probably because she could feel the blood draining from her face.

"He knows my nickname's Nine," she said in a calm voice that belied her churning guts. "He knows me. Not just from the newspaper article or my interview with Channel Seven. He knows me well enough to know what my close friends call me."

D'Annibal gazed at her levelly. "And maybe your classmates?"

"But this is . . . it's just not from one class. This is something else. He has to have access to my grade school . . . stuff. He has to be close to me, close to my family. Unless . . ." She pressed her lips together, sensing if she didn't that they might tremble.

"Unless," the lieutenant probed.

"Unless he was taking things of mine all through my school years."

Light glinted off the steely gray of his hair. There was a lengthy pause and then D'Annibal nodded once, as if he'd just agreed to a question that had yet to be answered. "Detective, I think you know what I'm going to say next."

Lost in her own whirling thoughts, she blinked at him. "Sir?"

"I'm taking you off this investigation, Rafferty. It's too personal and too dangerous."

September inhaled sharply. "No. Please, sir. No. I need to keep moving on this."

"It's time we turned the whole thing over to the feds," he disagreed, sounding tired. "If they want you to continue on, I won't stop you."

"They won't want me to. You know they won't want me to. You're as good as saying there's no chance!"

"You can keep informed through your partner. If Sandler learns anything, she can let you know, but I don't want you actively working on the case any longer."

"Please reconsider."

"Take it up with Bethwick and Donley. I'm sorry, Nine. You're in this guy's crosshairs. This last piece"— he gestured to the report that was still held by September's thumb and forefinger—"just proves it."

"But—"

"You can trade with Sandler and work on the

murder/suicide with Thompkins. That's all," he stated firmly, when she would have protested again.

September walked stiffly back to her desk. She couldn't be off the case. She couldn't. This *was* personal, and that's why she needed to stick with it, but there was no convincing D'Annibal.

Sitting down, she stared into space. Then she snatched up her cell from where she'd left it on her desk and put a call into Jake, her eyes watching D'Annibal through the glass just in case he suddenly came out of his office and overheard her.

It was hot and sweat dripped down his face and swept beneath his chin. He hadn't gone to work today. He'd been on the way and decided to swing by Nine's apartment. It was risky, but he got a hard-on being close to her and once or twice he'd caught her driving out of her apartment complex while he was parked at the curb. Had seen her face as she'd driven by on her way to work.

This morning he'd pulled into her lot. It was early and he parked in one of the farthest visitors' spots, against the far wall, training his rearview mirror on her parking space beneath the portico of her building. Her car was there, so he knew he hadn't missed her. He kept his hands on the steering wheel while excitement thrummed through him. He vibrated like a plucked guitar string.

And then the black SUV pulled into the lot and parked behind Nine's car, and Nine got out of the passenger side, signaling to the man who climbed from behind the steering wheel that he was parked illegally. And what did he do? He pulled her to him and kissed her and she laughed, pushed away, but looked at him in *that way*. Like she wanted him to fuck her. Probably already had. That's where she'd been all night! Screwing and moaning and rutting like Boonster's sheep.

Who was he? *Who was he?*

And then the bastard turned and it was *Jake Westerly.*

His chest hurt. Jake Westerly. He'd been there, too. On the playground. In the hallways. One of the laughers. Laughing, laughing, laughing.

His erection collapsed. She was screwing Jake Westerly.

He watched her open her door on the second floor and try to say good-bye to him, but he pushed his way inside and there was more laughing. Laughing, laughing, laughing!

The laughter rang inside his brain. He had to stop it.

Had to stop it.

Sinking back down on his couch he couldn't look at the sea anemone picture right now. He kept his eyes closed and pulled himself into a ball. Had to keep the beast contained.

He sat, unmoving, for a long, long time.

Chapter 17

"If you could just . . . if you could . . ." Marilyn Cheevers took a shuddering breath. "If you could stay here with her, just for a while."

Loni's mother was shaking all over. This had been a close one. He put his arm around her shoulders and she turned into him and started bawling, clinging to him.

"This isn't something I can fix," he told her. Words he'd told her many times.

They were on a slow moving seesaw together, down when Loni was down and wouldn't come out of her room except to shuffle across the floor and maybe take too many pills, up when she was effervescent to the extreme, her brain popping with ideas and plans, her body wired and in constant motion.

One or the other. A condition that had begun toward the end of high school, or maybe had just been too much for her to hide any longer, and then had progressively grown worse despite Loni's constant claims to the contrary. "I'm better," she'd told him. So many times he couldn't count them. "If we got married, I know this won't happen anymore."

He knew it for the lie it was.

Marilyn knew it, too.

"I know it's a lot to ask," she said now, "but I need someone to stay with her. I've got some things to do that I can't put off. I'll only be gone an hour."

Jake heard the emotional blackmail for what it was. And despite her words, Marilyn didn't think it was a lot to ask. At some level Loni's mother thought he owed it to her daughter. She hadn't forgiven him for walking away even though his relationship with her daughter had turned him into a caretaker and Loni into a patient. It was never going to work, and Jake had finally just recognized that fact.

Did he feel guilty about it? Sure. And it was that guilt that contributed to his dissatisfaction with his own life. Oh, he got it, all right. He just hadn't been able to act for a long time.

"I don't think I can stay, Marilyn," he said now, knowing he needed to, feeling like a heel anyway. "I've got a job."

"With flexible hours," she flashed at him in anger.

"I'm not dating your daughter. It's over."

"You could just stay for an hour. That's all I'm asking!"

"No. It's not."

"What?" Her gaze flicked from him to her unconscious daughter and her lips trembled.

"It's not all you're asking."

Immediately, her hot eyes turned back to him. "Did you ever care?" she asked, tearing up.

Before he could respond, his cell phone started ringing. When he pulled it from his pocket Marilyn Cheevers made a harrumphing noise, letting him know what she thought of *that*. He saw that the call was from September and he said, "Excuse me," and moved past her into the hallway.

"Hey, there," he said into the phone as he moved away from Loni's room.

"Hi, I'm . . . having . . ."

"Having what?" he asked when her voice disappeared. "Don't say second thoughts about last night." When she still didn't respond, he asked, "You still there?"

"Yeah, yeah . . . I'm sorry. I'm—D'Annibal took me off the case. Lieutenant D'Annibal. My superior."

"Why?" he asked, glancing back at the door. He wouldn't put it past Marilyn to follow him into the hallway, and almost as soon as the thought crossed his mind she was standing in the doorway. Catching him staring at her, her expression darkened and she ducked back inside.

"Jake, another piece of my schoolwork was sent to the station."

"*What?*" He forgot about Marilyn and Loni and everything, his attention zeroing in on Nine.

"It was my sea anemone report. I don't know exactly what grade it was. We were studying the ocean."

"Fourth grade. I did one on blue whale migration."

"My God . . . Jake . . ."

It was so unlike her to be undone that he wanted to hang up and run to her. He debated on just leaving, but decided he could at least tell Marilyn he was going. He started back to Loni's room, saying, "I'll be at the station in half an hour."

"No. Don't. I'm . . . let me meet you."

"Nine." He felt frustrated all to hell.

"Jake, he wrote 'nine' in a Roman numeral on the back of my report. I used to do that sometimes. I wrote my name like that. Everyone called me Nine, and I thought it was cool. But I didn't put a nine on that report. *He* did it. He knows me."

He stopped short, anxiety crawling all over him. "Then I'm glad you're off the case," he stated flatly.

"I have to figure this out. I can't just stand by and let it happen."

"It's for your safety, Nine. Don't you get it?"

"Of course I get it," she said in a low, angry voice. "And I just got out of an *interrogation* with the feds about my family! They think it's from them, and I don't know, but I'm not giving up. I know I'm onto something." She inhaled and exhaled. "Are you at your office? I can meet you there."

"No, I'm . . . not . . . let's meet in Laurelton?"

"How about Bean There, Done That? Do you know where it is?"

"Close to your apartment. I'll be there as soon as I can."

"Where are you?" she asked, hearing something in his voice.

"On the eastside. See you in thirty."

He clicked off and walked with long strides back to Loni's room. When he entered, he saw her eyes were open and they lit up with relief upon seeing him, "Jake, you came."

"I have to leave," he told her, feeling Marilyn's laser-like gaze boring into him though he wouldn't look at her. "I'm glad to see you're awake. I've got an appointment, but . . . I'll be back," he said.

"You can't stay?" she asked in a small voice.

"No, Loni. I can't."

They stared at each other a few moments, then her eyes filled with tears and she plucked at the covers. "I'm sorry . . . I know you don't want to be a part of my life anymore . . . but I'm really, really better."

Marilyn said, "If you could just stay for the next hour. Really, Jake."

He turned from Loni and gazed at her mother. "I can't," he said. "I really can't."

And then he walked out, feeling surprisingly okay. He'd finally set the boundaries on his relationship with Loni. Something long overdue.

September's cell rang as she walked through the coffee shop door. She recognized the ringtone as her sister, July. "Hey, July," she said, looking around for a table. She would have preferred something tucked away so that she and Jake could talk in private but the booths were taken and so she settled on a table in the rear, though it was near the short hallway to the restrooms.

"I need a favor, Nine. A big favor."

"Go ahead and ask. Don't think it'll happen, given my busy schedule, but go ahead. Ask."

"Okay . . ." July said, responding to September's sarcasm. "I need you to come to the house tonight. I want to talk to Dad about some stuff and I'd really like you to be there."

"No."

"I know about your fight with Dad. I was there."

"Then, you know about the note Verna wrote," September said. "Enough said."

"For what it's worth, I think you're right. Verna was having an affair with our father and Mom found out."

September was surprised by July's cold tone. Her older sister had always seemed "on the other side" with

March and their father. "I blame him," September said simply.

"So do I. Come to the house tonight. We'll have dinner. March is coming and Rosamund will undoubtedly be hanging around, and I've asked Dash, too."

"Have you and Dash gotten closer?"

A pause. "Yes, actually. We have."

"Is he baby-daddy material?"

"That isn't in the cards. So, can I count on you?"

"You make it sound a little like a command performance," September said.

"I want Auggie here, too."

September actually laughed. "Yeah, well, I'd like a villa in France, but I don't think it's gonna happen anytime soon."

"I'll call Auggie myself and get him here. I just need you to say you'll be here."

"Okay, now you've got me wondering what the hell is going on. I don't want to talk to Dad. I don't want to be anywhere near him."

"I understand, but this is important. Come for six o'clock dinner," she said. "I've talked to Suma and she knows I'm having guests. I just need to give her a head count."

"Anyone else you've invited?"

"Verna and Stefan."

"I hope you're kidding." At her silence, September said, "You are, aren't you? July . . . ?"

"No."

"Are you nuts? What for? Now you'll never get Auggie there. Whatever you're planning, count him out."

"But you'll come," she pressed.

September rolled her eyes. "Sure. How can I miss it? It's already been a shitty day. Might as well make it worse."

July took no offense, just said, "Good."

"You know the feds are asking me about the family. That's where their investigation is leaning because of the warning notes I've received."

"Yeah? Well, they've got a lot of people to look at, don't they?"

"You don't think there's anything there, do you?" she couldn't help asking, unable to quite fathom July's mood.

"You mean, do I think someone's stepped over the line from greed, treachery, adultery, and basic lying to murder? No. But then what do I know?"

"Are you all right?"

She exhaled heavily. "Yes. I'm all right. It's been an unbelievable week, that's all. Just, be there tonight."

"All right. Good luck with Auggie, July. Really. He won't come."

"He might," she said in a hard voice, then clicked off.

"You get him to do that, you're a better woman than I," September said aloud after she'd hung up.

She had to leave her table to stand in line for an iced coffee, keeping an eye on it, hoping no one would take it. She lucked out and was able to get her drink and save the table, and she took the chair that gave her a clear view of the front door. She spent the next few minutes feeling like a weight was on her chest. She wasn't going to give up on the investigation. She couldn't.

Her mind went back to when she'd been asked into another room again by "good agent" Donley, who'd then proceeded to ask question after question about the Rafferty family. September had dutifully answered, though she hadn't wanted to. Yes, she was angry at her father and Verna; their actions had led to her mother's death. But they, along with everyone else, just couldn't be part of the Do Unto Others case. She wouldn't believe it, and she kept that information to herself. She only offered up banal information and was only half into the conversation at all, until he brought up her sister May's homicide.

"Your sister was killed in a robbery attempt at a fast food restaurant in Laurelton when she was seventeen?"

"Louie's. It was a local burger joint, but it's no longer there."

"She and her friend were held up by a man with a knife?"

"Erin worked there, and May was just visiting her. She used to do it all the time."

"Do you know what happened? The sequence of events?"

September had glared at Agent Donley. First she was taken off the case, now she was being treated like a hostile witness, which, in fact, she probably was. She didn't see what May's death could have to do with her family's supposed involvement in this. "All I know is that Erin was working and May went to see her. Some guy came in with a knife and demanded money, and then he held the knife to May's neck and forced them both into the back room. It was about ten o'clock, and there was no one else there, although I think kids came in later and thought the place was empty and stole some things. It was caught on videotape, I believe. I was fifteen at the time."

He asked a few more questions about May, and then some about her two stepmothers, and then, sensing she was seething, he let her go back to work.

She had a cold feeling inside that the feds were trying to blame all this—May's death, too—on the Raffertys. It was nowhere near the truth. Nowhere . . .

Jake appeared a few moments later in blue jeans and a white shirt. He wore Nikes instead of cowboy boots and she recognized that this was his casual office attire, a perk of being your own boss. To her shock he actually came up and kissed her hard on the lips before he sat down across from her.

"There's a greeting," she said, smiling.

"I missed you." He reached across the table and grabbed her hand, holding on to it as if he couldn't bear to let go.

She was caught off guard by his mood. "Bad morning? I thought I was the only one."

"I'm glad you're off the case. Sorry. I'm worried about you."

She shook her head. "I can't stand the thought of someone else working it, *especially* because he's targeted me. I'm not going to quit."

"How are you going to stay on?"

"I'll just keep searching on my own. I've got leads to follow."

"Don't, Nine. Just back off."

She pulled her hand away, hurt and frustrated. "I called you for support. If you can't give it, I might as well leave right now."

He stared at her and she could hardly look at him without thinking about making love to him. "I'll help you," he said. "If you won't quit, then I'm in this with you. I'll come over after work and we'll start tonight."

"Jake, thank you, but—"

"He's got your fourth grade work as well. We can start by checking out the fourth grade class pictures. I'll ask my mother to find mine, since yours is missing."

She gazed at him helplessly. "You just can't know how much I want that, but believe it or not, I've got a dinner at my dad's tonight. I don't want to go. I don't want to ever see him again, but July twisted my arm, hard."

"Then, I'll see you afterward," Jake said. "I liked having you overnight."

She shook her head at the speed this relationship was traveling. "I like having you have me overnight," she admitted. To his flashing grin, she shook her head but said, "I'll call you as soon as I'm done."

By the time September arrived at Castle Rafferty—now she was calling it that, too—there were a number of cars in the parking area. She quickly scanned for Auggie's Jeep and was kind of gratified that it wasn't there. Whatever July's great mystery was, Auggie hadn't been convinced.

It had been a draggy afternoon. When she returned to the station after meeting with Jake, Gretchen and George were back. The probable murder-suicide was looking more like a slam-dunk. The husband had shot the wife as she was walking into the house carrying a bag of groceries, which tumbled down a short flight of stairs that led up into the kitchen from a back room off the garage. He had then walked past her and into his den where he turned the gun on himself.

"It's going to be mostly report filing from here on," Gretchen said, and that's when D'Annibal came out of his office and told the room at large, Bethwick and Donley included, that September was off the Do Unto Others case and showed them the anemone report with the red IX.

The only saving grace was that Gretchen said she would type up the notes on the murder-suicide as she'd been on scene, and George quickly agreed, so September was basically free to work on something else. Since the Zuma case was off the Laurelton PD's collective desk as well, she pulled out a report on the body of a man who'd been found half-naked, zip-tied to a flagpole some six months earlier. The tox report said he'd ingested a number of pills, including a roofie, and then died from the combination of pills and hypothermia when the late February temperature dropped into the twenties. There was a note hung around his neck, in his own hand: *I have to pay the price for what I've done.* The case was listed as a homicide, as the general consensus was that he couldn't zip-tie his hands behind his back without some help. But there were those who felt maybe it was an assisted suicide. The guy was a postal worker with a wife and teenage son, and everyone was completely baffled by his behavior.

There's a reason, September told herself, but it was a half-hearted attempt to get engaged in something other than Do Unto Others when everyone else was working the case. She knew she should bring Gretchen up-to-date on what Hague had said, but she didn't really have the opportunity and she was glad to leave at five to go home and change, even though the rest of them were staying on.

Now, she rang the bell and the door was opened almost immediately by March's ten-year-old daughter, Evie, whose big blue eyes and bright smile were a welcome sight. September gave her a big hug, which surprised Evie, since she didn't see her aunt that often, but she hugged her back.

"Dad and Aunt July and Grandpa are on the patio with Rosamund and Aunt Verna and Uncle Stefan," Evie said. "And Aunt July's boyfriend's here, too."

"Ahh . . . I guess I'll head to the patio." *Aunt Verna and Uncle Stefan.* Neither of them was any part of the Rafferty family anymore and September could have done without seeing Verna. She blamed her and Braden for her mother's death. Was it fair? Probably not. But she didn't really care what was fair. Her mother was gone and they'd kept the secret of their affair and how it had played into Kathryn's death for far too long.

"Rosamund's going to have a baby," Evie said, as if she were delivering big news.

"I heard."

"I'm going to have a new cousin," Evie said. "I only have cousins on my mom's side so far, but now I'll have one on my dad's!"

Strictly speaking, little Gilda/January would not be Evie's cousin, but her aunt, but the idea seemed to make the girl happy so who was she to point out the flaw in her logic. And anyway, if "Aunt July" were to get on the baby track, Evie might have another cousin coming along very soon.

She braced herself for walking out to the patio and joining the family. She didn't know what the hell she was doing here, especially given how she'd left things with her father, but she didn't really want to alienate July and she was seeing Jake later, so she could get through the next couple of hours by just thinking about last night, if need be. A vacation in her head. A lot better than thinking about the last eight hours.

March was actually standing by the barbeque while Suma brought out trays of food and placed them on the large outdoor table with its huge tan-and-white-striped umbrella. A pitcher of lemonade lay sweating on the table, and September saw there were two empty glasses left. Everyone else had one in their hands, so she stepped up and poured herself a glass.

"If you'd like something stronger, the bar's in the den," her father said diffidently. His eyes had tracked her progress from the moment Evie had led her to the patio.

"Thanks, this is fine," September said. She tried to keep her voice noncommittal but her tone sounded stiff to her own ears.

"I brought Cat's Paw, in case you change your mind," July said by way of greeting. "Best Pinot Noir around." She headed September's way, leaving Dashiell by the hors d'oeuvre tray of ahi tuna slices with sesame seeds, ginger, soy sauce, and scallions on the plate. She linked her arm through September's and led her away from the group toward the kitchen, but her move nearly ran her into Verna and her hovering son, Stefan. Verna and Rosamund were standing with their backs to each other so that neither of them had to look at the other.

On the heels of July's greeting, Verna declared, "Oh, Nine! I saw your interview on television. Have you got any leads on this monster? I swear, the whole world's getting worse. I don't know how you stand being a cop!"

Stefan was gazing down at the top of Evie's blond head, looking as if he were on some distant planet, or maybe just wanted to be. He felt September's eyes and looked up and nodded to her.

"It has its challenges," September said to Verna tensely. She didn't know why it bothered her that Verna called her Nine when she wasn't bothered by anyone else doing it.

Dash came sauntering over and said genially, "Good to see you again."

September felt a clock ticking in her head, counting down to a bomb. She wanted to blast Verna and creepy Stefan, too, though all he did was stand by quietly and observe. She didn't want to talk to them. She didn't want to ever see them again, but she was saved from answering by July dragging her away from the dining room and into the virulent lime green kitchen where they could be alone.

"What the hell are you doing?" September asked her sister when they were out of earshot.

"You're not the only one pissed at Dad, y'know," she said, dropping her smiling hostess act and regarding September with barely leashed anger.

"Are you mad at me?" September asked.

"I'm mad at Dad and Verna and Rosamund, too, just because she's such a bitch. I'm not thrilled with March, either. You and Auggie are the only ones I even like in my family."

"Well, it's mutual. What about Auggie? I thought you said—"

"He'll be here," she said. "How much do you know about Dad and all his women?"

"All his women? I . . . not much. I know about Verna, obviously, but that's it. I'm sure there were others," she said, releasing a deep sigh.

"There were others," July confirmed. "I kinda want to get into that tonight."

"Why?"

"Because he deserves it. And there's Rosamund parading around like she's the fairest in the land, and the only thing good about that is it infuriates Verna and she looks like she's been sucking on a pickle all night, her lips are so pursed with anger."

"Yeah, but . . . what's changed? Is this because I found the note?"

"It was nice to know you finally knew what I've known for years. Maybe not about Mom finding the note, but about Dad's lifestyle." She grimaced. "All I would like is a baby, and maybe a husband, too, sure, but nothing seems to be working, whereas Dad just threw it away and then he gets Rosamund pregnant!"

"What about Dash?" July dug her fingers into September's arm and September said, "Ow," and yanked it away.

"When Auggie gets here, we'll deal with everything. I'm

sorry that Evie's here. I didn't count on March bringing her, but hell, she's in this family, she might as well know."

"Auggie?"

"I told you he's coming. He's just late. I told him he could bring his girlfriend. I mean, what the hell, why not? But he's coming alone."

"But he is coming."

"Yes," she said as if she were tired of telling her the same thing. "Yes. Yes, he is."

"What's going on?"

"July?" Rosamund's voice preceded her into the kitchen as she appeared from inside the house. Twin spots of color suffused her cheeks. "Okay, I'm just going to say it. I don't appreciate the way you took over and made these plans like . . . well, like you own the place. You're staying here for God knows how long, but it wasn't by my choice."

September slid a glance at July to see how she was taking being berated, but her sister's face was shuttered as she answered, "Duly noted."

Which only pissed off Rosamund further. "This isn't your house!" she declared. "What part of that don't you get?"

"I've made plans to move out. Don't you worry. I'll be gone long before January arrives."

"Gilda," Rosamund grated.

Through the window September saw Auggie's Jeep wheel into the lot and park next to her Pilot. "You did it," she said in amazement and admiration to July, sliding past Rosamund, yanking open the front door and meeting her twin as he climbed from his car. "July said you would come. I didn't believe her. What the hell's going on?"

Auggie's gaze slid past her to the open doorway where

July now stood. "I guess she didn't give you the preview," he said.

"What preview? There was no preview."

"I hear you got pulled off the case," he said, looking down at her.

"Yeah, yeah. I'm sure you're doing a happy dance."

"I think it was the right move," he agreed. "D'Annibal told me about the newest message. Jesus, Nine. You know you shouldn't be on the case."

"Who better?" she challenged him, closing her ears to his concern.

"I wish I wasn't so entrenched in this other case, but I can't back out now."

"I'm not one of your damsels in distress," she gritted. "Now, what the hell are you doing here really? Tell me. Or, I'm going to think you're a pod person, or something."

"I'm not staying long," he told her as he moved to meet July. He gave his older sister a hug as he entered the house, and July looked past him to wave her hand for September to hurry up and join them. As September moved toward the house, she pulled her cell phone from a pocket and checked the time. Seven fifteen. Though she was curious to know what was going on, she wondered how long she'd really have to stay.

It took another twenty minutes before Suma brought the final dishes to the table, serving plates brimming with salads and vegetable dishes, all with an Asian flair. March had finished the barbequed, five-spice chicken and sat it in the center. The family was seated by then, with Braden at one end and Rosamund, her lips in a hard line, on the other. July sat across from September and nearer to Rosamund than Braden with Dashiell on her right and Verna and Stefan beside him. Auggie sat next to September, across from Dash, and with Evie beside him and March at the end near Braden, literally her father's right-hand man.

Braden's gaze was all over Auggie, but he was giving their father his profile. When Braden said, "It's good to see you, August," he managed a curt nod, but, whatever had gotten him to come to the house was clearly not meant for Braden to think it might be something more.

March began passing the plates around, helping his daughter with the heavier ones, and everyone began serving up except Rosamund, who was holding her glass of lemonade to one side, as she surveyed the group. "Okay, July," she said in a tsk-tsk tone. "Let's get on with it."

Braden scowled at his new wife, but managed to keep from saying anything. Verna, seeing the interplay, said, "What an interesting kitchen color choice, Rosamund? I don't think I would have thought of it."

July said loudly, "This is a momentous day. We're not a big, happy family. We never have been, and come to that, we're not even really a family. There have been a lot of tragedies, too." Her gaze swept from Braden to Verna, and September held her breath. Just where was this going? "I moved back to the house this summer because I was thinking of changing my life." She slid a half-glance to Dash, who was sitting quietly with a faint smile on his face, listening. For a moment September thought July had lied to her and she and Dash had decided to get pregnant together after all, but then she said, "I don't really know how to say this, so I'll just say it. You've all met Dash before, Dashiell Vogt. He came to The Willows a few months back and introduced himself and we struck up a friendship."

"Oh, you're getting married," Verna said with a conspiratorial smile. "Good for you."

Auggie drawled, "I wouldn't have shown up tonight if that's all it was."

"What is it?" Evie asked innocently. Her gaze turned to Dash, who gazed right back at her, and in that moment September saw the Rafferty blue eyes on his handsome face.

"Oh . . ." September said, setting down her fork.

July smiled at her and then at the table at large. "You've met Dashiell, but you haven't really met him. Not even you, Dad. But it's time you did." She turned to Dash and lifted a hand.

He took the cue, slowly rising from the table, lifting a glass. "Hello, Father," he said in a wry tone. "Glad to finally meet you."

Chapter 18

September glanced from Dashiell to her father, to Auggie, and back to July. Surprisingly, the first thing she thought was, *I don't have time for this*. Her anger at her father and Verna was still a bright ember, but the realization that she had some unrecognized sibling from a different liaison—given Dash's age he was before Verna's time and Verna was the type to flaunt her children, not bury their existence—was a complication that September wanted to deal with at some future date.

"You remember Dash's mom," July was saying to Braden when he stared at Dash silently for so long that it became uncomfortable. "She worked for you and Mom when March and I were just babies. Dash decided to meet me first, but he didn't tell me the whole story until just recently. I thought I should share."

Silence followed. Verna blinked rapidly, as if the act of moving her eyelids could get her brain processing faster, and Stefan sort of shrank away from Dash as if he might have cooties.

Auggie reached across the table, holding out his hand.

"July already told me, obviously. Welcome to the family, brother," he said ironically.

"Dash is your brother?" Evie asked, lost. "How come no one told me?"

"It's kind of been news to all of us," July said, looking at Braden, whose face had suffused with color, only to have it drain away again.

Rosamund stated flatly, "I don't believe it."

"I don't either," Verna said, flustered.

"You think you're the only one who had an affair with Dad? Stand in line," July shot back.

September choked out a laugh. She'd never been that close to her older sister, and she was beginning to think she'd really missed out.

"Dash is Dad's son," July said. "I even did a little thing called DNA testing, and guess what it proved."

"You can even see it," September observed.

Everyone took a hard look at Dash, who lifted up his palms as if to say, "Have at it."

"I think I'll get an independent test, just the same," Rosamund declared.

September knew she was just worried that there was now another person in line for the Rafferty inheritance.

"You'll waste your money," Auggie said.

"It's mine to waste!" Rosamund glared fire at all the Raffertys.

March seemed to stir himself, but he remained silent, waiting for Braden to speak. Braden took his time, and when he did, he warned July. "You shouldn't have done this."

"You mean because it's self-destructive? Because you'll take my job away from me? You blew that when you and Verna took my mother away from me. That's all on you!" Her voice cracked as she gazed from Braden, to Verna, and back again. Though she'd barely eaten a bite, she then dropped her napkin on the table, scooted back her chair, and stalked away from the table to the kitchen.

Dash didn't follow her. He'd clearly been given a script ahead of time and merely regarded his father coolly.

"You're not my son," Braden said coldly.

"I don't really like the idea, either, but DNA says differently. You know my mother, Anna Marie."

"Anna Marie worked for Kathryn, not me, and she was only here a short time," Braden stated flatly.

"Because she was pregnant with me. I know." Dash picked up his lemonade and drank a huge swallow. His fingers trembled slightly, the only giveaway to his emotions.

September was starting to wish she'd taken her father up on that drink. Everyone was looking at Braden, who was staring down at his plate. She wondered, idly, if he would try to deny the charge, but it was pretty clear July had already done her homework and facts were facts.

Auggie clapped his hands together and said, "Okay. If that's it, I gotta get going. I think I'm over my quota of Rafferty drama." He scraped back his chair.

"August, I want to talk to you," Braden said quickly.

"Seriously? You think this is the time?" Auggie asked.

"It's all the time you're giving me!" he growled.

"You want to talk about something? Something other than meeting your long lost son, that is?" Auggie swept an arm toward Dash. "Why don't you worry about Nine and the fact that she's in the killer's sights—"

"Auggie," September warned.

"—and that he's sent her her own grade school artwork with a message: 'Do Unto Others.' And a second piece, with the Roman numeral IX on the back. He put that there. She didn't. So, where the hell's her old schoolwork? It's not here. She's looked. Help her find it, before speculation that the doer's one of us becomes certainty in the minds of the authorities."

Braden had jumped to his feet in fury. "In *your* mind, *son?*"

"Wait . . . wait . . ." September moved closer to Auggie, hoping to defuse a situation that was rapidly getting out of hand.

"The FBI's on this one, *Dad*. Nine's been taken off the case because she's a target."

"Is this true?" Braden bellowed at September.

"Yes," she admitted.

"You should have said something when you came here!" He glared at her.

"I should've," she agreed. She just hadn't wanted all the drama, but she'd gotten it anyway.

"So, where is it?" Auggie asked. "All of our stuff is missing." He glanced around to March and July, who had returned to the table, and his hard gaze fell on Verna. "I would say someone destroyed it, but since some of Nine's schoolwork's been sent to her, I'm betting it's still around."

Unless the killer's had it all along. September didn't voice her thought, however.

Verna said, "You can't think I'm responsible," as she also got to her feet.

"Mom died and you moved in," July stated in a cold voice.

"Stop this nonsense!" Braden roared. He pointed a finger at Auggie. "I should have known the only reason you came here was to start a fight." He flashed a look at Nine. "I told you not to go into police work. This is exactly why. You mix with the likes of scum and you pay a terrible price."

"I didn't touch any of your things," Verna came back hotly to September, ignoring Braden entirely. "Some of Kathryn's were put in the attic. I thought that was where the rest of your childhood memories were."

"We found my mother's," September said woodenly.

"You should have found the rest. It was there!" Verna declared.

Stefan slid from his chair and moved behind his mother and out of the room. September's gaze flicked to him as he sneaked away. Evie looked about ready to cry and March put a hand on her shoulder, glaring furiously at Auggie.

"I think we've all talked long enough," he said.

They all started moving away from the table except for Rosamund who seemed frozen in place. As if realizing they were all standing, she lumbered to her feet. Some of the punch had gone out of her, and September stared at her and with dawning comprehension said, "You moved the boxes."

"What?" Rosamund didn't meet September's eyes.

"You moved the boxes. You knew it when I came here the first time and when I came back with Jake on Monday."

She thought for a long moment, and September could see she was trying to come up with an excuse. Eventually, she said with a hike of her shoulders, "I didn't know it was so important. You were just looking for some old stuff. You didn't say why you wanted it."

"Where is it?" September demanded.

Her eyes moved past her to Braden, whose own expression was hard to read. "Well, I didn't know!" she told him, as if he'd accused her.

"Where is it?" Braden repeated September's question.

"You know! I told you I was getting that storage unit at that public storage place off Western." She couldn't hold his gaze, and September suspected that she might just have purposely forgotten to mention that plan. "I had Suma's husband, Jorah, take some stuff over there. Just—junk." Feeling cornered, she added, "I can give you the key."

"Do it," September told her, and she started to move toward the stairs that led to the master suite set of rooms.

"Were you ever going to tell Nine?" Auggie asked Rosamund as she moved past him.

"I didn't know it was such a big deal!" She looked about ready to cry and Braden said roughly, "That's enough." As she headed for the stairs, Braden said pointedly to Verna and Stefan, "I think we've all had enough for tonight."

Verna made the mistake of putting a hand on his arm. In a voice only September could hear, as she was closest, she whispered to Braden, "I don't believe he's a Rafferty."

Braden put a hand in the small of her back and guided Verna and Stefan outside. September made a point of not meeting his eyes as he returned; she knew, as he did, that Verna's comment had everything to do with Rafferty money and that's why she was picking sides.

Rosamund was back in a few minutes with a folded piece of paper and a key on a ring with the unit number: C14. "This is the code to get into the place," she said, handing the piece of paper along with the key to September.

"Thank you," September said coldly.

"I'm sorry. I'm trying to help you," she declared, fighting tears.

"For God's sake, Rosamund. What were you thinking?" July said with a roll of her eyes.

"She gave you the key," Evie reminded September with

a touch of urgency, her blue eyes clouded with concern. "She just made a mistake."

"That was good," September agreed woodenly for Evie's sake. "We all make mistakes."

Dash took the following lull to say to Braden, "I'd like to meet with you at some future time."

Braden's nostrils flared. "You come into my house under false pretenses and expect me to accept you with open arms. . . ." He shook his head, as if he were beyond words.

"Hey, any pretenses, false or otherwise, are all my fault," July said airily.

March steered Evie away from the confrontation and toward the front door. "School tomorrow," he said vaguely as an explanation.

"Is Dash going to change his name to a month, too?" Evie asked just before the door closed behind her.

Auggie snorted. "That's a good point. What month were you born?" he asked Dash.

Braden suddenly moved up to Auggie, looking for all the world like he was going to hit his son. Auggie raised his brows and met his father's gaze deliberately, goading him with one arched brow.

September said, "Whoa, whoa. Let's all take a step back."

"No need," Auggie said. "If this is what he wants, I'm ready. Take your best shot," he challenged his father.

July said quickly, "Okay, I'm sorry. I should have handled this differently. Nobody's hitting anyone."

"It's your fault!" Rosamund stated to her with a bit of triumph, glad the focus was off her.

"That's enough." Braden was curt. His gaze bored into Auggie, who stared back, calm and cool and ready. After several tense moments, Braden said again, "I think we've all had enough for tonight."

Dash put in casually, "It's December, actually. The month I was born."

July looked at him. "Well, it starts with a 'D,' so I guess that counts."

"Next time you want to have a party at my house, think again," Rosamund sniffed at July. "Goodnight everyone."

At Rosamund's dismissal, September hurried Auggie outside. "What's wrong with you?" she demanded.

He turned to her. "Hey, you want to be mad at someone, be mad at July. She's the one who cooked this whole thing up after Dash told her the truth. I wonder how many more 'Dashiells' there are out there. Think how many Raffertys there could be."

"I gotta get outta here," September said.

They were walking toward her Pilot and his Jeep. It was dark by now and Auggie stopped and said, "Okay, maybe it's low of me, but I'm kinda glad to have it all out there. This is who we are. The real Raffertys."

"What's July thinking?" September muttered. "I mean, my God. Talk about burning bridges. She practically said she was going to lose her job. And she can't stay at the house anymore."

Auggie hiked his shoulders. "She just couldn't stand the bullshit anymore. And I think she likes Dash."

"What's the story there?" September asked, thinking how July had been considering having a baby. Now she knew why she hadn't considered Dash in her plans.

"He came to The Willows and introduced himself. He didn't say who he was at first and it kinda went from there, and then he told her, and she sat on it a while, I guess, but after your run-in with dear old Dad, she was pissed. I don't know what the hell's going on with her, really, but she convinced me to come." He half-laughed. "Glad I didn't miss it."

"What do you think Dash's agenda is?"

"Rafferty money?" He shrugged uncaringly.

"Yeah, well, just wait till Dash tries to take a slice of the Rafferty pie. Verna and Rosamund will be all over it, among others."

"He can have my slice," Auggie said. "Or, maybe he's just looking to connect with his family."

"Yeah, that's it."

They both laughed. Then September glanced back at the house. "I don't really care about any of this. It's crazy drama stuff, but I'd like to kill Rosamund. She knew why I was here before. She just didn't want to admit she moved my stuff out."

"Dear old Dad will never let her get away with that." Auggie grinned. "He may treat us all like shit, but he won't allow anyone else to."

"True," September said.

"I'm just glad I don't have to worry about you on the Do Unto Others case anymore." As the smile fell from her face, he added, "That said, I know it's a bitch to be taken off a case. I'm sorry about that. But this one's too personal. You know that." When September didn't say anything, he said, "I suppose you're going to look in the storage unit."

"Tonight, hopefully. I may be off the case, but I'm still going to find my own schoolwork," she said with a bit of heat. "*Our* schoolwork, since yours is missing, too."

"Okay." He shook his head. "Boy, did Rosamund miscalculate on this one. You can't get rid of us Raffertys that way."

"And now there's one more of us."

"At least," Auggie said.

The front door opened and Dash and July walked through. July wished him goodnight with a quick hug, then went back inside the house. Dash came toward them and stopped by a dark blue Nissan Pathfinder. The three of them stared at each other a moment, then Auggie said, "I'm so glad you met us on our best behavior."

That broke both Dash and September up, and then Dash shook Auggie's hand again. He looked at September and held out his arms, asking her silently if she wanted a hug.

September, who usually abhorred that kind of thing, walked into his arms and hugged him back. She didn't care what his agenda was; he was a Rafferty and an outsider, and that put him on Auggie's and her side of the ongoing family war.

Slightly embarrassed, she pulled back and exchanged phone numbers with Dash, who then did the same with Auggie. She then climbed back in her car and grabbed up her cell phone which she'd purposely left in the car, sensing earlier that whatever July had in store for her, she was better off not being distracted by phone calls from work or Jake or anything else.

There was one voice mail and two texts. The first text was from Sandler, asking her to call. She knew what that one was about; she wanted September's take on the interview with Hague Dugan. The second text was from Jake.

Meet at your apt. Be there by 9.

She didn't recognize the number for the phone message and debated on waiting to take it. She wanted to get to her apartment and maybe talk Jake into joining her on a hunt in the storage unit.

Sticking her earbud in, she listened to the message

while she put the car into gear. She had to punch in her code, but then she was driving and the message came on.

"Hi, this is Della Larson. Hague's caretaker. I got your number from the card you gave Hague. I worked for a very short time at Grandview Hospital myself. Hague was a patient there and that's how I first met him. Before you get any ideas, he was young and I barely noticed him. We met years later again, and I was looking for in-home work and well . . . everything just came together.

"I know you're looking for the person who murdered Glenda Navarone," her voice went on, "and you think it may have something to do with whomever she allegedly had sex with on her uncle's examining table. I should tell you that's an urban legend. If it happened, it was before either Hague or I were there. Here's my phone number if you want to talk more, but I think you're following a dead end." She then left the number.

September thought a moment, then decided to let it go. She could call her back later, but for now she wanted to meet Jake and have him go with her to the storage unit. She could call Della tomorrow, maybe. What she should do was talk to Gretchen about Hague and his caretaker, but then that aspect of the case would definitely be out of her hands, too. She wasn't going to let that happen yet.

As she drove into her carport, she saw Jake's Tahoe parked in a visitor's slot. He climbed out of the car and came her way as she stepped out and hit the remote lock. Her heart fluttered a bit and she muttered, "Down girl," to herself before he reached her.

"Hey," he said with a smile.

"Hey, yourself."

"I made some plans for us tonight. Pack a bag and let's have another overnight."

"At your place?"

"I've got somewhere else in mind."

"I have work in the morning," she said, though it made her chest feel heavy just thinking about showing up and not being a part of Do Unto Others.

"I'll get you there on time." He came up to her and put his arms around her, giving her a fierce hug. "This feels so good," he said on a heavy sigh.

She smiled against his shoulder. "If you want to compete for the bad day award, you're going to lose."

"Once this guy's in custody, it'll be okay," he said.

"Yeah . . . well . . ." She eased out of his embrace and headed for the stairs. "Okay, I'm ready to go wherever, but I need to make one stop first. Rosamund gave me the keys to a storage unit where she shipped all the Rafferty childhood stuff. She finally saw fit to tell me about that tonight."

"Huh. Was that why you had dinner with your family tonight?"

"Not really. That just sort of came out. I've got a lot to tell you," she said, threading the key in her lock and pushing open the door. "Come in while I pack, and I'll bring you up to date. . . ."

Thirty minutes later they were pulling into U-Store and More and September read the code to Jake and he punched it in on the keypad. The gate slowly lumbered inward, protesting with a whine of metal hinges, and then they were driving through, looking for C14.

They found the unit at the end of a long row where each unit was faced with an orange metal garage door. Jake parked in a nearby designated spot and they both walked toward Building C which was lit by a series of sodium vapor lights set on the walls between the garage doors.

Pulling out the keys, September grabbed the lock, intending to put the key in the keyhole but the lock unsnapped in her hand. It was just set to look as if it were locked. When she tried to snap it together, it wouldn't hold.

"Wonder how long it's been that way," Jake said, glancing around.

"Wonder if Rosamund even knows." She unhooked the lock and then Jake grabbed the rope that was tied to the door handle, yanking upward. The door clattered onto its rails and they were left staring into a dark, rectangular ten-by-ten box. "Have you got a flashlight?" she asked Jake.

For an answer he held up his cell phone, pressing a couple of buttons to engage its light function. A thin stream of illumination fell over stacks of boxes. Without further ado, September started combing through the boxes. Jake bent down to help her. It didn't take long to realize they were full of all the old Rafferty memorabilia. Six boxes in, September murmured, "She really cleaned the place out of all things Rafferty."

"Who's that?" Jake asked, pointing.

It was the portrait of Stefan Harmak that had hung over the fireplace prior to Rosamund's.

"My stepbrother," September said. "Rosamund got rid of Verna's things here, too, apparently."

They opened box upon box, and discovered March, July, Auggie, and May's pictures and schoolwork and other flotsam and jetsam from their youth, but there was nothing of September's. There was also more of Kathryn's things. Boxed up and labeled by Verna, September saw from the handwriting, and then shuffled out of the attic by Rosamund, who'd missed the box of books that September and Jake had found earlier. Probably thought it was Braden's, she surmised.

"So, this explains it," Jake said.

"I think so," she said, a chill feathering her skin. The

killer had her belongings from the storage unit, which was disturbing, but he hadn't taken them from her classroom when she was a second grader, which made her feel slightly better. Maybe he hadn't targeted her from her youth. Maybe it was, as she'd first thought, more recent. That seemed—less invasive—somehow.

Jake stepped out of the unit and said, "It would be easy enough to climb the fence. He scanned the area and said, "There are cameras."

"Maybe they keep a tape or digital copy," September mused, knowing she had no idea when the killer, or whoever, had stolen her belongings. Knowing also that the perp would most likely be wearing something to hide his features.

"Maybe," Jake said.

"How did he know about this place, when the only one who did was Rosamund?"

"Maybe he knows Rosamund?"

September shivered. "Could Rosamund be a target? I thought he was after me because I'm the cop on the case, or was, and maybe that was the kickoff. He started killing right after my picture was in the paper announcing my new position with the Laurelton PD. But maybe there's something more there. My father has a number of enemies . . . and Rosamund looks a little like me, too, and Emmy and Sheila and Glenda.

"Or, maybe not," she said, shaking her head. "He killed that prostitute, too, but everyone seems to think that's because she was available."

"He killed Glenda right after your interview with Channel Seven," Jake pointed out.

"What do you think?" she asked him as Jake pulled the garage door back down and replaced the faulty lock to make it appear as if it were secure.

"Maybe he works here?" he asked, glancing toward the darkened office.

September followed his gaze. "We can check in the morning."

"No." His abrupt tone caused her to gaze at him in surprise, and he reminded her, "You're off the case. You can tell your partner in the morning."

"Oh, to hell with that. I want to know. This is my family."

"Then talk to Rosamund. She's the only one who would have an idea. But tell your partner. Let her be the lead dog."

September pulled out her cell phone as they drove back through the gate and away. She didn't want to hear his logic. She wanted him to be on her side, come hell or high water, which was unrealistic, but it was what she wanted. "I'm calling July. I don't have Rosamund's cell number, and I'm sure as hell not talking to my father." She saw him smile in the darkness, but he didn't comment. "So glad I'm a source of amusement," she grumbled.

"I kinda like it when you're in a bad mood."

"Bad mood? You haven't seen me in a bad mood, but I'm getting there."

He chuckled and July's voice mail came up. "Hi, it's September. I don't have Rosamund's cell number. Would you have her call mine? I need to talk to her about the storage unit. Thanks."

She clicked off, and then realized they were heading south out of Laurelton. "Where are we going?" she asked suspiciously.

"Westerly Vale B&B," he said. "I got us the room that looks over the vineyards."

"Oh . . ." She sank back into the seat. She was bound to meet Colin and his wife, and they would then be aware of her relationship with Jake.

She felt her anxiety start to rise as they turned into the long drive that led to the winery and bed and breakfast, but when Jake opened the front door for her and they entered the welcoming front room, and Jake's brother came and clasped his hand, and September was introduced to his wife, Neela, who both seemed thrilled to have her with Jake, she relaxed. Jake introduced her as September, not Nine, which said something, she supposed, though she wasn't quite sure what, but Colin treated her like an old friend, which she was, in a way, and Neela was as warm as anyone she'd met in recent years.

There was a bottle of dessert wine and cookies on a tray and everyone had a small glass and there was a lot of talk about the winery. It couldn't have been better, September realized, somewhat surprised. It took her mind off the case and her family troubles, and by the time she and Jake were in bed, curling into each other and making love, she'd pretty much put the worst of the day behind her.

"I'm going to take a shower," he said, a few minutes later. "Don't fall asleep. There's some stuff I want to tell you."

"What kind of stuff?" She pulled the covers over her breasts.

"I'll tell you as soon as I'm back."

Alone, she stared up at the ceiling fan that was lazily swirling the air in the room around, creating a comfortable breeze. There was air conditioning as well. It was a really wonderful place and September wanted to smash her face in the pillow and stay there forever.

But then her mind started tripping along familiar pathways and she thought about calling Della back. She reached for her messenger bag and pulled out her cell, checking the time. It was after ten. Not a great time for placing a phone call, and yet almost as the words crossed her mind, her phone rang in her hand.

Another unfamiliar number. Maybe Rosamund?

"Hello," she answered cautiously.

"Detective Rafferty?" a male voice asked. "It's Phil Merit."

Not Rosamund. "Oh. Hello."

"You gave me your number and I've been debating on calling you back."

September sat up in bed. "You've remembered something about Sheila Dempsey, or . . . ?"

"I didn't tell you everything about Sheila. I've been kicking myself, but it seems so . . . it just can't be related. It doesn't make any sense."

"Let me be the judge of that."

"I had her make out a will," he rushed out. "I'm an estate lawyer and I just told her everyone should have a will. So, she did. She thought it was dumb because she didn't have anything, really, outside the marriage. Maybe a car. But she didn't want her husband to get anything of hers, so she wrote in the name of another beneficiary. I never filed the papers and I just sorta let it go . . . we were drinking at The Barn Door, and then at the house . . . and it wasn't supposed to be serious. Then when she was killed I knew I could probably be in trouble for half-assing the whole thing, and . . . God . . . I don't mean to try to excuse myself, it's just my thought process, y'know. I just waited too long."

"Okay."

"I should have told you earlier. It's meaningless, but I should have told you earlier."

September felt her heart start to pump heavily. "The

beneficiary?" September asked, but she didn't need to. She knew. She knew already.

"Jake Westerly. The guy she was so wild about at that time. She thought it was fun to put his name in, like they were connected, or something. But like I said, it's meaningless. I just should have told you earlier."

Chapter 19

September sat at her desk, staring straight ahead, watching Bethwick's mouth move, only picking up one or two syllables at a time. ". . . cord . . . small fibers . . . all four victims . . . Demp . . . blinds . . . must bring with . . . his kills . . ."

It was Friday morning and she wasn't on the case, which now was just as well, after Phil Merit's bomb dropped last night. In her gut she knew he was right: it was meaningless. Jake was about the last person to have a reason to kill Sheila Dempsey for what she'd supposedly left him. He was wealthy, a self-made man, probably with a net worth in the millions. It made no sense at all. It was just one of those curve balls that happened in an investigation that could make you lose focus. She wasn't going to let it happen.

But she'd lain awake in the dark listening to Jake's breathing and thinking about all the coincidences, the numerous points on the axis where Jake crossed into her investigation. They'd gone to the same elementary school, and junior high, and high school. He remembered both the falling leaves artwork and that he'd done a report on the migration of blue whales while she'd written a report on sea anemones. He'd known Sheila Dempsey as a friend, in grade school and from meeting her again at His and Hers Hair Salon. He'd joined her and several friends at The Barn Door for drinks, and he'd even faced off with Sheila's estranged husband, Greg Dempsey.

She shook her head and glanced down at the note on her desk. Channel Seven was trying to get another interview with her. They didn't know she was off the case, and she wasn't going to tell them. Wadding up the note, she threw it at her waste can and was gratified when it bounced off the rim and in.

Staring ahead of herself, she felt a seething anger building. Though it was completely off point, she found herself furious with Deputy Dalton. He hadn't interviewed Phil Merit and therefore it *wasn't* all in the report, like he'd claimed. He'd stopped at Greg Dempsey and hadn't learned about Sheila Dempsey's will.

Her head ached. All of this was such little stuff, really. They'd gone to school together so it was likely he would remember some of their art projects. He had a passing relationship with Sheila, one of Do Unto Others's victims, who had then, on a lark, named him as her beneficiary.

She doubted he even knew what Sheila had done.

And there was something else now, too, which while irrelevant to the case, said something about Jake. He'd wanted to talk to her about something, but she'd faked being asleep when he came out of the shower. Then, this morning, as they were waking up, he'd received a call on his cell phone that had made his expression turn grim when he saw the number. She'd felt her heart begin to pound, wondering what now? She was holding so much in. What they'd shared, physically and emotionally, was so new and precious that she'd been loath to chance destroying it.

He'd clicked off the call without answering it, then caught her eyes on him. She could almost see the calculation running across his mind.

"What is it?" she'd asked, almost afraid to know.

He moved his head slowly, from side to side, as if weighing how to tell her. Fear shot along her nerves. She subconsciously braced for something devastating.

"This is what I wanted to tell you. That was Marilyn Cheever, Loni's mother. Loni's in the hospital. She overdosed on a combination of pills that she'd probably been hoarding . . . she's done it before. Marilyn wants me to come see her again, and it's a cycle I need to break. That's where I was yesterday when you called."

September had just stared at him. It was such a complete left turn from what she'd feared that she hadn't known how to respond. Misinterpreting, he'd added, "It's over with Loni. Has been since January, like I told you. She's bipolar and it started after high school, or maybe even while we were in high school, I don't know. Sometimes she's fine and well . . ." He sighed in frustration. "You know the drill. But don't . . . please . . . let this affect what's happening between you and me." He moved his hands to include her and him together. "This is good. I spent way too many years with Loni. A lot of it out of guilt. Don't let this ruin it for us."

"I'm not worried about Loni," September had said truthfully, but then had quickly climbed out of bed and run through the shower, dressing in haste, unable to really meet his eyes, so she knew she'd given him the wrong impression.

She tried to act like nothing was wrong on the way to her apartment and her car, but he'd grown progressively quieter while she'd become a magpie, chattering about every inconsequential thing that entered her mind.

Now, she didn't know what to do. Though she wasn't supposed to act on the case, she needed to at least appear alert and taking in information at every meeting, and she could feel the feds' gazes touch on her, along with Gretchen, George, and D'Annibal's. Luckily, she'd gotten enough, if asked. Though she'd only heard bits and pieces, she understood that the feds had gotten the lab report back on the type of cord the killer used as his method of strangulation. It was identified as a common cord used in window coverings, specifically blinds.

"We also interviewed Emmy Decatur's parents," Bethwick said, turning his flat stare accusingly at September and Gretchen. "They asked why we were interviewing them again. They thought we would be checking with Grandview Hospital, since they'd revealed that Emmy went there for several years."

September saw Gretchen's face flush dark red, but she was too involved in her own personal hell to really react. Let 'em be mad. She didn't much care. Gretchen quickly explained how they'd spoken to Dawn Markam-Manning, who'd been a nurse at Grandview, but that she hadn't offered up any real information. She invited the agents to recheck with Dawn, and then allowed that maybe it would be better if they checked with someone else who'd worked at the hospital, someone who might remember Emmy Decatur better.

Silence followed. If September had been more involved, she would have enjoyed Sandler's inherent snappishness, for once.

The meeting broke up shortly afterward and Gretchen came steaming over to September's desk. She was pissed, mostly at herself for getting caught, but eventually she realized September wasn't feeling the same slap down. She gazed at her hard. "You okay?"

"Never better," she said, to which Gretchen snorted her disbelief.

"You look like you're not even really here," she said. "What gives? What did you do yesterday?"

September almost snarked back, "Nothing," but stopped herself. It wasn't Sandler's fault she'd been taken off the case. Deciding she needed to be a team player, she said, "I actually learned a few things."

"Yeah? Like what?"

Keeping her voice down, September said, "Oh, let's see. I had a visit with Hague Dugan about 'Wart.' I had dinner at my father's and, what do you know, I have another brother. Half-brother, actually. And then I found out that my latest stepmother didn't tell me that she shipped all of our stuff—us Rafferty kids'—to a storage unit, and when I went to see what was in that unit, the only box missing was mine."

Gretchen sat down at her desk, looking at September thoughtfully. "Wow. That's a lot in twenty-four hours. You think our doer took your schoolwork from the unit?" She kept her voice low as well.

"Looks like he took the whole box."

"That puts a different spin on it." She gave September an assessing look. "So, you're still working on the case."

September shot a glance around the room, but the agents were gathering their stuff and heading out and not paying any particular attention. "Just tying up some loose ends."

Gretchen, in turn, threw a glare at the two agents, a hard look at George who was on the phone, and another one toward D'Annibal's office for good measure. The lieutenant was also on the phone. "Tell me more."

"Uh . . ." September waited till the agents were gone, and as they left, she heard George's heft creak in his chair. He was off the phone, but he got up and moved slowly toward the hall, probably heading toward the break room. As soon as they were alone, September told Gretchen everything she could recall from the moment yesterday had started until Phil Merit called her, though she left his phone message out. She needed to talk to Jake first, and she didn't want to send the investigation down what she figured was a blind alley, unless she had to.

When she was finished, she sat back and let Gretchen digest everything. She was still processing when George came back and eased his bulk into his protesting chair.

"Well," Gretchen said, leaning back in her own chair and speaking in a normal voice. "I went to The Lariat and Gulliver's again, this time with *George*, and we didn't learn jack shit."

George said, his gaze on his computer screen, "Don't blame me. You're the one who pisses people off."

"No niceness?" September asked. She felt the best she'd felt all day.

"They didn't deserve niceness. Suffice it to say, nobody knows nothin'." But there was no real heat in her words, and a few moments later, she said casually to September, "I could use a break and you look like you need an iced coffee."

September glanced at the clock and asked, "How'd you know?"

"Sometimes, I'm just clairvoyant."

Fifteen minutes later they were at the nearest Starbucks. They got their coffees, iced for September, hot and black for Gretchen, and as they took their seats, Gretchen said, "So, you have a new brother. That's wild."

"Wild," September agreed.

"And your stepmother shoved all your stuff in a storage unit that got ripped off, probably by our doer. When Frick and Frack learn that, maybe they'll ease off your family."

"Don't count on it."

She squinted her eyes thoughtfully. "But even so, the most interesting part of what you told me is that Hague Dugan mentioned Wart, and that his fuck-buddy called you and warned you that you were on the wrong track."

"Caretaker," September corrected. "Della Larson. Yes."

"Why bother?"

"I don't know," September said. "I'm going to call her back and try to figure it out."

"How much are you telling the feds?"

"I'm telling you," September said firmly. "You can decide how much you want them to know."

"I don't want them to know nothin'." She pressed her lips together and thought hard. "I think you should go see Dugan again. Forget the caretaker. Go see him in person. He's the source."

"But I'm not on the case."

"Not officially."

"I could call Hague's sister, Liv Dugan," September said slowly, waiting to see if Gretchen was going to go with this, like she was indicating.

"Yeah. And if you learn something, just call me. I can't know what you're doing, so if this is your choice, I didn't know about it until it was over."

"Gotcha."

"For what? We didn't decide anything, did we?" Her smile was a faint smirk.

Back at the station, September placed a second call to U-Store and More. She'd phoned as soon as she'd gotten to the station and was connected to a recorded message that gave their hours as ten to six. As it was long after ten, she hoped to actually talk to someone this time, but again she had no luck. She left her name and cell number and hoped for the best.

Jake called in the afternoon, sounding diffident as he asked her if she would like to get together that evening. When she immediately agreed she could tell he was glad, if a bit confused.

What the hell. She needed to talk this out, and she was feeling stronger now that Gretchen had given her tacit okay to forge ahead. Sure, she had no real authority but it was nice to think her partner had her back.

For the rest of the afternoon September tried to keep her attention on the homicide of the man tied to the pole, but it was nearly impossible. She was plagued by other thoughts that ranged from the highly charged scene at the Rafferty house the night before, to the rather cryptic message from Hague's caretaker, Della, to thoughts of Jake and how she was going to approach the information Phil Merit had dropped on her.

Just before five, she walked outside to place a call on her cell that she didn't want overheard. She could feel sweat form on her scalp and she looked for some shade in the heat of the afternoon. Fat chance. The Laurelton Police Department was surrounded by low-growing plants and one spindly white dogwood tree that offered no respite.

Walking to her car, she slipped inside and blasted the air conditioning. Gretchen was right. She should bypass Della and try for another face-to-face with Hague, as Della would likely be a roadblock. She briefly thought about calling Auggie before Liv; Della had clearly liked him. A lot. But that was problematic, too. Auggie knew she was off the case and wouldn't be as understanding as Gretchen.

But Liv might go along with her, if she played it right.

What the hell. It was worth a shot.

She put in a call to Auggie's home where she hoped Liv would answer the phone as she and Auggie had moved in together. Liv didn't own a cell phone. She was almost as much of a technophobe as Hague himself. A Luddite, she called herself, referring to the term coined by a group during the Industrial Revolution of the nineteenth century who banded together and protested industrial automation. In Liv's case, she'd never really been against technological advancements. She'd just been afraid that the insta-speed of today's communications would help bring a killer to her door.

Now, September pulled the phone from her ear to look at it and thought, *If those Luddites could only see us now.*

Liv's voice answered and she quickly placed the phone back and said, "Liv?" only to realize that her voice was in a recording on Auggie's voice mail. September waited to leave a message, and when she heard the prolonged beep, she asked Liv to call her back on her cell phone as soon as she could.

Now she was waiting for Liv's call and Rosamund's. Peachy.

She walked back into the station and headed to her locker. Gretchen was already there when September entered the room. She said, "I'm going to Xavier's and plan to get mildly drunk. Maybe medium drunk. And then I'm going home with Dom." She slammed her locker shut. "What about you?"

"I'm . . . meeting Jake Westerly."

"Ahh. Good luck with that."

September was climbing in her Pilot, heading home,

when her cell phone rang. She scrabbled for it, knocking her messenger bag into the footwell in the process, swearing as she grabbed for it. She managed to get to the cell just in time. "Hello? Hello?"

"Nine . . ." Rosamund's angry voice answered.

"Hey, I wanted to talk to you about the storage unit. The lock's broken and—"

"I'm getting the boxes back! I've already got them coming back! Everybody's on me. You didn't have to sic the FBI on us! What do you think we are?"

"I didn't sic them on you."

"Yeah? Then, how come they're here. Talking to Braden. Oh, he's *really* pissed at you and Auggie. How could you?"

"Rosamund, an investigation goes, where an investigation goes," September said tightly. "It's out of my hands."

"Well, isn't that just such a convenient excuse!"

"Who knew about the storage unit?" September asked, trying to get to the point of her call. "Besides you."

"Your father. I did tell him, no matter what he says. He just doesn't remember."

"Anyone else?"

"Suma's husband, Jorah, did the moving."

"That's it?"

"Yes!"

"You're sure?"

"Yes. I remember because we were finishing the remodel and I didn't want to leave the house while the workmen were here. Suma and Jorah were taking the boxes out then. I gave Jorah the lock and he set it up, came back, and gave me the keys."

September knew Jorah, a big man with a huge smile

who radiated nothing but good feelings. She didn't believe he had anything to do with the theft. "Okay, thanks."

Rosamund made a sound of exasperation. "Yeah, whatever." She hung up.

September called the storage unit office again and was surprised when someone, a woman, finally answered. "This is Detective Rafferty. I left a message this morning," she said, irked.

"Ah . . . yeah . . . Burton got the message but he had to leave. He didn't know what you were talking about."

"Burton's the manager?"

"Yeah, he's the man. Been here for a hundred years. No one works here but him and me and I've been here for the last couple of years. He said you can come on over anytime and talk to him or me. Except for lunch. We're out from noon to one, or thereabouts."

"I might do that."

"Sure thing."

That didn't sound promising, September thought. She didn't believe the doer was a woman, and if Burton had worked there for "a hundred years" she got the sense that he might not be in the right age range. For the moment she set that aside.

Her cell rang just as she reached her apartment. Putting the vehicle in park, she pulled her phone from her bag and saw that it was Auggie's home number. "Hello," she answered.

"Hi, September. It's Liv. You left a message asking to see Hague again?"

In the back of her mind she registered that Liv Dugan was one of the only people she knew who called her by her true name. "I have a few more questions, but I have the feeling that if I go through Della it just might not happen."

Liv snorted her agreement. "You got that right. Is this still for the Do Unto Others case? I thought you were off that one."

"I am. Reluctantly. This is more for my own edification than for the case."

"Meaning?" she asked.

"I'd really rather have Auggie find out after the fact," September admitted. "He'll try to stop me, but I just feel I might shake something loose if I go by myself, er, with you."

"If we go tomorrow morning before ten, they'll still be there," she said slowly. "If I call and give them too much of a heads up, Della will come up with some excuse."

"So, what are you saying?"

"How about I pick you up a little after nine tomorrow, and I'll call on the way."

"Great. What about Auggie?"

"He's been working late nights. I'll just sneak out for a bit. No big deal."

"I don't want to get you in trouble with my brother," September said.

"The one he's going to be mad at is you," she pointed out.

"That, I can handle."

With her plans set, September gathered up her messenger bag and climbed the stairs to her unit. She heard a car motor start up in the lot below as she threaded her key in her lock. She'd just opened her door, when she had a sudden prickling of her scalp, a sense of being watched, and she carefully glanced around. A vehicle was just exiting the lot; she caught the tail end of it as it passed the side of the building. A van of some kind, she thought. Her eye traveled carefully all around her, and apart from a maple leaf drifting down from one of the trees that lined the back edge of the complex, she didn't see anything out of place.

Her cell rang again, causing her to jump. This time she recognized the ringtone as the one she'd assigned to Jake. She closed the door and locked it behind her, then answered the call. "Hey, there."

"Where are you? You home?" he asked.

"Yep."

"We're okay, right? I meant what I said about Loni being in my past."

"I'm okay with that. Really. It's . . . oh, a lot of things."

"You want to go to dinner and clue me in?"

"Why don't you come over, and I'll order a pizza or Chinese food?"

"How about I pick up sandwiches at Wanda's and come over?"

"Sounds good. I'll take a tuna and cheese on rye, and a Diet Coke."

"See you soon."

September walked into her bedroom, stripped off her clothes and ran through the shower, letting the hot water nearly scald her. She was not looking forward to this.

Chapter 20

Jake took the steps to her apartment two at a time, carrying the white bag with the two sandwiches, two small bags of Lay's potato chips, and a Diet Coke for her, a regular Coke for himself. She answered the door on one knock, as if she'd been waiting on the other side.

"No surprise, there was a line at Wanda's," he said. He glanced at her, seeing she'd unclipped her hair and changed into jeans and a white tank. She was barefoot, and her feet looked small beneath the frayed hem of her jeans. When he looked at her, she shifted her gaze away. She seemed tired, he thought, and, as if to answer that silent question, she pushed her dark hair away from her face and sighed.

As she took the bag from him and started laying the sandwiches onto plates and searching for glasses for their drinks, he asked, "What's wrong?"

"Nothing, really. I just . . ." She trailed off as she grabbed a tray of ice cubes from the bottom freezer and plunked two cubes into each of their glasses. She handed him a glass and his Coke, and placed his sandwich on the small table pressed against the wall. He took one of the two chairs and then waited as she brought over her own sandwich and drink, and placed the two bags of chips between them.

"You may be the detective, but I'm detecting that you've got something on your mind," he said. "If it isn't Loni, what is it? You haven't been yourself since we were at Colin and Neela's."

"I got a call. From Phil Merit." She looked straight at him, her blue eyes serious. "He called me on my cell when we were at the B&B."

"Okay." Jake popped his Coke and poured it over the ice cubes. It fizzed and sparkled and he picked up the glass and took a long draught.

"He said he forgot to tell me something. He'd kept it to himself, and he didn't think it mattered. He's pretty sure it's meaningless. He said Sheila did it on a lark."

"I'm listening."

"He told her she should make out a will. She was leaving her husband, and he's an estate lawyer, and she did. Sounds like they were having a few drinks and it's just something they did."

Jake had unwrapped his sandwich, and he noticed she'd not done one thing to prepare to eat. He waited himself, taking another drink from his Coke, his gaze searching her tight face.

"Sheila named you as her beneficiary," September said.

He blinked. "She did?" he asked in disbelief. "You're kidding."

"No. Phil just left the will at his house, apparently. He said he half-assed it. Looks like she never had a copy herself. But it's probably still valid. I don't know. You'd have to check."

"I don't want anything of Sheila's. That's . . . bizarre. I

hardly knew her." He peered at her closely. "What are you saying?"

"I'm saying . . . I don't know. It doesn't look good. I haven't reported it, because I just don't want to. They've already taken me off the case. This just feels like a dead end."

"Who are you trying to convince?" Jake asked. He'd picked up one half of his BLT, but now dropped it back to the plate. "Is that what this is? You think this means . . . I had something to do with—"

"No. I know you didn't."

"Yeah?"

"But they'll ask you about it, if I tell them. The feds. They'll probably put you on the hot seat because that's what they do."

"And you're afraid of that?" He could feel the heat rise up his throat.

"I'm just warning you."

"You think I had something to do with Sheila's death," he stated coldly.

"No! I told you I don't. Stop putting words in my mouth."

"To hell with this," he muttered, getting to his feet. He felt angry and frustrated. "You take this cop thing way too far."

"You make it sound like my career choice is a joke!" Her face was flushed and her eyes flashed blue fire.

"Nope. I just think you're trying to make your career be everything. Everything you are. You don't want there to be any Nine Rafferty in there anymore," he said, pointing at her. "It's all *Detective* Rafferty."

"That's hardly fair," she snapped.

"Yeah? Well, the guy you're looking for is out there," he grated, swinging his arm to point through her living room window. "Not here. He's probably planning something more right now. Something against *you*. And you're thinking I had something to do with this?"

"That's not what I'm saying." Her jaw was tight.

"It is what you're saying. You just don't want to believe it." He stalked to the door. Twisting the knob, he hesitated a moment, looking back at her wide eyes and stubborn chin. "I'll call you," he stated flatly, and then he went out the door and down the steps, wanting to slam his fist into the wall at the back of her parking lot, managing to hold himself back with the shreds of his self-control.

As soon as he was gone, September felt herself grow hot with regret and anxiety. That had gone about as badly as she'd expected it to. And the way he'd said, "I'll call you," didn't much sound like he meant it.

"Peachy," she said to the hollow emptiness of the room, fighting back a sting in her nose and eyes. She shook her head and inhaled several deep breaths. She'd warned him. That's all she could do. At least now if—when—the federal agents came to interview him, he'd know what it was about.

The guy you're looking for is out there, not here. He's probably planning something more right now.

September turned her gaze to the window, knowing Jake was probably right.

He stood in the center of the field, staring up at the stars flickering in the black sky. His head was pounding, his nerves sending hot messages up his limbs and through his body to his brain, which felt about to explode.

He'd followed her and Westerly to the vineyard, Westerly Vale. He'd been afraid to pull into the long driveway behind them, so he'd pulled into a dusty turnout down the highway and hiked back, being careful not to be seen as he sneaked through the trees and vines and hedges that lined the drive.

They were already inside when he got close, and he'd been glad for the binoculars he kept in the van. He'd grabbed them up before he started his trek, and then he'd lifted them to his eyes just as a light switched on in one of the upper rooms of the house that faced the rolling acres of vines. He'd seen a faint outline of two people. Something indistinct, but in his mind's eye he saw them embracing. Their silhouettes frantically groping as they fell to the bed.

He'd heard the howl of pain and realized it issued from his own throat, so he'd quickly and stealthily moved back to the van, firing it up, his hands on the wheel, his foot pressed to the accelerator. The beast took over and when he finally wrested control again, he was twenty miles in the wrong direction. He'd turned around and driven back to his place, throwing a glance toward the old lady's house when he arrived, but there were no lights showing.

Good.

But he'd been sick with fury and hate, lying on his cot, as if he were in a fever.

Westerly Vale. Jake Westerly.

He wanted to plunge his knife into his chest over and over again. Cut out the bastard's heart. Castrate him. Feed him piece by piece to the vermin that roamed in the fields.

He'd skipped work again this morning, but Mel had called him on his disposable cell phone, demanding to know where he was. He'd told the truth: he was sick, but Mel didn't want to hear it. He'd given Mel the number; he'd had to. But now he would have to ditch this phone and get another. Mel had the old lady's address, but it couldn't be helped. If things got too close, Mel may have to have an accident, but he feared that may bring them down on him too soon. *September* down on him too soon.

He wanted her now.

But was now the right time? Would it be the end? He'd expected to hear that she'd received his latest message, but there'd been nothing on the news. He had cable and wireless Internet, courtesy of the old bitch if she but knew it, but though he'd waited and searched and ached for news, it felt like he'd been cut off.

Now, trembling as if he'd aged a thousand years, he got up from the cot and went to his treasures. It took all his willpower, but he bypassed the box with September's special gifts and instead pulled out the rest of what he'd saved.

Closing his eyes, he tried to drag Sheila Dempsey's image to his mind, but it was nearly impossible. September was always imposed over all of them, but with an effort, he pushed September back and pulled Sheila forward and now his mind could see her again, standing with a group of friends at The Barn Door.

She was beautiful. Trim dancer's body in a low-cut, white lacy top and denim jeans. The dusky hollow between her breasts mesmerized him. He should have turned away and left as soon as he saw her, but the beast's eyes were locked onto those mounded breasts. It was too late. She saw him and frowned, then her brow cleared and he knew she recognized him. He couldn't back out. He had to try and pull it off, to talk to her, but he should've known better. That never worked with the laughers. He told her that her skin was smooth, and she said, "Still have your knives?" as she backed away. Her

words filled him with rage, and he made the mistake of
reaching out and brushing a hand along her hip. He wanted
to touch her breasts but he couldn't be that obvious. She
moved away as if repulsed and the beast—always so hard
to contain—lifted up and roared. He said something else,
and she snapped back at him to leave her alone, and
then a man was there, asking if she needed help.

He quickly left, but he watched for her to leave, noted
her car. The next time she came back to The Barn Door,
he pulled his van in beside her car and waited. She came
out of the place with friends, but they parted and she took
her time, searching in her purse for her keys. He was
crouched in front of his van, and was wondering if he
would have to wait, but her friends backed out and turned
onto the highway just as Sheila reached her car. He leapt
forward, slipped the noose over her neck and pulled, all
the while moving her in his arms to his van, as if he were
helping a drunk. She struggled, but it was over before she
could make a sound. He slipped her limp form into the
passenger seat of the van, and no one saw.

He took her to the cot and made love to her . . . to September . . . dreaming of sea anemones. He kept the noose
tight and every time September came to and begged to be
free, he pulled it tight again until she was gone.

He lay with her for hours. At least that's what it felt
like. But then he awoke as if doused in ice water and saw
the beast had marked her flesh with the knife. He felt as
if he should understand, but he didn't. He just knew he
had to get rid of her body. Not September. Sheila. He had
to keep reminding himself.

When he was rid of her, he felt empowered. The red
mist he saw through when the need was on him was gone.
He'd sent the beast back to the cave once again.

He blamed September for it. Like the bad thing he'd

done . . . the bad thing that had gotten him sent away. It was her fault. Her false kindness was a torture from which there was no release.

He thought he'd vanquished the beast once again, like he had so many years ago, but he was wrong. This time, with Sheila, he'd given it a taste of pleasures that could no longer be denied.

He trolled other bars, watched other women, and then, there was Emmy Decatur, dancing and flirting and rubbing her body up and down all the men in the bar. The beast took it as a sign. She was a laugher, too. A different place. A different time. But she'd teased and taunted and she was tight and firm and the beast watched her parade herself on the dance floor. Again, he knew better than to be seen, so he left the bar before she could remember him from Grandview.

But he couldn't stay away. The beast wouldn't let him. It was dangerous, but he was drawn back. This time he followed her to her apartment. It was dark. The parking lot light was out. Before he really thought it through, he pulled his van up beside hers and as she got out, she saw him.

"Hey, Wart," she called loudly.

He glanced around in fear but no one heard. He came up to her and slid his arms around her, as if they were in an embrace. Surprisingly, she was drunk and seemed willing, so he lured her into his van and to the cot room. At Grandview he'd tried to have sex with her in the bathroom, and she'd freaked and called holy hell down on him, but now. . . . Then she stumbled at the stairs. Tried to change her mind, but he wasn't going to let her, this time. He tamed her with the noose and took her upstairs, threw her down and rode her. And then . . . and then . . . she called him *names*! Told him he was a fucking joke

and they all laughed at him! He thought he was such a
stud at Grandview. Strutting around like a cock. He
should still be in Grandview! That outpatient treatment
he moved into was just their way of getting rid of him.
Nobody wanted him. *Nobody.* He never got cured, like
she did. Never even improved. He was always telling the
newbies what a badass he was, when he was just a sick
fuck. Then and now.

Her mouth was grinning. September's mouth. He
could hear the laughter.

He pulled the noose until his arms ached, but then he
killed her too quick. He never reached full pleasure. In a
fury he carved into her flesh **DO UNTO OTHERS AS
SHE DID TO ME**. The words came out of the beast but
when he saw what he'd done, he knew it was right.

And then Glenda . . .

He'd seen September on the news, speaking Navarone's name, and it threw him back to his nights with
Glenda in the examining room. He'd half-believed he
loved her. He was over September! It was finished! He
almost cried with the relief of it. Here was someone
who cared about him, and he could bury the laughers
forever.

But then he learned that Glenda was only interested in
fucking if she thought her uncle might catch her, and
before long, she was gone. No longer hanging around
Grandview, her dark eyes searching through the sick
rubble of her uncle's patients for a quick screw.

This summer he'd found Glenda at The Lariat, but
after his experiences with Sheila and Emmy, this time he
was very, very careful to keep her from seeing him before
he was ready. He watched from deep in the shadows of
the bar. Watched her line dance, her attention only on
learning the steps. The wild child he'd known had turned

into someone aloof, someone *respectable*. Ha! He knew her . . . he knew her . . . and then after September spoke to him through the television, he knew it was a message. It was time to take her. So, when all the shit was raining down on her uncle, he followed Glenda home and reminded her of who she really was.

But after Glenda he couldn't wait. He went for the whore. And he didn't want to take her back to his place so he used her in the field.

And now . . . ? He pressed his fingers to his temples, feeling the beat of the beast's heart within him, suffocating him. *Is it time for September? Is it?* He thought he would know for certain by now, but he was unsure.

Just thinking about her got him worked up. His head was pounding and he couldn't see for the red mist in front of his eyes. The beast wanted a woman. Dark-haired. Like September . . . but not her yet . . . *not yet.*

In a wild panic he ran outside to the van, fired it up, headed back toward Laurelton. No . . . not Laurelton . . . too soon . . . Portland.

He drove with controlled passion, forcing his foot from the throttle. Couldn't get picked up by the cops. The cops . . . the fucking cops . . . like September.

He surfaced long moments later to recognize that he'd driven to Grandview Hospital. Only it wasn't a hospital any longer. It was an old persons' home. Grandview Senior Care. He could see a stack of wheelchairs through the doors that had once led to the hospital, and several older people shuffling along.

His fury was sudden and unexpected. Why couldn't the old lady be here with them? The house, the land . . . all of it should be his. *She* should be at Grandview, while *he* should own all the acreage.

He drove away from Grandview to the nearest bar. It

was swanky, compared to his usual haunts. Had the air of a British pub and mullioned windows and outside tables with candles and propane heaters, unused tonight, as the heat felt thick enough to wade through.

It wasn't his kind of place but he couldn't stop himself. The beast was making the choices and there was a woman just inside the open door, sitting at the bar, her head turned toward a male companion.

September . . .

He found a parking place at the far end of the lot and backed in carefully. The lot was crowded and he needed to be able to get out fast. He moved into the bar and pushed himself behind a group of people so that he could see the woman, but she couldn't see him. He wished she would get up and dance. He wanted to see her move.

Sidling a bit closer, he saw that the bar stool behind her had opened up. He stared at it, wondering if he dared. She was leaning toward the guy next to her, giving him a full shot of her breasts. Taking the chance, he slid onto the stool. He couldn't see her face but he could hear her conversation and the way her dark hair was clipped back, and the angle of her shoulder and neck and waist . . . She could be September.

And, oh, God . . . there were red highlights in her hair, glistening under the low lights.

He felt an erection coming on and pulled his attention back to the bar. He rarely drank, but he needed camouflage in this room. He was too exposed. He never let himself be seen, but . . . it was so good . . . so good.

"A beer," he croaked out.

"What kind?" the bartender asked a bit impatiently.

Behind him, he saw they had Bud on tap and that's what he ordered. When the beer was served to him, he wrapped his hand around it and tried to appear casual.

". . . see there's two types of seriously sick fuckers: the psychopaths, and the sociopaths," she was saying drunkenly. "They're both total whack jobs, if you know what I mean. I'm doing a paper on it. And you know people get 'em confused all the time. Like, what's the difference, you know what I mean? Psycho, in Latin, means one, whereas, Socio, is many. Like society, y'know? We live in a society of many people. But the main difference is a nature versus nurture thing. Psychopaths just come out that way. It's like . . . you play the percentages, and a certain amount are just gonna be rotten eggs. Psychos. Period. But psychos know what they're doing. They know it's wrong, but they just don't have the capacity to give a shit. Sociopaths, on the other hand . . . they've been influenced by their upbringing. Like if they were abused, then they turn around and abuse someone else. For instance, sexual abuse? If that's what happened, then they turn into sexual abusers themselves."

She paused to slurp down half of a martini. He found himself staring into the mirror across the bar, his mouth open. He closed it quick. His nerves were sending hot messages of panic. He needed her to shut up. SHUT UP!

"Okay, so sociopaths," she began again, never turning his way. Her companion's eyes were looking around the room like maybe he was getting bored. "They're not as organized. They might think they are, but they're not. Cracks'll start to show. They can't move through society like a psychopath can. They can't be charming. They're just a mess, and sooner or later, they fuck it up, and everybody's onto them. But they can form attachments to a few people. The ones closest to them. But just wait." She wagged her finger in front of the guy's face. "If they think you've turned on them, spurned their affect . . . affection. God, that's a hard word to say." She gave a little trill of laughter. "Affection," she repeated with more punch. "If they think you've spurned their *affection*, then suddenly you're at the top of the hit list."

This was her come-on line? He wanted to scream at her: *Like you know, bitch!*

Suddenly she didn't look like September any longer. She looked like a crone. A hag. Like the old lady.

He got off the stool and shoved his way out the door, leaving one kind of steaming heat for another. The weather had been blasting hot for over a week and there seemed to be no end to it. He was hot inside and out.

He went to his van and sat in the dark, his hands on the steering wheel. He wanted her. He was going to have her. But he didn't think he could have sex with her. She wasn't September. She wasn't even Glenda, or Emmy, or Sheila, or even that whore.

It took two more hours before she stumbled out of the bar with a different guy. He was trying to peel her off his arm and he practically ran away from her as soon as she was weaving by her well-used Ford Mustang. She was stumbling on her heels, just like the whore. He didn't know anything about her and he didn't care. All he wanted was to see her die.

He followed her back to her home, across the Hawthorne Bridge to the east side of the Willamette. She was living in one of the older homes that didn't have garages, some didn't even have driveways. Everyone parked on the street. She bumped the car in front of her, trying to park. The first sign that she was inebriated as she'd been very careful driving home.

It took her a while to get out of the car. He pulled up next to her and said, "You gonna leave a note on that car you hit?"

She looked around at him, then at the vehicle in front of hers. "I barely touched it," she declared with disdain.

She started to walk away, heading toward the back of his van and a house apparently somewhere down the block. The neighborhood was dark. Not a light on. Quickly, he snatched up his noose and stepped onto the road, then moved to the back of the van, opening the door with a soft screech. She was on the sidewalk and she glanced his way, stumbling a bit.

He darted at her, surprising her, the noose over her head before she knew what was happening. He pulled hard and she made a strangling sound and he hustled her into the back of the van, climbed in beside her and held the cord on her until she was gone. Not dead. Just passed out.

Feeling a clock ticking in his head, he climbed back out of the van and into the driver's seat just as a car turned onto the street behind him, moving slowly his way. The road was narrow, cars on either side, so he eased the van into drive, knowing the car could not get around him.

He drove back toward Grandview Senior Care and past its grounds. There was a park on the far side. He'd spent a lot of time there waiting outside the hospital for his outpatient treatment. Stupid doctors. They'd kicked him out of the hospital and back to the old lady because there was no money to pay for his treatment any longer. They told him all he needed was outpatient treatment anyway. It was a scam. Navarone was the worst. He wanted to experiment on all the freaks. Navarone had told him that it was important that he continue his treatment and for a while he had. The bad thing had troubled him. Troubled him because he wanted more. He would never tell the doctor about it. He would contain it himself. Control the beast.

But he made sure each time he showed up at Grandview that he would detour from Navarone's office to the common room and watch the other freaks in the hospital. He thought about taking them to the park. In the open fields, under God's eyes.

He stopped the van toward the back of the park. Where the grassy area turned up a hill to a thick stand of Douglas firs. He couldn't go back toward Laurelton because he would give himself away. Maybe already had.

He'd left the noose around the bitch's neck. Now, he grabbed his knife and walked around to the back. She was lying as he'd left her but he could make out the shallow rise and fall of her breaths.

He pulled her out by her feet, slung her over his shoulder, quickly took her to the trees, and laid her on the needle-covered ground. She looked peaceful and his mind moved back to September. Yes . . . she *was* September. The words she'd spoken at the bar crowded his mind anew and he almost lost the moment, but then he saw her hair, remembering the red glints he'd seen under the lights. He stripped down her pants and ripped open her blouse. He kept glancing around, his heart pounding with excitement. This was closer to other houses than he'd been. There was more danger.

Quickly, he pulled a condom from his pocket, and pulled down his own pants. His member shot out and suddenly there was a shriek and she sat up and clawed his face, her nails ripping the skin in front of his left ear.

Shocked, he grabbed the noose and pulled and pulled and pulled until she flopped around on the ground and finally lay still. Fury kept him holding the cord. It actually bit into his skin and he had to stop before blood could fall, though he wanted to kill her again and again.

He had tools in his van. And solvents. And bleach. You just never knew . . .

With cold fury sliding through his veins, he ran back to the van, pulled out a bottle of bleach, popped off the child-proof top, took it back to the bitch and poured it over her hands, then her face. He stopped then, holding his breath, listening, but all was quiet. Picking up his knife from where he'd dropped it, he glared down at her bare torso.

Do Unto Others screamed across his mind.

He stabbed downward into her soft flesh and then he heard the noise. Voices. Soft laughter.

Laughter.

No time. No time.

Swiftly, his thoughts on September, he moved the knife, making his mark. Dragging her by her feet, he slid her out into the grass.

. . . in fields where they lay . . .

Lightly he ran across the grass, jumping into his van, twisting the ignition and sliding out of the lot. He glanced into the rearview mirror and saw the dark line on his face where her nails had dug, filled with his own blood.

As he drove away his mood grew darker. The reckoning was coming sooner than he'd expected. It was time for him and Nine to make their last stand together.

His last disquieting thought was that the bitch he'd just killed had been right: he'd screwed up.

Chapter 21

September hadn't said a lot on the way over to Hague's apartment. She and Liv didn't know each other that well, and after the sleepless night September had just had, she wasn't much in the mood for chatter. Now, as she and Liv walked into the building and the elevator cage, she turned off the sound on her cell phone so she wouldn't receive a call that could possibly disturb Hague.

"Auggie was called out to a crime scene early, so I didn't have to lie about what I was doing," Liv told her.

"I'll call him as soon as we're done, I promise," September said. "Sorry to put you in this position. I just didn't want to hear about it before I talked to Hague."

"I hope you get what you're looking for," Liv said as she shut the accordion-like gate of the elevator and pushed the button for the third floor. "Della's not going to be very welcoming."

September understood the implied message: this is your last shot. Liv had used September's cell to call Della on the way over and from what September could hear of the conversation, she knew they were lucky to be getting past Della, the gatekeeper, at all.

At the door Della's icy blue eyes glared at them, and September wanted to roll her own eyes, but managed to keep from doing it. She'd debated on what tack to use with Hague, and decided to go straight to the heart of things. If he faded out on her, well, that was that.

Della warned Liv, "Every time you come you upset him."

"I wish it were different," Liv responded, as they were reluctantly led to Hague's room. "But you're holding the reins, not me."

"I'm the only one who knows what's best for him," Della declared.

"Keep telling yourself that," Liv muttered softly.

September shot a glance at Della, but she'd moved toward Hague's chair and had missed the remark. She kinda thought she might like Liv more than she'd expected.

"Hague," Della was saying, leaning over him in a motherly manner.

"Give me some room," he said, shooting Della a dark look.

She snapped up straight, hurt. "Your sister's here, with that detective."

"September Rafferty," September introduced herself, taking a step forward.

He regarded September stonily beneath bushy brows. Without looking over, he said, "Hi, Liv."

"Hi, Hague," Liv answered. "You okay?"

His eyes held September's. "So far."

"Mr. Dugan, the last time I was here, you mentioned the name Wart, and then you went away."

"I went into a fugue state," he corrected her. "It's Hague." She nodded. "Who is Wart?"

"He was Navarone's patient. I had Dr. Tambor."

September had that much already. "Wart was a friend of yours?"

Della made an involuntary movement, but pressed her lips together. She was trying hard to let Hague tell his tale in his own way, but it was against her nature.

"Friend . . ." Hague said, as if trying out the flavor of the word. "I thought so. I was fourteen or fifteen and messed up."

Della put in, "We all know this. And we know whose fault it is."

"*I* don't know," September reminded her.

"Wart told stories," Hague said. "He didn't listen to me about the government. He *pretended* to, but he didn't listen. He doesn't know. He wanted to talk. That's all."

"What's Wart's real name?" September tried. She didn't want to send Hague down some obsessive path.

Hague stared off into space for nearly a minute. September was afraid she'd lost him, and she had so many more questions. Della started to say something, but Liv grabbed her by the arm in a death grip. Della's eyes shot fire, but Liv ignored her.

"I heard someone call him Peter once," Hague said carefully.

"Peter," September repeated, feeling a jolt of excitement. Finally, she was getting somewhere. "He had Dr. Navarone," she reiterated, trying to keep him going.

"Jeff had him, too." He made a face and seemed to pull in on himself.

"He doesn't like talking about Navarone, and this Wart wasn't even there at the same time Hague was," Della burst in. "He was older. He wasn't at the hospital when Jeff and Hague were there. And his being with Glenda Navarone is an urban legend. I told you that."

"No, it's true," Hague said. "It's true." He looked at September as if for support. "Wart took her on the examining table. He wanted the girls with dark hair." Hague's eyes zeroed in on her auburn tresses that September had clipped back. "The doctors . . . out of the sides of my eyes . . ." he said, glancing sharply around the room.

"Hague," Liv warned.

"But he had a knife," he said. "He could cut the receivers out of his head."

His hands started to come up again like blinders, and Della bit out in a low voice, "He does this when he talks about Wart. It's a shield, I think." To Hague, she added more loudly, "He's not here. Wart is not here. You're safe."

"Safe," he said, his lip curling as he stared past her. "He came to the west hallway. He waited till they were gone and then he would tell us about them. The bad things. He said he took both of them behind the counter."

Della shook her head. "There was no examining table. There was no counter. Whoever Wart was, he scared Hague," she said. "I never saw him, but his name comes up sometimes when he's under stress."

September understood that Della didn't believe there was a "Wart." But she knew someone with that nickname existed. "Does Peter have a last name?" she asked Hague.

"No." His gaze had been wandering around the room, but now it came back to her. "No, it's Louie!" he suddenly shouted, making September jump. "Louie took the girls behind the counter. They screamed, but he had the knife." He looked around wildly. "The government tells him to do it. They put receivers in the folds of your brain, so they know what you're thinking. They KNOW."

"Louie?" September repeated a bit breathlessly.

"He never told them about the bad thing, the doctors . . . They aren't real . . . they keep their hands in his pockets. They have rigor smiles and they keep their hands in their pockets."

Della shot Liv and September a fulminating look, then said, "Shhh, Hague. Don't think about it." She grabbed September's arm and practically spun her around, dragging her back to the door. "I'm not going to let you torture him anymore. He doesn't know anything. You're just poking at his fears!" She whirled on Liv, who'd come up quick, thinking apparently that she needed to save September. "This is over, Olivia. I won't have it again. Don't come back."

"Don't leave, Livvie!" Hague yelled at Della, angry.

"I'll be back, Hague. Don't worry," Liv told her brother.

"You can't—" Della started.

"Shut up, Della," she cut her off, getting in her face.

"I—" Della sputtered.

"My brother's my brother," Liv told her in a low voice that nevertheless packed a punch. "I'll see you both again. I won't let you stop me."

Della's mouth was open as September and Liv left the apartment and got into the elevator. Liv muttered about Della's highhandedness all the way out to the street, then she took a hard look at September. "What's wrong? What happened?"

"Nothing." She heard her own voice and it was a stranger's.

"You look like you've seen a ghost."

September let out a breath. She felt like she was floating. "No . . . no . . . it's good. He said Wart's name is Peter."

"Or Louie. Hague's not very clear at the best of times," Liv apologized for her brother.

September lapsed into silence. She couldn't talk anymore. She could feel Liv's eyes studying her, and it was all she could do to act normally after Hague's comments.

Louie took the girls behind the counter.

She felt sick with a chill. Starved for air. She had to get to her car, and the station, and talk to Sandler, and Jake. . . .

I'll call you.

She wanted to laugh hysterically and cry and ululate. Jake didn't want to talk to her. But she could call him. She should call him.

But what she was thinking was crazy. She knew it. She knew she had a weakness for making connections too soon.

Yet . . . yet . . . Louie's was the burger spot where May and Erin had been killed. Erin worked behind the counter and the killer had a knife.

He's good with a noose. Hague had said that about Wart—Peter—too. And May and Erin had been subdued and killed by strangling first.

No . . . no . . .

Wart and the Do Unto Others case . . . it wasn't about *her sister*!

Liv dropped her off at her apartment and like an automaton September drove to the station. It was Saturday. She wasn't supposed to work, although she knew everyone else would be clocking overtime on Do Unto Others. Vaguely she saw Guy Urlacher's mouth moving but there was only white noise in her ears. Fugue state . . . she thought distantly.

The people in the squad room seemed watery and elongated. Agents Bethwick and Donley weren't there, but George Thompkins seemed to have lost thirty pounds and Sandler looked stern and rail-thin but kind of loopy, too, as she leaned into September.

Through watery pools and ripples she heard: "*Did Auggie reach you? He called the station.*"

"No . . ."

"*How—did—you—hear?*"

"What?"

Did she say that? Was it her voice? She wondered if she was having some kind of breakdown.

Gretchen was frowning at her. "How did you hear about Georgia Friedman? Your brother and Frick and Frack are on the scene. How did you know?"

"Who?"

"Nine, what the hell?" She snapped her fingers in front of her face.

September came back slowly. She was following her own internal dialog so closely that the world faded away. "Who's Georgia Friedman?"

"The vic found at Haverly Park in southeast."

"I didn't know. I just came in," September said.

"Auggie called on the station line, looking for you. The 911 call went to the Portland police."

"I'll call him, but—"

"It's our doer, Nine," Gretchen said grimly. "He caught up with her outside a bar. But he screwed up this time. She scratched him and though he poured bleach on her, there's flesh under her fingernails. Might be able to get some DNA anyway."

"Good." She shook her head, clearing her mind. She needed to *think*.

"There's something else," Gretchen said, shooting a look to George, who shared something unspoken between them.

"What?"

"He carved into her skin."

She got a cold feeling in the small of her back by the way she was acting. "Not 'Do Unto Others,' I take it . . ."

Gretchen shook her head, her almond-shaped blue eyes serious as they gazed into September's. "This time, he carved the Roman numeral nine into her skin."

"Oh, shit . . ." September expelled, and sank into her chair.

He stared stonily at the face in the mirror. The vertical lines beneath his left ear were a dark branding. Sociopath . . .

You screwed up!

There was no more waiting.

He'd been following Nine around all summer. It was time to stop.

It was time for them to be together.

September stared across the squad room. Concerned, Gretchen had brought her a cup of hot coffee, but she hadn't touched it. She couldn't process. It was too much information. The doer had carved IX in the latest victim's torso. That was another message to her, no doubt. But did any of this have to do with May's death?

Feeling herself trembling inside, she inhaled and exhaled several times, then put a call in to Jake. She didn't care if he didn't want her to call. She couldn't wait. When the call went straight to voice mail she ground her teeth, and sent him a text:

Please call. I need to talk to you. I'm sorry.

It was pathetic but she was past caring. There were so many pieces of information vying for attention inside her head she was shut down and overwhelmed. She sat quietly at her desk as they waited for more information from the federal agents. Auggie called again and was relieved to get hold of her. He'd been working with the Portland police and was called out to the scene with Donley and Bethwick. He wanted to make sure she was all right, and September assured him she was. She didn't have to tell him about visiting Hague; he was too absorbed in what he was doing.

Off the phone, her gaze traveled to the bulletin board with the first three victims' pictures and bullet points. Lulu Luxe had been added under her real name, Dolores Werner, and now Georgia Friedman had joined the board.

And what about May Rafferty? Should she be there, too?

September had planned to spill the information to Gretchen as soon as she walked in, but she'd been blindsided by Do Unto Others's latest kill. Now, she got up from her desk and walked down the hall to the break room and went to her locker. There was nothing in it. She hadn't even put her messenger bag in.

She stood there a moment, thinking hard. Then she turned quickly and found the steps to the basement and the evidence room. There was a uniform at the counter reading a copy of *People*. Seeing her approach, the man quickly put it aside. September showed him her badge and said, "I need the evidence box on a cold case from fifteen years ago."

"Write down the date and name," he said, sliding her a form. She filled it out and slid it back to him, and he punched the information into a computer, stared at it a minute, then headed through a steel door. Before it closed behind him, she saw row upon row of metal racks filled with boxes that held information on unsolved cases.

It took him a while, but he returned with a box, and said, "You wanna take this upstairs, we gotta couple more forms to fill out."

September was staring down at the name, MAY RAFFERTY. "Maybe. I'll just stay here for a minute and see." She took the box to a counter on the far wall and opened the lid. Inside were plastic bags with her sister's bloody clothes and sneakers. She'd been casually visiting her friend at the burger spot. There was no knife; the killer had brought it with him and taken it away. The thin cord he'd used to strangle her was in a separate plastic bag, however. She glanced at it, shying away from the sight of her sister's dried blood.

It was the report that interested her that was nestled in the box alongside the evidence. It, too, was in a plastic bag, but that was mainly for safekeeping. She wouldn't be contaminating evidence by looking at it as it had been created by the detectives who'd worked the case.

She read through it quickly. Knowing it was her sister's, she found each word stung her even more than other homicide cases. It didn't take long, and she slipped it back in its plastic sleeve.

"Thank you," she told the uniform.

"That all you need?"

"I think so."

She was barely at the stairs when she was already dialing her cell phone, punching in the number for the Rafferty house. Her father picked up a few moments later, and before he could say more than, "Hello," she answered in a flat, grim voice, "It's September. I'm on my way over to see you. Don't leave. Just . . . stay there."

"What's this about?" he asked, surprised.

"May, Dad." She could scarcely control the tremor in her voice. "It's about May and the fact that you lied to me."

September's emotions were all over the place as she drove to Castle Rafferty. May? Had Wart killed *May*? It couldn't be that far back.

But didn't you think this went all the way back to grade school?

But that was before the storage unit, she argued with herself.

Then how did he find the storage unit? He was watching . . . watching the house . . . watching for you.

"No," she said aloud. "That doesn't fit."

Unless May was first . . . and you were second . . .

She wanted to clap her hands over her ears, but she kept focused on the road. By the time she wheeled into her father's house, she was a bit calmer. Not much, but some.

Braden opened the door for her as she stalked inside. Rosamund was there, one hand protectively cradling her belly. September could scarcely stand to look at her and would have preferred to be alone with her father, but apparently it wasn't to be.

"You never told me the truth about May," she bit out.

"What has this got to do with May?" he asked, clearly feeling this had come out of left field.

"There was no robbery. You always said it was a botched robbery, but you knew it wasn't. You knew it was a straight homicide."

He shook his head, but his gaze fell from the accusations in her eyes. "There was money at the scene."

"But none taken. I pulled the evidence box. I saw the report. Nothing was stolen from the store. May and Erin were forced into a back room and he tied them up with a cord that they believed he brought with him. He *meant* to kill her. He went there to kill her."

"You don't know that. You and August were fifteen!" he came back at her, his face red. "You'd lost your mother, and now your sister was killed. Forgive me for wanting to spare you some of the horror."

"You should have told me," September said stubbornly. "Later, if not then. You should have told me."

"I'm sorry, Nine," Rosamund put in diffidently, "but aren't you overreacting just a little? Your father wanted to spare you."

"Stay out of this." September couldn't even look at her.

"Well, excuse me for trying to help. I'm part of this family, too, whether you like it or not!"

"Rosamund," Braden said flatly. A warning.

September forced her gaze away from her father and to her stepmother. She wanted to blast her for so many things, but it wasn't really about her.

Rosamund ignored the warning. "All your stuff's in the garage. It's safe, okay?" she told September. "I brought everything back that was there. Sorry, I didn't go with Jorah to the storage unit, but that workman was sneaking around and I didn't feel that I could leave. Ask Suma. She stayed with me, too." She waved a finger at September. "I called Mel about him, too, and believe me, I sure got a discount!"

September barely heard her. Her mind was on her sister and the way it must have come down at Louie's that night. If Wart/Peter had killed her sister and her friend then she needed to tell Sandler. Maybe get Frick and Frack going on it.

"I told you about that guy, when I told you about the

storage unit," Rosamund was whining to Braden. "I can't believe you don't remember."

Braden snapped at her, "I remember you going on and on about Mel's and I told you to use a reputable company next time. That's what I remember."

"Sorry if I'm just trying to save money!" Rosamund threw up her hands.

"It's not saving money when none of those blinds work. Discount? You should have got every penny back."

September turned to Rosamund. "Blinds?"

"Yes, blinds," Rosamund said through her teeth. She was glaring at Braden. Then she lifted her chin and marched from the foyer into the kitchen, breaking into little mewls of despair.

Braden waved a hand after her in disgust, then turned back to September. "We don't know what happened that night. It could have been a robbery, but I see you're convinced it was premeditated murder. I don't agree with that, and . . . oh, now where are you going?" he demanded.

September had drifted after Rosamund. She caught her pressing her nose to a tissue, but though it sounded as if she were crying, her eyes were dry. "In what rooms did you put the blinds?" September asked.

Rosamund made a strangled sound of disbelief. "Your father's den? The garage? What do you care?"

"The den?" she repeated.

"And a bedroom," she said. "And we weren't even re-doing it!"

"Which bedroom?"

"The blue bedroom."

"My old room," September said woodenly.

"Okay, your old room." She hiked her shoulders, then thought a moment. "He gave me the willies. I walked in and he was just looking at one of the boxes that I was taking to the storage unit, real intent-like. I asked him what he was doing and he didn't answer. That's when I told him he should leave, and I got on the phone to Mel."

"Who does Mel work for?"

"Mel's the owner. Mel's Window Coverings. Why do you care?"

September turned away without answering. Her mind was racing and she had no more time for Rosamund, or her father, either, for that matter. She swept past Braden, who'd come to stand in the archway to the kitchen and had to step back when she suddenly charged away.

"Hey," he called to her.

She headed outside. She'd seen Mel's Window Coverings around somewhere. It had been around for a long time, and Laurelton wasn't all that big. Her mind just couldn't seem to focus on it, but her GPS would pinpoint it for her.

"Hey!" her father yelled again. "What's the matter with you!"

She lifted a hand in good-bye but didn't turn around as she climbed into the Pilot. Switching on the ignition, she spent a few moments programming the GPS. It popped up with the address, and she peeled away from the house with a little chirp of tires.

On the way across town her eyes kept moving from the road to her GPS and back. She thought about calling someone, but she was flying by the seat of her pants. As soon as she got corroboration from someone at Mel's, then she would know.

What if he still works there?

Okay. No. She would call as soon as she was parked.

Her pulse thrummed with extra adrenaline. She reached Mel's in twenty minutes, a low, concrete building that stretched from the back of a utilitarian storefront. There was a chain-link fence around the property and several white vans parked inside the perimeter. Driving past the entrance, she parked on the street, then plucked out her cell phone and called Sandler, who didn't pick up. September suspected the agents had probably returned with their findings from the latest crime scene, and Sandler would call her as soon as she was able. Quickly she related where she was, then cut the connection . . . and then realized Jake had texted her back.

Tried to call. Didn't get through. Call me.

She saw she had a missed call and realized she hadn't turned the ringer back on. She felt tense as she punched in his cell number, and then was a little unnerved when he answered on the first ring, "Hey, there."

His voice sounded a bit circumspect, so she rushed in with, "I know you said you'd call, and I know I'm jumping the gun, but I needed to talk to you. Lots of stuff is happening."

"I saw breaking news, Nine. I know another body's been found."

She could hear the worry in his voice and though she was glad he was concerned for her, she knew it was not a good idea to tell him where she was and what she was doing. "Where are you?" she asked him.

"On my way to my parents'. Mom found my grade school stuff, so I'm going over there to pick it up."

"Good. That's right. You were going to ask her for it," September said, her eyes on Mel's parking lot. There was someone inside the office, she was pretty sure. She was glad they apparently worked on Saturdays.

"Are you at the station?" he asked.

"No, I'm following a hunch."

"A hunch?"

"We'll see if it pans out. Everyone is working the case today. County, too. I'm still supposed to be sidelined, but I went into work anyway, and now I'm checking another angle."

"I want to see you," he said suddenly.

"I want to see you, too," she answered in a rush of feeling. "Jake, I'm so sorry about last night."

"Forget it. I know you had to ask."

"I knew it was all coincidental. I just . . . I just want to see you and then I've got . . . a lot to tell. How about I meet you at your house? I'll call you when I'm done here, and then we'll talk."

"Okay," he said, and she wished she could reach through the phone and kiss him.

"I think this thing is breaking, Jake."

"Because of this latest victim?"

"Yeah, among other things. I've got a call in to Gretchen. She's wrapped up dealing with this new victim."

"Okay. Be careful," he said.

"Always." She was so relieved she wanted to say something more, something to let him know how she felt. "Jake, I don't want to mess things up between us. That's the last thing I want. I'm just—deliriously happy."

"Deliriously?"

"Yes, yes," she said, responding to the amusement in his voice. "I'll be by later."

She clicked off before she got all sappy. Then she phoned Gretchen again, but once more got her voice mail, so she ended the call without leaving another message. A man was walking from around the back of the building to one of the white trucks. She watched as

he placed a magnetic sign on the door that said MEL'S
WINDOW COVERINGS.

White van. Like the one seen at Richie's Bar the night
Lulu Luxe disappeared. Mel's didn't paint their trucks.
They used magnetic signs.

She stepped from the Pilot, her gaze on the man.
Could this be Wart? He was around thirty, she guessed.
She wouldn't know until she was closer.

She heard the scrape of a shoe and cocked her head.

Then hands grabbed at her, jerked her violently backward. She tried to turn around but something went over her
head. A rope. No, a cord! Her hands came up but it was too
late. The noose was choking her. She struggled to get a
look at him, struggled to save herself. Struggled to *scream*!

But nothing came out. Spots showed in front of her
eyes. God, no. God, no! She couldn't pass out. She
couldn't. She had to stay alive!

But the edges were fading. Fading . . .

With a last effort, she lifted a foot and slammed her
heel into his shin. He grunted and swore.

"Fucking bitch, I love you," he whispered in her ear.

And then the world went dark.

Chapter 22

"The box is right over there," his mother said to Jake, pointing to a large cardboard box stacked by the back door. "You're going to have lunch, right? You're not going to just run out of here with your hair on fire."

He gave her a bear hug, and said, "'Fraid so."

"Oh, Jake."

"I promise that soon . . . very soon . . . I'll come back and I'll bring Nine with me."

"Nine?"

"You know. September Rafferty."

"Ahh . . . yes. I overheard some of that when you were talking to your father."

"You gonna warn me off the Raffertys, too?"

"Oh, I suppose your father was clear enough on that for the both of us. And I'm sure September's a nice girl, it's just we have a history with her family, you know."

"Nice girl," he repeated with a grin.

"What?"

"Well, yeah. Maybe she is. But she's a cop, Mom. It just isn't how I'd describe her."

"I can't see any of Braden Rafferty's children being police officers," she said with a shake of her head.

"And you just put your finger on one of the biggest problems dividing that family. Oh, well, there is the Dashiell Vogt issue," he added. When his mother just raised her brows in a question, Jake said, "This is going to take way too long for the amount of time I have, but I promise I'll make it up to you."

She snorted, but half-smiled.

He was relieved that he and Nine had gotten past the surprise of Sheila's will. The whole thing was all dumb anyway, but that's how fights were sometimes. Nine had reacted like a cop, and he'd seen it as a breach of trust. It had taken him a while to get over it. The fact that it mattered so much showed him how much he'd fallen for Nine Rafferty, and that was something he needed to give some serious thought to.

But for now, he was just glad they'd jumped that hurdle.

Jake went to the box and lifted it to the kitchen table. He opened the flaps and looked inside. Right on top was his second grade classroom picture, and he pulled it out and looked at it again. "I saw this on the school computer recently. Mrs. McBride stays in assisted living now. It's kind of hard to believe. She was such a—disciplinarian—back then."

His mother came to stand beside him and look down at the photo. "She was fit to be tied that year. I remember her telling me to be careful and not let you become like those other boys. She probably should have retired long before she did."

"She said something like that to Nine. What other boys?"

"Well, T.J. was one. You were friends with him, and she was worried you'd be as disruptive as he was."

"T.J.," Jake repeated. "T.J. moved to New Mexico right after high school."

She gazed at him, confused by his non sequitur. "Doesn't mean he wasn't 'high energy.'" Her eyes moved back to the photo. "Davey Marsh was another one. He pantsed another boy and was suspended for a while," she said, pointing at a red-haired boy. "It's amazing how I can still remember some of these things. The boy he pantsed isn't in the picture. He was in a different homeroom than yours. You had him in homeroom later, maybe third or fourth grade. I think he was picked on because he wet his pants a time or two."

"I remember that," Jake said. His mother was pulling things from his own memory long buried.

"Kids can be so cruel, but he was kind of an odd duck," she said with a slight shrug. "A loner."

"Cargill," Jake said suddenly. "Peter Cargill. He moved away before junior high."

"That sounds right. I don't really remember his name."

"It was Cargill." Jake quickly dug through the papers until he found a manila envelope labeled fourth grade. He pulled out a stack of papers, thumbed through them, and found the classroom photo. Scanning the smiling amalgam of faces, his gaze fell on Peter Cargill, whose thousand-yard stare was evident even in the old picture. He felt a frisson of apprehension slide down his spine. Dropping the photo back, he hefted the box into his arms. "I gotta go, Mom. Thanks."

"You're welcome," she said, but he was already past her, opening the door and striding to his SUV.

As soon as he was inside the Tahoe, he yanked out his

cell phone and scrolled through his saved numbers. T.J.'s
was there, but he hadn't talked to him in over a year. Still,
people hung onto their cell numbers with their life, so
he punched in the number.

"Jake, my man," T.J.'s voice answered as if no time had
passed since last they'd spoken. "I was gonna call you.
Freaky. I know it's weird, but I need a best man. I'm getting married, man!"

The news momentarily derailed Jake. For a heartbeat
when his mother had named T.J., Jake had wondered
wildly if his old friend had been involved in sending September the messages, maybe even the homicides, somehow. But almost instantly he'd dismissed the idea. T.J. was
an ass, but he was just that kind of guy. Still, hearing he
was getting married was a surprise.

"Uh . . . yeah . . ." Jake said. "You sure you want me?"

"Who else? And when you and Loni finally pull the
trigger, you'd better remember to invite me and my lady,
Belinda."

"Loni and I aren't together anymore."

T.J. made a sound of disbelief. "Yeah? What happened?"

"It just . . . ran its course. T.J., I want to ask you something else," he said before T.J. could steer the conversation in another direction.

"Shoot, brother."

"Do you remember Peter Cargill?"

"Cargill. Yeah. The pants wetter? What a fuckin'
weirdo. Marsh was always screwin' with him. You remember Davey Marsh? He was just always on him, and
Cargill would scream and glare and we'd all laugh. Remember?"

"Maybe . . ."

"But that's when we were little. Later on, he'd just

glare like he was killing us with his laser-like stare. His parents were all fucked up or something, so he moved in with his grandparents. I don't think it helped, though."

Jake had a bad feeling in his gut. "How do you know so much about him?"

"Man, Davey and Cargill were always in trouble, and I was kinda there, too, y'know? Our parents were always at the school and I saw Cargill's old man whack him across the head when he didn't think anyone was watching. But I saw. That was right before he moved in with the grandparents, I think. Maybe fifth grade?"

"Do you know where they lived?"

"The grandparents? Sure. You remember Erin Boonster? Got killed in that robbery with Nine's sister? May or June or something?"

"May," Jake said, his mouth suddenly dry.

"Yeah, well, the Boonsters' farm is right next to Cargill's grandparents'." When Jake didn't immediately respond, T.J. asked, "You still there?"

Jake found that he was holding his breath. "Do you know if Cargill was ever called Wart?" he asked after a moment.

"God, why are you so interested in him, man? What'd he do? Kill somebody?" He laughed at his own joke. "Yeah, he called himself Wart."

"He nicknamed himself?"

"Yeah, as far as I know. 'Cause his middle name was Wharton," T.J. explained. "That was the grandparents' name. Wharton. I was with Marsh at a Pop Warner game against Twin Oaks—I think Cargill had already switched schools by then—and he was there, and he saw Marsh and came over and said something weird . . . hmmm . . . don't remember exactly, but he said to Marsh, 'Call me Wart when you talk to me.' Made Marsh and me just crack up. Oh, yeah, now I remember what he said. He said he knew who the laughers were. I guess he meant us."

Jake's head was flooding with memories. He remembered Peter Cargill, always alone, always slightly off. "T.J. I gotta go. Thanks."

"Hey, Belinda wants to be a June bride. I'll call you."

"Yeah . . ."

He clicked off, then immediately called September. Her cell phone rang and rang, then went to her voice mail. "I know you're busy," he said urgently. "But I think Wart might be Peter Cargill. Peter Wharton Cargill from Sunset Elementary School. Call me."

September slowly came to, aware that she was being bumped and jostled, aware that her throat was hot and hurting inside and out. Vaguely she recalled the chain-link fence and the concrete building and then someone had come and—

Her heart lurched and she gasped. She tried to move her hand. She wasn't tied but she was being rattled around.

"I can pull this from here," a voice said, and she felt tension and searing pain at her neck as something tightened against her. The cord from the blinds. He was pulling it from where he sat in the front seat.

Immediately she collapsed back down. She was in a vehicle, a van—the white van!—and her captor had her in his grasp. He'd been following her, she realized dimly. She hadn't been wrong when she'd felt a presence all summer long. He'd been the one following her. Wart . . .

And the cord . . . the noose . . . he was also following the path of another killer who'd strangled women and left them in fields. . . . That was why this case seemed so much like the Zuma one. There were similarities in methodology, but they were separate doers.

Who was he?

She dared not lift her head. She was dying of thirst.

"Won't be long," he told her. "You know where we're going, huh? You know?"

His voice was unfamiliar.

"We're going to Westerly Vale Vineyards. You couldn't wait for me, though, could you? Y'see, I know. I know you were there with *him*."

Something rattled loudly and September's eyes flew open. She was staring at a large toolbox. A pair of bolt cutters lay beside it and the motion of the van made everything jump and clatter.

"We're going to be together," he said on a loud sigh. "The time has finally come."

She tried to speak but it hurt to try. Better to save her strength. Better to save it till they got to Westerly Vale. She assessed herself and realized he'd taken her gun but her cell phone was still in her pocket. She tried to move her hand, but he demanded, "What are you doing?" and she froze. He was watching her too closely in the rearview mirror, but there might be another time and she didn't want to give herself away.

If only she could call Jake.

Jake left a text on September's phone: Call me. She needed to get back to him, but she was clearly not answering her phone. What was she onto? A hunch, she'd said. A hunch about what?

He thought about her partner, Sandler. He didn't have

her cell number, but he could call the station and ask for her. Or, would that be getting Nine in hot water? He knew she wasn't supposed to be working the case and it had sounded like she was flouting that edict, some aspect of it anyway.

With a frustrated growl meant for the world at large, he checked the Internet on his cell, searching for a phone directory. He tried Peter Cargill in and around Laurelton and failed. Then tried the name Wharton and also failed except for an unlisted number. He thought a moment, then plugged in Boonster and was rewarded with Avery Boonster's number and address on Farm Hill Road, which was not all that far from where one of the victims'—the prostitute's—body had been located.

Should he go there himself? he wondered. Would that foul up the investigation? Piss off the authorities? He did a quick search of his feelings and realized he didn't give a shit. He wanted answers, and he wanted Nine to be safe.

After plugging the address into the Tahoe's GPS, he turned the vehicle's nose southward, toward an unincorporated area outside the Laurelton city limits that was dotted with rolling farmland and small stands of timber. He knew approximately where he was going, and he felt his attention sharpen with each passing mile.

He had no weapon; it wasn't his deal. He sure as hell hoped things didn't come to that, but he knew there was a slim chance he could meet Cargill face-to-face if the guy had stayed on at his grandparents' house.

Just to the right of the Boonsters' address was a narrow gravel drive with a tuft of brown grass growing down the center. The track branched off toward another building right before the hedge that divided the two properties. A garage of sorts, with an upper story, was on the west side; the main house on the left. The hedge, spotty in areas, ran between the two buildings, mostly blocking the view of each place from the other.

After a moment of indecision, Jake decided to drive up to the main house, which was a sorry affair that looked as if any and all repairs had stopped somewhere in the eighties. A satellite dish sat on the roof of the house, the only new thing about it.

Pulling the Tahoe to a stop beside the dilapidated porch, he tucked his cell phone in his pocket and then stepped out and walked up the creaking wooden steps to the front door.

His knock wasn't answered, so he tried again, louder. He thought he heard someone moving around inside, and wondered if he was being ignored, but then the door slowly swung inward. A stooped woman with steel gray hair and glasses that magnified her eyes in that owlish way of the elderly looked him up and down. "What'cha selling, mister?" she asked with asperity.

"Mrs. Wharton?" Jake tried.

"Yes?"

"I was actually looking for Peter Cargill," he said.

"Peter?" She glanced toward the hedge that divided the garage from her house. "You got the wrong house. He's over there." She pointed with an arthritic finger.

"You're his grandmother."

"Yep. All he's got left. How do you know Peter?"

"We went to school together."

"Then you know about my husband's daughter and that criminal she married. He's dead and so is she, thank the Lord. My husband loved her, but she was an addict and so was he. Put Samuel in an early grave."

Jake got the feeling this was something of a mantra for her. Something she told everyone who crossed her path. "Is Peter home?"

"I don't keep track of him. He comes by to adjust my satellite and steal my change." She *humphed* in disgust.

"Okay. Mind if I leave my car here while I check in on him?"

"No, mister. Ya gotta move it. I might have to leave. I don't let no one park in my drive."

"Oh. Okay, thank you."

He got back in the Tahoe, reversed, and then headed down the other lane. His nerves were stretched thin. He'd just telegraphed his approach and, if Peter Cargill truly was Wart, this could be one really bad idea.

There was a carport around the back and, from his angle as he climbed from the Tahoe again, he could just see there was no vehicle there. Drawing a breath, he walked purposely toward the front door, which he suspected had been put in place at the time the garage door was removed and the building turned into a separate residence. He knocked several times, loudly, but there was no answer. He was pretty sure there was no one home.

Cupping his hands, he tried to look through the windows, but the curtains obscured his view.

T.J.'s words crossed his mind again: *He said he knew who the laughers were. I guess he meant us.*

From some distant part of his brain he recalled that a different serial killer had once said he'd been deeply embarrassed when he'd been teased in grade school by kids saying, "Your epidermis is showing." He hadn't known it had simply meant his skin and he'd carried that moment of humiliation into his adulthood.

He wanted to see inside Cargill's place, but apart from breaking in, he didn't see a way. He walked all around the place, looking for anything. Finally, he noticed there was the tiniest of slits at the bottom of a living room window where the lower blinds hadn't flipped completely down.

Squinting, he peered inside and saw a television and DVD player against the far wall. Above them, he caught the bottom edge of a picture. The ocean, he thought. Sea anemones.

Sea anemones.

Could it be a coincidence?

Jake half-ran back to the Tahoe, pressing the button for September's cell again. He had to interrupt her. Had to. When she didn't answer, he yelled in frustration, "Pick up, pick up," but the call went to voice mail.

Climbing into the Tahoe he backed out of the drive, the tires spinning a little. She wasn't at the station. She said she was following a hunch, but what did that mean?

Where the hell was she?

Westerly Vale Vineyards had a few cars parked in the lot and a number of people nosing about. He hadn't counted on that and it made him furious. He drove right past the first building with its sign that said TASTING ROOM and around the back of the house that they used as a bed and breakfast. He parked in the shade from the building beside an Impala sedan.

Twisting, he looked back at Nine, who was feigning unconsciousness. "Hey," he said. "Come on." He gave the cord a couple of hard tugs, but apart from a stutter in her breathing, there was no movement.

Grabbing up his knife, he climbed into the back with her, examining her closely. Her hair had come loose from its clip and he brought a handful of it to his lips.

He was instantly hard.

For a wild moment he thought about taking her right then. In the back of the van!

But that wouldn't be perfect.

"Get up," he told her. "I know you're faking."

She still didn't move.

He glanced back at her gun that he'd left on the passenger seat, but he wasn't as comfortable with a gun. Dropping the cord, still holding the knife, he roughly turned her over. "Get up!" he yelled. "GET UP!"

But she didn't move and he realized she was truly unconscious again. He'd pulled too hard.

Frustrated, he glanced out the front windows of the van. Had to get her inside the house, but how?

In utter shock he watched as the back door of the building suddenly opened and a curvaceous blond woman descended the steps, heading to the Impala. She was pulling out her keys as she drew near, and she shot a curious look toward his van.

Panicked, he snatched up the gun, then threw open the van's back doors and jumped out. The blond woman recoiled, her eyes taking in the knife and the gun. She started to turn, but quick as a flash he brought the knife to her neck. "Unlock the trunk," he said in her ear. "Scream and I'll slice your throat."

For a moment he thought she was going to disobey. He pressed the blade tighter. With shaking hands, she popped the trunk.

"Give me the keys."

She held them out and he growled, "Get inside."

"Please . . ."

He smacked her alongside the head with the gun. She crumpled forward and the keys fell to the ground. It was a simple matter of sliding her bottom half in, and slamming the trunk.

It had taken all of fifteen seconds.

He put the gun and knife down on the van floor, then

dragged September out by her heels, throwing her in a fireman's carry over his shoulder. Snatching up the knife, he slammed the door on the van then headed up the stairs to the back door. When he tried the knob, it was locked. The bitch had locked up when she left.

"Fuck." Setting September down, he ran back for the keys. In that moment she staggered to her feet, but he was back in a flash, the knife to her throat. "You're mine," he snarled. She didn't have the strength to do anything but lean against the building.

Turning the key, he popped a head inside. The door led to the kitchen, which looked to be empty. Hauling September up again, he next sat her down on the floor, propped against a wall. Then he gathered up the keys, his knife, and the gun again. Once they were inside, he turned the lock on the door from the inside.

There could be people staying at the bed and breakfast. He knew that. He looked down at the gun in his hand. He was going to take September up to the top floor where he'd seen her with Westerly. If he had to kill others on the way, he would, and though he preferred the knife, the gun was a better instrument if there was a crowd.

Carefully, he pushed his hand against a door that swung into the dining room, cracking it about an inch. He peered through. It was quiet. Not a breath of air. In the light from the front windows, he could see faint dust motes.

He savored the moment, the pause. There had never been enough time with the surrogates, even when he'd taken them back to his cot.

But now he was in control. He had time. And he was with September. One way or another, they were going to be together. Eternally. Starting now.

Turning back, he saw she was staring straight at him, her blue eyes taking him in coldly.

"You killed my sister," she rasped out.

"Where's Nine?" Jake demanded into the phone. "Do you know where she is? I need to talk to her." He'd had to call the station since Nine was not picking up. He'd insisted on speaking with Detective Sandler, and when he'd been told she was unavailable, he demanded that he speak to her and told them to give Sandler his name. Finally, he'd been connected.

"Detective Rafferty is not here," Sandler told him carefully.

"I know she's not there," he said with forced patience. "She's not answering her cell. She told me she was going to call you. I need to tell her something."

"I'm sure she'll get back to you—"

"Wart is Peter Wharton Cargill. He lives in a garage apartment on the Wharton property on Farm Hill Road."

A pause. "How do you know this?"

"I just need to know where September is!"

"Mr. Westerly, I don't know where she is. I'll try to find her."

"You do that, and call me back."

He clicked off, feeling impotent. He was sitting in the Tahoe at her apartment parking lot. He needed a direction.

Nine, where the hell are you?

"Do you remember me?" he asked her with a faint smile.

Yes, she remembered him, September realized. He had

been in her second grade class. The boy who'd wet his pants. One of the three Amelia McBride had said had caused so much turmoil and trouble.

"Peter . . . Cargill," she said, finally coming up with the name. Her voice sounded thin and it was hard to talk.

"You do remember," he said, and the way he smiled at her made her blood run cold.

"You weren't in the second grade picture, but you were in my homeroom."

"I missed that day. I missed a lot of things in grade school." He shook his head at her. "You found me at Mel's," he said in disbelief. "How did you do that?"

"You hung blinds for my stepmother."

"She told you."

"Sort of. You saw my schoolwork at the house and you knew it went to the storage unit. You followed Jorah."

"Yes. It was an opportunity. She called up. Mrs. Rafferty." He was pleased with himself. "I knew then I had to be the one to go there. I traded with someone to get the job."

"But why . . . ?"

"You know."

He came very close to her and she had to fight herself to keep from shrinking back. She was sitting on the floor, bracing herself with her hands. The phone was in her pocket. If she could distract him for just long enough to place a call . . .

"You're the one," he told her. Then his expression darkened, and he said hatefully, "But I haven't forgotten that you laughed."

"I laughed?" she repeated and suddenly he had the knife to her throat and they were nose to nose.

"Don't act like you don't know."

After a few moments he pulled away and September

racked her brain to keep him talking. "Why did you bring me here?"

"You already know the answer to that, too. Because you came here with him," he hissed. "Upstairs." He waggled her gun to indicate the floor above. "Jake Westerly."

She silently thanked the gods she'd turned off her cell phone ringer and left it off, because if Jake were to happen to call her now . . . The idea made her shudder inside.

She had to be careful. She wanted to scream at him about May, but she couldn't upset him. Her life was in the balance. "You sent me—the leaf artwork."

"I liked the sea anemone report better." He stared at her unblinkingly, in a way that clutched her heart.

"What else do you have of mine?"

"Your *All About Me* book. I've had that piece of your hair until now. I have all your treasures."

"You did kill May," she repeated, unable to stop herself. She kept her voice even, the emotion out of it.

She stared at him and watched his expression darken again. "I didn't mean to," he said angrily, glancing away, pacing. In that moment she slipped her hand into her pocket and clasped the phone. "I thought she was you," he said dreamily. "I saw you and I followed you. Except it wasn't you, and I . . ." He shook his head. "And then I saw Erin. I knew she would tell you about me. I couldn't let that happen! You understand, don't you?"

September froze as he looked her way. She'd pushed the buttons on the phone from memory, hoping she was making the right moves, sliding through the screens to the call list on her phone.

"She saw the fur," he said, sounding disgusted. "She knew it was her cat."

September's throat throbbed. She was having a little

trouble following. "You—killed her cat?" she asked in horror. She purposely shook her head, moving her body in the process. As she did so, she hit her thumb to the top of the phone screen, where her last call, either in or out, had been made. The top two calls were Jake and Gretchen. If she reached either one of them they should be able to hear her.

God, she hoped so.

"She lived right next door," Cargill was going on. "I thought she was you, y'see? I thought she was you! Then they looked at me . . . they both looked at me and started *laughing*."

"May and Erin. You're talking about May and Erin Boonster. . . ." She remembered driving near the Boonster farm when she and Gretchen had gone to talk to Stuart Salisbury and his mom. She'd mentioned to Gretchen that they were near May's friend's house. Erin Boonster.

She slid her hand from her pocket, afraid he would notice soon that it wasn't on the floor. She lifted it to her face, just to prove where it was. She didn't have to fake its trembling.

"Put your hand down!" he barked, and she immediately dropped it.

Was the phone on? Had she connected? She hoped she'd calculated correctly and hit the right button. She needed to talk, to give whoever was listening some clue to her whereabouts. "But this is Westerly Vale Vineyards," she said. "Someone will come. There are people around. Colin Westerly or Neela . . ."

"Neela," he repeated.

"Colin's wife. They live in an apartment here, on site at Westerly Vale Vineyards. There are people at the tasting room. You can't get away."

He gazed at her hard and her heart pounded. It felt like he was looking right through her. "There is no getting away. This is where we belong. Outside . . ." His eyes looked past her. "At the end . . . in fields where they lay . . ."

When Nine's number popped up on his screen, Jake snatched up his cell and wanted to scream into the phone. But Nine was already talking about her sister May and Erin Boonster. And then she was saying ". . . Westerly Vale Vineyards . . ." and he knew instantly it was some kind of message. He'd been sitting in his car at her apartment, sick with anxiety. And then when he heard a man yell, "Put your hand down!" he'd known. He'd covered the bottom microphone of the cell with his hand and slipped the Tahoe into gear.

He kept the cell to his ear as he drove madly, wildly. He should call someone but he didn't want to lose his tenuous hold to Nine. And as the conversation went on, his insides grew colder and colder. Cargill had her at Westerly Vale. *And he'd killed May Rafferty and Erin Boonster!*

September's heart raced. "What about Sheila Dempsey? And Emmy Decatur? And Glenda . . ."

His pacing had intensified. "I had the beast under control," he hissed. "But then you started playing games with me. You did that. I saw your picture. You became a cop! You set the beast free!"

September gazed at him helplessly. The beast? "You saw the article in the *Laurelton Reporter*."

"Yes. You put it there. And I couldn't control the

beast any longer. The hunt started and there was Sheila. At that cowboy bar. She looked like you and she knew me. She knew about the knives. The beast wanted her. You started it."

"Tell me about Emmy," she said, licking her lips. Her throat was on fire.

"She was at Grandview. Thought she was better than me. Got me in trouble, but I almost got her to the park."

"The park?"

"I wanted to take her to the park, but . . . I had to wait . . . years. And then I saw her again. At that other bar. There she was, dancing, grinding away on those men." He gazed at September, dead-eyed. "They all go to bars and dance. She recognized me and she wanted to have sex. She was begging for it. I took her home, but then . . . but then . . . she started fighting. Changed her mind. But she wasn't you, either."

"Peter, I think you might have the wrong impression of me."

"Wart," he stated flatly. "Dance for me."

"I wasn't trying to play games with you."

"DANCE FOR ME!"

"I—I'm no dancer," September protested.

"C'mon. Get up. Get on your feet."

He grabbed her by the arm and yanked her up. September swayed. Her head was woozy and thick. Her throat ached and burned.

"Dance!" he commanded.

She took two steps forward and stumbled. He caught her and pulled her close. She felt bile rise in her throat and tried to hold it back. He stroked her hair and started crooning to her. "Lovely, lovely hair. You want it, don't you, Nine? You and I. I always knew it. Come on. We'll go outside. Forget upstairs. That doesn't count with *him*. You and I . . . we'll go into the fields."

He was fifteen minutes out when his phone cut out and Nine was gone. Had Cargill found out about their connection? Did he know? Jake didn't know, but he didn't hesitate. He phoned the Laurelton PD station again and barked that he needed to speak to Detective Sandler. This time Sandler came on the phone faster. "Yes?"

"She's at Westerly Vale Vineyards. I'm on my way there. He's got her."

"If that's true, you need to stand down, Westerly. You need to—"

"Bullshit. Just get there!"

He clicked off.

A faint sound was heard. A tinny voice. Oh, God, the phone! Did he hear?

September was still in his embrace, fighting an inward battle with herself. She wanted to knee him in the crotch, or punch him in the nose, kick and spit and fight. But she knew she was more likely to infuriate him than incapacitate him for long. She needed some space. A way to run. And a weapon.

Hearing the voice, Cargill suddenly thrust her to arm's length. He cocked his head and September realized at the same time he did that it was coming from outside, not from her phone.

"Fuckin' bitch," he muttered furiously. He stood her on her feet, then suddenly pulled the cord from her neck, over her head. September eyed him warily, but then her hopes sank when he grabbed her hands behind her and reused the cord, red with her own blood, binding her hands together behind her back.

"Sit down," he snarled at her.

She glanced around the room looking for something—anything—that she might be able to use to fight him.

And then from down the hall, a male voice called: "Neela?"

Colin!

Oh, God.

Cargill clapped a hand over her mouth and slowly sank with her to the floor. He'd set the gun down on the work-table in the center of the kitchen, but now, as he pulled away from September, he snatched it up. He pointed it at her briefly, his eyes silently warning her not to make a sound.

Colin's footsteps neared, but then made an abrupt turn before they reached the kitchen. The apartment, September realized with relief. He wasn't coming into the kitchen.

Cargill held the gun in front of him, aimed at the door that Colin would come through if he did. September could tell how unfamiliar he was with it. But the knife was another matter. It was in his other hand and he twirled it unconsciously, a familiar old friend.

She couldn't let Colin meet his doom without any warning. She inhaled to take in a breath, ready, should he decide to keep coming. But then his footsteps retreated toward the living room and the front of the building.

Cargill left her and moved almost silently from that door, back to the swinging one that led to the dining room. He opened it a crack, putting his eye to it. "He's going," he said with satisfaction. "Along with those fucking tourists."

September gathered herself, poised for flight, but then he suddenly turned back to her and she didn't move. He was lean and tough and had the blankest eyes she'd ever seen. Had she gotten through to Jake? Or Gretchen? There was no way of knowing if she couldn't look at her phone.

The tinny voice was heard again, along with some soft pounding. Cargill swore and looked through the back window. "I'll have to kill her," he said, as if he were talking about the weather.

"Who? Neela? You're talking about Neela?"

"If she's the blonde in the trunk," he said, then dragged September by her bound hands over to the table. Quickly, he worked the bonds until he had enough cord to tie her hands to the table leg. "Make a sound and I slit her throat," he said, then he headed for the back door.

"Don't hurt her," she burst out.

He'd opened the door, but now he paused to look at her hard. "It's our time, Nine. Only ours."

"Wait, Peter! Wart!"

He swept back and hit her with the gun and she saw stars and slumped down.

Time seemed suspended. She heard something outside, but she couldn't place it beyond the ringing in her ears. *Bastard,* she thought suddenly, violently. *Bastard.*

She fought the dizziness.

The phone. In her pocket. Could she still reach it with her hands bound?

She struggled, but she was tied to the table leg. Fighting to get her feet under her, she put her shoulders beneath the table and then she strained and pushed, lifting it with an effort, till it suddenly tumbled over with a loud crash. Staggering, she yanked her hands free of the leg, then looked anxiously around the kitchen.

There was a wine bottle opener on the counter. Her eye had passed over it before, but now she could see it had a small foil-cutter knife tucked inside. She backed over to it and maneuvered it between her hands, then quickly lay back down on the floor and began to moan as he returned noisily inside the back door.

He yanked her forward by her feet, breathing hard. "Bitch!" he cried. She dared not open her eyes, just moaned and moved her legs as if in pain. He threw himself on her, pulling open her eyelids. "You think you can get away from me?" he snarled.

"What?" she said. "What?"

She saw then that there was blood on his knife. Blood on his shirt.

"You're playing games. It's your fault."

"Neela . . ." September asked unsteadily, staring at the blood.

"Not her. Westerly's brother. She's just . . ." He didn't finish his thought as he grabbed her by her upper arm and yanked her to her feet once more. "It's our time now," he said.

Westerly Vale looked deserted in the late afternoon sun. Bronwyn only worked in the mornings and it looked like Neela had closed the wine tasting room early because no one was around. Nine had said she was at the house, so Jake parked outside the tasting room and made his way toward the back of the building, though he knew anyone looking through a window would be able to see him.

But the first person he saw was Colin. On the ground.

Unconscious and bleeding from a knife wound to the chest. He ran forward, scared and sick. "Colin? Colin?" he asked anxiously.

His brother made no response, but he was breathing!

With shaking hands, Jake dialed 911 and before the dispatcher could ask him what the nature of his emergency was, he spit out the address and demanded an ambulance, telling her there was one person with a critical knife wound to the chest and possibly more victims. He left the phone on and placed it next to Colin, then he moved in a crouch to the back door.

They were heading into the vineyard, he was half-dragging, half-carrying her. September was heartsick and afraid. She needed to call for help.

She'd managed to pull out the knife blade from the opener, but the pace was too fast and she couldn't manipulate it to free herself. Maybe when they stopped, she could stab him. An elbow to the nose was another defensive move that could give her a few moments, except her hands were tied and it would be difficult. He had the knife in his free hand and the gun in his pocket.

And then she heard the sirens.

He grabbed a hank of her hair and jerked her head up. She cried out from the pain but he shook her. "What the fuck? What did you do? *What did you do?*"

He threw her down in the dirt and jumped on her. The wine opener popped from her grasp. Her arms felt like they were breaking as he dug in her pocket and ripped out her cell phone.

"You called them!" he screamed.

She felt the opener at the end of her fingers. She worked

it closer, pulling the knife blade to her bindings. "I don't know. I couldn't call. I didn't do it," she babbled.

"Liar."

He pulled out his blade and cut open her blouse, exposing her bra.

She gazed past him toward the house and the road and seeing her eyes, he jerked his body around as well. She sawed with all her might. The cord was thin but taut. *Puk.* She felt one strand release. Then, *puk, puk.* She was free!

She pulled her arms out just as he turned back. "You!" he cried in outrage, lifting his knife. But she was faster. She swung her arm up in an arc and stabbed him in the lower neck, driving the little knife home, feeling his blade slice into her shoulder at the same time, biting deep.

"Augh!" he cried, reaching upward to the knife.

She pushed him hard with all her strength, toppling him back.

Then she scrambled to her feet and ran.

Jake heard Cargill's scream of fury and bounded through the front door of the house and across the porch. He was running full speed in the direction of the vineyard as a Jeep slid to a stop on the tarmac of the parking lot followed by more police cars. Gretchen had called the cavalry.

September felt Cargill behind her, ran, tripped, ran some more. He grabbed at her hair, bellowing. She slashed backward and he grabbed her hand and twisted, throwing her down. His eyes blazed with fury and he raised his knife.

She grabbed his wrist, fighting with everything she

had. Then suddenly he was pulled off her by strong hands and the knife skittered into the vines.

"I'll kill you," Jake's voice snarled. "You hurt her. I'll kill you."

Seeing him, Cargill scrabbled for the gun.

"Jake!" September screamed.

Jake jumped him and they crashed past September. She was trying to get to her feet, trying to help. Footsteps were pounding and then suddenly:

Blam! Blam!

"Oh, God . . ." She got her feet beneath her, her gaze focused on the two men on the ground. Cargill was on top. There was no movement.

Then Gretchen was there, holding her gun on Cargill. September smelled the cordite and realized it was Sandler who'd fired. "Don't move, motherfucker," she snarled.

"Jake," she said brokenly.

Then blood bloomed on the back of Cargill's shirt in two spreading red pools, and Jake moved from beneath him, working his way free.

As he got to his feet, he murmured, "September . . ." in a scared voice.

She saw the growing red stain on her own shoulder and felt the hot pain beneath it. "I'm okay. I think I'm going to be okay."

And then her eyes fluttered closed.

Chapter 23

There was something about the smell of a hospital that seemed to permeate everything. September was only half awake during the ambulance ride, and then was put under for the surgery to mend the knife wounds. When she came to, they told her she was remarkably lucky and she felt it, especially when she learned Colin Westerly's surgery was far more extensive as he'd been stabbed in the chest and suffered a collapsed lung and nicked artery. Jake spent time with her but was beside himself over Colin, and Neela, rescued unhurt except for minor cuts from the trunk of her Impala, couldn't stop the flow of silent tears until she heard that he was going to be all right.

They wanted to keep September overnight, but she couldn't bear the thought. She was in a post-op room and told them she wasn't going to a hospital room, but in the end her decree was overridden.

"You've got a nasty neck wound here, too," she was told by one of the emergency room doctors. "Damn lucky whatever damn near garrotted you didn't sever your carotids."

She didn't tell him that it had done the job Cargill was looking for by choking her to unconsciousness.

Gretchen was the first one to come see September. "Took forever to get done with them," she said. "Them" were the IAD agents who investigated officer-involved shootings, and as soon as they'd gotten Gretchen's report she'd come to the hospital. Peter Wharton Cargill had died from his gunshot wounds and Gretchen had been placed on administrative leave as was the policy of the department.

"Wes called," Gretchen told her. "He wanted to know if he should come to the hospital."

"I'm going to be out of here by tomorrow," September said.

"Well, it looks like he might be your new partner until I'm cleared. As soon as you're ready to go again."

"I'm ready. And thank you," September told her, with heartfelt gratitude.

"Save your thanks for your boyfriend," she said with a smile.

She had thanked Jake, but he'd tried to minimize his part in the Do Unto Others capture. As Gretchen left, he returned to her room.

"Colin's in ICU," he said. "But he's awake. It's good."

"I think I could go home," she said.

He gazed at her tenderly. "You've got a bandage wrapped around your neck and your left shoulder is taped across your chest. You look like you've been in a war."

"It's not that bad."

"Worse," he said. "Is there any way I can talk you into another profession? I don't want to sound like your dad, but since we're going to be living together, I just want to at least be able to vent."

"I don't recall agreeing to living together?"

"Oh, I asked you. And you said yes. You don't remember?"

She gazed into his teasing gray eyes. "Oh, yes . . . maybe I do . . ."

He grinned and she chuckled and it kind of hurt, and when she moaned, he placed a kiss on her forehead and said seriously, "We're together, you and I."

She heard the unspoken question. "We're together."

His mouth had moved to her lips when she heard an "Ahem" from the doorway. She and Jake both looked around to see Auggie and Liv.

"You get stabbed, on your first big case?" Auggie gave her a look.

"Second big case, sort of. And I was pulled off both of them."

Liv said with concern, "But you're feeling okay?"

September slid a look Jake's way and he threaded his fingers through hers. "I'll live," she said with a smile.

"Then I guess you can take the—kinda bad news—we're here to bring you."

"What bad news?" September asked, her heart clutching.

"Someone set fire to the house," Auggie said. "It started in the garage and spread. Dash was there with dear old Dad and he helped contain it before the fire department came."

Jake inhaled on a sharp breath and September asked, alarmed, "Is everyone all right?"

"Yes," Liv assured her. "Everyone's fine."

Auggie said, "But Rosamund's lovely green kitchen is a disaster." He flashed her a grin.

"Wow," September said.

"Do they know how it started?" Jake asked.

"Looks like arson," he said matter-of-factly.

"Arson!" She'd expected Auggie to say it was faulty wiring or a gas leak, something along those lines. "Not . . . Dash?"

"Nope," Auggie assured her. "He was with Dad, and they saw someone running away but they don't know who."

"Knock, knock." September looked around them to see July poke her head in the room, holding up a bottle of Cat's Paw. "For when you're better."

"Did you hear about the fire?" September asked her.

"Just heard from Dad. Guess he's forgiven me enough to want to keep me informed. What the hell was in those boxes from the storage unit anyway?" she asked with a shake of her head.

"What do you mean?"

"Dad said that's where the fire started," July explained. "Someone threw gasoline on them and torched them. My money's on Rosamund. If she can't move the boxes out, she'll just burn 'em up."

September knew July was being facetious, but she looked from Auggie to Liv to July and then back again to Auggie. They all had the same *I don't really get it* expression on their faces.

"I'm going to check on Colin again," Jake told her and she watched him leave, feeling warm inside. Reading her expression, Auggie snorted and then he and Liv took off. July watched them go, then came to perch on September's bed.

Before she could speak, September asked, "Do you know about May?" She wasn't sure the word had gotten out past Jake and the Laurelton PD.

"Yeah, I do. Dad talked to Auggie and I guess you had it out with him before you found Peter Cargill."

"Seems like a long time ago and it's only been hours," September realized.

"Hey, little sis," July said. "After hearing about May, it just made me realize even more that you and I haven't spent enough time together."

September was pleased that she felt the same way she did. "Well, we have some Cat's Paw to get started with."

July smiled. "I haven't been completely honest with you, and when I heard you were stabbed I just went batshit with worry. I don't want to lose you, too."

"Haven't been honest with me?"

"I'm pregnant. I already went and picked out my little sperms and had the whole procedure. I just was . . . I couldn't be straight with you at first."

"July . . ." September felt a rush of emotion. "When are you due?"

"May. If it's a girl, I think I'll stick with tradition no matter how lame I think it is."

September reached out to embrace her, and July carefully returned the hug, not wanting to cause her pain.

"So, who do you really think set fire to the boxes?" September asked her when they'd broken apart and were smiling at each other.

"Stefan," July said without hesitation. "He's just too damn weird."

Epilogue

Stefan Harmak sat in his van outside the mall, his eyes glued to the doorway where the girls would come through. It was raining, finally, a break in the streak of hot weather, and he supposed it was a blessing, but he didn't want anything to spoil his view of the beautiful girls. Beautiful . . . beautiful girls . . .

His mind drifted while he waited. He'd had to set the fire at the Rafferty house. He'd been sick with fear that his treasures would be found. That stupid cow Rosamund had shipped off all their belongings to the storage unit before he'd been able to retrieve them, and then when Nine had asked about them, Rosamund had brought them back. He was half-relieved that they were somewhere he could get to them, again. Finally. He'd spent endless hours worrying that someone would find them. Then he'd had his opportunity when no one was home and Suma was gone as well, and he'd let himself in with the key he still possessed.

He'd sneaked into the garage from the kitchen, but then Braden and that Dashiell guy had decided to have a meeting at the house, and he'd been trapped in the garage for what felt like hours. He'd gotten scared others would start showing up, so he'd grabbed a can of gasoline that was just sitting there, poured it all over the boxes, and then struck a match to it. The fire had served a dual purpose: it destroyed the evidence and it created a diversion so he could get away.

But he'd lost his treasures. Pictures of Evie naked, when she was about eight. Pictures he'd taken when she was getting ready for the bath. He'd snapped them in a hurry when March and Evie were staying at the house. No one had seen him. No one knew but Evie, and even she wasn't sure as he'd pretended he was just fooling with the camera. He'd hurried away before anyone realized he'd been in the bathroom after she'd taken her clothes off.

But now, with the way she'd last looked at him at dinner the other night when all he'd tried to do was stroke her hair and touch her, he couldn't trust that she'd keep her mouth shut if the pictures were found. Everyone would wonder what was up. There was no choice but to steal the photos back, but in the end he'd had to destroy them.

Now, he drew a breath and shuddered. He had to get over his obsession with Evie. She was out of reach to him. But one of these days he was going to find one girl alone, a straggler from the pack. All he had to do was wait.

The mall doors opened and a group of them came out, giggling and walking arm in arm. If he could think of a way to snatch just one, and if he could only be with her a little while . . . just a little while . . . that's all he would need.

A shadow fell over the side of his window. A woman in a parka. Her face stared at him from beneath the hood. He glared at her through the sheeting rain and when she tapped on his window his heart seized a bit. But she couldn't know what he was thinking. She couldn't know.

Pushing the button to lower the window, he glared at her, pissed that rain was falling inside the van.

"Who the hell are you?" he demanded, sizing her up. He saw a movement, and then her arm suddenly rose, and he recognized the stun gun just before she pressed it to his neck.

"I'm Lucky," she said, and then every nerve inside him started shrieking with pain as he flopped around uncontrollably on the seat.